THE WOMEN OF ABBEY PLANTATION

*Ordinary Lives and
Unexpected Enchantment*

NANCY ROGERS

HERE I AM
PUBLISHING, LLC

ISBN 978-1-958032-11-4
Printed in the United States of America.
Registered in the Library of Congress.

Front cover art by Lura Lauer
Page formatting by Levi Stephen, 303 Pixels LLC (303pixels.com)
Edited by Yvette Kilgore, Editor, Here I Am Publishing, LLC.
Cover formatting and placement, Jeremy Cannada, Here I Am Publishing, LLC

Published by Here I Am Publishing, LLC.
info@hereiampublishingllc.com
Sandi Huddleston-Edwards, Publisher
780 Monterrosa Drive
Myrtle Beach, SC 29572

Dedication

To
Janet Wright and Judy Bednar

I couldn't have done this without you....

Contents

MARIAH'S STORY

Preface

ALTHOUGH I THINK OF *The Women of Abbey Plantation* as a sequel to my first novel, *Sarah's Secret*, I have to admit that it's more than a continuation of Sarah's story. It takes place along the Waccamaw River, just as the first story does, but it's a much larger story. Instead of being one book, it should have been three or even four separate novels. I would have done it, but I was afraid I'd never get them published. So, I shortened the story and split it into two parts: *Sarah's Secret* and *The Women of Abbey Plantation*.

Sarah's Secret takes place on a former rice plantation named True Blue. Today True Blue Plantation has been folded into a gated golf community called Heritage. Historically there wasn't a plantation named The Abbey. I invented it to have a location where I could build a logical story out of true events, rumors, and out-and-out fiction.

Everything that I could take from history is true. I used real names, real families, real events, real ways of doing things, real weather events, real tragedies, and real dates whenever I could, and I don't mind telling you that it required some of my best writing to build a compelling story and to be true to historical events at the same time.

The names of the characters in the book are fictitious, but they are based on real people who actually lived along the river at that time. In some cases, I had to change the names so they wouldn't conflict with the characters' names in *Sarah's Secret*.

In other instances, I needed new names for my fictional characters, so I drew from old plantation census records. However, one name stands on its own: Renty Tucker. Renty was a real person who in real life was an enslaved carpenter at Hagley and True Blue Plantations. Renty was an extraordinary builder credited with having built the Hagley Plantation Slave Chapel that I renamed St. Mary's of the Field in The Women of Abbey Plantation. The real-life Renty Tucker also built a summerhouse for the owners of Hagley Plantation. The structure that still stands on Pawley's Island is now called Pelican Inn. After freedom, Renty became the coroner in the City of Georgetown and built his family a handsome, white-clapboard house with black shutters.

Hattie Wineglass's character was inspired by the legendary Ruby Middleton Forsythe (1905–1992). Miss Ruby, as she was called, was an elementary school teacher who provided education to the African-American community during the Jim Crow era. Born in Charleston and buried in Mount Pleasant, Miss Ruby was an extraordinary woman honored by all.

Those of you who live in present-day Pawleys Island are certainly familiar with the surname Wineglass. One of the older Wineglass gentlemen on the island once told me the story about his ancestor's selection of the name, Trumpeter Wineglass.

I hope I captured Miss Ruby's spirit in my tale of Miss Hattie. In many ways, Miss Hattie is the soul of the book, and her spirit stretches throughout the book in surprising ways.

Donna "Jackson" Phillips was a real person, too. She was the granddaughter of True Blue Plantation's caretakers during the1950s. Donna told me hundreds of stories about the plantation, including the ones about lightning boring a hole through their freshly mopped kitchen, the story about her granddaddy trying to kill the excess alligators in the pond with dynamite, and the fact that the interior of the entire house was painted Fannie Farmer Green. She also told me that although she and her grandmother loved the Pawley family cemetery, Granddaddy Jim said it gave him the creeps.

Donna was an artist and singer and the owner of The Island Sign Company along with her husband. We used to eat cookies together. She died in 2017 and I still miss her. I made up the part about her winning the writing contest, but if she had entered a contest like that, she would have won it for sure. No one knew more about True Blue or loved the plantation more than Donna and her grandmother did—not even me.

CHARLOTTE'S STORY

Hunker Down Chil'

The Abbey Plantation
Pawleys Island, SC 1829

CHARLOTTE AND HER FATHER, Thomas Dunhill, set out on their two-mile journey toward the rice fields. Thomas's side of the Dunhill family had owned The Abbey for five generations. But they weren't alone. Eleven additional plantations along the river were owned by other members of the family.

The Dunhills were successful planters and prolific breeders. The family tree was a mess. A generation earlier, one of Thomas's uncles changed his surname from Dunhill to Dunnhill, certain that the additional *N* would clarify legal and genealogical matters. It didn't; it only made matters worse.

Papa and Charlotte were quiet most of the way, and that suited Charlotte just fine. Natural-born farmers like she and Papa didn't rely on words. When they neared the fields, however, Papa got to carrying on about the river and the trunks and the dikes. He was rattling off things so fast that Charlotte had a hard time keeping up.

Just then, screams coming from the women in the fields. "The rice birds is on de way!" the women shouted, pointing to the horizon just beyond the river. And there they were, millions of birds turning the color of the golden sky to soot.

"Ring the plantation bell!" Papa shouted, jerking at his mare's reins.

"Tell everyone to get here fast." As the workers rushed to sound the alarm, Thomas told Charlotte he was going to drop her off at the duck stands next to Old Luther's trunk, and she was to stay there until he came back to get her.

"Jubilee's right over there," he said, pointing to a female hoe hand standing about twenty feet away. "I'll tell her to come stay with you, and under no circumstances are you to leave her side. I'll be back soon."

The birds began their descent only moments after Jubilee came sloshing through the swampy fields. "Hunker down, chil'," Jubilee shouted. "We's gonna hunker down together."

Then Jubilee wrapped her skirts around Charlotte and the two of them knotted up like a ball of yarn. Soon the air crackled with cawing and flapping sounds akin to devils being driven out of their hiding places on Judgment Day. "Biblical chaos," was how Jubilee described it the next day. "The Devil done opened the gates of hell, he surely did."

It took less than five minutes for the birds to arrive in full, millions of them gnashing and scratching at each other in an act of shared madness. Fortunately, they weren't interested in anything that Old Luther's trunk had to offer, nothing much grew there, so Jubilee and Charlotte were free to stand up after a time, and take a good look around. They couldn't believe what they saw. The birds were so thick that they looked like a sea of molasses with flapping bird feathers sticking out of it. There were so many birds that Charlotte couldn't distinguish one from another, only millions of flapping wings.

"What do we do now, Jubilee?"

"We start to shouting and waving our skirts, missy. We gotta scare off the birds so they don't eat up the rice." So, she and Charlotte started flapping and hollering and chasing off the birds, and causing as big a ruckus as they could.

A gang of teenage boys came running into the fields banging pots and pans. Others had muskets and bullwhips, anything that would make enough noise to scare the birds away. The men and women from the quarter were there too, all raising as much cane as they could.

"Shoo, you ol' birds," they shouted.

Almost as suddenly as the birds had appeared, they began to leave. Then Papa arrived, brandishing his jacket at the last of them, as he made his way toward Old Luther's trunk. He dismounted and thanked Jubilee for minding Charlotte during the bird attack.

"I'm sorry I had to leave you here," he said. "We were close to losing the whole field, and I couldn't have done what I had to do with you on my horse. It would have been too dangerous."

"That's alright, Papa. Jubilee and I scared away millions of birds, and it wasn't as scary as I thought it was going to be. Next time I want to use a bullwhip."

"Let's hope there's not a next time."

"Right, Papa. I hope we never see another rice bird, not ever."

Charlotte loved Old Luther. He was the oldest person on the plantation and he knew more about growing rice than anyone on the river. He'd been the plantation's head trunk minder when Papa was a boy, and although he'd gotten too stove-up for trunk minding, it didn't affect his memory, any. He could tell the same story a hundred times without changing a single word.

"Back in the old times, if you wants to eat rice on Sunday, you got to pound it on Saturday. You put a mop-bucket full of rice in the mortar and start to pounding it with the pointed end of the pestle. Then when the husk starts to falling off, you commence to pounding it with the flat end. It takes about three hours to pound enough rice to eat two, three days."

Even though Luther was nearly ninety when he started sharing his stories with Charlotte, he could still recall a story his own mother had told him about harvest time.

"Mamma tell me that after the rice been finished, it been poured into great big wooden barrows. When the last of the rice been all barrowed up, now that was a time of rejoicing. Mamma say everybody would get on them old flatboats and go up and down the river singin' and dancing and playin' the washboard. The first year Mamma work in the fields, her mamma wouldn't let her go rejoicing because she was only fourteen. When Mamma tell me that story, she cry so hard. I cry, too."

As the long days of summer stretched into September, anticipation started to build. Harvest time was coming, and even though everyone on the plantation would have to work double shifts, there was just something glorious about harvest time.

"Oh, Papa, look how beautiful the fields are. They're golden just like it says in the Bible. Do you think this could be heaven?"

"There are too many mosquitoes to be heaven," Papa said, laughing, "but I think it's pretty close. I can't think of another place I'd rather be. How about you?"

"Me neither," Charlotte said.

CHAPTER 2

Edgar's Funeral

The Abbey Plantation 1829

TWO WEEKS INTO SEPTEMBER, Old Luther's great-nephew got Charlotte into the worst trouble of her whole life. It would be fairer to say that he indirectly got Charlotte into trouble, and he got himself into a whole lot more, because he ended up being dead.

His name was Edgar and even though he was missing part of his right hand, Papa said he was the best damn bootblack in South Carolina. The little cracks around Edgar's knuckles were stained the color of Papa's boots. The stain made his hands look like they belonged to an old liver rather than fifteen-year-old boy.

"You don't talk much, do you, Edgar?" Charlotte said to him once in the tack room beneath the big house.

"No, miss," he replied. "I don't talk much."

Charlotte wanted to ask him why, but he turned his back on her and walked from the tack room into the gun room. Charlotte used to look for him after that, but seldom saw him. When she did, he'd lower his eyes and turn away. Charlotte asked Papa about Edgar one day, and Papa jumped all over her.

"Edgar is none of your business, Charlotte."

"I was just curious, Papa."

"You have no business being curious about Edgar or any of the other People at The Abbey, especially the men."

"But why?"

"Because we own them just like we own the livestock on the plantation."

"Oh, Papa," Charlotte said.

"That's the way of it, Charlotte," Papa replied firmly. "The People of The Abbey will spend the rest of their lives working here, and in return, we will give them everything they need."

"What if Edgar doesn't like his job or wants to live somewhere else?"

"He may ask the overseer to apprentice for a new job. He also may ask to be sold to another owner."

"I think Edgar looks sad."

"It doesn't matter. He is much better off living here than in Africa," Papa said, clearly tiring of the conversation. "If he were back in Africa, he'd be living in a house made of thatch or mud, and killing his own food. I've been to Africa, Charlotte, it is the most ungodly place on earth. Here he is given blankets and food and clothing and a decent place to live. He should thank God every day that we rescued him from such a place."

Papa was through; he'd explained himself more than he wanted to, so Charlotte gave him a little curtsy and left the stables. She still didn't see how Edgar was better off at The Abbey. 'Seemed to her he'd be better off back in Africa with his people.

After spending most of the summer living in a glorious rented cottage in New Paltz Village, New York, the family returned to The Abbey. Flat boats carrying cotton, sweet potatoes, collards and marine stores dotted the Ashley River on their way to markets in Charleston, and The Abbey was a flurry of activity.

Everyone was in high gear, including Edgar. Charlotte was surprised when she spotted him after the long summer. He'd grown about a foot since she'd last seen him, but he treated her with the same indifference, so she didn't acknowledge him other than to nod her head.

Edgar hated the master's daughter. The last thing he needed was to have some spoiled brat following him around asking stupid questions. He hated her and everyone else living in the Big House. He hated all white people, and he hated black people, too, especially his own father for the sin of giving him life when all he could offer him was slavery. It could be worse. His treatment at The Abbey was better than at some of the notorious plantations along the river. He heard rumors. He listened to gossip. He was fifteen and plenty big enough to keep company with Old Lucy, a woman who was three times his age and one of the biggest gossips in the quarter. Pillow talk was worth the investment, and he was going to need it.

He was making his escape from the plantation in two days. In forty-eight hours, he'd be free. His plan, however, was as guileless as it was reckless. He was going to steal a jon boat and work his way up river, hiding by day and traveling by night. It was the oldest trick in the book, and the first place they'd look. At least Edgar had selected a good night for his escape. The moon was in its darkest phase and he could barely see his own hand in front of his face. He was off to a good start, but his luck wouldn't last. The trouble began in the boathouse where the boats were kept under lock and key, so the first thing he had to do was to break one of the locks and to do it without being discovered.

With him he'd brought an iron bar, which he wedged into the hole in the lock face, and then he twisted. Several tries later, the lock snapped open and he was able to disengage the chain that was looped through a ring on the front of the boat. The chain slipped effortlessly into the water and Edgar stepped into the boat. He didn't know anything about boats. Idiots operated boats. How hard could it be?

Then he missed his step causing the boat to tip hard to one side, and he went flying. He landed on his side on the edge of the dock, and the pain was excruciating. Edgar alternately cursed and cried, as he pounded the dock with his fists. He'd busted his ribs. He was only fifteen, but he knew that much.

Edgar woke up the following morning to learn that he'd been found unconscious and that his chest was black with bruises. He'd broken some ribs, his father said. Three, maybe more, and one of them had punctured the skin. During the night, his mother had extracted a three-inch bone from his chest with a pair of pliers.

Edgar's mother and sisters took turns tending to him. Infection set in, however, and despite the round-the-clock application of poultices and tinctures, Edgar's condition worsened. Edgar's father notified Master Dunhill that Edgar had injured himself falling from a tree, but no one, including the master, believed anything of the kind. They all knew that it had been Edgar who had tried to steal the boat. Considering the seriousness of his injuries, though, Master Dunhill let it go and sent the plantation nurse to check on Edgar. She gave him several doses of her homemade turpentine-laced elixir coupled with and a healthy dose of laudanum and bragged to the family that Edgar would be better in the morning.

Only he wasn't better in the morning or any day after that. He just laid in his bed and festered. Green goo started oozing out of his chest on the fifth day, and on the sixth day, he died.

An hour or so after sunset that night, his body was carried to the People's cemetery. The sky was pink and golden by then, and as Charlotte and her father sat on the piazza, they could see the procession of torches weaving its way through the fields.

Like a necklace of fireflies, it made the twists and turns through the fields in absolute silence, and it was spellbinding.

"Papa, what happened to Edgar?" Charlotte asked. "Why did he die?"

"I don't have the entire story, Charlotte, but I'm certain that it was Edgar who tried to steal that boat last week. Somehow, he hurt himself."

"Is his family going to get in trouble because of what Edgar did?"

"No, I think they've suffered enough, don't you?"

"Yes, Papa, they have. They've lost their only son. It's kind of like Jesus."

"Well, not exactly," Papa said.

"What are the People going to do at the graveyard tonight?" Charlotte asked.

"They're going to have a funeral, just like we do when one of our people dies."

"But they don't have a church, Papa."

"It doesn't matter; a funeral can be held anywhere."

"Will they talk about how hard Edgar worked and all of that?"

"I suppose they will, and then they will pray that God will let him into heaven. Then they'll start singing and dancing, and it will go on most of the night."

"Dancing? The People dance at funerals?"

"Not the kind you think. I shouldn't have even used that word, but I don't know another way to describe it."

"Can we go watch?"

"Absolutely not, Charlotte. As the master of the plantation, I must acknowledge the boy's passing, but if I were to take you with me, it would be disrespectful. This is a serious matter and it's not for your amusement."

Papa left for the cemetery a few minutes later, and Charlotte was right behind him. He'd be extremely angry with her tagging along, so she stayed back. She didn't have her own torch or lantern, of course, so she had to make her way in the dark. She'd never done such a thing before, and she was so frightened that she was trembling. She wasn't even certain that Papa could hear her if something awful were to happen. What if she ran into an alligator or a snake, or raccoon? Alligators move from pond to pond at night—a lot more than you'd think, and if you get between a mother raccoon and her babies, she could bite your face off.

As Charlotte drew nearer, she had to negotiate through saw grass that was way above her head. The grass's heavy heads roiled and swayed like witches around a bonfire. She was about to turn around and head for home when she spotted the cemetery through an opening.

The light from the People's torches reflected off of a small pond that defined the southern edge of the cemetery. The light enabled her to find a good hiding place among the cattails, but the gurgles and croaks and splashes coming out of the pond terrified her. Rice plantations came alive at night. Everything with teeth, fangs or claws bellied up to the supper table after the sun went down, and Charlotte felt like a plug of ham.

Charlotte was wearing a gray wool shift, black cotton stockings and a pair of short boots. It had been a warm day, and she had complained umpteen times to anyone who would listen that she was miserable and needed to put on something cooler. Cook told her to quit bellyaching.

"Nobody's gonna listen to a whiny little crybaby," she said.

Cousin Margaret was even less sympathetic. "Part of becoming a lady, Charlotte, is learning to soldier on."

Well, Charlotte wasn't hot anymore; she was freezing; and there was scummy stuff floating on top of the water and everything stunk to high heaven. And to make matters worse—if that were possible—she had to crouch down, so the funeral-goers couldn't see her. Did leeches have teeth? She didn't think so, but she knew alligators did.

All-y, All-y 'outs' in free....

Moments later she saw Papa. He stepped out onto the edge of the cemetery and stood for a moment with Edgar's family. Then he tipped his hat, stepped back onto the shadows, and he was gone. He hadn't spoken a word. Sneaking away to watch Edgar's funeral was the stupidest thing Charlotte had ever done, and yet she would have done it all again to witness what she saw that night.

Edgar's body was wrapped in what appeared to be a quilt top without the stuffing, and he was resting on blocks of wood. The People gathered around him, reached for each other's hands, and began to sing "All Hail the Power of Jesus' Name," but they didn't sing it like they did at St. Philips. They sang it slowly, so slowly that each word sounded as though it was going to be the last.

Then some men took Edgar's body out from under the quilt top and lowered Edgar into a narrow grave and covered it with dirt. All the while, there was more singing going on. Charlotte couldn't tell who was leading the singing, but she got the impression that no one was in charge. Everyone just knew what to do. After the second hymn, the funeral-goers stood so quietly that for a moment Charlotte thought the funeral was over. Suddenly, three men appeared, and she knew that it was just changing gears.

The men were carrying long tapered drums made out of tree stumps. They were joined by another man clutching a pair of rib bones, probably from a cow, and another holding two long pieces of scrap iron. Although Charlotte knew practically everyone on the plantation, there wasn't enough light to recognize any of the musicians. She was kind of glad since she was trespassing and all. While the men took their places, the dying torches were replaced with fresh ones. Their brilliance, however, didn't bring more light; instead they cast ghoulish shadows on everything, including the humblest blades of grass.

Well, that was it, she thought. *Snakes were going to appear from everywhere, and the earth was going to rise up in a lava-encrusted mound, and then it was going to crack open and Satan was going to step out. He was going to strut among the People sticking out his pointed tongue and giving nasty smiles to the women, while he slapped the backs of the men and called them by their names. It was the end of the world.*

The Bible was right about heaven and hell, and Charlotte was going to witness the whole thing whether she liked it or not because she was stuck in pluff mud up to her knees. At that moment, she started to pray harder than she'd ever prayed in her life, not the *Now, I lay me down to sleep* kind of praying, but the *Save my retched soul from the belly of the beast, Lord Jesus!* kind. Ol' Scratch was on his way, and he was going to melt her backside with one flick of his finger, and she was going to be a pile of ashes before Jesus could save her.

Then the most astonishing thing happened. The land didn't mound up, the torches stopped their grotesque light show, and everything got quiet, really, really quiet. Then the funeral-goers formed two concentric circles around Edgar's grave, and the drums and bones and scrap iron instruments started beating softly. As the drumming intensified, the People began to sway from side to side in unison. It frightened Charlotte, but at the same time, it was strangely beautiful.

Satan hadn't shown up that night. It was the God of Abraham or maybe the god of Africa who came calling. Charlotte didn't know, but one of them was there, and the People knew it, too. As they moved in and out of the circles, they stomped their feet at certain times, causing dust to puff up around the circles. The women clapped their hands above their heads, and the men beat their hands on their thighs and chest. Pattin' juba, it was called.

They sang one of their own songs this time, a song with shouts and heel stomping, and it was repeated again and again. Charlotte didn't recognize the song, but she did remember that it was something about wading in water. As the song was sung, sung again, and sung another time, the dancing became more graceful, and it was plain to see that the dancers were dancing with Jesus, not with each other. They were twirling and stamping and shouting and spinning and it was glorious!

Charlotte was so caught up in the excitement that she didn't pick up on the first small wave of water that rippled around her waist, but she felt the second. Something, something big, was right behind her, and she was going to die! And then a hand grasped her shoulder, sending a bolt of electricity down into her toes, and she turned her head to see Papa. He had his finger up to his lips cautioning her to keep quiet. And then he grabbed her under her arms and pulled her out of the mud, leaving her boots to stay as a reminder of her disobedience and forcing her to hobble home in her stocking feet. As spoiled as she was, nobody spoiled her that night.

On the way home, Papa threatened to give her a whipping, and if he had she wouldn't have blamed him. She didn't realize it, but she had been gone for three hours, and Cousin Margaret and Papa had been frantic to find her. Cousin Margaret even had to be carried to her bed after having a fainting spell in the downstairs parlor.

"I'm sorry," Charlotte said, realizing how she had worried everyone. "I'm really, really sorry."

"That's not good enough. I think you know that."

"Yes, Papa, I know."

"We'll talk about this in the morning. Right now, I want you to go upstairs and get cleaned up before you say goodnight to Cousin Margaret. You smell like the swamp."

Cousin Margaret had taken a sleeping potion, and by the time Charlotte was clean enough to see her, she was groggy, but she knew that Charlotte was home, and she hugged her more fiercely than she could ever remember.

"I love you, Cousin Margaret," Charlotte whispered. "I'm sorry you were worried about me."

"I love you, too, Charlotte. Don't ever scare us like that again."

"I won't. I promise."

Papa's study was the first room on the left as you entered the house, and it was the logical place to put the master's office. Oftentimes, there was a stream of overseers and businessmen from Charleston sitting on overstuffed horsehair settees, waiting their turn to speak to him. Unfortunately, the settees were empty that morning, and Charlotte had to enter the study all by herself. Like a prisoner going to the gallows, she walked in as slowly as she could get away with, with a hangdog look on her face and her ribbon-less hair stringing down. She tried to look as sad sack as she could, although she was certain that Papa wasn't going to fall for it.

"Sit down, Charlotte," he said from behind his desk.

"Yes, sir."

Then he ignored her. He did it on purpose, of course, and if he was trying to make her nervous, it worked. Two steps into the office, Charlotte suddenly found herself completely paralyzed except for her eyeballs. Stuck to the carpet and struggling to breathe, she tried to undo the spell by looking around the room. The study was a relatively small room compared to the rest of the house, but it had a high ceiling, and there was something about the room that made it special. For one thing the color of the walls was unlike any she'd ever seen before. It was greenish-gold, the color of a tobacco leaf, and it glowed in the sunlight. Leather-bound books lined the wall to Papa's right—first editions—many in Greek and Latin.

"A library defines the man," Grandfather Dunhill always said. Papa's desk was in the center of the room facing a window that looked out onto the plantation. Behind him was a fireplace with a marble surround carved in a neoclassical pattern like the freeze found on a courthouse. If she hadn't been temporarily paralyzed, Charlotte might have been about to make out what the figures that were depicted on the freeze were up to.

Six panel doors flanked the fireplace. The one on the left led to a hidden stairway, enabling Papa to escape the room in case of fire or an altercation of some kind at the front door. The door on the right was even more interesting. It opened onto a small closet, and the architect who designed the house noted on his renderings that to his knowledge the closet was American's first. Charlotte didn't know what Papa kept there. It could have been maps or plats, or his silver handled pistols, or even whisky, but it had a sterling silver lockset just as the rest of the doors throughout the house, and Papa was religious about keeping it locked.

Papa cleared his voice, and Charlotte's paralysis disappeared as suddenly as it had arrived. It wasn't much of a consolation, though, because judgement was at hand. Was she to be locked in her room for the next ten years or tethered to a post? She had no idea.

"Charlotte" he said, "I'm extremely disappointed with you."

"I know, Papa. I'm disappointed with me, too."

"You put yourself in danger last night, and you spied on the People after I'd told you not to. I don't know which offense was worse, so I'm going to punish you for both. You will be confined to the house for the next two weeks — one week for each offense, and you will be put to work in the kitchen," he said, taking time to reset the clock on the mantelpiece.

"You will peel potatoes, mop the floor, tend the fire, churn butter, dip candle wicks, whatever cook tells you to do, and you will do it without complaint, won't you, Charlotte?"

"Yes, Papa. I will do it without complaint."

"And don't think that because you're my daughter that anyone is going to go easy on you. It's because you are my daughter that you will be expected to do the dirtiest jobs. In the Bible, it says to 'whomsoever much is given, of him shall be much required.' Much has been given to you, Charlotte, and you need to learn to appreciate it. I know you're still a young girl, but you will be a young woman one day and mistress of a plantation and, God willing, the mother of many children. My tutor used to say that forced discipline leads to self-discipline. You and I are going to test that theory. Now change into something suitable to work in, go say good morning to Cousin Margaret, and then meet cook in the kitchen. She's expecting you."

"Cousin Margaret," Charlotte said as she timidly opened the door to her cousin's morning room. Cousin Margaret was sitting at her desk, looking disheveled. Her hair was loose, and it had that slept-in look.

Her dressing gown was untied and her feet were bare. For a moment, Charlotte didn't recognize her.

"Cousin Margaret, are you alright?"

"I'm fine. I'm just having some difficulty waking up."

"It's all my fault, and I'm terribly sorry. Papa told me not to go to the funeral last night, and I went anyway. I won't ever do anything like that again, I promise."

"We were so frightened. Do you have any idea how dangerous it was for you to do what you did? It isn't as if you could have stumped your toe or torn your dress. You could have drowned or been bitten by a snake or a spider or an alligator. We might not have ever found you. Promise that you won't ever do anything like that again."

"I promise you won't have to worry about me ever again."

A few minutes later, Charlotte walked out into the yard on her way to the main kitchen. She'd meant it when she apologized. Being a child was a big responsibility.

The kitchen, a separate building from the house, was a large clapboard building with a long porch and two columns holding up a pedimented roof. Plantation kitchens were always separate from the main house. *Dependency kitchens* they were called, and they were separated for good reason. It kept cooking smells and smoke out of the main house, and it cut down on the chaos that took place there, but the main reason was because of the threat of fire.

Plantation owners like Papa worried more about fire than anything. A fire could happen anytime or anyplace on the plantation, and if one got out of control, the only way to stop it was to let it burn itself out. The Chimneys, a plantation just up river from The Abbey, caught on fire one Christmas morning a few years back. The guests and servants fought valiantly to control the fire, but it was a lost cause, so its owner did the only chivalrous thing left open to him: he had the furniture in the parlor brought out onto the lawn along with the contents of the liquor cabinet so everyone could watch the fire in comfort.

One spark from the fireplace could set fire to anything—a baby walker, a wicker basket, or sewing box, and then the entire kitchen could go up with it. If the fireplace and chimney were old, say a hundred years or more, the bricks themselves could catch on fire. Another worry with old fireplaces was that the chimney could collapse and bring down the entire kitchen. The chimneys attached to the slave cabins in the quarter had been intentionally built to slant away from the cabins. Logs cut from sycamore trees braced the chimneys in place. If a chimney caught fire, the support log could be pushed out of the way to allow the chimney to fall to the ground rather than onto the cabin.

Charlotte liked the plantation kitchen a whole lot better before she showed up for work that day. She'd always just breezed in and out whenever she wanted to, but now she had to spend the entire day there, and Papa wasn't exaggerating when he said that she'd be put to work. Cook's given name was Zephaniah, which she didn't like on account of it being a boy's name and all, so Charlotte was told to call her Baby Sister. Charlotte hadn't been there five-seconds before Baby Sister sat her down at the work table and handed her a big yellow potato. Then she gave her a paring knife and told her to teach herself to use it. There wasn't much of the potato left by the time she was through, but she got it peeled. She nicked her thumb once, but it didn't break the skin, so she kept going.

"If you cut yourself next time, just stick the bleeding part in your mouth 'til it stops," Baby Sister said. "If you think you're going to bleed to death, come show it to me."

Charlotte's next job was to sweep the floor beneath the biscuit table. The floor in that part of the kitchen was made of four-by-four-inch pavers nearly two-inches thick. Charlotte knew how thick they were because she'd seen some of them pulled up and repositioned earlier that year. Baby Sister said they get lopsided over time since they're laid up dry, and if they're not lined up good, someone will eventually trip, and the pot roast would end up on the floor.

Over the next two weeks, Charlotte must have done every dirty job in the kitchen except cookin' on account of Baby Sister not trusting her to do it right, but she did stir every pot and kettle. She polished Mamma's silver with lemon juice and salt. She cleaned copper with ketchup, scrubbed tabletops with vinegar, and learned that you can soak off cooked-on crud in a bath of water and soda ash.

"Valuable lessons," Baby Sister proclaimed.

Charlotte was a miserable failure, however, at whipping egg whites because her muscles weren't strong enough; at swinging a kettle over the fire, again, weak muscles; and at gutting a fish. That was her biggest failure by far. She'd never even seen fish guts before when Baby Sister handed her a washtub containing a fish big enough to put a saddle on. She named him Jonah.

When Baby Sister told her to cut an opening along the bottom edge of Jonah's belly and then to dig out his guts, Charlotte started gagging. "Just keep at it," Baby Sister told her. "You'll get used to it," but she didn't. She gagged again and ran out the door to throw up. Jonas landed on the floor, guts and all, and Charlotte only got as far as the porch. After her stomach settled, she expected sympathy. Instead, Baby Sister handed her a bucket and a scrub brush and told her to clean up the porch.

She was good at other jobs, though. She learned to separate egg yolks from the whites, snip white sugar, sift flour, measure molasses sugar—you have to press it into the measuring cup to get it measured right—grind coffee, tell the difference between flat and curly parsley, get butter out of a butter mold, and with some assistance from Baby Sister, she even trussed a turkey.

CHAPTER 3

The Dove Cote

The Abbey Plantation 1829

ON THE LAST DAY of the two weeks, Baby Sister told Charlotte that she had a special job for her. Papa was entertaining that evening, and Cousin Margaret had asked Baby Sister to serve squab, a fancy name for baby dove (a pigeon if you're English), and it was going to be a tough order. Squab were small and a pain to clean, and it took a mess of them to make a decent meal, but orders were orders.

One guess who Baby Sister expected to collect the birds—Charlotte of course! Fowl houses stunk to high heaven, and it was a smell that stayed with you for days. Until then, Charlotte had done every job without complaint, unless you count a quivering lip or two, but she performed every one of them. This time, though, she said, "No." As many as two hundred pigeons lived in the dovecote that time of year, and they flapped and fluttered around in terrifying disarray at the slightest disturbance. Charlotte was certain she could go mad in there.

"You've just got to send somebody else," she pleaded. "I'm afraid. The birds will get stuck in my hair and poop all over me. You just can't send me in there. I'll have a heart attack and die, and it will all be your fault, and Papa will be angry. I'm sure you see how important it is not to send me."

"Well, missy, I'm sure that you don't want me tellin' your papa that you refused to do an important job, 'specially after I asked you so nice and all," she relied. "So, I'll be leavin' it up to you. You go collect the birds, and I won't mention it to your papa, or we'll go speak with him right now. No pressure, Miss Charlotte. It's all up to you. Now, what's it gonna be?"

"I'll go get the dang birds," Charlotte said.

"You'll what, Miss Charlotte?"

"I'll go get the adorable little creatures out of the dovecote."

"And you'll do it with a smile on your face, right?"

"Yes, ma'am. I'll do it with a smile on my face, but you can't make me like it."

"I didn't ask you to like it. I only asked you to pretend yourself a smile."

Charlotte left the kitchen by the back door, flashing the toothiest grin anyone had ever seen. Her fists were in knots, and she was mad enough to go in there and rip that whole birdhouse apart. She could have found the cote in the dark or with her eyes closed because it stunk a hundred times worse than the other fowl houses.

It didn't look anything like a chicken house, though. It was a two-story brick cylinder the size of a small grain silo, but it reminded her of a tower in a fairytale where the fair damsel waited in distress. Rapunzel would have been right at home there. A small door with a rounded top was the only access into the cote, or as she liked to think of it, the hell hole. From the exterior, though, the dovecote was beautiful, kind of like a tall gazebo with solid walls. It had a conical roof with a huge finial at its peak, and the roofline was so steep that there wasn't a hawk in the county that could perch there long enough to waylay a pigeon. Plantation owners always maintained dovecotes. Some were cylindrical like the one at The Abbey; others were simpler wooden structures, but everybody kept pigeons because all they required was a place to nest and some grain, and the birds did the rest. You could eat the adult birds, although they were stringy and tough, but the baby birds, squab, were delicious and were fat enough to eat in only four weeks.

Doves also could be raised for their down, but Cousin Margaret said that people were skittish about doing it because there was an old saying that if you had even one pigeon feather in your pillow when you were on your deathbed, your passing would be long and painful. The best reason for raising the birds was for the guano. Papa said it was the best damn shit you could find. "A little goes a long way." That was good, of course, because like all birds, pigeons were pooping machines, but they were so small that their poop didn't add up very fast.

Wearing short leather boots, a dress that she planned to throw away, and a tea towel tied onto her head, Charlotte was as ready as she was going to get. The one good thing was that she didn't have to go into the cote alone. Baby Sister ordered a teenaged kitchen helper named Cicero to go with her.

"Are you ready, miss?" Cicero asked politely.

"I guess so," Charlotte said on the verge of tears.

One last look and they slowly opened the door to the cote. It creaked open like a castle door leading into a dungeon, and it smelled worse. Rotten corpses would be nothing compared to pigeon poop. The moment they stepped inside the door, the birds flew to the top of the cote in mass, flapping and fluttering and setting off a blizzard of feathers and poop.

Unaccustomed to the darkness, Cicero and Charlotte bumped into each other, almost knocking each other into the slushy, stinky guano in the bottom of the cote.

"Watch out for the snakes, Miss Charlotte," Cicero whispered.

"Snakes!"

"Black snakes and coach whips. They love pigeons. Don't you know anything?"

"I just know I want to hurry up."

"Alright, then, let's do it."

More than a hundred small nesting boxes, not much larger than building bricks, lined the walls of the cote, forming rows of concentric circles. To reach them, you had to climb a revolving ladder called a potence. The ladder had a long arm at its top that was attached to a pole in the center of the cote. The arm enabled the ladder to revolve around the pole, something like a library ladder sliding along a wall.

Just as Cicero was about to mount the ladder, they saw something slithering beneath the guano. "A snake!" Charlotte screamed. "A snake!" As if they were joined at the hip, Cicero and Charlotte sprang for the door in unison and escaped out into the sunlight.

Charlotte ran around going: "Eeee!" and Cicero, bent at the waist, put his hands on the dovecote's brick front and took a deep breath.

"That like to scared me half to death, Miss Charlotte."

"Me, too," Charlotte gasped. "I'm not going back in there no matter what."

"Maybe you can do that," he said, "but I gotta go back, or I'll get a lashing."

When Charlotte heard that, she had to go, too. That was the kind of self-discipline Papa was trying to teach her. She just didn't know why she had to learn it in snake-infested guano. "Alright," she sighed after a long pause.

"I don't want you to get a lashing, Cicero. I'll go with you, but what do we do about the snake?"

"We kill it. I'll go get a machete. Do you know how to use one?"

"No," Charlotte said. "I've never even touched one."

"It ain't hard," he assured her. "I'll teach you."

He returned with a machete half as tall as he was. "This machete's too big for you to even pick up," he said, "so I'll have to do it. You stay here until I holler for you, so I don't hit you by mistake."

Hesitantly he entered the cote, dragging the heavy machete behind him. Then it got as quiet as a tomb inside that cote, and Charlotte wondered if Cicero was still breathing, when all of a sudden, she heard a big thunk! She poked her head into the darkness of the cote and found herself nose to nose with Cicero.

"I kilt him! Look!" he said, tossing the snake into the yard.

"I reckon he's a five-footer, Miss Charlotte. That's the biggest one I've ever kilt."

"You've killed snakes before?"

"Well, o'course I have. Snakes is everywhere."

"What kind of snake is this?"

"A black snake. They ain't poisonous, but they're mean tempered, and they'll chase you and bite the tar out of you. 'Make you sick, too."

"Are they like garden snakes? I've seen lots of garden snakes."

"Sort of," he said, "only they're bigger an' meaner. I'm going back into the birdhouse. Are you coming?"

"I'm going, too," Charlotte said, cinching down her tea towel. "I'm scared, though."

"Me, too."

Cicero climbed the ladder and reached into the first nesting box searching for the baby birds. He found two, which is what he ended up finding in most of the other ninety-nine nests. Without even speaking to each other, they worked out a system. Cicero would hold the birds out to his side, and then on Charlotte's cue, he'd drop them into her outstretched basket. The most time-consuming part of the job was moving the ladder, and both of them praised Jesus as they captured the last of the chirpy little birds.

As they walked the hundred or so yards back to the kitchen, Cicero and Charlotte gave each other a grin, and then they parted ways. They had just gone into hell together, but their bond was severed the moment they had harvested the last of the chicks. Baby Sister was waiting on the porch of the kitchen, and she took the basket of birds from Charlotte with one hand and held her nose with the other. "Go 'round back, child," she said. "There's a girl there who's gonna help you get cleaned up. We're gonna bury that dress. I hope you ain't fond of it." Charlotte shook her head from side to side, and stuck out her bottom lip. "Don't you cry. You did good. Your papa's gonna be real proud of you."

"Are you going to make me clean the birds?"

"No, I ain't. You done enough. Now, skedaddle."

The girl in the backyard had fashioned a little tent out of bed sheets, and she had Charlotte stripped down in no time. Then she made her stand in a washtub of cold water and scrubbed her down with lye soap. "You close your eyes, good," she cautioned. "This soap'll sting like the dickens if you get it in your eyes."

So, Charlotte squeezed her eyes shut and held her breath as the girl nearly scrubbed the hair right off her head. Charlotte had heard about lye soap all her life, but the only soap Cousin Margaret used was French-milled soap made from lavender grown at the Abbaye Notre Dame de Senanque in Provence. The homemade lye soap burned her skin, and it smelled a little bit like bacon grease, but it wasn't nearly as bad as she expected, and she had to admit that it got her as clean as a baby's butt.

With wet hair and a clean hide, Charlotte was wrapped in one of the bedsheets, and the girl walked her back into the house. "Thank you," Charlotte said as they walked.

"You're welcome," the girl replied. "You smelled terrible. You ever smell alligator guts?"

"Fish guts, I've smelled fish guts."

"Well, alligators like to eat rotten stuff, so their guts smell a whole lot worse. That's what you reminded me of."

"For true?" Charlotte said, impressed.

"For true."

When Charlotte saw Cousin Margaret upstairs in her morning room with some of her supper guests who were staying over for the night, she proudly told them the story about the birds and the snake and the alligator guts, and Cousin Margaret's friends thought it was hilarious. Cousin Margaret, however, saw no humor in the incident.

"Cook sent you into the dovecote?" she asked.

"Yes, ma'am," Charlotte replied, sensing that she had just gotten Baby Sister in a world of trouble. "It wasn't Baby Sister's fault, though. Papa told me that I had to do every dirty job that Baby Sister needed doing, and you told her that you wanted squab for supper. She had to send someone to get the birds, so she sent me. She trusted me enough to do it, and I did it. I was scared, but I did it anyway, and Papa's going to be really proud of me. 'Forced discipline leads to self-discipline,' you know. It's in the Bible. You told me that Mama believed that just because you're a girl doesn't mean you can't do something. I trussed a turkey, peeled potatoes, and even gutted a fish, a giant fish named Jonah."

Oh, no. Papa must have kept the details of her punishment to himself, and she'd forked over more information than Cousin Margaret wanted. Charlotte needed to disappear, so she gave everyone a small curtsy in her mummy outfit and said goodbye.

"Charlotte," Cousin Margaret called out, "I'd like for you to stay in your room the rest of the afternoon."

"Yes, ma'am."

Charlotte was certain that Cousin Margaret and Papa must have had words over the extent of her punishment because Cousin Margaret never brought it up again. Charlotte understood both points of view, but her heart was with Papa on this one. Her two weeks of kitchen duty gave her a profound appreciation for everything that made it to the supper table, and although she never ever wanted to gut another fish, she had had a wonderful time and learned some valuable lessons, just like Baby Sister said.

She learned about keeping her word, minding Papa, and showing respect for others. She also learned that an apron without a pocket wasn't worth the time it took to tie it on.

The following day Papa again called her into his office but this time to congratulate her.

"Thank you, Papa," Charlotte replied, confident that she had earned his praise.

There were three men sitting on the horsehair settees, so she understood that her time with him was limited. So, she hurriedly said, "Papa, may I ask you something?"

"Something about your punishment?"

"No, sir, it's about something else."

"Alright. What is it?"

"Remember when I asked you about Edgar, about him feeling sad, and you told me that he was none of my business? You also said that the People were the same as livestock."

"I remember."

"Well, did you really mean that, Papa?"

"No, Charlotte, I didn't. I was just trying to make a point. Our slaves certainly aren't livestock; they're living, breathing people."

"Like us, Papa?"

"No, Charlotte, they aren't like us, but we certainly shouldn't treat them like livestock."

"Do you think they'll ever be free, Papa?"

"If they were, where would they live, and how would they feed their families?"

"I don't know, Papa, but I'd like to think it will happen someday."

"Why is that, Charlotte?"

"Because while I was working in the kitchen, I got to calling Baby Sister, *ma'am. Yes, ma'am, No, ma'am.* She didn't tell me to call her that; I just did it automatically. On my last day, though, she told me not to call her that anymore."

"Why?"

"Because it ain't fittin," Baby Sister said, waving a spoon in my face.

"Was she right, Papa?'"

"She was, Charlotte. You mustn't address any of the servants like that again. Do you understand?"

"No, Papa, I don't."

"You will when you're older. You're a very thoughtful girl, aren't you, Charlotte?"

"There are just so many things I want to know."

"Well, don't be in too big a hurry to grow up."

"Do you wish I had been a boy, Papa?"

"I wouldn't trade you for all the boys in the world."

CHAPTER 4

Mama, Please Don't Die!

The Abbey Plantation 1820

COUSIN MARGARET WAS ASKED to join the family after Mistress Anne's passing, but Cornelia was The Abbey's real boss. She ran the house and servants who worked there. There wasn't nothing that Cornelia didn't know about and nothing that she wasn't a part of. She knew her place, of course; she was one of the People, but her importance at The Abbey couldn't be overstated.

As Cornelia watched Charlotte growing into the image of her mother, she thought more and more about that dark day when Charlotte was born. It was 1820—almost ten years ago. Charlotte was six-weeks early, but she had all of her fingers and toes, and everyone in the birthing room was relieved. Cornelia was on edge, though. She knew that the tree spirits were drawn to the warm, soft breath of newborns and that Charlotte had to be protected from them, or they would suck the life out of her tiny lungs. Cornelia's white family didn't believe in the spirits as much as the People did, so she had to act in secret.

Cornelia placed Charlotte in her bassinet, quietly reached into her apron pocket, and hurriedly rubbed her thumb against a small cake of blue chalk.

Then she reached under the baby's gown and pressed her thumb in the middle of the baby's belly, leaving a bright blue thumbprint. "Praise Jesus, Amen." Cornelia whispered to herself, knowing that the incantation and the blue chalk mark would protect Miss Anne's precious baby from the spirits.

Spirits always showed up during birthing time, so protecting the baby was one thing, but getting them out of the house was another difficulty. So, Cornelia had her maids draw blue chalk lines around some of the mansion's largest windows and doors. Chalk lines were enchanted. Cornelia knew that the chalk lines served as portals to help bewildered spirits to find their way out of the house and return to safety of the cottonwoods. Cornelia repositioned Charlotte's gown, walked to the other side of the nursery, and handed the infant to her father.

"Did you mark her, yet?" Master Thomas said, looking down at his new daughter.

"I did," Cornelia replied, realizing she'd gotten caught.

"How long does the chalk take to work?"

"It pretty much works the minute you put it on," Cornelia said, authoritatively. "You're not goin' to be mad at me for doin' it are you, sir?"

"No," Thomas said wearily. "I know you did it to protect her, but I did think you were a Christian."

"I am a Christian. and I know that Jesus does what He can, but the spirits ain't Christians, and they're ever-where."

As Charlotte gurgled in the background and the baby nurses gathered up the birthing rags, Dr. Bednar allowed Thomas back into the birthing room to be with Anne.

"She's so pale," Thomas said.

"It's a miracle she lived long enough to deliver a healthy baby, but she's known all along that she wouldn't survive this pregnancy. It's time to call in the family. There's nothing left to be done," Dr. Bednar replied. The doctor reached for Anne's wrist and a hush fell over the room. Even the baby held her cries because it was at that moment that Thomas accepted the inevitable: Anne was going to die.

Staring down at Anne's delicate face, Thomas began to weep.

"Master Dunhill, I'll do the calling if you wants me to," Cornelia said.

"No, I'll do it."

"Then, I'll just stay here in case you needs me."

Anne's family, most of whom lived near Charleston on Johns Island and Stono, had already been summoned. Two days earlier Thomas had alerted them by messenger that Anne's prognosis was grim. "Pray that she will surprise the doctor and return to us," he wrote. Thomas swore under his breath as he told the family that Anne was not expected to survive the night. The pain was almost more than he could bear. Cornelia stood in the shadows as Anne's loved ones tiptoed in and out of the room.

"Can she hear us?" one of the cousins asked.

"Probably not," Dr. Bednar said, "but it's possible, so skip the last-minute confessions."

A few moments later, a hush fell over the sorrowful gathering with the arrival of Anne's favorite cousin, Sarah Vaux. Sarah Vaux was the mistress of True Blue, the plantation that shared its northern border with The Abbey, and she entered the room with the dignity of a swan.

Sarah Vaux descended from the Lowcountry's equivalent of Huguenot royalty, and she didn't disappoint. She gracefully leaned over Anne's small body and softly whispered something into Anne's ear. Thomas thought it was a mixture of English and island French, but he couldn't hear the actual words. It left a faint smile on Anne's lips, though, and that was gift enough. Sarah kissed Anne's forehead and left the room as regally as she had entered it. That was the last time Thomas saw Sarah Vaux until he attended her funeral at True Blue Plantation four years later. The official cause of Sarah's death was malaria, but that was the least of the story. There was a tantalizing rumor about the last years of Sarah's life that was whispered during gatherings like this.

According to the story, Sarah had escaped a massacre in Haiti during which time her second husband—a mysterious Englishman from New Zealand or India or Aruba—had died, and soon after, Sarah had married one of her Huguenot cousins, Henri Hebert. That part of the story would cause one to roll his or her eyes but was believable enough. But then the story became the thing of fairy tales: It was said that Sarah and Henri and some of their extended family members traveled more than six-thousand miles to visit the Czar of Russia

Thomas had no difficulty believing that Sarah married her Hebert cousin or that she spent most of her final years living at the Hebert's palatial compound in Mt. Pleasant but a visit with the Czar? That sort of thing simply wasn't done in South Carolina; it simply wasn't done.

It was finally time for Anne's children to say goodbye. Anne tried to soothe them, but darkness had now overtaken her, and she felt weightless as though her body belonged to someone else. She began to spin downward inside a giant funnel where there was a great light. Then she burst through the darkness to soar above the room like an enraptured bird. How she wanted to tell her family the indescribable joy of it all.

Anne and Thomas's oldest son, George, was the first to say goodbye. Poised beyond his twenty-two years, he kissed his mother's cheek and quietly left the room. His decorum wasn't wasted on his extended family that day. They were fairly busting with pride. Someday he'd be the plantation's master, and he would do it well.

Anne's eldest daughter, Margaret Anne, didn't restrain her grief. "Mama!" she screamed as her father led her into the room. "Mama, please don't die."

Ten-year-old Haddrell held back his tears as he snuggled up beside Anne and whispered into her ear. "I will miss you, Mama, and I promise to study hard and become a great man just like Papa. You will be proud of me, I promise." Then he kissed her cheek, climbed down from the bed, and left the room.

A procession of house servants and other slaves from the plantation were then allowed to file into the room to get one last look at their mistress. The women curtsied and the men bowed their heads, and some of them used their shirtsleeves to wipe their tears. Dr. Bednar watched in silence. Later that evening he told his wife that many of the People had demonstrated more dignity that day than some of the members of the family.

Anne died at five o'clock that evening. "Thomas," Dr. Bednar said as he solemnly covered Anne's face with the bedsheet, "she's gone." Thomas made no acknowledgement. He simply continued to stroke Anne's hand.

"Cornelia," Dr. Bednar said, looking over at Cornelia. "Could you…?"

"Yes, sir."

"Master Dunhill, Master Dunhill," Cornelia said softly. "Miss Anne's gone; she's gone to Heaven to be with Jesus an' the babies," referring to the couple's three children who had died as infants.

"The children," Thomas whispered. "I need to speak to the children. Take care of Anne while I'm gone, Cornelia."

"I'll be staying right with her, Master Thomas. I won't go nowhere."

Despite their wealth and access to the best doctoring, the members of the great South Carolina planter families were experts at burying their dead. Dying was a fact of life that was often unexpected and far too commonplace. The planters stored coffins of varying sizes in concealed rooms in their barns. Black and purple funeral finery, including ostrich feathers, were quietly stored beneath their beds. Some families even had black patent-leather trimmed carriages and patent-leather tack for their horses. Funerals for the planter elites were well-orchestrated, well-rehearsed productions that oftentimes bordered on theatrics, but that's how folks back then liked it, so it was a thing done.

Anne's funeral, however, was bare bones out of necessity. Anne had had the misfortune to die at the onset of the fever season, and even the loss of someone as loved as she, was no match for the fever. A hurried service was held in the ballroom that Thomas had added to the manor house ten years earlier. An anniversary gift for Anne, the thirty-five-foot-long room was oval-shaped and beautiful by anyone's standards. Thomas had taken his inspiration from a similar ballroom that was added to Hampton Plantation near McClellanville to celebrate a visit by George Washington in 1791. Both ballrooms had soaring walls and coved ceilings.

The ceiling at Hampton Plantation was painted pale blue. Thomas had the ceiling at The Abbey gold-leafed. It had cost a small fortune and had required months of scaffolding and artisans traipsing in and out of the house. But it had been worth it. The Abbey's ballroom was renowned throughout the Lowcountry.

After the service, Thomas ignored his family and other guests, wiped his tears with the back of his hand, and slowly made his way to a small, cozy room just off the bedroom that he had shared with Anne. He came to see the new baby, Charlotte Layton Dunhill. He found her in a small cradle suspended from a wicker stand that enabled the cradle to be rocked by pressing a small foot pedal at the head of the cradle. A baby nurse was fussing with the infant when Thomas entered the room and almost toppled over when she found the master standing beside her.

"I just came to see the baby," Thomas said apologetically.

"She's a fine baby, Master Dunhill. We done checked ever thing on her this morning, and she's real fine," she said, taking more credit for the checking out process than what was due her. "Here, you can see for yourself." Then the girl reached into the cradle and gathered Charlotte into her arms as gently as if she had been picking up a cloud.

"Gratulations, sir," she said with a bob of her head.

Then Thomas held his hands outstretched and felt the tiny baby squirm in his arms. "She's getting more beautiful with every passing moment," he said more to himself than to the nurse.

"She surely is," the nurse replied, noticing that Cornelia had entered the room.

"Leave us," Cornelia said to the nurse with her eyes.

"Yes, 'um," the girl replied, disappearing down the adjacent hallway.

"Cornelia, Anne would have been so proud," Thomas said smiling down at the little bald baby staring back at him. "She looks like Anne, don't you think?"

"She does; she looks a lot like Miss Anne—especially around the eyes—but she looks a might like you, too," Cornelia replied. "Do you want me to take her?"

"I don't know what I want, Cornelia," Thomas said with a voice made raspy by crying. "I want Anne back."

"She didn't want to go, but it was her time, an' she ain't never coming back," Cornelia said in her pragmatic way.

"I know, Cornelia. I've not become unhinged. I just miss her."

"We're never gonna get used to Miss Anne being gone," Cornelia said. "Today was the saddest day of my recall."

With that Thomas gently handed Cornelia the baby and left the room. Thomas had three older children, a two-year-old, and a newborn to care for. George would soon return to Harvard for his final year of college, so Thomas's primary responsibility to him was to pay for everything, an easy enough job when you're one of the richest planters in the Lowcountry.

Margaret Anne had finished boarding school and was living at home again. She had always been self-centered, but now she looked down her nose at her provincial (although extremely wealthy) father and siblings in her dash to land a husband from one of THE leading Charleston families. Thomas should have understood that Margaret Anne's behavior was commonplace among girls raised in expensive boarding schools, but he always excused it because she had lost her mother so young. Even so, Thomas's disappointment with Margaret Anne was beginning to eat at him. He couldn't remember a time when she hadn't been awed by wealth and star power. Now she had her cap set for one of the Drayton cousins.

"Pie in 'd sky," Cornelia said after hearing Margaret Anne's plans. None of the Drayton cousins had made requests to formally court her, however, so Margaret Anne was trying to drum up support by corresponding with one of her former Drayton classmates.

Haddrell needed less fussing over than the other children. He was a loving child, and Thomas was extremely proud of him. As long as he had a microscope and the odd assortment of slides that he'd bought through mail order, he could entertain himself for days on end. A DO NOT ENTER sign was affixed to his bedroom door, and he meant it.

As for Baby Charlotte and James, the two-year-old, Thomas knew he was in over his head. Even with Cornelia and a houseful of maids and baby nurses, the children still needed mothering. So, after consulting with Anne's family, Thomas asked his great aunt, affectionately known within the family as Cousin Margaret, to make her permanent home with him and the children. Three weeks later she arrived at The Abbey in one of her brother-in-law's schooners packed to the gills with crates, trunks, valises, and grips.

"I left most of my things with Sister," Cousin Margaret laughed as she gave Thomas a smothering hug.

"How IS Matilda?" Thomas asked politely.

"She's fine."

"And Augusta Georgia?"

"She's fine, too. The whole damn family's fine," Margaret said with an infectious giggle. A spinster lady by choice, Cousin Margaret was soft and round, witty and sassy, and everyone who knew her adored her. Permanently stuck in high gear, she was a fireball of unruly curls and starched petticoats, and her cheeks were as pink as shrimp roe. She knew the words to every hymn in the hymnal but believed that a good walk in the woods was a better way to talk to God than to take up a pew on Sunday mornings. She insisted that she was too fluffy to play hide and seek, but she never turned down a high stakes game of horseshoes with Thomas and his friends. She also loved Anne's children. She sang to them when they were sick and helped the little ones learn their ciphers. She taught them to fly kites, bake Indian pudding, bait a hook, dig for doodlebugs, skip rocks, and say their prayers. Most of all, she read Anne's letters to Charlotte so many times that she could recite them by heart.

CHAPTER 5

The Fairy Godmother

The Abbey Plantation 1838

DESPITE COUSIN MARGARET'S protestations, Papa refused to send Charlotte to boarding school. He would miss her too much, he said. So, between the ages of six and seventeen, she attended All Saints' Academy, an exclusive school located on the grounds of All Saints' Parish Church.

Cousin Margaret had vehemently opposed Thomas's decision, fearing that Charlotte would "grow up as dumb as a doorknob," but Thomas wouldn't budge. Cousin Margaret was forced to come up with a compromise. During the six months of the year when the family lived away from the plantation, Charlotte would be instructed by a private tutor; the rest of the year she would attend the academy.

Charlotte excelled at school, but she'd never paid much attention to her appearance. She was far more interested in being in the fields on horseback than prancing about in front of a mirror. It all came to a screeching halt one evening when she appeared an hour late for supper. Cousin Margaret took one look at her bounding through the front door with the hem of her skirt tucked into her waistband and immediately suffered one of her patented fainting spells.

"Oh, my," she said, gasping for breath. "You are seventeen and you look like the daughter of a potato farmer. What have you done! Your father is one of the most respected planters in the entire state, and you present yourself at his table looking like a vagabond. You aren't a child anymore, Charlotte. You're a marriageable young woman with an enormous dowry."

"It's my fault, Meggie," Thomas said as he walked into the room.

"Charlotte is so like Anne, I've spoiled her. We'll work on it together, but for now let's enjoy our meal."

The work Papa referred to got underway in earnest the following week with the arrival of Madame Estelle, whose sole purpose in life was to transform potential spinsters into marriageable young butterflies. As four servants struggled to carry Madame Estelle's voluminous luggage to her room, Madame Estelle asked to interview Charlotte alone in the drawing room. Once there, Charlotte turned and twirled as she was told to do, and Madame Estelle emitted a groan that made the furniture shake. Then she rolled her eyes and let out a painful aaah...and said, "Where is your corset, child?"

"I don't wear one," Charlotte said defiantly.

"Well, I certainly have my work cut out," Madame Estelle said as Charlotte sheepishly left the room. "It's not completely hopeless, though. I've seen worse."

Charlotte's transformation got underway the following morning with a supervised scrubbing from head to toe and an inspection of her shameful sun damaged skin and hair.

"You are not to go out into the sun ever again without a proper bonnet and gloves, my dear," Madame Estelle began. "And Cornelia must see to it that buttermilk is applied to your skin every night at bedtime without fail. The sun will turn you into a gargoyle before you know it, and beauty is far too fleeting as it is," she said, sounding like she'd said the words a thousand times.

"At best, we women have but a few good years, so there is no need to hasten it. This is a battle we have to fight, knowing it is one we are destined to lose."

During the next few hours, Madame Estelle examined every petticoat, pantalette, chemise, stocking, and mantilla that Charlotte owned.

The examination was as critically performed as a diamond cutter study-ing the crown jewels, but it turned out to be pointless because Madame Estelle ended up discarding everything anyway.

Once Madame Estelle cut a swath through Charlotte's unmentionable drawers, she moved on to her outerwear. The best, however, was yet to come. After Charlotte was confined to the house for three days because all she had left to wear was her night clothes, a carriage arrived from Charleston. Charlotte stuck her head out of the window of her room to discover half a dozen dressmakers, two hat makers, and one scrawny shoe-maker, wearing pink satin shoes, packed into the carriage like firewood.

The entourage descended on the mansion, arguing and squabbling like geese. To add to the confusion, another carriage loaded with dress-maker forms, sewing notions, pattern books, cobbler's tools, and enough fabric to reach to Charleston and back again arrived moments later. Charlotte watched the invasion from her perch at the top of the stairs, hoping that no one could see through her dressing gown that was all she had left of her former wardrobe.

In the past, Charlotte had always been able to worm her way out of Cousin Margaret's attempts to turn her into a girl, but the only one who showed her the least bit of sympathy this time around was Cornelia. Even so, there was little Cornelia could do other than to assure Charlotte that it would all be better when morning time came, which they both knew was a lie.

Cousin Margaret was as proud as a peacock as she and Madame Estelle scurried about assigning rooms to the members of the onslaught, and Charlotte didn't have the heart to complain. Both women were in their glory. After all, they were rescuing a naive child from a life of certain spinsterhood. The next few days dragged by and dress patterns were scrutinized with surgical precision: "It needs a dart here, a nip there, a tuck here, and a flounce there."

Necklines, sleeve lengths, covered buttons, pearl buttons, grosgrain ribbon, satin ribbon, silk flowers, embroidered flowers, French silks, Belgian lace, stripes, dots, and brocades — Charlotte couldn't have cared less, but she held her tongue, hoping that her obedience would make everything end.

Selecting a hat should not take an entire afternoon, but according to Madame Estelle, there was no more important expenditure of time. "The bonnet," she said, "makes or breaks an outfit. To make the proper selection, one is required to take one's time." Not surprisingly, she felt equally strongly about the selection of mantillas, shoes, corsets, gloves, ribbons, jewelry, stockings, petticoats, cloaks, muffs, wigs, and hair combs.

Then there were dancing lessons, hair styling lessons, and etiquette lessons that Charlotte had been too obstinate to learn from Cousin Margaret. Six weeks later a triumphant yet tearful Madame Estelle climbed into her carriage and waved goodbye. She was off on another rescue mission, this time to Benton Hill Plantation to save three aging sisters from spinsterhood just as she had Charlotte.

Charlotte's first opportunity to show off her freshly honed man-snaring skills was Easter Sunday services at All Saints'. Looking as fresh and enchanting as a paper white and brimming with confidence thanks to her newly discovered breasts, Charlotte accompanied Papa to the family pew with nerves of tempered steel. She was poised for battle and she knew it. *Mothers, guard your sons. Madame Estelle's masterpiece has arrived.*

Charlotte could feel every eye trained on her, and to her surprise, she loved it. She surveyed the room with her chin up, and her eyes slightly lowered (to create an air of remote indifference), and then her eyes rested on the only male in the building (besides Papa) who wasn't lustily staring at her—Nicholas Prior—who was just back from college. Tall with dark curly hair, dark lashes, and pale blue eyes, Nicholas was beautiful.

Every girl in the parish had had a crush on him at one time or another, including Charlotte, but there was something disquieting about Nicholas, a preoccupation of sorts. Although his manners were impeccable, and he was of planter stock through his mother's side of the family, Nicholas always looked as though his thoughts were somewhere else. With Charlotte's newfound female prowess, his disinterest was as alluring as a drug.

Following the services, she saw Nicholas near the back of the nave and made a beeline in his direction. "Nicholas, I understand you have just graduated from medical school," she said, batting her eyes just as Madame Estelle had instructed her. "Congratulations."

"I did recently graduate from college, Miss Dunhill," Nicholas replied, "but not from medical school. I earned an advanced degree in botany, and I intend to do research."

"What kind of research, Nicholas?" Charlotte said, exhibiting a flirty smile.

"Plant research with special emphasis upon the hybridization of rice," Nicholas said, uncomfortably. "I hope to make a hybrid that is more resistant to disease, but I'm certain that is all very boring to a young lady like you."

"Oh, Nicholas," Charlotte squealed, forgetting everything Madame Estelle had drilled into her head. "You couldn't be more wrong. All I've ever wanted to do is grow things, and rice is the most interesting thing of all. Please tell me everything!"

After a few minutes, Papa walked over to the couple and quietly suggested that it was time to head home.

"Why don't you invite Nicholas to supper sometime, Charlotte," he added, seeing the look of disappointment on his daughter's face. Nicholas agreed to join them the following day, and on the ride home, Charlotte could barely control her excitement.

"Oh, Papa," she squealed, "I'm so happy. Nicholas is so handsome and so, well, handsome, and you know what, Papa? He likes the fact that I'm interested in botany. He says I know more about rice than he does and that being a female has nothing to do with how intelligent I am. Can you imagine that, Papa?"

"I can't imagine, Charlotte," Papa said, laughing. "I just can't imagine."

Seven months later in a beautiful wedding held on the east lawn at The Abbey, Charlotte and Nicholas were married. Charlotte didn't wear a bonnet the entire day nor did she wear buttermilk to bed ever again.

CHAPTER 6

Rogue Rice and Waterbugs

The Abbey Plantation 1840

AT PAPA'S INVITATION, Charlotte and Nicholas moved into the south wing of the big house at The Abbey following their honeymoon trip to Boston. Someday, of course, Charlotte's older brother, George, and his wife would inherit the plantation, but for now, they were happy living elsewhere, as were the rest of Charlotte's siblings, so Papa said he could use the company. Unlike their friends, however, Charlotte and Nicholas spent little time attending parties. They could usually be found traipsing through the rice fields together gathering specimens to put under Nicholas' microscope. Nothing was beyond their interest.

They studied and catalogued rice seeds, soil samples, and rice plants in all stages of development; they analyzed weeds and rogue rice, saw grass, insects, and water samples, but they spent most of their time comparing the subtle differences between the variety of rice grown at The Abbey and the other varieties grown on surrounding plantations.

"Nicholas, I'm having such fun," Charlotte said one day, as she organized a series of slides. "You don't supposed God will punish us, do you?"

"Punish us for what?" Nicholas asked. "You have me completely graveled."

"I'm worried that He will punish us for spending our days collecting weeds and insects and molds," Charlotte replied. "Maybe He'd rather have us build an orphanage or houses for the homeless."

"He gave you the mind of a scientist, Charlotte. If He didn't want you to use those skills, why would He have given them to you?"

"I didn't think of it like that," Charlotte said thoughtfully. "Perhaps we will do something important someday, but until then, do you think it's alright for us to just be happy?"

"I certainly do," Nicholas laughed.

Before long, Nicholas and Charlotte had assembled an impressive laboratory in a small room near the back of their living quarters, and Charlotte 's botanical drawings had transformed the walls of the laboratory into a gallery. Several months into their experiments, however, Charlotte's involvement in the laboratory was curtailed when she proudly announced that she was pregnant, and Nicholas banned her from the laboratory as a precaution to protect the baby. Charlotte had put her foot down when Cousin Margaret brought up the notion of confinement.

"Cousin Margaret, I'm not sick. I'm merely pregnant," Charlotte said. "Having babies is a natural thing, and I'm a modern woman. I'm not going to spend the last part of my pregnancy in bed."

"But it's safer for the baby," Cousin Margaret insisted.

"No, it's not," Charlotte replied. "Women have been having healthy babies for centuries without being confined," Charlotte argued. "Most of the women at The Abbey work right up to their due dates, and their babies are healthy, healthier than ours most of the time."

"But you're an aristocratic young white woman," Cousin Margaret replied. "You're more delicate than the plantation women, and besides, what would your friends think, seeing you rushing around like you do?"

"Meggie, I promise that if I have any problems, I will do whatever you say, but until then, I'm going to live my life the same as always."

"You promise to take good care of yourself," Margaret said, realizing that she had been defeated.

"I promise," Charlotte said, laughing. "I want a healthy baby, too."

Charlotte's predictions about having a healthy pregnancy came true, and it was a happy time. Cornelia fussed over Charlotte just as she had over Anne, and everyone eagerly awaited the arrival of the baby. Papa and Cousin Margaret even had a wager on the sex of the child. Cousin Margaret was convinced that it was going to be a boy, Papa, a girl.

Papa didn't get to collect on his bet, though. Cousin Margaret died without warning three days before the baby arrived. One morning she had been instructing a young servant as to the proper way to dust Papa's study when she complained of a stabbing pain in her left temple and collapsed.

"Master Dunhill! Master Dunhill!" the maid screamed. "Miss Margaret's had herself a spell!" But her warning had come too late. By the time Papa and Charlotte reached Cousin Margaret, she was gone.

Nicholas' father, Dr. Prior, concluded that Cousin Margaret had died of a seizure. "A blood vessel in her brain burst," he said, "killing her instantly." Thomas was devastated, and when Cousin Margaret's burial in the family cemetery was over, he took to his study. When Charlotte heard the bolt slide on the lock to the study door, she pleaded with Nicholas to make Thomas open the door. "Let's give him a little time to himself," Nicholas advised. So, Charlotte had a chair placed outside the study door, and she waited.

Hours later when Thomas finally unlocked the door and allowed Charlotte to enter the room, he admitted that he had cared about the old girl more than he'd realized. "She drove me crazy, but the house will be empty without her. It reminds me so much of losing your mother."

"Oh, Papa, please don't suffer so," Charlotte cried, kneeling down beside him. "Cousin Meggie was so full of life she wouldn't have wanted us to grieve like this." Charlotte was about to continue when a hot pain suddenly shot through her abdomen.

"Oh, Papa," she said, grabbing his hand. "It's the baby. I think it's time for the baby."

With that, Thomas sprang from his chair and shouted so loudly for Nicholas and Cornelia that the laundry maids heard him all the way out in the laundry yard. "The baby, the baby!" Papa shouted. "The baby's coming, Nicholas! Send for Dr. Bednar, Cornelia. Let's you and I get Charlotte up to her room. We're going to have ourselves a baby."

Thomas Dunhill Prior arrived seventeen hours later, and within minutes, was placed in the arms of his grandfather. "He looks just like your mother, Charlotte," he said in a half whisper. Then the baby scrunched up his face and offered Papa a tiny gas-induced smile. "Oh, and I think I see a little of Cousin Margaret in him too."

Thomas had six other grandchildren by now, but he'd never had a chance to spoil them, so little Thomas's every accomplishment was cause for celebration. The day he called out "Poppy!" as Master Thomas was entering the house, the elder Thomas threw a party for everyone on the plantation.

"Has there ever been a more amazing child?" he exclaimed as he crisscrossed the lawn introducing Thomas Dunhill Prior to the People.

"No sir, I reckon I ain't never seen one," was the usual reply. "He be a mighty fine young 'en. Mighty fine."

Thomas Dunhill didn't have the stage all to himself for long, however. Just two days before his second birthday, Charlotte gave birth to a daughter, Margaret Anne. If Master Thomas hadn't made a big enough fool of himself over his grandson, he more than made up for it after the birth of Margaret Anne.

Master Thomas was seldom seen after that without one or both of the children thrown over his shoulder like sacks of meal. He stole cookies for them from the kitchen and apples from the cellar. He tucked them into bed at night and made each of them a red, white, and blue whirligig for Christmas. But he was at the same time very strict with them when it came to demonstrating good manners and respecting their elders.

CHAPTER 7

Golden Jasmine

The Abbey Plantation 1848

AS CHARLOTTE AND NICHOLAS' family grew to include another son named Henry, so did their research. They compiled stacks and stacks of in-depth studies about the various varieties of rice grown along the river and were experts in the field.

"Where do we go from here, Nicholas?" Charlotte asked one night. "I feel like we're a couple of mad scientists. We probably know more about rice than anyone in the world, but we're not growing it; we're just studying it."

"I know," Nicholas said. "We've been so busy with our research and raising children, it seems like we've just been standing still. We haven't been, though. A few minutes ago, I checked on our cross-breeding samples, and they were all positive. It looks like we've done it, Charlotte. We've just propagated one of the best varieties of rice ever produced. I think we're going to get rich."

"Oh, Nicholas, are you certain?" Charlotte whispered.

"Of course I am," he replied, laughing. "I'm one of the world's leading authorities on rice. Didn't you know that?"

As it turned out, the rice performed even better than they dared dream. It not only produced more rice seeds per plant, it produced a shorter, stronger stalk that made the plant less prone to toppling over during the last few weeks of growth. They called the new hybrid *Golden Jasmine* because it was primarily a combination of Carolina Gold and Jasmine, the variety of rice commonly grown in the Far East.

Nicholas and Charlotte—the only female in the room—introduced the new hybrid to their fellow planters at the annual meeting of the *All Saints' Agricultural Society,* and it was an overnight success. Everyone wanted to grow this hearty new rice, and it couldn't be produced fast enough.

Charlotte and Nicholas made a fortune from their discovery, ten times more than they needed to buy their own plantation. The old Vereen plantation just across the river from The Abbey had recently gone up for sale, and Charlotte and Nicholas jumped at the chance to buy it. It was one thing to create a new variety of rice, but it was another to actually grow and harvest it.

Although Thomas was happy for Charlotte and Nicholas, he was still upset by the news because he was afraid that he'd never see his grandchildren again. "Papa, don't be silly," Charlotte said one afternoon as they strolled the gardens together.

"You can practically see the plantation from the upstairs piazza; it's just across the river. It's less than a mile away for heaven's sake."

"It won't be the same," he said. "Besides, you have everything you need right here at The Abbey. Why would you want to leave?"

"Papa, you know Nicholas and I love The Abbey. You're here, Mama's here, Cornelia's here. Someday this plantation will belong to George, though, and that's the way it should be. Besides, Nicholas and I need our own place, our own land that belongs to us. We've spent years preparing to grow rice, and now we need the resources to produce it. I'll make a deal with you," she said. "It's going to take months to get the plantation in shape—it's Ben Vereen's old place, you know, and the big house was wiped out in a fire two years ago. So, if it's alright with you, we'll continue to live here for the next year or so until we get things up and running. After that, I promise to send the children to see you any time you want to see them. I promise, Papa."

"You have yourself a deal, Charlotte. Cornelia, what's for supper?" he roared. "I'm as hungry as a horse."

As Charlotte and Nicholas gradually turned their focus upon building a new house at their new property, aptly named Jasmine Plantation, Charlotte's youngest brother, James, showed up for supper one afternoon to ask Papa if he would be opposed to him moving back home to The Abbey. James had recently graduated from the Medicine University of South Carolina in Charleston and had spent the past three months living with Haddrell at Oakhampton Plantation.

Unfortunately, Haddrell seldom said more than three words to anyone unless he had to, and James said he couldn't take it anymore. "Besides," he said, "I want to start my own medical practice, and Oakhampton is just too isolated. Living at The Abbey would be perfect for me, Papa."

Master Thomas, of course, was delighted at the prospects of having his youngest son back on the plantation and so was a certain young woman named Katherine Fitzsimmons. Katherine was the sixteen-year-old daughter of a South Santee River planter. She'd met James at her cousin's wedding at Mt. Holly Plantation and had told all of her friends that day that she was going to marry young Dr. Dunhill, and so she did.

Katherine and James were married six months later on the lawn of the big house. Katherine would have made a beautiful bride that day except that she was two months pregnant and sick as a dog most of the day. At one point, she even threw up on her wedding gown, but Cornelia and Charlotte whisked her off to the kitchen and cleaned her up so fast that no one was the wiser. Fortunately, by the end of the day, Katherine had lost most of her greenish cast, and everything ended on a high note with fireworks over the river and six raucous stanzas of "Sitting on a Rail."

Charlotte and Nicholas had finally finished their new house and were in the process of moving when Charlotte began to notice a change in Papa. Master Dunhill had always been an avid equestrian and spent most of his mornings at the stables inspecting the tack and tending to his horses, but he seldom went there anymore. He tended to spend most of his days in a large wicker rocking chair on the piazza, overlooking the river. When he did move about, he did it slowly.

After supper that evening, Charlotte mentioned her concerns to James, and James promised to look into it the next day. As promised, the following day James joined his father out on the porch and asked him about how he was feeling. "You're not yourself, Papa."

"Son, you're talking like a doctor again," Master Thomas replied. "I didn't send you to medical school so you could nag me about my health. I admit I do run out of steam faster than I used to, but it's nothing to worry about, and I don't want to be preached to anymore." Thomas wasn't fine, though. In the fall of 1846, two months after his sixty-sixth birthday, Thomas Dunhill died in his sleep.

Charlotte fell to her knees and sobbed when one of James's servants brought the news. "Nicholas," she wailed, "I've always had Papa to turn to, and now I'll never see him again."

"I know, dear," Nicholas said, trying to comfort her. "We have to be grateful for the time we did have with him and for the fact that he died peacefully. And there's another thing that I didn't tell you about. Last Sunday after supper, he told me that he was ready to go, Charlotte. He said he wanted to be with your mother."

Two days later, Charlotte, Cornelia, and the rest of the family stood by as Papa's body was placed on a small barge that was draped with black silk crepe and covered with flowers from Anne's rose garden. Charlotte had invited Cornelia to attend the funeral with the family, but she declined, explaining that she would rather do her grieving in private. So, she stood on the landing as the barge containing Thomas's body was rowed the three miles north to All Saints' Church for the funeral.

The sanctuary, there, was overflowing with more than two hundred of Thomas Dunhill's friends and fellow planters. The men who had rowed the barge weren't allowed to enter the church, of course, so they stood outside in the churchyard. After the funeral, Papa's body was brought home, back to the family cemetery at The Abbey and buried next to Anne. It was there that the People of The Abbey were allowed to pay their final respects.

The following day, Charlotte and her siblings gathered in their father's study where his attorneys took turns reading the various provisions of his will. As expected, Papa had been extremely equitable with the distribution of his estate. The Abbey was bequeathed to George, along with the London townhouse and Thomas's silver handled pistols. Oakhampton Plantation, the most productive of all of Papa's plantations, was to go to Haddrell. A smaller plantation known as Lower Plantation was bequeathed to James, along with the creek house on Pawleys Island, and to everyone's surprise, Charlotte was devised a sizable plantation on the Pee Dee River known as Swamp Plantation.

As the attorneys stopped for a moment to review their paperwork, Charlotte whispered, "Nicholas, did I hear that right? Did Papa leave me the plantation, or did he just leave me the income from the plantation?"

"He left you the plantation," Nicholas replied. "Swamp Plantation is yours to do with as you wish."

"But I'm a female," Charlotte said.

"You're a planter."

After regrouping, the attorneys went on to explain that the will prohibited the sale of any of Papa's plantations for three years and that his slaves—three hundred and twenty strong—were to remain on the plantations where they were currently living for the stipulated three-year period. After that time, if any of the plantations were sold, Papa requested that they be sold with their slaves, if possible, so as not to split up families. Large sums of cash (much of it from Anne's estate) were bequeathed in equal shares to Charlotte and her siblings, and then another sum was divided equally among the grandchildren.

Papa's personal effects were also bestowed: his long guns, family heirlooms, and jewelry, family portraits, his globe, and collection of antique maps, his pocket watch, his surveying instruments, and his cherished spyglass. The attorneys went on to explain that Master Thomas had made no additional provisions for the People, with one exception. Then they stopped their reading and requested that someone find Cornelia and ask her to step into the room. Cornelia arrived a few minutes later, and as she entered the room dressed in a traditional mourning dress and black kerchief, she looked puzzled by the urgency of the summons. She had diapered most of the people in the room and had rubbed salve on their skinned knees, but at that moment, she felt like she was surrounded by strangers.

"Come in, Cornelia," one of the attorneys said. "You may take a seat if you wish."

"No, sir, I won't be a' doing that if you don't mind," Cornelia replied as the door to the study was closed behind her, and she retreated into the shadows at the back of the room.

"Then we'll continue with the reading of Master Dunhill's will," the attorney said, "and this part concerns you, Cornelia."

I will and desire that my woman named Cornelia and her issue should from the time of my death have and enjoy full freedom in consideration of the faithful service performed by her to myself and children and that she be allowed to continue to live at The Abbey, if that is her wish, and to receive an annual sum of $100 for the remainder of her natural life.

A hush filled the room. It was against South Carolina law to emancipate a slave. Thomas Dunhill had known it; his lawyers knew it; everybody knew it, including Cornelia. As her weight shifted toward the wall behind her, Cornelia heard nothing beyond the word freedom: "Freedom for Cornelia and her issue."

As Cornelia tried to clear her head, she heard George in the background asking the attorneys how Papa expected them to fulfill his wish to free Cornelia if it was against the law. "Your father was a clever man," the older of the two replied. "Six months ago, he advised us that he wished to sign an affidavit stating that Cornelia's husband, Blue Russell, had secretly purchased his family's freedom. Two weeks later, Blue Russell drowned in an accident, so no one had known about the transaction except your father."

Unless she had been rocking a fussy baby or shelling peas in the kitchen, Cornelia had never allowed a member of her white family to see her seated. Slaves and their masters didn't sit together, ever. When James and Charlotte placed a chair next to her, she sat.

"Will it stand up in court?" George asked.

"I think so," the attorney replied, hiding his own thoughts on the subject. He opposed the idea of freeing slaves, thinking them little more than savages, but he had a job to do. "They're the words of a gentleman and a dying man," he said. "I don't think the courts will reverse them even though they do sound suspicious. We've seen it before. As far as we are concerned, Cornelia and her daughters are freewomen as of this moment," he said as if he were making the final argument to a jury. "As I said before, your papa was a clever man."

The rumor was that Cornelia's husband, Old Blue, paid eight hundred dollars for the freedoms, but he didn't have no eight hundred dollars; he barely had two nickels to rub together most o' his life, but now his girls were free, now and forever free like the paper said.

CHAPTER 8

I Don't Want to be Called Mammy No More

The Abbey Plantation 1848

"I'LL TAKE YOU HOME," James said, after helping Cornelia to her feet.

"No, Master James. I can be taking myself home," Cornelia said, "but I thank you all the same. Miss Charlotte, I'll be taking the rest o' the day off, if that's alright. I have a lot ta think on. Oh, an' before I go, I want ta be thanking Master Thomas. That was a kindly thing he done."

Cornelia left the room as quietly as she had entered it, but she was a changed woman; she was free. She had waited her entire life to hear those words, and now the thing was done. She just wished that Blue Russell had been alive to enjoy it. She hoped he was up in Heaven right now laughing at the snafu Master Dunhill pulled on the lawyers. Cornelia could go and do whatever she wanted to do for the first time ever, but she was nearly sixty years old. She was beginning to get her mother's rheumatisms, and besides, where would she go? The Abbey was her home.

Cornelia spent two days sitting alone in her house, ignoring the knocks at the door and the faces pressed against the windows. Then on the morning of the third day, she stepped out onto the porch and set out for the big house. When she got there, she went directly to Master Dunhill's old study and knocked on the door. "Master George, I'd like to speak to you if I could," Cornelia called out.

Through the door she heard George's voice: "Come in Cornelia, the door's unlocked." After accepting a seat facing George's desk, Cornelia said she was there to discuss her future plans.

"And what are they?" George asked.

"Well, sir, I've decided that I wanna stay on at The Abbey if you'll have me. I wanna keep on living in my own house an' I wanna keep on workin' in the big house, but I wanna be paid for my work now, Master George. I want to be paid two dollars cash money ever month."

"I think that can be arranged," George replied. "Because of Papa's will, it will be at least three years before any changes can be made here at The Abbey, and I can't imagine trying to run this place without you. Is there anything else I can do for you today?"

"Thank you, sir. That's mighty kind of you. Oh, and there's one more thing that almost slipped my mind. I don't wanna be called Mammy no more. From now on I wanna be called Cornelia."

CHAPTER 9

This Plantation is My Home

The Abbey Plantation 1855

SEVEN YEARS AFTER PAPA'S DEATH, the plantation bell at The Abbey began to ring off its hinges. "Who died?" the People asked each other as they nervously ran to the front lawn at the big house. The People didn't like change. They were uncomfortable with it because they had no control over who might be doing the changing. They waited.

Within a few minutes, the entire Dunhill family solemnly filed out onto the lawn: Master George and his wife and their children; Charlotte and Nicholas, and Master Haddrell from Oakhampton Plantation, and James and his wife. Cornelia brought up the rear. Everyone had swollen eyes, red noses, and handkerchiefs in their hands.

After a long pause, George held up his hands and said that he had an important announcement to make. "We've decided to sell the plantation," he said in a faltering voice. "We've finally come to the realization that each of us has too many other responsibilities to keep the plantation in the family any longer."

George owned several businesses in Charleston, a plantation on the Pee Dee, and managed three of his wife's plantations in Berkeley

County; he couldn't continue to manage The Abbey without help. He certainly couldn't turn it over to Margaret Anne; she was a Middleton now and thought that properties on the Waccamaw River were beneath her.

Haddrell was a brilliant plantation master, but he had his hands full overseeing his massive plantation on Sandy Island, and James ran his practice out of Georgetown. Charlotte was George's last hope, but they had a thriving rice hybridization business to manage, a growing family, and their home was at Jasmine Plantation. It was time for the Dunhill family to move on.

"I just signed the papers," George said with his lip quivering, "the papers selling the plantation to Plowden Weston. Master Weston already owns the three plantations just to the south of The Abbey, and many of you already know him. I can assure you that he will be a good master, and he has agreed to keep The Abbey just as it is."

Master Weston then stepped through the door of the big house, walked across the lawn, and took George's hand. "Thank you, George," he said. "I promise to take good care of The Abbey." Then he looked out over the crowd. "Nothing will change, here," he promised. "Your lives will go on just as before."

The People were stunned. The Abbey had been in the Dunhill family for nearly a hundred and fifty years. "How could it be so," they asked themselves as they slowly returned to their homes. "This is the saddest day of my life except for the day Papa died," Charlotte told Nicholas, as they watched the People walk away. "We shouldn't have done this. We should have kept the plantation no matter what."

"The ultimate decision was your brother's," Nicholas said. "We'll be right across the river, and you can visit whenever you want to. As for the cemetery—it will always be a part of this family, you know that. I'm just glad that it was Mr. Weston who bought the plantation. He's a fine man and one of the richest men in South Carolina. He'll spend whatever it takes to keep the plantation just as it is."

"I know," Charlotte said. "I'm grateful, too, but I'm worried about Cornelia. I know she's retired now, but I'm going to ask her if she'd like to move to Jasmine Plantation, if that's alright with you."

"Of course it is," Nicholas replied. "I know how much you love her."

Charlotte caught up with Cornelia as she was making her way along the path leading to her cabin. "Cornelia," Charlotte cried out. "Wait for me."

Cornelia knew what Charlotte was going to say even before she said it, and she had her reply all ready. "No, darling," Cornelia said. "I'm too old, and this plantation's my home. I don't want to leave. Besides, who's gonna tend your mama's gardens lessen I do? You go on home now, chil'. You can come visit me whenever you want to."

CHAPTER 10

Miss Cornelia's Last Days

1860

EVERYBODY ON THE PLANTATION knew the story of Miss Cornelia and how she had been given her freedom by old Master Dunhill and the fact that she was a wealthy woman on account of her saving all the money Master Dunhill had given her over the years. But she didn't socialize much, especially during the last few years. She was usually seen sitting on her porch. Folks were welcome to wave passing by, but they knew that Miss Cornelia wasn't one for gossip, so they just kept on going. During her last days, she was bound to her bed. Charlotte stayed with her night and day, sleeping on a pallet on the floor and taking real good care of Cornelia—lots better than those "spoilt daughters" of hers who lived in fancy houses in Charleston.

"Imagine, an' her being a fine lady an' all," the People whispered to each other about Miss Charlotte. They'd never seen a white lady do something like that, and they commenced to feeling genuine respect for Miss Charlotte.

As Miss Cornelia's body weakened, she was chilled most of the time, even on sunny days. Fall was coming with its eerie shadows that the children in the quarter called witch's fingers, and Charlotte was worried about keeping Cornelia warm. She'd begged Cornelia to come to Jasmine Plantation where she had enormous fireplaces that she could keep going all day, if necessary, but Cornelia wouldn't hear of it.

"I've lived in this cabin most o' my life," Cornelia said. "Why on earth do you think I'd think about leaving it now? I just got it broke in good. Besides if I was ta leave, Jesus might not be able ta find me when it's time ta go. God's got many mansions—plenty good room, missy. I'll get a bigger house when I go ta Heaven."

Cornelia's body might have been worn out, but there was nothing wrong with her resolve, so Charlotte quit trying to manage her and decided instead to just make her comfortable. That's when she remembered Cornelia's special quilt.

"Cornelia, where's your quilt, your Tree of Africa quilt?"

"It's in my grip under the bed. What do you want with it?"

"I'm going to wrap you up in it. You're cold and it's the warmest thing you have. I should have thought of it sooner." As Charlotte retrieved the grip out from under the bed, unlocked its latches, and pulled out the quilt, Cornelia let out a long sigh. Although practically every family in the quarter had a similar quilt, no two Tree of Africa quilts were alike. Cornelia's quilt was dominated by a stylized tree in the center with gnarled roots and big green leaves.

Brown stick figures representing Cornelia's ancestors were embroidered onto each of the leaves, and a four-inch band of blue denim appliquéd with smiling elephants, zebras, tigers and snakes formed a border around the quilt. At the bottom of the quilt in bold letters was the name: *Cornelia*. Someday, Cornelia's grandchildren would use the quilt to teach their children about Africa, just as Cornelia's mother had taught Cornelia.

"Promise me something," Cornelia said.

"Of course," Charlotte said.

"Promise me you won't bury me in that quilt. Promise you'll keep it for my grands. I got eight head now."

"I promise," Charlotte said, unfolding the magnificent quilt, "but for now, we're going to use it to keep you warm."

"Promise?"

"Promise."

"Well, now that we got our promisin' done, it does feel awful good. It's the warmest quilt I've ever worn. I've always worried 'bout wearing it out, but I won't be wearing it long; I'm feeling pretty poorly today."

"Oh, Cornelia, you're going to live forever," Charlotte whispered, turning her eyes away from Cornelia's gaze.

"I ain't sprouted wings yet chil', but I recon I will any day now."

Cornelia died four days later, two weeks shy of her sixty-ninth birthday. Miss Lillian and some of the other women from the quarter were with her when she passed. Nicholas and the children were in the yard. Cornelia's daughters had elected to stay in Charleston.

Cornelia was buried in the People's cemetery at The Abbey, and the wake was attended by practically everybody in Georgetown County. They came to pay their respects to Miss Cornelia, of course, but they also came to get a good look at her rich daughters, and the pair didn't disappoint. They showed up wearing black satin dresses and black velvet capes trimmed with real muskrat. Charlotte helped the daughters select a burial plot for Cornelia, but it wasn't as simple a task as Charlotte had anticipated. Unlike the Dunhill family cemetery where the graves of Charlotte's ancestors were laid out on a precise grid, the graves within the People's cemetery more closely resembled seeds that had taken root wherever they wanted to. When Cornelia's grave was dug, the gravediggers could have disturbed the grave of someone already buried in that spot. The possibility of overlap, however, wasn't the least bit troubling to Cornelia's daughters, so Charlotte kept her feelings to herself.

When it came to picking out Cornelia's burial outfit, however, Charlotte tactfully resigned from the selection committee. She had hoped Cornelia's daughters could have agreed on something suitable—even dignified, perhaps, but they had other ideas. They were determined to send their mother into eternity in the latest style. Cornelia went to her grave wearing a bright blue satin dress, silk stockings, a double-strand of fake pearls, blue satin shoes, and a cottage-style bonnet trimmed with pink satin roses.

"Help me, Jesus," Cornelia must have cried.

The funeral was held at dusk in the new slave chapel that Master Weston built on The Abbey's southernmost tip. Completed less than a week before Cornelia's funeral, St. Mary had a marble font and brilliant stained-glass windows. The chapel had been the dream of Master Weston, and was thought to be the largest People's chapels ever built.

It was large enough to easily seat as many as two hundred people, but it nearly burst at the seams during Miss Cornelia's big day when more than three hundred mourners squeezed together to say their goodbyes. The protocol for the service was unusual, to say the least. St. Mary was a slave chapel, a church designed specifically to accommodate the People and an occasional visit from Master Weston and his family, but Miss Cornelia and her family fell somewhere in-between. They were freed blacks. They weren't enslaved, but they weren't white, either, so where were they to sit?

They could have been asked to sit in the back of the church and would have had little recourse. At Master Weston's insistence, however, Cornelia's family was invited to sit on the front row to the left of the pulpit, while Charlotte and Nicholas and their brood of four occupied the pew just to the right. Margaret Anne sent her regrets, but George, James, and Henry were there, and they sat directly behind Charlotte and the Westons.

Because of the overcrowding and the disagreeable air that it generated, the service was mercifully cut short, but as the minister beseeched Heaven to open its gates to receive Sister Cornelia and the choir sang Cornelia's favorite song, "The Angels Are Coming," no one there could recall a finer send-off.

Cornelia's white family said goodbye at the chapel; only Africans had business in the People's graveyard after dark. So, Charlotte and the rest of the family made their way back to the big house, while the African mourners followed Cornelia's body through the fields and on to the cemetery.

The cemetery sat on a rise overlooking the river on the border that separated The Abbey from True Blue Plantation. It was a long walk from the quarter at The Abbey and an even longer one from St. Mary, so Miss Cornelia's body was carried to the cemetery aboard a mule-drawn wagon draped with black and purple crepe paper. The sky was the color of ink that night, and Charlotte's children were spellbound by the procession of torches weaving their way through the fields.

At dawn, Charlotte quietly slipped out of the big house where she and her family had spent the night and set out for the People's cemetery. She had to say goodbye to Cornelia one more time, no matter what. She and Nicholas were planning to return to Jasmine Plantation that afternoon, so this was her only opportunity. She made her way down the steps of the piazza and choked back tears as she passed beneath an enormous arbor formed from the branches of her mother's Saskatoon Serviceberry bushes that she had grown from cuttings given to her by Cousin Sarah at True Blue. Beneath the bushes, there was a profusion of chocolate lilies.

The familiar path started out at the carriage house, and then it went on to the smith shop. From there, it continued for another two hundred yards or so until it forked. Charlotte took the path to the left, the one that led past the tea garden and her mother's old rose gardens, and then into a pecan grove that Emily Weston had planted in one of the plantation's former indigo fields.

She continued past the rice mill and winnowing house and then along the top of the dike that ran parallel to the river. Each step was precious. She was saying goodbye to Cornelia, but she was also saying goodbye to The Abbey. She'd always be welcome to visit the plantation, of course, but now that Cornelia was gone, it wouldn't be the same.

She entered the cemetery the way everybody did, by removing a small section of fencing. Installing a proper gate would have made more sense, but it seemed to work just fine as it was, so that's the way it stayed. Charlotte then looked over a small rise in the center of the cemetery, and just beyond, she spotted Cornelia's grave.

Beneath the shade of a giant sycamore, the grave was covered with bouquets of flowers in every color and variety even though the funeral was held the last day of the year, 1860. Some of the bouquets were held together with ribbons, most with colored yarn. The flowers were from Mama's winter gardens. She'd be so pleased.

Large sea shells rested upside down at the head of the grave, and dozens of smaller ones had been placed at the foot of the grave. There was a jar of honey, a crystal from a chandelier, an empty pepper sauce bottle, and a wooden headstone that read

CORNELIA DUNHILL/ FREEDWOMAN / 1860

Kneeling beside the grave, Charlotte slowly traced the letters on the headstone, remembering Cornelia's gentle spirit. Her heart was broken. "Goodbye my dearest Cornelia," she whispered, and then from her pocket, she pulled out a triple strand of coral beads. She placed them on top of the grave.

"These are from Mama."

HATTIE'S STORY

CHAPTER I

Ladies in the Big House
is Mighty Spoilt

The Abbey Plantation 1848

HATTIE WINEGLASS KNEW THINGS. By the time she was six, she was advising folks to suspend egg shells above their fireplaces to keep the hens laying and to chase away the miseries with pokeberry wine. She had her grandmother's gift, alright, and Miss Lillian's powers had come straight from Jesus.

Hattie was born on The Abbey during the summer of 1848, and she and her family lived with Miss Lillian in a whitewashed cabin near the far end of the quarter. Hattie's mother, Sheila Wineglass, ran the children's nursery. Miss Lillian's best friend was Miss Cornelia, who was the only freedwoman on the plantation besides the white folks. Freedom didn't change her all that much, though. Cornelia was the same tough-as-nails hard working woman she'd ever been. But the old master had promised her money every year—round about a zillion dollars, everybody said. So, Miss Cornelia was rich—maybe richer than the master, hisself.

Hattie's papa was Trumpeter Wineglass, the plantation's youngest trunk minder, which was a source of pride for the family because trunk minding was one of the most important jobs on the plantation. Master

Weston held Trumpeter in high esteem. The year before, Trumpeter had saved more than half of the plantation's rice crop with his quick trunk minding, and Master Weston rewarded him by allowing him to select a title: his own surname.

Enslaved people like Hattie and her family were the property of their owners and were of such little consequence that their names weren't entered into census records. They were simply given a first name to differentiate them from the other slaves living on the same plantation. It wasn't surprising then that being allowed to select one's own surname was an enormous honor. In recent memory, only the plantation's head carpenter had been allowed to do that.

Everyone had expected Trumpeter to take Master Weston's last name, all except Trumpeter. He respected Master Weston and all, but he'd spent months thinking about his new name, and he was having none of that. His plantation name was Lil' Jacob, but Trumpeter didn't want to be Lil' Jacob or Big Jacob or any other kind of Jacob, anymore. So, when the time came to reveal his selection to Master Weston, Trumpeter didn't hesitate. He picked Trumpeter Wineglass.

"That name goes into my records," Master Weston said, seated at his desk with his ledger book in front of him. "It's going to be official, so make sure it's the name you're going to keep."

"Oh, I'm gonna keep it alright," Trumpeter proudly replied. "There won't be no need to change it, not ever." When Trumpeter arrived home to tell his family what had transpired in Master Weston's office, Sheila couldn't believe her ears.

"Trumpeter Wineglass? What the hell kinda name is that?" she blurted out. She was mad. You could tell by the way she had her hands mounted on her hips and her feet dug in. She was itching for a fight.

"You should'a picked a powerful name like Hercules or Zeus. Hercules Weston, now that's a proper name. Trumpeter sounds like a bird. You gotta go back an' change it, Lil' Jacob. I don't want to go through the rest of my life bein' called Sheila Wineglass!"

"It's my name, and I'm keeping it."

"Where'd you come up with a name like that?" Sheila asked, refusing to call her husband by his new name.

"My granny had a wineglass she got from the big house once, and it was nearly as big as a trumpet. Granny said it was shaped like Gabriel's horn, and it had magical powers. I don't know if it was magic, but Granny loved it, and we put it on her grave when she died. It's a done deed, Sheila. I'm keeping the name."

"It's a stupid name."

"I don't care. It's done."

Miss Lillian's cabin was ten paces wide and fifteen paces long with windows on either end and two more overlooking the porch, which was a recent addition. Just like the other houses in the quarter, the cabin sat on tree stumps aimed at improving air circulation and cutting down on uninvited guests, namely snakes. Velvety mosses and Lady Ferns grew in the cracks between the roof tiles, and in summertime, the yard was a profusion of lilies of the field. The cabin had a fireplace, a kitchen table, two chairs, a shelf to hold dishes, and two beds, one for Miss Lillian and one for Sheila and Trumpeter. Hattie slept on a pallet on the floor with her older sister, Rachael. The baby, four-year-old Lacey, slept with Miss Lillian.

Earlier in the year, Master Weston let Miss Lillian retire from her seamstress duties due to the rheumatisms, but she kept busy. She was the plantation doctor, and when she wasn't puttin' on splints and passing out tonics, she was busy performing spirit consultations. Tree spirits, conjures, magic spells, and witchcraft plagued the plantation, so Miss Lillian was in heavy demand from daylight 'till dark. Everybody on the plantation was petrified of the spirits, all except Miss Lillian, or so she said. She said spirits wasn't anything to be afraid of because "they wasn't real."

"Brain figmentations," that's what she called them, but when a cat yelped or an owl screeched in the middle of the night, her eyes got as big as everybody else's. Then she'd whip up one of her special elixirs or incantations, and come morning, the spirits would be gone.

Miss Lillian and Hattie were experts at everyday things, too. Spiderwebs inside the house were good luck, but don't never toss a hat on a bed. That simple act could conjure up a curse that could only be broken by sticking a pin in the crown of the hat and hanging it above the bed overnight. A few prayers to Jesus wouldn't hurt, either.

Knowing when to plant was another specialty. Cotton had to be planted during a new moon when the soil was warm and the air smelled like rain, but sweet potatoes grew best when planted on a cooler night during a waning moon.

Everybody wants something they can't have, and Hattie was no different. Miss Lillian taught Hattie practically everything in the whole world that was important, but the one thing that Hattie wanted more than anything, Miss Lillian couldn't give her. Hattie wanted to learn to read. Ever since the day she watched Daddy Tom reading to the people from the steps of the chapel, she had had an itch to learn to read. Reading was magic; she was certain of that because how else could anyone turn squiggles and lines and circles and little rat tails into words? How else could you explain thoughts and ideas jumping off the page like chiggers on a griddle without the notion of magic?

So, why couldn't Miss Lillian teach Hattie to read? She could fix broken wings, clear the croup from babies' lungs, and sometimes, she could even make it rain, but Miss Lillian said she didn't understand the wonderment of reading, and it would take an act of God or Jesus or the Father of Israel to teach Hattie that. It would be easier to make pigs do cartwheels than to conjure up a reading potion, she said, but she'd surely try.

Hattie took to sulking. She was going to find a way to learn to read, or she was going to die trying. Nobody ever wanted anything more than Hattie wanted to learn to read. She would have given practically anything just to get to touch a book and to get to look at its pages? Well, she didn't even have words for that.

Going to the Big House

The Abbey Plantation 1853

JUST AS HATTIE WAS about to celebrate her seventh birthday, she caught the attention of the plantation overseer. Mr. Turner was new at his job, and he was out to impress Master Weston. He was a man with big dreams, little education, and no prospects.

Turner was the typical overseer, and he was expected to run the plantation doing whatever it took to grow every last grain of rice possible, just as long as he didn't offend the sensibilities of Master Weston in the process. One of his many responsibilities was to assign slave children to their first jobs. By the age of six or seven, most of the children on the plantation worked on trash gangs, small groups of children that did odd jobs, such as toting drinking water to the field hands or weeding gardens. As they got older and stronger, most of them were sent to work in the fields.

Sheila had always been comforted by the fact that Hattie was on the scrawny side and too small to work on a trash gang. Sheila had an uneasy feeling, though, when she looked up one afternoon to find the hated overseer standing in the doorway to the nursery. He smelled like horse piss, and his beard and teeth carried the stain of tobacco. If bats were the souls of the Devil's children, Miss Lillian had once postulated, then Mr. Turner had grown up in a cave somewhere suspended by his feet.

"Sheila, I jest spotted two boys out in the yard who are big enough to go to work," he said in his usual nasty way. "Tell me their names, so I can add 'em to my list."

After identifying the boys, Sheila held her breath, hoping that Mr. Turner hadn't noticed Hattie, who was playing less than ten feet away. Just as she was about to let out a sigh, the overseer said in his low-class, white-trash voice, "Oh, and have that little gal of yours report to the big house in the morning. Misses wants someone to comb her hair. You jest keep in mind if she don't show up, her little black ass will end up on a trash gang. You remember that, now."

That evening Sheila told Miss Lillian about her conversation with Mr. Turner. Miss Lillian said she was sad about Hattie having to go to work so young and all, but she'd be mighty thrilled if Mistress Weston took a liking to Hattie and wanted her to continue working in the big house.

"Ain't no snakes or gators in the big house like there is in the fields," Miss Lillian shouted. "No Siree!"

Sheila broke the news to Hattie the next morning, and she and Miss Lillian didn't even wait for a response before they stripped off her nightgown and shoved her into the wash tub.

"Ladies in the big house is mighty spoilt," Sheila said in between passes with the scrub brush. "You got to treat them with respect, or they kick you out in the fields. With you being nothing more than a little slave chil', you best figure on being scared the whole time."

Pink from all that scrubbing and wearing her Sunday dress, Hattie walked with Miss Lillian to the end of the avenue, and then they continued halfway up the walkway to the back of the big house. Then Miss Lillian stopped and said: "This is as far as I can go, Hattie. Now, you go to the kitchen behind the house and knock on the door. Cook'll be there, and she'll tell you where to go. Just do 'xactly what you is told."

Hattie stood like a statue as she watched her grandmother walking away from her. She was too scart to move. Maybe if she just stood here long enough, the angels would swoop down an' take her to glory.

So, she stared down the lane, but nothing happened, no wing flapping or angel voices, just a little girl standing so still she looked like a garden ornament. Hattie had to get on with it. It was up to her and her Sunday meeting dress to break the statue spell she'd put on herself and get to moving. So, she tiptoed past the master's gardens and terraces and climbed the steep wooden steps leading to the kitchen. She did it somehow, but once she was there, she was too scart to knock, so she just stood quiet-like until one of the kitchen maids spotted her and dragged her through the kitchen door.

Then Cook took Hattie by the arm and spit-washed her face. Then she tried to smooth down Hattie's wild head of hair. It was sticking out in all directions, making Hattie look like a wild thing, Cook said. So, she slapped a little lard on the sticking out parts and stepped back. "Much better." Then she ushered Hattie into the interior of the big house through a large paneled door. Hattie followed Cook down the hallway where she smelled beeswax combined with the scent of lemon oil. It reminded her of her Mama's funeral cake she always made when someone in the quarter died.

If Hattie hadn't been so frightened, she would have noticed the dining room, and she would have been awestruck. The room's ceiling was decorated with richly carved festoons and medallions, and the walls were covered with silk wallpaper hand painted to replicate the gardens at Versailles. The room's enormous shutters were called box shutters. Their clever design enabled them to be adjusted from inside the house rather than having to bother with going outside. Above the shutters were gold leafed cornices, and draperies made of the finest Italian silk. The draperies were held in place by tassels the size of a man's forearm.

There were enough place settings on the table to feed a small army. If Hattie had had her wits about her, she might have noticed. She also might have noticed that the dining table was made of three smaller tables placed end-to-end. The table in the center had leaves that reached to the floor and were made out of single planks of mahogany. The buffet to the left of the table was more than eight-feet-long and much taller than Hattie. Had she been on stilts, she could have seen the china stored there. Exotic birds decorated the center of each plate, tea cup, saucer, and serving bowl, while wide bands of gold and burgundy decorated the outer portions of the plates. The china pattern was called Laurel Hill, after the plantation where Master Weston had grown up, and it had been created exclusively for the family. The room's piece de resistance, however, was a crystal chandelier. Cook liked to point out that it had come all the way from Paris, France.

"See that ober there?" Cook said referring to the mistress's collection of silver serving pieces. "That's worth a go-zillion dollars. Mistress got spoons for coffee and different ones just for choc-let. See those big things ober there?" she said, pointing to a table containing domed platter covers. "They's big enough to hide a brace of ducks. Don't you go touchin' nothing though; you'll get your ass in a world of trouble."

"Yes, ma'am," Hattie whispered.

They arrived at the stairway, and Cook looked down at Hattie and said, "Do everything the mistress tells you to do and you be alright. Now, you git on up them stairs. Miss Emily's door is the first one on the left. You do know which side is the left?"

"Yes, 'am, I do," Hattie said softly.

"Then get goin'. You'll be alright, girl. Just mind the mistress."

As Hattie turned to look at the enormous stairway, she tried to take a big swallow, but she was out of spit by then, so she just kept studying the stairs. They went straight up to Heaven; she was sure of it, just like the preacher, Brother Abraham, described in his sermons about Resurrection Time and going to Heaven to rest in the bosom of the Lord. She would have rather gone to Heaven at that moment than to have climbed those stairs, but she was told to go up 'em, so up 'em she went.

Once she got to the mistress's dressing room, she saw a pair of small gilded chairs upholstered in silks and velvets, draperies dripping with fringes and lace, a looking glass almost as tall as the ceiling, and fancy little bottles filled with something that smelled better than anything she'd ever smelled before. Wardrobes lined the far wall, spilling over with dresses in more colors than Hattie ever knew existed. To the left was another kind of the wardrobes with glass doors. On one shelf, there were gloves all neatly sandwiched together in carefully arranged stacks. Some of the stacks contained white gloves; others contained black. Broaches, feathers, beads, and handkerchiefs were also displayed there.

My, Miss Weston must be a mighty important woman. The rest of the wardrobe was taken up with large round boxes. Hattie took them to be hat boxes. Then she spied more than a dozen hats without their boxes, all in velvety colors. Who knew that there were so many shades of purple or blue or brown, and where did all the trimmings come from? Hattie wondered as she studied the netting and feathers, ribbons and laces.

Hattie just couldn't imagine having so many beautiful things to choose from. Why one of those fancy purple feathers probably cost more than everything Hattie owned. Jesus must think a whole lot of Miss Weston to give her such wonderful things. Hattie was just about to touch a delicate blue hat that was sitting on a pink and yellow striped settee when she realized that she wasn't alone. She turned to her left, and it was then that she found herself eyeball-to-eyeball with the mistress who was sitting on another of those fancy little chairs. Hattie attempted to curtsy, expecting her heart to beat right out of her chest at any moment.

"Good morning, Hattie," Mistress Weston said, but Hattie couldn't speak. The devil had her tongue. "Hattie," Mistress Weston said again, "it's alright, child. All I want you to do is to brush my hair. No one is going to hurt you."

"Yes, ma'am," Hattie mumbled.

The mistress's hair was the color of a brindle calf, and when she removed her night cap, it fell down the back of her chair halfway to the floor. *This is not the way the Lord made people hair. The mistress has corn silk sprouting out of her head.* Hattie was afraid to touch it. *Did white people's hair carry a curse?* She'd never heard of one, but you could never be too cautious, so she just stood there praying for lightning to strike.

Then the mistress handed her a fancy gold brush, and Hattie lost her resolve. She'd probably get whopped with the brush if she didn't start to brushing, so she walked over to the cursed hair and started to lightly touch it with the bristles. Then she decided that she had started in the wrong place, so she tried to pull the brush away, and that's when everything went wrong.

Suddenly Mistress Weston's silky hair was one big tangled mess. Hattie tried to brush it out; she tried really hard. She must have tried too hard, though, because in the middle of things, Mistress Weston let out a yelp! Then Hattie got to crying and wet herself on the mistress's rug, and she knew she was in big trouble. Not knowing what else to do, Hattie knotted up in a ball on the floor, waiting for the first lick of the hair brush when the mistress told her in a soft voice that she wanted her to go. When Hattie got home and told Mama what had happened, Mama pulled down her drawers and whooped her good.

She had good reason. After a disaster like that, Hattie would end up working in the fields for the rest of her life. Sometimes, though, the strangest things happen. Mr. Turner showed up the following morning as friendly as you please to tell Sheila that Hattie was to become one of Sheila's apprentices in the children's house. "And this is from the mistress," Mr. Turner said, handing Sheila a blue and white stripped hatbox. Mr. Turner never said another word about the incident at the big house, and no one ever knew where his generosity had come from or why the mistress had given Hattie the blue-ribboned bonnet.

"It's just one of the Lord's sweet mysteries," Miss Lillian used to say to explain away Mr. Turner's behavior, but she wasn't completely sold on the motive behind the bonnet, it being a white person's hat and all. To be on the safe side, Hattie was only allowed to wear the bonnet indoors. "No sense in upsetting the spirits," Miss Lillian said.

"I thought there weren't any spirits," Hattie remarked one day. "You said they were brain figmentations."

"Most of them are brain figmentations," Miss Lillian said thoughtfully. "But it's possible that there are one or two real spirits out there. It's unlikely, but it's possible, so until I'm certain, we're gonna keep you and your new bonnet indoors."

CHAPTER 3

Beautiful Rachael

The Abbey Plantation 1858

FOLKS IN THE QUARTER were solicitous toward Hattie. Practically every evening someone would stop by and ask about the tide or the soil or the best time to plant daffodils or potatoes. People just seemed restless until they were assured by Miss Lillian or Hattie that they was doin' the right thing. Behind their backs, though, some people said there was something unnatural about them, something they couldn't wrap their minds around. "Maybe Hattie and Miss Lillian descended from witches? Miss Lillian had knots beneath her coarse gray hair where her ancestors had had small horns," they said. They didn't do their snickering and postulating in front of Miss Lillian, though. They were always on good behavior around her, trying to keep their heads clear of dangerous thoughts. Sometimes Miss Lillian could read minds.

One day a group of children just coming off a trash gang saw Hattie in the yard of the children's house. They were hot and sweaty from carrying water out into the fields all day, and they were ticked off by Hattie's seemingly cushy job, so they started taunting her. "Jest 'cause you're a witch don't mean you're better 'en us," one of them shouted. "There you are sittin' on that porch lookin' all high and mighty in de shade, while we's out in de fields bustin' ourselves. It ain't right. We know what you done; you put a spell on the oberseer, an' we're gonna tell him about you."

"I'm not a witch," Hattie yelled back at them, "and I work jest as hard as you."

"Oh, sure Miss Prissy Pants. Sure. We can't get you some lemonade?" another yelled back before they disappeared down the lane. Hattie watched them. Her lower lip quivered, and she tuned up and cried. She didn't blame them. Her job was easier than theirs, but she didn't put a spell on Mr. Turner to get it. Miss Lillian might of, though. Hattie hadn't thought about her granny slapping Mr. Turner with a spell, but she might of. There were a lot of spells out there zipping this way and that, bouncing into each other and fragmenting. A broken spell was a dangerous thing; they could crash into other broken spells and make new ones. Magic was dangerous business.

Hattie was a natural-born seer and spell caster, but her older sister, Rachael, hadn't inherited any of her grandmother's gifts, and as far as she was concerned, the belief in potions and charms and incantations was poppycock.

Rachael had her own gift. Rachael was beautiful. Her dark skin wrapped around bones that looked as though they had been sculpted by an artist. Her nose, her cheekbones were perfect. Her black eyes were the size of dresser drawer pulls, and she wore her hair pulled back in a knot to emphasize her long, graceful neck.

Rachael had delicate hands and narrow feet, and Hattie couldn't point to a single spot on Rachael's entire body that wasn't perfect. Even her teeth were small and white and not all crammed together like Hattie's. Rachael may not have had Hattie's gifts for the supernatural, but she was still the envy of every girl in the quarter.

Rachael and Hattie weren't especially close, at least when Hattie was little. They seldom even saw each other. Rachael worked as a seamstress, and Hattie was assigned in the children's house. Evening times, Hattie was usually off with Miss Lillian learning spells and such, and Rachael was with her friends. They shared a pallet at night, though, and some-times Rachael would talk about her dreams. Rachael was searching for something. She was unsettled; it might have been a better way to put it. She wanted more than her lot, and she was beginning to figure out how she just might get it.

Rachael was assigned to the laundry house where her every day job was checking garments for missing buttons and torn hems, but she also excelled at appliqué and tatting, and Mistress Weston often found special jobs for her to do in the big house. Rachael was going on fifteen, and just like a fertility doll, she was ripe with possibility—and there was this boy. The boy was Mistress Weston's nephew who was visiting from Charleston. He was a Middleton and spoiled even by Middleton standards.

His features were pinched and his manners insolent; even Rachael could see that, but he was smooth-tongued when it came to talking girls into doing things they never dreamt of doing. He also had the experience of a well-oiled alley cat. The boy had been caught sneaking out of his younger sister's room in the wee hours, and he refused to tell his father what he had been doing there. The decision to ship him off to military school was quickly made, but making the necessary arrange-ments would take time. His parents couldn't risk having him remaining in the same house as his sister even for one more day, so they prevailed upon Emily Weston to allow him to spend his last two weeks at The Abbey before heading off to school.

Cousins to Emily through her father's side of the family, the Middletons weren't exactly forthcoming with the reasons for the rather odd request, but Emily took it in stride. Childless, Emily Weston attracted strays of all kinds, including a pet raccoon that terrified her staff but delighted its owner.

Rachael crossed paths with the boy a time or two before she took much notice, but that was going to change once the boy figured out a way to get her alone. So, he started nosing around the laundry house and the path leading between the laundry house and the big house.

"Pretty girl, come here," he said one day as he found Rachael walking up to the big house. Rachael turned a deep shade of purple and kept on going. "Come here," he whispered. Again, Rachael ignored him. So, he followed her a little ways until she came into view of the big house;

then he backed off. Their game continued until Rachael gave herself away by cutting her eyes toward the boy just as he was looking up at her. "Meet me at the winnow house," the boy said. "I'll give you something that will look real pretty around your beautiful neck."

"I can't," Rachael said, astounded that she had managed to speak.

"There are other pretty girls on this plantation," the boy said, teasingly. "I'll give the necklace to one of them, instead."

Now Rachael had been expecting something like that. Boys in the quarter offered her gifts all the time, but they were as poor as she was, and they had little to give. One boy had offered her a pair of silk ladies' shoes, but even at a distance, she could tell that they were worn over and stained. Another boy wanted to give her licorice from the general store, and another had drawn her picture in charcoal on the back of a feed sack. She wasn't interested in trash from poor boys; any fool would turn down offers like that.

A necklace from a Middleton, however, was something altogether different. Rachael was a pretty girl; she knew it, but pretty girls didn't last long in the rice fields or even in the laundry house. She knew she was already on the list of marriageable females; she could even be sold into a marriage, although she'd never known Master Weston to do such a thing.

Before that happened, she was going to take a chance. "I'll meet you," she said, taking the boy by surprise. "Let me see the bobble."

"Did I say it was a bobble?" the boy asked.

"No, but I won't meet you if it's not."

"Why, you little tramp," the boy said, revealing more of himself than he had intended.

"The bobble, please," Rachael said.

"Oh, the bobble. Yes, the bobble," the boy said as he searched his pocket.

"Ah, and here it is," he said, holding the necklace up for Rachael to see. "You want it? You're going to have to meet me. Meet me at seven tonight," the boy whispered, smiling.

"The People don't keep watches," Rachael said, almost in a taunting way.

"Then sundown," the boy said. "Meet me at sundown."

"I'll try," Rachael replied, disappearing into the rear door of the laundry house. As Rachael settled into her chair near the smaller of the two fireplaces, an older laundry maid named Matilda said, "Well, Miss Rachael, looks like you're gonna be the talk around here."

"What do you mean?" Rachael asked.

"Iffen you do what I think you're planning to do with that Middleton boy, you're gonna be the source of dirty talk. Dirty girl, dirty talk."

"I didn't do anything wrong," Rachael whispered. "I didn't do anything."

"A pretty girl like you doesn't have to do anything wrong, at least not anything sinful. Just talking to a white boy like that is wrong; don't you know that, girl? What do you think he wants from you? He wants to put his fingers in places they don't belong, and then he'll put his thing there, too. That's what white boys do, you stupid girl. What did he promise you?"

"He didn't promise me anything," Rachael said, defensively.

"I know he promised you something 'cause I saw him," Matilda said. "Ain't nothing he got that's worth losing your purity over, girl. Ain't nothing worth that except a good, honest husband."

"I don't want a husband," Rachael said. "I just want to have something exciting happen to me, that's all. I see all them pretty things the mistress has, and I want 'em, too."

"We all want 'em, you stupid girl, but we ain't gonna get 'em because we was born into slavery. You want somethin' fancy to happen to you? Well, imagine telling your mama that yo' is knocked up with some white boy's baby. Then see how much excitement you're havin'. 'But, Mama, he's a Middleton.' Don't be a fool, girl. Half the women in the quarter have been chased by some white boy, and lord only knows how many was caught. You know how much white blood there is in the quarter? Buckets of it. Do you think light skinned babies just fall outta the sky?"

"No," Rachael said on the verge of tears.

"Well, yo' be right," Matilda said.

"Look, girl. As long as there's slavery, there will be mixed babies. There will always be sons and nephews and uncles lurking about ta tell you lies and ta get under your skirts. They'll slobber all over you, and then they'll tell their friends that you gave them fleas."

"How do you know all of this?" Rachael said.

"'Cause it happened to me," Matilda said, with a down-turned smile that exposed a large gap between her middle teeth. "I grew up on a plantation on John's Island, and I had me a fling with a couple o' the master's sons, sometimes one right after another. Their daddy was rich and powerful, and I thought I was just about the fanciest gal there ever was 'til they gave me fleas and a baby that was born dead. No decent black man would have anything to do with me after that," the woman said. "I got too fancy for my britches and sold myself cheap. I had a husband, once, but he was no good and he beat me when he got liquored up. You know what he called me when he was drunk? 'Trash,' and there wasn't nothin' I could do about it. I was trash. I was fifteen when I made that life-altering decision, and I'm still payin' for it. Don't you do that, darlin.' Ain't no man on the face of the earth worth being called names for, and I should know."

Matilda gave Rachael a kiss on the forehead, and picked up a basket of wet laundry and set out for the clotheslines. Rachael was both relieved and ashamed. She hadn't even told the woman about asking to see the bobble. She hadn't told her how coy she was or how emboldened she was or how trashy. She'd been wooed by a snake, and the part that scared her was that she'd liked it. That evening, she stood up to the boy by not showing up at the winnow house. He was probably plenty mad.

Rachael and Matilda became friends after that, and over the next several days, Rachael grew to trust her with her secrets. She also learned that it was natural to have feelings in your lady parts when a man gave you a compliment or looked at you a certain way, but it didn't mean you had to romp around in the hay with him.

"Your body belongs to you."

"My body belongs to Master Weston."

"It's 1858, and it ain't gonna be like that forever," Matilda replied patting Rachael's knee. "Freedom's coming. I can feel it, but freedom won't change somethings all that much, and taking care of yo'self is one of 'em. You are precious in Jesus' sight, but it don't work unless you're precious in your sight, too."

"Precious in my own sight?" Rachael asked, laughing.

"You know what I mean. You just go on and treat yo'self right."

"Thank you," Rachael said, smiling.

"Yo' is certainly welcome."

Having a rich white boy flirting with her had made Rachael feel all prancy inside, but even before her conversations with Matilda, Rachael knew that it was dangerous to think that a colored girl could have anything to do with a white boy, especially one from a family as wealthy as the Middletons. The Middletons owned hundreds of slaves, maybe as many as a thousand. When you own someone, you have complete control over her, including her future. In this instance, the Middleton boy had all power, and she had none, so the only thing Rachael could do was to stay away from him and hope that he had moved on to someone else. The Middleton boy hadn't been privy to the wisdom being passed on in the laundry house; he only knew that a little black bitch had stood him up. He was pissed, and he was going to get even before he left for home the following week. He'd be gone by the time the story got out, so who cared.

Of course, there were other Middletons who weren't as lucky as he was. Being born on the wrong branch of the family tree made you invisible. He had siblings and cousins in the quarter back home; everyone knew it, and there was every chance that he had fathered a few of those little black bastards himself. He'd gotten off to an early start, after all; but this girl was different. This one had stood him up, figuring she could wait it out until his stay at The Abbey ended, and he was shipped off to school.

He had one more week at The Abbey, and that would be plenty of time to get even. He knew that Rachael worked in the laundry house, so he laid in wait. Huge serviceberry bushes separated the back of the laundry house from the path leading up to the big house. They were perfect cover, so that's where he waited. Two days into his wait, he saw her. Her beautiful face and starched white apron made him all the more determined as he watched her round the corner of the laundry house on the path that skirted the serviceberry bushes.

He grabbed her before she could even let out a scream. It was easy; he just reached out, and there she was. As he locked his hand over her mouth, her black eyes glistened and a sob rumbled up from her throat, but it was trapped beneath his hand. She was terrified, and he liked it. He should do this more often. He dragged Rachael away from the path and deeper into the berry bushes with one hand over her mouth and the other around her waist. "Now, aren't you sorry you didn't meet me?" he growled. Rachael could only shake her head, but at that moment, it wouldn't have mattered what she did.

Then the boy threw her to the ground and tore the front of her blouse, leaving deep scratches across Rachael's chest, but she fought back. That's when he hit her the first time, slugging her as hard as he could in the stomach. She cried out, and he grabbed her wrists to keep her quiet. Then he tore at her skirts, and she screamed, and he hit her again, this time catching her in the jaw.

In the process, he had to let go of Rachael's wrists. It was a mistake. Rachael reacted within the blink of an eye by attacking the boy's face with her fists, and that time it was his turn to cried out. He covered her mouth again, but she bit his hand. Then he delivered a searing blow to her head.

Rachael reeled as pain shot out of every pore. It was beautiful, and the boy stopped for a moment to admire his handiwork. He'd like to do that again, too. He grabbed at her again when suddenly he was hit with a blinding blow across the bridge of his nose and a thunderbolt to his crotch. Out cold, the boy fell forward, landing on top of Rachael. His eyes were dull, and blood was spurting from his broken nose.

"Get up!" a voice cried. "Get up!"

Rachael's left eye and jaw were badly swollen, and the boy's dead weight had her pinned, but her rescuer pulled the boy away until she had enough room to roll out from under him. Then, keeping her eyes locked on the boy, she stood on shaky feet, trying to cover herself with her tattered blouse. It was then that she looked up at her rescuer. It was Matilda. She was holding a mop, the weapon she had used to crush the boy's nose and privates.

"Get outta here," Matilda said in a whispered scream. "Get out!"

"But what about you?"

"It ain't nothing to me."

"But what are we going to do? We could be whipped for this. Or sold! We could be sold."

"It ain't nothing to me," Matilda repeated. "Now, get!"

Rachael obeyed, but not before whispering "thank you." Then she was off, grateful that dusk had set in hard, and she could make her way home unnoticed. Rachael's jaw was so swollen by then that she had difficulty breathing as she made her way home. It was a moonless night, and she could barely see enough to put one foot in front of the other. She wasn't going to make it. Everything was spinning, and she couldn't breathe. Her insides felt like they were going to spill out all over the lawn.

She stopped to steady herself and looked out on the river when pain shot through her gut, and she collapsed onto the path. Moments later, Papa scooped her up into his arms and carried her home. "What happened to you, daughter?" he cried. "We been lookin' everywhere for you."

"The boy, Papa," Rachael mumbled. "The Middleton boy. He hurt me, Papa. He hurt me."

"We'll be home before you know it, and Mama and Miss Lillian will take care of you. We'll be home in a minute."

When Trumpeter came staggering up the lane, Sheila frantically ran to meet him. Miss Lillian, however, stayed on the porch, stone-faced.

Trumpeter's warrior face was stained with tears, and Hattie clung to her grandmother. As gently as he could, Trumpeter placed Rachael's bruised body on Miss Lillian's bed.

"What happened?" Sheila cried. "What happened to her, Lil' Jacob? She's bleeding. What happened?"

"I don't know, woman. I found her on the path next to the old Cuba Garden. She said that a boy, a Middleton boy, had hurt her, but that's all she said. Now, she can't even hear us," Trumpeter said, looking up at Miss Lillian. "Mama, tell me she ain't gonna die."

"She ain't gonna die, boy," Miss Lillian assured him. "She's broke up, but she ain't gonna die. Sheila and me have to figure out how much she's hurt so's we can fix it, so shoo, boy. Wait out on the porch."

Rachael whimpered as Sheila and Miss Lillian looked her over as they would a new born, but first they covered Rachael's breasts with a kitchen towel, so nobody who might happen to be out on the porch could stare. Hattie put tea towels over the other windows, and then they removed Rachael's skirts. Sheila and Miss Lillian were certain that Rachael had been raped, of course, and they wanted to know how badly she might be bleeding.

"Nothing," Miss Lillian whispered, after gingerly studying Rachael's lady parts. "The chil' wasn't raped. No wonder she's so beat up; she must 'a held the boy off'n her."

They moved on to the obvious injuries. Rachael's jaw was purple and so swollen that Miss Lillian couldn't tell if it was broken or not. Her ribs were extremely tender in two places, and there was another purple bruise at the bottom of her ribcage.

Her internal injuries could be life-threatening if something inside had been broken into jagged pieces, but there was nothing Miss Lillian could do about it, other than to keep a careful eye on them, so she moved onto the cut over Rachael's right eye.

"Hattie," Miss Lillian called out, "get me my doctoring bag." But Hattie sensed it before her grandmother could finish her words and set it down at Miss Lillian's feet.

"Sheila, this cut won't get well 'lessen I sew it shut," Miss Lillian said. "Don't cry, now," she said as Sheila bit her lip. "We got to do this, and we've got to hold her real still. Hattie. You hold this shoulder; Sheila, you hold the other one.

"Oh, Hattie, I forgot. I need you to thread the needle."

"I already did, Granny. It's right there in the pin cushion."

"Did you remember the alcohol?"

"Yes, Granny, it's there, too."

"Watch close, Hattie. You're gonna be doin' this someday," Miss Lillian said. "Sheila, you best close your eyes."

"Granny," Hattie said. "If I could read, we could get a book to tell us about doctoring."

"Hattie Wineglass! What is the matter with you? We're in the middle of a delicate operation here, and you are skylarking about books! Could yo' let go of it for five minutes? Do you think you can do that?"

"Yes, Granny, I just thought we could...."

"We could, WHAT? We could waste our time reading words?"

"No, Granny, I guess it was a stupid idea."

"Well, stupid is, stupid does, missy. Now get on with helping me, or I'll chase you outta here."

Miss Lillian deftly moved her needle, making stitches even enough to show off in a sampler, and Rachael did little more than moan.

"Is it over?" Sheila said.

"Almost, Mama," Hattie assured her. "Granny's doing real good. Rachael will be as pretty as ever. Don't cry."

"Hattie, did you see how I tied off the threads?" Miss Lillian asked.

"Yes, Granny."

"Good."

Trumpeter was seething. His daughter had been beaten, and he wanted to know who'd done it. It was almost impossible to keep a secret on the plantation, though, and within a few minutes, there was a group of friends and neighbors on the porch demanding to know what had happened.

"Somebody beat my girl," Trumpeter said, drying his tears with the back of his hand. "Somebody beat her bad."

"Who done it?"

"She said something 'bout a boy, a Middleton boy, but she's too broke up to say any more than that. Somebody did it, and I'm gonna kill him when I get my hands on him. I'm gonna kill him."

"There's a boy staying with the Westons," one of Trumpeter's oldest neighbors said. "I've seen him. I don't know if he's a Middleton, but it don't make no difference. You can't even take a swing at a white boy; you know that. You'd be whipped for sure, and you wouldn't be no help to your girl if you was busted up, too. Master Weston's the best master around; everybody knows that. The only thing we can do is to wait."

"I don't want to wait. I want to kill somebody," Trumpeter said.

"I know, boy, but there ain't nothin' you can do. It's in de Lord's hands, now."

Up at the big house, one of the servants had just rushed into the master's study to tell Master Weston that his nephew had been found in the serviceberry bushes behind the laundry house. "He's broke up, sir. He's bleeding!"

"Charles!" Master Weston shouted to his valet. "Get a torch, and follow me on the path."

The night was inky black, and even with the torchlight, Master Weston was barely able to find the boy. With his head pointed toward the river, the boy was hidden beneath the bushes except for his feet, and he was kicking like an upturned palmetto bug. When he heard his uncle's voice, the boy started wailing.

"What happened, boy?" Master Weston asked.

"Somebody hit me," the boy said, spitting out his words. "Some bloody molly hit me. I'm going to kill him!" he screamed.

Plowden Weston was known above all for his civility. He was a poet, as well as an orator, and he had never had to rely on profanity to make his point. This sniveling boy with his filthy mouth and equally filthy sense of entitlement was almost more than Master Weston could bear.

"Charles, pull the boy out of the bushes and into the light, so we can see the extent of his injuries," he ordered. The boy screamed upon being touched, and Charles hesitated.

"Pull him out, man," Master Weston said. "Get him by the feet if you have to, and pull him out onto the path."

"But Master Weston."

"I said pull him out!"

"Yes, sir."

Charles then grabbed a hold of the boy's feet and dragged him toward the path. The boy howled and hit his fists on the ground in pain as the man servant did as he was told.

"You merkin," the boy screamed! "I'll kill you for treating me like this," he said to Charles. "I'll have your butt on a pike."

Master Weston made quick note his nephew's injuries as a number of servants rushed to help. Mistress Emily joined them to announce that she had sent for the doctor. "It could take hours, though," she pointed out, "so I sent someone to get Miss Lillian to take care of things until the doctor gets here."

A dozen or more men were gathered on the porch to Miss Lillian's house when the messenger arrived. "What are you here for, boy," some of them asked in unison.

"I'm here to get Miss Lillian," the boy cried out. "The master's nephew got beat up, and he needs doctoring. I gotta tell Miss Lillian.

Master said to look Miss Lillian in the eyeballs and to tell her to come, 'mediately."

"She's busy," Trumpeter growled.

"Don't make no difference," the boy said. "Master say she gotta come with me to the big house."

"Get outta my yard, boy," Trumpeter said, stepping out into the light. "You get your butt outta my yard."

A long pause followed the standoff, which was like two duelists squaring off, only one was a boy and one was a great big angry man. The boy was going to get pounded, killed, maybe. Then Miss Lillian stepped out onto the porch.

Mr. Middleton's Winky

The Abbey Plantation 1858

"TRUMPETER," SHE SAID using his new name for the first time. "I'm the doctor on this plantation, and I've got to go see what's wrong with the hurt boy. How'd the boy get beat up?" Miss Lillian asked, cooly.

"Nobody knows, and nobody knows who done it," the boy replied. "They just found him in the bushes all busted up."

"Is this boy from one of the Middleton plantations?" She turned to ask the messenger.

"Yes, Ma'am. He be visitin' from Charleston."

"Well, now, that I know he's a Middleton, I'll hurry," Miss Lillian said with a cagey smile. *I think the canary done ate the cat this time,* she thought to herself. *God certainly does work in mysterious ways, now don't he?*

"Hattie," she called out. "Bring me my doctoring bag and come along with me. As for the rest of you, stay here. I'll let you in on everything as soon as I can."

Hattie and Miss Lillian reached the path leading to the big house within minutes. "Where's the boy?" Miss Lillian asked the messenger.

"Don't know."

So, they continued up to the big house where they were greeted by Master Weston's man servant. "The boy's in the master's dining room."

"De dining room?" Miss Lillian asked. "What's he doin' there?"

"'The light's better in there,' mistress said. Just don't hurt the table or nothin'."

Miss Lillian made her way towards the dining room, with Hattie right behind her. She hoped she'd never have to go to the big house again, and there she was, tiptoeing down the hallway like she had good sense. Later she'd have to ask Granny what any of this had to do with a canary eating a cat.

The dining room was lit up like the sun. Hattie didn't know you could get that much light all in one place. She figured she'd never see anything like that again. The boy was surrounded by kerosene lanterns and laying on a quilt stretched out in the center of the table. He was howling and cursing and generally acting insane, but that was nothing compared to how he reacted when he was told that Miss Lillian was going to treat him.

"No black woman's going to touch me!" he screamed, trying to break the hold of the servants who were constraining him.

"Nephew," Miss Emily said in her velvety voice, "this will go much more quickly if you cooperate."

"She's not touching me!" he screamed, "And neither are you!" he said pointing to his aunt. "Nobody's touching me!"

"Then we'll just walk away and let you bleed to death," Miss Lillian said. "We'll just get on back home." Then she and Hattie got halfway to the door, and the boy said, "No."

"Were you speaking to me?" Miss Lillian said, innocently.

"Yes, I was speaking to you," the boy screamed. "I'm bleeding."

"Well, if you'd ask me nice, I might take a look at your injuries, but then, if you don't want me to, I'll just be getting on home like I said."

"Alright, I'll ask you nicely. Make me stop bleeding, please."

"Master Weston," Miss Lillian said looking across the table. "Do you want me to continue?"

"Certainly, Miss Lillian, I would appreciate whatever you can do."

"We'll start with the top of his head and move down."

And so began the systematic humiliation of the Middleton boy. Beginning with a close inspection of his ears and scalp, Miss Lillian took her time to be thorough; after all, she was treating the master's nephew. Then she moved on to the bridge of the nose, which was still squirting blood, despite the rags used to put pressure on it.

"The nose needs sewing up," she said. "It won't heal without it. Hattie, fix me up a needle and thread just like before, and someone get me some alcohol. As big a bottle as you have."

When the boy heard the words needle and thread, his eyes got the size of salad plates, and he started howling again.

"I know this is going to hurt, boy, but your nose is broke, and that cut's gonna keep on bleeding if we don't patch it up," Miss Lillian said. "Now, you just hold on to something—the edge of the table, maybe—while I reset your nose and get a couple of stitches into it."

Six people were constraining the boy by that time, and they could have used another six. It could have been worse, though, because the boy fainted during the nose resetting process and missed the first couple of stitches. The last few came pretty tough, though, but Miss Lillian just kept stitching until she got to the end where she tied off the threads.

"Did you see how I tied off the thread, Hattie?" she asked.

"Yes, Granny, I did."

Once Miss Lillian was satisfied with her handiwork, she moved on to the boy's chest and ribs, both front and back, his feet and knees, and his buttocks. The only spot yet unexamined was the boy's pizzie—third leg, John Henry, pink cigar, tallywacker, and skin flute—the royal penis.

"Get the women out of here!" the boy commanded.

"We need them to help hold you down," Miss Lillian said clinically.

"I'll be still," the boy said, capitulating.

"No, I don't think you will."

"I promise!"

"Do you think he'll hold still, Hattie?"

"No ma'am."

"Well, I don't either."

"Of course, it's your decision, Master Weston," she said, deferentially.

"The women will remain," he responded, clearly enjoying the subtle way in which Miss Lillian was torturing the filthy-mouthed boy. "Carry on."

"Hattie, I'm going to leave this up to you. Do you want to stay? Do you think it will help you doctoring someday, or are you uncomfortable about seeing Mr. Middleton's man parts?"

"I'm staying, Granny," Hattie said, stoically.

"Good girl."

The boy howled obscenities while the team of doctors removed the towel obstructing the view of his penis. No wonder he was howling. The end of the penis had a one-and-a-half-inch gash on it that would have made a grown man queasy.

"No wonder you're in such bad sorts, boy," Miss Lillian said. "You've got a nasty gash right on the end of your manhood. That's gonna take some sewing up, too. Hattie, make me up another needle—a bigger one this time, and you over there," she said pointing to one of the house servants, "we're gonna need another towel and a tumbler full of alcohol."

The men in the room gasped as Miss Lillian plunged the end of the boy's penis into the alcohol, but no one heard the gasps because of the boy. *This is for you, Rachael,* Hattie thought, hoping that everyone in the quarter could hear his cries.

The gash was sewed back together, and Miss Lillian saw to it that the boy was properly cleaned up, so he'd be presentable when the doctor got there and gave the mistress a piece of folded linen that contained a potion that would make the boy sleep.

"Is it alright to move him to his bed?" Miss Emily asked.

"Yes, ma'am, he'll be fine to move. He's gonna be bruised up in a few hours, but he's gonna be fine. He's such a fine boy and all."

Miss Emily almost busted out laughing when Miss Lillian called her nephew a fine boy. Emily detested him just as much as everyone else in his family did and was counting the hours before she could safely send him home.

Back in the quarter, Rachael was sedated, yet conscious, and grateful to be in her granny's warm bed. Trumpeter, however, wasn't grateful for anything other than his daughter's life. With the stitches above her eye and her swollen jaw, he barely recognized her, and he was livid. He was still out on the porch with some of the neighbors when Hattie and Miss Lillian returned from the big house. "What happened, Mama?" Trumpeter asked. "What happened to the boy?"

"Somebody broke him up pretty bad," Miss Lillian replied. "Got a big gash on his manhood. I had to treat it with alcohol and put a whole lota stitches in it, and I had to fix his broke nose, too. He passed out, it was so painful."

"He was screaming and hollering the whole time, Papa, and everybody got to see his winky."

"Hattie!"

"I'm sorry, Papa, but they did, and he was howling and carrying on. You should have been there."

"I wish I had been, Hattie. I wish Rachael had been there."

"When we soaked Mr. Middleton's winky in alcohol, I said a little prayer for Rachel, Papa."

"Well, it's late, Hattie. Go inside and give your sister a kiss, and then go to bed. Mama, Sheila and I are sleeping in Uncle Bob's shed, so you can take our bed."

"You sure, boy?" Miss Lillian asked.

"We're sure, Mama. Good night."

Miss Lillian ended up sleeping in her rocking chair that Hattie dragged in from the porch. That way she could keep a better eye on Rachael. She didn't tell anyone else, but she was worried about the girl's internal injuries. If she had busted ribs and an infection set in, she'd probably die. The only way Miss Lillian knew how to gauge an internal injury was to check Rachael's chest for swelling and temperature. She seemed fine through the night, though, so even though Miss Lillian was exhausted when morning time came, she was a tiny bit more confident that Rachael would survive. It'd take another two or three days before she'd know for sure. The hardest part of doctoring was the waiting.

Hattie went to bed thinking about how much easier Miss Lillian's job would be if she could read about temperatures and internal wounds and such. Surely, there were books out there that talked of such things.

CHAPTER 5

Get Me the Big Needle

The Abbey Plantation 1858

THE BOY WAS SILENT in no time after taking Miss Lillian's potion. *What a disgusting person,* Miss Emily thought as she checked in on him before going to bed. *My raccoon possesses more grace than that boy does. God may have a plan for his life, but I certainly don't see any redemption.*

Master Weston was still up, and he planned to stay awake until he knew what had transpired. The only place he knew to begin was with the young boy who had spotted his nephew in the bushes.

The boy related that as he walked along the path leading up to the big house, he'd heard moaning. "Then I seen some legs thrashing all about and hear some curse words. That's when I run for help."

As Master Weston was listening to the boy's story, one of the older men from the quarter was escorted into the master's study. With hat in hand, he said he had some news from the quarter, news about the Middleton boy.

"What have you heard, man?" the master asked.

"There's a girl, Trumpeter Wineglass's girl. She was brought home tonight all broke up. She said the Middleton boy done it."

"How is she?"

"I don't know, sir. Her daddy found her on the path beside old Miss Anne's vegetable gardens. Then he carry her to his mama for to be doctored. I don't know how she is now, sir."

"His mama is Miss Lillian?"

"Yes, sir, Miss Lillian."

Master Weston stood at his window and went over the information he had just been handed. His hoodlum nephew had attacked Trumpeter's girl, but who had intervened for her? He'd call in both sides in the morning, he decided, wondering if he had ever held such contempt for another living soul as he did for his nephew. The next morning Master Weston decided to visit Trumpeter and his family at their home rather than to call them to the big house. He was hoping the girl would be well enough to tell him what had happened. He didn't want to get information like that secondhand.

The People couldn't remember the last time Master Weston had visited the quarter, but early the next morning, there he was on foot, dressed in his usual country gentleman attire. Having the master show up on her front porch, nearly croaked Miss Lillian. When she heard that he was asking to speak with her, her head went soft for a moment, and she couldn't breathe. Then she gained her composure as best she could and said that it would be a pleasure to have him visit.

"Would you rather talk on the porch, Miss Lillian?" Weston asked.

"No, sir, ain't no privacy on the porch. The porch has big ears." With that settled, he entered the cabin and thanked Miss Lillian for being willing to speak to him.

Would he like to take the rocking chair?

"No," he said. He'd rather stand. "I wanted to ask you about last night. I want to know about your granddaughter. How is she feeling today?"

"She's asleep right now," she said, pointing to the other side of a sheet that had been rigged up in the center of the room to afford Rachael some semblance of privacy.

"Her face is all swollen, and she's got some nasty bruises, but I think those things are gonna heal in time. I'm not sure about her ribs, yet, but her breathing's good so far. That's a good sign."

"So, what do you know about what happened last night?"

"My son, Trumpeter, came walking up the lane last night carrying Rachael. She was so still in his arms, we thought she was dead at first, but then we heard her cries."

"When was that, Miss Lillian?"

"It was right after dusk had set in good."

"Did she say anything?"

"Yes, sir, she did. She say she was hurt by the Middleton boy. She say that a couple o' times. O' course, we didn't know who she was talking about at first, but when you called me to the big house last night, I figured it out pretty quick."

"Did your granddaughter say anything about who stepped in for her? Did she see who hit my nephew?"

"No, sir, she said she didn't see nobody. By then her face was all swollen up and she was havin' a hard time breathing. She couldn't see much o' anything. She just say that a voice tol' her to jump up and get outta there, so that's what she done, 'ceptin' she got all dizzy after that and passed out on the path."

"I'm going to ask you a very personal question, Miss Lillian," Master Weston said. "I need to know if your granddaughter was raped."

"Me and her mama checked all of her lady parts, and we didn't see nothing that looked like rape to us. I think she got hit keeping him off'n her. I think she was a brave girl, sir."

"I think so, too."

"If you don't mind telling me, sir, what's gonna' happen to the boy, now?"

"We're sending him back to his parents in Charleston just as soon as he can be safely moved. I hope you don't think all my kin behaves like that, Miss Lillian. I'm extremely ashamed of what he did to your granddaughter and of how he behaved when you treated him last night. By the way, the doctor arrived about an hour ago, and he said you are a good doctor. He also said that you made the finest stitches he's ever seen."

"Thank you for the compliment. It means a lot to me to hear that. So, when did you say the boy was goin' to be sent home, sir?"

"Two days from today," Master Weston replied. "If I could send him home today, I would."

"Thank you, sir," Miss Lillian said, as he stepped out onto the porch to see a dozen or more people milling about with farm tools in their hands.

"This porch does have big ears," Master Weston said, laughing. "I see what you mean. Goodbye Miss Lillian."

"Goodbye, sir."

"Oh, and have Trumpeter stop by my office, Miss Lillian. I need to speak to him."

"Yes, sir, I surely will tell him to meet with you, sir. I surely will."

As Master Weston walked back from the quarter, he was reminded of how much Anne Dunhill's old rose gardens, orchards, and grape arbors meant to him. He and Emily once considered removing the rose gardens and replacing them with a formal English-style flower garden, but they just couldn't bring themselves do it.

Trumpeter rushed home from his trunk minding station when he heard that Master Weston had been to meet with Miss Lillian. Trumpeter couldn't think of anything good that could have come out of the meeting, but he was hopeful all the same.

"Mama," he said as he entered the cabin.

"Shush," Miss Lillian whispered back. "You gonna wake the girl. Go back out on the porch if yo' want ta talk."

"I heard that the master was here this morning, and I couldn't think of anything good to come out of it," Trumpeter said.

"Well, it was good," Miss Lillian said. "He was checking on the girl, and he wanted to apologize for his rotten nephew. Mostly, though, I think he wanted to know who stepped in to beat on the Middleton boy. I got the impression it was fine with him that somebody done that. He asked me if I knew who done it, and I said I didn't even think that Rachael knows. She might, a' course, but she never tol' me nothing. I tol' Master Weston the truth, son. I just tol' him the truth. He say the Middleton boy is so rotten that he and Miss Emily are gonna send him home as soon as possible — one, two days. He said if he could send him sooner than that, he would. Oh, an' I forgot; he say he wants to see you at the big house."

"What about, Mama?" Trumpeter asked, worried.

"He didn't say. He just said he wants to see you."

Trumpeter went straight to the big house. Master Weston had always been kind to him and had never been crossways about anything, but Trumpeter was still so nervous about his summons that his shoes were all squishy from sweat by the time he knocked on the back door to the mansion. A young maid showed him in and reminded him to remove his hat before stepping into the master's study just like he was an idiot or something, but Trumpeter didn't say anything and just did as he was told. When he entered the study, he realized that Master Weston couldn't have been mad about anything because he stood to shake Trumpeter's hand, which he couldn't recall the master ever doing before. He took Trumpeter's worn hand in his soft one, and they stood there for a second separated from one another by the master's desk and more than a century of tradition.

"I'm sorry to call you away from your work, Trumpeter, but I wanted to apologize for my nephew's behavior. He'll be leaving the plantation the day after tomorrow, and he'll never be invited to come here again. How is your daughter today?"

"Mama says she's doing 'well as can be expected, which is pretty good, I guess," Trumpeter said. "She don't look like herself, yet, but Mama says she will when all that swelling and stuff goes away. Just take some time. Mama'll get her well. She's a pretty good doctor."

"She certainly is," Master Weston replied. "She's a damn fine doctor."

Trumpeter had to laugh after that, and then he asked if there was anything more.

"No, there's nothing more, Trumpeter. I just wanted to apologize for my nephew in person."

"Well, thank you sir," Trumpeter said, reaching down to get his hat that he'd accidentally knocked onto the floor. "I'll be getting along, sir, but I'll be sure to tell Granny what you said. She'll be mighty pleased."

Miss Lillian was right about Rachael's face going back to being pretty again. Once the bruising and swelling went away, she was pretty as ever, pretty enough that the little scar over her eye almost looked like a beauty mark. She returned to work three weeks after the attack and was glad to get back to her normal life. She was excited about seeing her friends and was even looking forward to returning to her sewing. *It's funny how you can miss your life,* she thought, *even if you think you don't like it all that much.*

CHAPTER 6

Just Keep Rockin'

The Abbey Plantation 1858

THE MOST IMPORTANT GIFT Miss Lillian ever passed on to Hattie was the notion of respecting things that couldn't be seen. For example, Miss Lillian believed it was bad luck to meet a woman walking early in the morning; so, if you had to go someplace, you had to slip through the woods and avoid the lane. And hawks were a sure sign of death if they were spotted flying over your house. A hawk could call out to corpses as it flew by. To avoid the curse, one needed to take a two-fold approach. The first was to never stare at a hawk, but if you accidentally spotted one, you were to quickly call out, "O' Hawk, stay away from me!"

Hattie was sitting out on the porch with Miss Lillian one day when a young woman from the quarter came to Miss Lillian, complaining that bad luck had been following her around since before Christmas. Her sow had been stolen, her stew pot cracked open like an overripe melon, and her husband was catting around with a new girlfriend. Things had gotten so bad she was afraid to go to sleep at night. Could Miss Lillian help?

"I reckon I can, but it sounds like a pretty tough nut to crack; it might take a while," Miss Lillian replied. Then Miss Lillian motioned to the young woman to sit in one of the rocking chairs on the porch and over a cup of sassafras tea, spent more than an hour asking her questions. Then Miss Lillian took to rocking, ignoring Hattie, as well as her confused patient. She rocked and rocked and rocked some more. Then she stopped, looked at the young woman, and asked: "Along about Christmas Time, did you borrow salt and forget to return it?"

"I might have," the young woman replied. "I was doing lots of cooking."

"That's it," Miss Lillian proclaimed. "You got a curse on you because you didn't return the salt. Go home right now, and take back twice as much as you borrowed, and your bad luck will be gone. Don't never be doing that again."

"Yes, ma'am, Miss Lillian," the young woman replied. "I won't."

After the young woman left, Hattie studied Miss Lillian closely and asked, "How did you know that, Granny?"

"It was as plain as the nose on your face once I got to thinking about it," Miss Lillian replied.

"I'll never be able to do that, Granny," Hattie said.

"Yes, you will, Hattie," Miss Lillian assured her. "The secret is to keep rocking until the answer just comes to you."

Other consultations took less time. Come planting time, Miss Lillian always had a gaggle of people—mostly men—showing up at the door to discuss the best days to plant. They didn't ask about planting rice, of course, because that was up to the master and the overseer, but the People grew their own corn, sweet potatoes, collards, butter beans, tomatoes, and peanuts, and if one planting day was better than the next, they wanted to know. Miss Lillian didn't have to use her rocking chair to figure out the best dates for planting; she just called upon her knowledge of the moon. There were rules for planting everything.

"Why don't the People figure it out just like you do?" Hattie asked.

"'Cause their brains get in the way," Miss Lillian said, after a long day of consultations. "They'd rather come here an' pay me a penny or a dozen eggs or a mess of fish, than to figure it out on their own. Besides, I'm always right 'cept for when there's an unexpected hurricane or freshet. I can't be held accountable for no storms."

"What if a storm does come?" Hattie asked.

"I keep the money anyway."

A Man Come Courting

The Abbey Plantation 1858

RACHAEL AND MATILDA continued to be friends. Rachael didn't have much to do with anyone else in the laundry house, though, at least not at first because of her feeling like a dirty girl and all. But after a time, she was her old self. Rachael begged Matilda to tell Rachael's parents what she had done to the Middleton boy.

"They could thank you," Rachael argued.

Matilda wouldn't hear of it, though, insisting that things were better the way they were. Rachael finally stopped asking. Something good did eventually come out of it, though, something that nobody saw coming. A man came courting, and he wasn't knocking at Rachael's door; he had his eye on Matilda.

Matilda lived alone in one of the oldest and smallest cabins in the quarter. It hadn't even started out as a cabin; it had been a shed of some kind. One of the old-livers said it was a potting shed used by the mistress who kept the Cuba Garden, but no one knew for sure. It was really old. It had layers of roof shingles, and the horizontal planking in the cabin's interior had been added on to at least twice. There was a small fireplace, though, so it was livable, and Matilda thanked God every day that she didn't have to share it with another living soul.

Matilda heard a knock at her door, her suspicious nature kicked in, and then she saw that it was Homer Lee standing on the porch. She knew his sister; they worked together, but Matilda had only met Homer Lee once, and that was weeks earlier when he came to help the women in the laundry house stir the enormous cauldron during soap-making time.

It had been so long since Matilda had passed the time with a man that she didn't even know what Homer Lee was up to at first. There he was, a fine-looking man dressed in his Sunday suit, rubbing a shine on the toes of his shoes with his pant legs, and she got to smiling. Could it be that he had come courting? Just thinking about it gave Matilda a case of the vapors. All this time she'd bragged to Rachael and to the other woman in the laundry house that she could do just fine without a man to complicate her life, but when she saw a living, breathing one standing at her door, she changed her mind in the time it took to say, "Thank You, Jesus."

Courting didn't come naturally to Matilda, but then it didn't come all that naturally to Homer Lee, either. That was just as well; that way they didn't embarrass themselves or each other, as their first conversation out under the tree sputtered a time or two before they got the hang of it. Homer Lee was plain spoken about his intentions. He was interested in having a woman to share his evening times with and to maybe even have a family with. He liked the looks of Matilda, and if she was interested in sharing her evening times with him, then they could just try it on for size.

Matilda said she hadn't thought about sharing her life with a man and that she was pretty happy living by herself, but he was a fine-looking man in his suit and all, and he seemed like good company, so she was willing to give it a try. Then she accepted Homer Lee's flowers and disappeared inside her cabin.

When she stepped back outside, she was carrying the flowers in a blue Mason jar, and he could tell that she had pinched her cheeks to make them rosy and had taken off her apron. He was mighty encouraged.

They talked, and Matilda learned that Homer Lee had been married once. He was sixteen, and the girl had been fifteen. The girl died in childbirth a year later, and Homer Lee took up with the whiskey. He accepted Jesus three years ago, though, and gave up the bottle. He was twenty-four now, and he wanted himself a wife and family.

Matilda had grown up on Arundel Plantation on John's Island, and she'd also been married. "My husband was young he liked whiskey, too," she said, "but he died. He'd been working on the chimney of the smokehouse, when a roof tile gave and that was the end of that. He was eighteen-nineteen, I can't remember, anymore. I'm twenty-seven now, and I was pregnant once, but the baby, he was born dead," she said sparing Homer the details.

"How'd you get to The Abbey?" Homer Lee asked.

"The husband I tol' you about wanted to move to Laurel Hill because his brother was there, so our old master made a trade with Master Weston. When we got to Laurel Hill, my husband died. I didn't know nobody, so when Master Weston asked if any of the domestic women wanted to transfer over to The Abbey. I said, 'Why not?'"

"How 'bout your family, Matilda?"

"You mean my people?"

"Uh-huh."

"I still have cousins on the island, but my Mama's dead, and my Papa was poorly when I left for Laurel Hill, so I reckon he's way gone by now. I had a brother. He was a sweet boy, but he and another boy ran away from the plantation when they was seventeen, and I never heard from him after that. I like to think about him livin' in a mansion in Texas or Russia or somewhere, but he might be dead. I don't know."

"I was almost dead from the drink," Homer Lee admitted, "but here I am in my Sunday suit sitting under a tree talking to a handsome woman. God's been pretty good to me, I reckon."

"What do you do on the plantation, Homer Lee?"

"Mostly I repair the dikes, but sometimes I do other jobs, too. I know a lot about making turpentine and the like, so I do some timber work now an' then. When I was a boy, I was assigned to the ram's run."

"The ram's run?"

"Yeah, that's where we kept the rams. They had to be separated from the lady sheep 'cause they wouldn't leave them alone, so we kept 'em in a run where they could spend their time waiting to visit the ladies."

"The ladies?"

"The lady sheep," Homer Lee said, laughing. "Ol' rams love de ladies."

"What do you want to do when freedom comes?" Matilda asked , taking Homer Lee by surprise.

"Well, o' course, I think about that a lot. Don't ever body, but I'm not really sure, yet. If I ain't too old when it gets here, I guess I'd go into the lumber business. Can't be too old for that, though. That's a young man's job. I've thought about sharecropping, too, but I could make more money in the timber business. What about you, Matilda?"

"I always dreamed about owning a hat shop," Matilda admitted, cautiously.

"A hat shop!"

"Yeah, I'd just like me a little store where I could sell pretty hats an' such. I've always liked hats. I know it's silly to dream o' something like that, but I can't help myself from thinking how nice it would be to spend my days surrounded by hats."

"You got a hat?"

"Oh, I got an old sorry-ass one that my mama give me, but that don't count. You know, a hat is a lady's crown, her crowning glory. A woman can't be a real woman without a beautiful hat on her head, something with feathers and ribbons — red maybe. I don't know. And it'd have to have a box to come with it, a white box with yellow stripes."

"Woman, you sure does have a fertile 'magination. I can practically see that hat on your head."

They finished their sweet tea, and Homer Lee said it was time for him to be getting on home. His sister and mama would be expecting him for supper, but he wanted Matilda to know that he had had a first-rate time and that he'd like to come around again, soon.

How about coming for supper the day after tomorrow? she said. "I fix good chicken an' a rutabaga and strawberry pie that's mighty good. It's rutabaga season, you know."

"I thought a rutabaga was a turnip, woman. Who ever heard of a turnip pie?"

"Well, you just come at supper on Tuesday, and I'll show you all about it. There ain't nothing better than rutabaga and strawberry pie, and I ought to know. I invented it."

"You invented a pie?"

"I surely did," Matilda said, laughing. "I surely did. Now, you get on home to yo' family, but don't forget about having supper with me on Tuesday. I'll be waiting for you."

"Can I bring anything?" Homer Lee asked.

"You could bring a chair and some more flowers," Matilda replied. "I've only got one chair, and I ain't never had a man bring me flowers before. I liked it."

"I'll be here, Matilda, and I thank you for everything. I felt happy talking to you today."

"I felt happy talking to you, too, Homer Lee. I'll see you Tuesday."

Matilda arrived at the laundry house the next morning, and Homer Lee's sister, Augusta, had already told everyone within ear shot that Matilda and Homer Lee were sparking.

"Sparking?" Rachael asked. "I don't even know what that means."

"Oh, sure yo' does, Rachael," Augusta fired back. "It means courting or wooing or whooping it up. Making sparks fly, you dumb girl. Making sparks fly. Ain't you never made sparks with a boy, Rachael?"

"No," Rachael said, thinking about the Middleton boy. "I never sparked with nobody."

"Well, one of these days yo' should," Augusta said. "You is a pretty girl. I see boys flirting with yo' ever-day. Yo' need ta' whoop it up a little. Git yo'self some fun."

"I will one of these days," Rachael said, trying to end the conversation. "I will, but now it's Matilda's turn, and I can't wait to hear if she likes that brother of yours."

"O' course she's gonna like him. Homer Lee's the best man on this plantation. Any girl would set her cap for that man. If he wasn't my brother, I'd go after him, myself."

"You would not!"

"I would; I swear. He'd have to beat me off with a stick. No lie."
"For true?"
"For true."

St. Mary of the Fields

The Abbey Plantation 1858

ONE DAY MASTER WESTON summoned his head carpenter, Renty Tucker, to his study. Dressed in work clothes and covered with a fine layer of sawdust, Renty Tucker had no idea what Master Weston wanted to discuss with him, but a summon from his owner wasn't to be put off.

"Morning, sir," Renty said, hat in hand.

"Good morning, Renty," the master said. "I hope I didn't pull you away from something important."

"No sir, I was just cleaning up my shop," Renty replied, wishing he'd used the term the shop instead of my shop.

"Renty, I called you in because the mistress and I have decided to build a chapel for the People, and I wanted to know if you think you could do the work. We don't want an ordinary chapel, Renty. We want it to seat at least two hundred people, and we want it to be the best chapel in all of South Carolina. What do you think?" Weston asked.

Renty almost keeled over from shock after hearing Master Weston's proposal. He was capable of building a chapel like those he'd seen on other plantations. Except having to figure out how to build a steeple, he could easily build a chapel like that, but a church that could accommodate two hundred people....

Renty swallowed hard, but the last thing he wanted to do was to admit that he might be over his head, so he said, "I'm pretty sure I can do it, Master Weston, but I'll need some pictures or something to go by, seeing as to how I never built a chapel before."

Master Weston said he had a better idea. He said he was going to send Renty to England for a whole year to learn to build chapels in the English way. Renty was relieved that he was going to get some on-the-job training, but he was so surprised at the prospects to traveling all the way to England that the cat got his tongue. He'd never heard of such a wild idea as that one, but he kept that part to himself. "I'd be mighty pleased to go to," he finally managed to say.

Master Weston said, "Good." He had the arrangements all worked out, and Renty was to leave the next week. The meeting ended, and Renty waited at the entrance to the study for a servant to accompany him to the front door when he got an idda.

"Sir, is it alright iffen I ask a question?"

The master nodded, and Renty posed his question. "Do you have a name for the new chapel, sir?"

"Mistress Weston wishes to name it *St. Mary of the Fields*."

Now, Renty didn't know much about church names. In fact, he didn't know anything about that sort of thing. The People's churches were usually named after the plantation they sat on, such as Laurel Hill Chapel or the Chapel at Midway. He wasn't sure, but he'd be willing to guess that none of the chapels for miles around had so sweet a sound as St. Mary of the Fields.

"That's a right nice name," Renty said.

"Do you think the People will like it?" Weston asked, surprising Renty with his openness.

"Oh, I'm for certain they will, sir."

Renty got back to the street and told his mother and the rest of the People what had happened. Everyone agreed that *St. Mary of the Fields* was a fine name for a chapel, but not one soul believed he was shipping out for England. Who would send a slave halfway around the world for a whole year and expect him to come back home? "We've heard some tall tales, Renty, but that one takes the cake," the People said. "Why didn't he just up and send you up to visit the rabbit in the moon?"

Mama Delilah, though, didn't appreciate folks talking to her boy like that even though she doubted him, herself. "You musta got the story wrong, Renty," she said. "Who ever heard o' such a thing as that. Ain't nobody fool enough ta send a slave off on some cockamamie trip like that."

"Well, Mama, that's what the master tol' me. An' iffen he say it, it must be so. I'm gonna pack my grip just in case." And it was a good thing because the very next week Renty left for England right on time. The People were drop-jawed. They just couldn't believe it, and Renty could barely believe it himself. Except for a half-dozen trips to Charleston, he'd never been twenty miles from the plantation, and he knew nothing about boats, especially ocean-going ones.

He occasionally went to Georgetown by skiff to pick up something for the carpenter shop, but crossing an ocean was a whole other thing.

His insides were jittery, and his ears were ringing. He was afraid of getting lost and accidentally ending up in China. He was also afraid of falling off the boat and drowning. He was afraid of being struck by lightning, and he wasn't a thousand percent certain that the cannibals who had once lived on an island in the middle of the ocean were really gone. Colored people were considered a delicacy, his granny used to say.

"They boil you up with onions and yams and eat your little black butt."

Renty's adventure began at the plantation landing where Master Weston and the People said goodbye and waved to him until the schooner he was aboard disappeared on its way to Georgetown. Master Weston had given Renty an envelope containing the necessary itinerary, bank checks, and other important documents, and he was told to guard it with his life. Renty said he would.

Renty blessed his half-sister for teaching him to read so long ago, and marveled that the question of whether or not he could read never came up. Did Master Weston know that Renty could read, or did he just assume? It kind of made the hair on the back of Renty's neck stand on end when he thought about it, but then he figured he'd never know, so he tried to keep it from his mind. Renty had more important things to think about. He had train schedules and steamship schedules to keep up with; he had bank checks to pay for the tickets and enough letters of reference to get him an audience with the Queen of Siam. He was an actor in a dream. He was an enslaved man—another man's property—and yet he was traveling halfway around the world on his own recognizance. He had money and tickets, and he was free to go and do as he pleased. The only thing that was holding him to the plantation was his own word. In a way he'd thought that Master Weston was the most gullible man there ever was, but on the other hand, Renty deeply respected Master Weston for his trust in him as a man of his word.

From Georgetown, Renty prepared to board the Gloucester, a three-masted schooner that would take him to New York. As the gang plank was locked into place, the ship's officers gathered nearby. They were smartly dressed in dark blue uniforms with brass buttons and crisp white shirts. Their air of authority intimidated Renty, and he stiffened up like he was bucking a heavy wind. He knew that he was going to be mistaken for a runaway and put in irons. He would be back on the plantation in less time than it had taken him to pack his grip. He presented his ticket when it was his turn and felt nauseous as he handed over the accompanying paperwork and stared at the officer's mustache.

"Where are you headed?" the officer said.

"England, sir."

"What do you plan to do there, boy?"

"To learn to build a chapel, sir, a Gothic-style chapel."

"A chapel?" the man said, clearly not expecting such an answer.

"Yes, sir, a chapel."

"Are you a freedman?"

"No, sir," Renty replied, knowing where the conversation was headed.

"Who's your owner?"

"Master Weston, Plowden Weston of Waccamaw, sir."

"Are you traveling alone?"

"Yes, sir. I am."

As the exchange continued, a dignified looking man who Renty took to be the ship's captain, interrupted the conversation with a gruff, "Let's get a move on it, Richards."

"But sir, this man is enslaved."

"Does he have a valid ticket?"

"Yes, sir, but…."

"I don't care who he is or where he's going as long as he has a valid ticket, Mr. Richards."

"Yes, sir," the officer replied, and with that, he shoved Renty's paperwork into Renty's hand and told him to get aboard.

"Yes, sir," Renty muttered.

Plowden Weston had paid for a full fare ticket, but Renty didn't understand that his fair also included a small cabin, so he found a space below deck and stayed there until a crew member stumbled upon him and invited him to use a spare hammock and to take his meals with the crew. Renty was reluctant to speak to the members of the crew, though. He couldn't understand them. He got the gist of their conversations, but he was used to people letting their words roll off of their tongues, not men who spit out their words like they were something nasty.

Master Weston had instructed Renty to stay at the wharf upon arriving in New York and to ask someone in uniform where he could buy a ticket for London. Five hours and two uniforms later, Renty was ready to board the Great Western, a steam-powered paddle wheeler noted for its speed. His two weeks passage cost a hundred dollars, plus an extra five-dollar steward's fee. Renty didn't know that there was that much money in the world. As he prepared to board the paddle wheeler, the feeling of trepidation crept into his brain again. He was prepared to be sick at his stomach, but it couldn't have gone more smoothly.

There were odd and interesting looking people all around him: Sheiks of Araby, Catholic nuns, women wearing black veils, English gentlemen wearing spats and bowlers, and children chatting to each other in languages that hurt Renty's ears.

No one even looked at him, much less questioned him about his ticket. They simply took his ticket and told him to go aboard. Halfway up the gangplank, he was told that he was to go to Cabin 31 near the center of the ship, which meant that he would be near the magnificent paddle wheel. Renty was thrilled. He was fascinated by the paddle wheel but even more by the steam mechanism that powered it. He would spend hours studying it during his journey, wondering if a similar machine could be adapted to process rice.

In London, Renty boarded a train for Dover that turned out to mystify him even more than the paddle wheeler. Given time he might have been able to replicate the paddle wheeler, but the locomotive was completely beyond his understanding. It was a thing of wonderment. In Dover, he transferred over to a horse-drawn wagon for the short ride to Dover Castle, where he was to apprentice under a Scotsman named Burke.

CHAPTER 9

Angus Burke

Dover Castle, Scotland 1858

RENTY STEPPED OUT of the wagon and was knocking off the road dust when a man came up to him and said, "I was told to expect a young colored man, and you must be the one seeing as how you're probably the only one in Dover," the man said.

"My name's Burke, Angus Burke," he added as he extended his hand.

Renty understood that shaking hands with another man was a sign of respect and equality—warrior to warrior, that sort of thing, but enslaved men were unaccustomed to it. When he saw Burke's huge hand waiting to receive his, Renty extended his own, hoping that he was doing it properly. Burke did all the shaking, however, so Renty just kept his hand in Burke's until it was released.

"The name's Renty, Renty Tucker," Renty said following Burke's lead.

Burke was a barrel chested-man with thighs the size of hams and a thick mantle of red fur. Renty couldn't take his eyes away, and then he noticed the kilt. Angus Burke was wearing a dress! It was a kilt, Renty was later told, and beneath the kilt Burke was wearing nothing but his hairy arse.

"'Tis good for the lads to be free," Burke joked when a gust of wind caused his kilt to sail and expose his lack of underwear.

"I'm sorry," Renty said.

"Have you never seen a kilt before, man?"

"No sir, there ain't no kilts in South Carolina."

"Well, there should be," Burke said, laughing.

"Makes the bollocks grow, you know."

"The bollocks?"

"The acorns, man. The acorns."

Burke reported to a gaffer hired to oversee the restoration of St. Mary in Castro, a small Saxon church on the grounds of Dover Castle. The main portion of the chapel was more than a thousand-years-old, Burke explained, but its bell tower was a former lighthouse built by the Romans. The church had been rebuilt by practically everyone who had ever lived at the castle, so it was a bloody mixture of architectural styles. From the Saxons, the church received its cruciform shape with a central tower the same width as the nave. Medieval additions included vaults and the altar recess in the nave's southeast corner. In 1252, three bells were cast at Canterbury to be hung in the bell tower.

"Edward III and a couple of the other Edwards pumped money into the ol' girl for a time after that, but the church finally fell on hard times and was boarded up," Burke explained. "Our job's to restore it."

Renty stayed at St. Mary during his stay, sleeping in one of the small cells hidden within the walls of the church. Nuns and priests had lived there before him, and Renty was struck by the lives that they led. In some ways, they were enslaved to the church, but it had been their choice, and Burke told him once that even though leaving the church was frowned on, it was a thing that could be done. Renty would never understand the tenants of the Catholic church, he'd never learn to like haggis, and he'd probably never understand more than half of the words that poured out of Burke's mouth. But it didn't matter because of his love for St. Mary. Each time he stepped into the chapel, he was humbled. The workmanship displayed there had to have been inspired by God, himself.

There was no other explanation for how the ancient stonecutters had formed perfect puzzle pieces out of the granite that they quarried from an outcropping near the castle's wall. Only divine intervention could explain the symmetry of the vaulted ceilings and the strength of the buttressed walls. Renty had never seen flying buttresses or stained-glass windows before, but even before Burke pointed them out, he noticed that the windows depicted stories from the Bible. One day, the sunlight streamed into the chapel at a perfect angle and fell onto Renty's hands. Its unexpected beauty made him weep.

"Let this be a blessing, Jesus," he prayed. "Let this be a blessing on me."

It was a turning point. Renty studied his worn hands and knew the truth. Even on his best day, he was a second-rate mason, and according to Burke, his stone cutting skills were worthy only of the skirts (the outskirts of the town). He had no business working on a royal chapel, and as for building a chapel for the People, it was a pipe dream. He'd been so flattered when Master Weston approached to him about building chapel, that he got all puffed up and stuck on himself, and he would have said he could'a built a palace, 'cause at that moment he believed he could. Now, he was halfway around the world, standing in the midst of Medieval perfection — him, a no account n....

"I can't do it," he said after finding Burke in the yard.

"Ye can't do what?"

"I can't build a chapel. I ain't good enough carpenter to build a fowl house. In a hundred years, I couldn't build a chapel."

"Ah, but you can," Burke replied. "You just have to figure out what kind of chapel you plan to build and learn the skills necessary to build it. For example, you're not planning to build a stone chapel like this one, are you?"

"Of course not."

"Well, then what will you build it of?"

"Lumber and brick," Renty replied.

"Then those are the skills you need to work on, man. Your bricklaying's terrible, so you sure as hellfire need to work on that one, but you're real good at cutting and fitting lumber. Do you know how to render?"

"Render?"

"I thought so," Burke said. "Renders are pictures of what you plan to build. You know, drawings. Your master will be expecting them. Only a crank head would pay for a chapel he ain't seen. Are you hoping to have lancet windows?" Burke asked.

"Oh, for sure I am."

"Then you need to learn to frame them out. And what about lancet doors or interior walls with lancet arches? Oh, and you'll also need a narthex, a nave, a transept, an ambulatory and aisles."

"I know what aisles are, but what's an ambulatory?"

"It's just a name for a fancy kind of aisle, boy."

"How many will I be needing?"

"Come to think of it, you won't need any. Let's just take that one off our list."

As Renty began to get a clearer picture of the skills he would need to build St. Mary, he felt more confident about the process.

"Learn one thing at a time," Burke advised. "You're terrible at laying brick like I said, and the chapel needs a new walkway, so why don't we start there? After that I'll show you how to use a compass and a T-square. They'll make your job a whole lot easier."

Renty followed Burke's lead, and he began to learn his trade. He was exhilarated.

Burke was a methodical tradesman, meticulous about each cut or drive of a nail.

"Remember, you're not driving a nail; you're building a chapel. There's a shit load of difference between 'em, lad."

Once Renty had worked his way up to framing walls and building doors and window frames, he allowed himself to daydream about being back on the plantation, back to his old life. The images came clearer with each day, and one jarring truth began to surface. In England, he was free to do as he pleased. Back home he'd return to being a slave. Renty needed someone to talk to about his predicament, someone he respected, and someone who would keep his secret. He wanted to tell Burke, but Burke could self-ignite if he were fired up enough, and knowing that Renty was enslaved might just do the trick. It was a risk, but Renty figured that the person Burke would be most pissed off with would be Plowden Weston, and Master Weston was two thousand miles away — pretty good odds. So, Renty broke the news, rendering Burke speechless for the first time in his thirty-one years.

"No bloody way!" he shouted.

"It's true," Renty insisted. "My master owns four rice plantations and more than nine hundred and fifty slaves. He's one of the richest men in the county."

"You should go back and slice open his gullet," Burke said, with eyes flashing.

"That's the complication of the whole thing," Renty said, staring up at the chapel. "He's good to me. He gave me a pocketful of money an' sent me here all by myself. I coulda escaped to China; I had enough money, but he trusts me to come back to build the chapel. I owe it to him to come home, and I owe it to the People to build the chapel."

"My ancestors were slaves," Burke said, surprising Renty. "They were called serfs, but they were slaves, same as you. If they left the land, they were punished with branding irons or worse."

"Branding irons?"

"Aye, lad, branding irons right on their foreheads. Sizzzzztz! "

"Do they still have slaves in Scotland?"

"No, not no more, but there'll always be the haves and the have nots. I still think you should slit your master's throat, Renty. I've thought on it, and that's what you should do."

The look on Renty's face made it clear that Renty had no intention of doing such a thing, so a long silence set in between the men, disquieting both of them in the process. Renty cleared his throat and studied his hands, and Burke hacked up some spittle and sent it flying between his front teeth.

"Can you put pen to paper?" Burke suddenly asked.

"I'm literate enough," Renty replied, surprised.

"Well, then I have another thought for you. How much wage have you earned so far working at St. Mary?"

"Seventeen pounds, seven," Renty replied, curiously.

"Then send your master a letter telling him that you wish to buy your freedom. Make it official. Have a judge witness it or a priest and offer the master seventeen pounds, seven. That's a lot of money, Renty, a whole year's wage."

"Master Weston would spend more than that on a pair of riding boots. It'd only insult him."

"Then sweeten the deal, lad. Offer to buy your freedom AND promise to return and build the chapel."

While Burke was doing all of his talking, Renty was leaning up against the ruin of the ancient lighthouse. When the words about buying his freedom came out of Burke's mouth, Renty almost went ass end over teakettle. He had dreamed of freedom every day of his twenty-four years, but it had never occurred to him that he could initiate its arrival. He'd always pictured freedom falling out of the sky like a blanket made out of clouds. And yet, this beast of a man with the muscles of a stonecutter had just planted a seed in Renty's head that shot out from his ears like a beanstalk rooted in magic elixir.

Renty had never hugged another man in his life, but he suddenly reached out and grabbed the Scotsman in a bear hug that took Burke by complete surprise.

"What are you doing, man?" Burke asked, pushing Renty away. "Are you daft?"

"No," Renty shouted. "I'm not daft. I'm going to be free."

With Burke's help getting the words just right, Renty sent the following letter to Master Weston:

Master Weston, Esq. Waccamaw
South Carolina
July 4, 1858

Your Lordship,

 I have a matter to discuss with you, Sir. I am intending to make a bisiness offer to you concerning My freedom, for wich I am prepared to pay £17 and 7 shillings current money.

 As part of the offer, I am willing to indenture myself to return to Waccamaw & to build a fine chapel at The Abbey. I wil build it to my ability & it will be well made. I wil expect to be paid current money for my labor, but I wil build it to your liking.

I believe this to be a fair & worthy offer. Because of your generosity, Sir, I have lived as a free man for these past months, & I know it is a thing I can do proudly.

Yours truely in the name of Jesus Christ,
Renty Tucker
Witnessed: Father Joshua, Brother St. Mary of Castro, Dover

Plowden Weston received Renty's letter and was completely taken aback. It hadn't occurred to him that Renty would desire more freedom than he had already extended him.

I've given Renty Tucker and the other Negros on my plantations every-thing they need, and in so doing, I've rescued them from their former lives of savagery, Weston wrote in his journal that day.

I have even allowed Renty to select his own surname. If he were freed, his life would be far more complicated than it is now under my protection. I have treated him with more respect than a freedman should expect, even though we are clearly not equals. My Negroes are my children, and I have treated them with benevolence, understanding and indulgence.

I guarantee them from poverty and distress from all conditions, and they are supremely happy. In return, they owe everything to my generous nature. I have been kind to them and just. I have taught them skills and trades in return for their labor, and now I am being thanked for my generosity with demands.

I will not be made to give in to such things. I refuse to grant this demand.

Over the next few days, however, Plowden Weston rehashed Renty's request. He thought about it, he raged, he prayed, and he talked it over with his horses. Granting Renty's freedom didn't stick in his craw, as much as the fact that it had been Renty's idea. Plowden Weston was not accustomed to being told what to do, ever. He was in charge of every aspect of his life, and he was going to keep it that way. He was a man of deep conviction and as chivalrous in his manner and behavior as a crusading knight, but he bowed up when it came to being told what to do. He didn't live in a cave. He knew what was going on in the rest of the world, and he was well aware that the institution of slavery was at its end.

It was a ridiculously expensive proposition, anyway, and his Negros were constantly at odds with each other over something. He'd do away with the lot of them if he could, but the plantation system ran on the backs of its labor force. His hands were tied. He was irritable over Renty's audacity, but he admitted that there was another side of the story. Renty, after all, was a product of Plowden Weston's good works, and he was without question, a good Negro and a hardworking one.

I made him, and If I were to grant him his freedom, he would serve as an inspiration to my other Negroes. As for his promise to build a wondrous chapel, I have no doubt that Renty would do as he says.

Weston could rant all he wanted to, and he could feel slighted until the sky fell in, but he couldn't change anything. Renty didn't need Plowden Weston's permission to do anything, anymore. Westons' high-minded notions of chivalry and duty weren't worth a three-pence beyond the plantation. If Weston turned down Renty's offer, Renty would simply refuse to come home, and then who would build the chapel? The next day, Plowden Weston wrote the following letter:

August 23, 1858
Renty Tucker Dover Castle Dover, England

Dear Renty,

I read with interest your letter requesting the granting of your freedom in exchange of your promise to return to Waccamaw and to oversee the construction of the People's chapel.

After much consideration, I have decided to accept your offer and to sponsor your manumission upon your return to the plantation.

When you arrive, I will have the necessary paperwork ready for your signature. You will receive your freedom in exchange for your promise to build the new chapel, and I will agree to pay you a commensurate wage.

Sincerely,
Plowden Weston, Esq.

Renty opened the letter in Father Joshua's office in the rear of St. Mary de Castro Chapel so that Burke and Father Joshua could be with him. Burke was the first to speak.

"That's wonderful news," he shouted. "Bloody wonderful, begging your pardon, father."

"It is bloody wonderful news," Father Joshua's replied. "Bloody wonderful indeed. I was afraid you were going to be disappointed, Renty. I did some research into the issue of slavery while we were waiting to hear from Master Weston, and I learned something very interesting. Trading in slaves was made illegal here in England in 1807, and in '34, it was banned altogether. If you refused to go back to South Carolina, Master Weston couldn't come after you because as long as you remain in England, you are a free man. He knows that; he just thinks that he created a perfect world for you on the plantation and truly can't imagine why you would want to leave it. When men are born into freedom, maybe they're incapable of knowing what it would be like to be enslaved."

"Master Weston was born with a gold spoon up his arse, huh, Father." Burke interjected.

"It appears so," Father Joshua replied, trying not to smile.

"I thought Master Weston agreed to my offer because I had him over a barrel, me being so far away and all," Renty said. "He's got a library that takes up two whole rooms. He had to know about slavery being banned. Now, I don't know what to think of him, Father."

"He may be a fine man in some ways, Renty, but when one lives in such a small, elite community of like-minded people, they lose perspective. That's certainly the case here in England. It may be seen as a gentlemanly thing to do in America, but as far as I'm concerned, it was the only godly thing he could do."

"God bless you, Renty Tucker," the priest said. "I've never taken part in a manumission before, and I must say, it feels pretty good."

"Begging your pardon, father, but exactly what does manumission mean? Does it mean being freed?" Burke asked.

"Aye," the priest said. "Manumit means to set free. Manumission is the process by which it is done."

"I have another question for you, Father," Burke continued. "Renty's master didn't mention the seventeen pounds, seven, and he didn't send manumit, manumission papers. It seems to me that Renty ain't free yet."

"That's true, Burke," the priest replied thoughtfully. "There are no documents attached to this letter from Master Weston, Renty. Do you trust him and his word enough to go home without a signed document?"

"I do, Father. Master Weston's letter is all I'll need. He's a man of his word."

"What if Master Weston dies or changes his mind between now and then?" Burke asked.

"Burke has a point, Renty," Father Joshua said. "I think I should attach my own letter to Master Weston's, and I'll ask the bishop to sign it. With the bishop's signature, no one would dare question its authenticity."

"Thank you, Father," Renty said, standing. "I'm going to be a free man, and it's all because of you and Burke."

"You already are a free man," Burke said in his loud, jovial voice. "You were born free in God's eyes. Ain't that so, Father?"

"Well, God certainly doesn't condone slavery, Burke. He surely doesn't."

"Then he's a free man?"

"Aye, he's a free man."

"Then let's all go to the pub for a pint," Burke said.

"And why ever not," the priest said. "A good pint to celebrate a good man's freedom."

CHAPTER 10

Time to Go Home

Dover Castle, Scotland 1859

THE CHAPEL AT DOVER CASTLE was completed three months later, and it was time for Renty to go home. He'd missed his family and was eager to see them again, but he broke down when it was time to say goodbye to Father Joshua and Angus Burke.

"All good things must end, Renty," Burke said, trying to hold back his own tears. "I won't be forgetting you, not never."

"That goes for me as well," Father Joshua said. "You're a rare man, Renty Tucker. A rare man, and it was an honor to be part of your life. Will you write to us, lad?"

"Yes, sir, I will, I promise."

"And name your first son after me," Burke shouted as Renty turned to leave.

"I'll name him Joshua Burke Tucker," Renty shouted back.

"A good solid name," Father Joshua said. "A good solid name."

The westward crossing of the Atlantic was longer than the easterly one had been but only by a few extra days. Renty safely arrived in Georgetown three weeks and four days after leaving Dover. The trip had gone smoothly enough and had had a familiar ring. Renty's perception of himself, as well as the world around him had changed more than he thought possible. Renty arrived in Georgetown and hired a young boy in a rowboat to go to the plantation ahead of him to announce his arrival.

"Don't make a fuss, boy," Renty said. "Just tell the men on the landing that Renty Tucker is on his way home."

"Home to the plantation?"

"Yes, boy, home to the plantation."

Renty arrived that afternoon. It was November 13, 1858. In Georgetown he'd learned that a heavy frost had come early that year. Swamp fever would be gone again for another winter, so Master Weston should be back living in the big house by now. He hitched a ride aboard a passing schooner and arrived at The Abbey in less than an hour. It had only been a year since Renty had left the plantation, but it felt like a lifetime. He had underestimated the excitement that his return would cause among the People.

In the time it took him to thank the boat captain, the plantation bell started ringing wildly, and the People rushed to greet him. He was embarrassed. In the middle of it all he found his brother, Amos, and their mother, Delilah.

"You look different," Amos said as he reached out to hug Renty. "You look like an Englishman."

He just had new clothes on, Renty said, but the People said, no, he was different in more ways than that. Maybe it was the food. English people ate kidney pie and pig parts that the People fed to their animals.

"Are they poor?" Delilah asked?

"No, they're rich, almost as rich as Master Weston. They just didn't know what tastes good, but they sure knew how to build chapels," he assured them.

Amos said, "Well, I don't care if you do look like an Englishman; let's go home to see the family."

"I'll have to meet you there, Amos. I have to see Master Weston, first. I have business with him," Renty said, not wanting to tell Amos about being a freedman in front of the People, "It's important, Amos."

"Oh, sure," Amos said, impressed. "You and Master Weston hav' chapel business to attend to."

"Chapel business," Renty said. "We have chapel business to discuss. Then I'll be on over to see everybody."

Renty hoped Master Weston didn't mind that the People had taken the liberty to ring the plantation bell. It was unheard of, but then Renty's return was a one-of-a-kind event, so to speak. Master Weston probably didn't mind too much; besides, Renty didn't want to wait another second before he signed his manumission papers.

Even though Burke and Father Joshua had told him that he was already a free man, Renty wouldn't feel it down deep until the papers were signed. Master Weston was waiting for him.

"The year has changed you Renty," Master Weston said, reaching for Renty's hand.

"Aye, I seem to have changed, some," Renty said, not even realizing that he had said, aye. "My brother, Amos, said I look like an Englishman. That may be, but I'm surely glad to be home, sir."

"Well, Renty, we have some business to take care of."

"We do indeed, sir," Renty replied, noticing how much the master had aged. Plowden Weston's meticulously trimmed hair and mustache was starting to gray, and his eyes were surrounded by a new set of wrinkles. He was thinner than he had been, too. His gate was strong and lively, however, and Renty was glad to see him.

"Do you wish to begin with the manumission or the chapel," Weston said.

"The manumission, sir."

"I thought so, so I have the papers all prepared. Before we sign them, though, I will tell you that I was surprised with your request, Renty."

"I'd never thought about asking, sir. In England, though, I worked with men who couldn't read or write or understand renderings, but they were free. They didn't know anything about the rest of the world, and I had to explain everything to them, but they were free, and I was a slave. It didn't bother me all that much here on the plantation. It was a thing I was used to, and I had all the freedom I needed to get my work done, but it's a thing that eats at you if you've come close to having it.

I don't mean any disrespect, sir. You treated me real fine, sending me to England and all. I just got to thinking that as long as I build you the best chapel I know how, maybe it just won't matter all that much whether I was free or not."

"I agree, Renty. Just think, if you'd stayed in Africa, you'd be building wattle and daub huts instead of English-style chapels," Weston said, insulting Renty without even knowing it.

"Yes, sir," Renty replied. "I reckon that's so."

The manumission papers took Renty less than two minutes to sign. Undoing a lifetime of slavery had boiled down to four signatures and two sets of initials. It was a thing done. In the eyes of the State of South Carolina, Renty was a free man. It didn't change his skin color, and it still didn't make him equal in the eyes of the law, but he and his issue were now and forever free. Scarcely able to breathe because of his excitement, Renty realized that they hadn't discussed the seventeen pounds, seven shillings.

"Sir, the money, you haven't asked me for the money, the money to buy back my freedom."

"I don't want your money, Renty," Weston said. "I'm a wealthy man. I don't need your money. Put it to good use. Have you decided where you want to live?"

"No, sir," Renty replied. "I haven't thought beyond this moment."

"If you want to continue to live on the plantation, you're free to do so. I'll include it in your salary. You're also free to leave the plantation, of course, but the nearest town is Georgetown. It would take you hours to get to and from work every day."

"What if I was to build me a little place next to the carpenter shop?" Renty suggested. "That way I wouldn't waste time coming and going. I don't need much. I could probably build something in two-three days that would do just fine."

"I like the idea of you living next to the carpenter shop," Weston said. "You can keep a close eye on everything that way. Do you have the supplies you need to build your house?"

"I'd have to check since I haven't been here in a while, but I'm guessing everything I need'll be right there, sir."

"Then let's move on to the chapel. Do you have a list of materials you think you'll need to build it?"

"Yes, sir, I have a number of renderings here and an inventory of the supplies I'll be needing," Renty said, handing Master Weston a large envelope. "I'm sure there'll be some extras, but I worked hard on that list—my Scottish friend back in Dover helped me—and I think it's pretty complete. You never know what's gonna happen when you work with wood, though. It has a mind of its own."

"I guess the last thing we need to talk about is your salary," Weston said, impressed.

My salary, Renty thought, hoping Master Weston couldn't tell how excited he was at the prospects of earning a wage just as he had in England.

"I'm prepared to pay you $700 for the completed project, not counting the windows, of course, which will be installed by a firm in Charleston," Weston said.

With his heart beating out of his chest, Renty asked if Master Weston could tell him how much money that would be in British Sterling.

"£145," Weston said.

"That would be a fair price," Renty finally managed to say, "A fair price, indeed."

Did Renty need an advance?

"No, sir. I have seventeen pounds, seven in my pocket. That will last me a long time." Renty thought the meeting was over, but he hesitated to move without Master Weston's signal. After all, he'd only joined the ranks of the free a few moments earlier. Master Weston rose from his chair behind his desk and Renty followed suit. This time it was Renty who extended his hand.

"I promise to build you a fine chapel, sir."

"I know you will. We'll set up a schedule to meet periodically to discuss the progress on the chapel, but we'll do that after you get settled."

"Thank you, sir," Renty said, exiting the office. "Thank you for everything. I won't disappoint you."

"Renty."

"Yes, sir."

"Wait just a moment, and someone will show you out."

"Oh, yes, sir. I will, sir."

Renty stepped out into the sunlight, and he felt twelve-feet-tall. The big house looked less intimidating, the trees looked shorter, the walkway narrower; the scale of everything had changed. It was as if Renty was suddenly larger, and everything around him had gotten smaller. Being free was a wondrous thing.

Renty stopped by the carpenter shop before heading on over to his brother's house.

He'd designed the shop and had built it himself, and he was concerned that it may have been changed or neglected during his stay in England. His concerns had been justified.

Lumber was randomly stacked near the front of the door, and the exterior of the shop needed painting. A hinge was missing here and a window pane there. Everything within the shop was covered with sawdust, and the hand drills that Renty kept in perfect order along the right wall were thrown about helter-skelter. The disorder was troubling to a meticulous man like Renty, and he'd been so eager to get started on his new life. He cursed, he tripped over a rusted hand tool, and then he cursed again.

Anxiety was filling his head with doubt. He was bedeviled, but there was a solution. His first job wasn't going to be to build himself a house; he could sleep on the floor of the shop, if need be. His first job was going to be to put the shop back in order. He couldn't build a proper chapel out of chaos. He couldn't begin his new life that way, either. Everyone Renty had ever known was there to greet him when he arrived at his brother's house. He was slapped on the back by kin and near kin so many times that his back was sore. He was glad to be home, though, and he was thrilled to see a spread of fried chicken and ham, sweet potatoes, pickled pigs' feet, butter beans, collards, cornbread, white flour biscuits, and chess pie sitting out under the trees ready to fill a street full of empty bellies.

"Thank you," Renty said after being asked to say a few words. "I'm mighty glad to be home, and I'm mighty glad to see y'all. I've missed the plantation, and I've missed my family."

"Then let's get ta eatin'," a voice rang out from the crowd, and everybody got down to it.

The only thing on Renty's mind that day was his reservation about having the People learn about his freedom. It would be one thing to tell his brother but another to have everyone in the quarter asking him about it, so he got to thinking that he'd keep it to himself for a while. When he came up with that plan, he was relieved. He needed time to get used to things again and time to figure out how to break the news to his family. It wasn't every day that someone from the quarter got his freedom. The only other person that had happened to was Miss Cornelia. Miss Cornelia was an old-liver now, and Renty often wondered what had prompted her to remain on the plantation.

Her daughters lived in Charleston; she could go live with them whenever she wanted to, but she stayed on at The Abbey. That's when it hit him. *Cornelia HAD exercised her freedom of choice. She lived on the plantation because it was where she wanted to live, not because someone had forced her to stay.* Renty was free to do the same. He'd keep his freedom to himself, at least for the time being. Then he got to worrying about how he was going to build the chapel. Thanks to Burke, he was confident in his ability to design the chapel and to oversee the construction of the various elements, but he was daydreaming if he thought he could find local men to do the work. He needed a real craftsman, a man like Burke.

The following day, Renty gathered his former assistants to begin the job of rebuilding the carpenter shop. He kept his hands in his pockets for fear of showing them his fists. He was really mad. A year was a long time, he'd grant them that, but even so, they'd wrecked the place, and he wasn't a forgiving man. During the third day into the project, Renty was surprised to see Master Weston approaching on horseback.

He'd just stopped by to see how things were coming along, he said. "I'd expected to see you working on your new house."

"That'll have to wait, sir. I wanted to get a handle on the workshop so I can get started on the chapel," Renty said.

"Was anything amiss?"

"Oh, just little things," Renty said. "We're about done."

"I ordered the supplies you asked for," Weston said. "They'll probably start being delivered in a week or so. Do you need to speak to me about anything else while I'm here, Renty?"

"Yes, sir, I do," Renty replied. "It's about my men, sir. They're good men and all, but they ain't very good carpenters. If I'm gonna build the chapel right, I need at least one man who knows as much about this kind of building as I do. I was thinkin', what if I was to ask my overseer from Dover to come to work on the project with me? He taught me everything, and we're friends; we get along good. We could split the $700, sir. Seventy-five pounds is a lot of money to a Scotsman."

Master Weston said he'd been concerned about getting good local assistants, too, and he thought it would be a good idea for Renty to ask his supervisor to come to work on the project. "Do you think he'll come?"

"I don't know, sir," Renty replied, "but I'm willing to try."

"Offer him $500."

"Five hundred dollars, sir?"

"I want it done right. By the way, that's the equivalent of a hundred-and-two-pounds sterling."

"Yes, sir."

"Write your letter, and bring it to me in my office to look it over. If we're lucky, we can have one of my factors deliver the letter to insure it gets into the right hands."

The following day, Renty handed his letter to Master Weston.

November 25, 1858
Angus Burke Dover Castle Dover, England

Dear Burke,

I got home safe to the plantation, and I have come up with a bisness plan that includes you. If I'm going to do the best job I can building the chapel, I wil need another carpenter as good as you.

Master Weston agrees and has offered to pay your travel expenses plus $500 when the chapel is done.

I hope you wil consider coming to America to help me, Burke. I have missed you and Father Joshua. If you can come, don't delay. We plan to commence as soon as our supplies are delivered.

Fondly,
Renty Tucker

"Perfect," Plowden Weston said. "It's to the point. I like that." He'd include his own letter, just to make things sound more official, he said, along with a bank note to cover Burke's travel expenses. One of Weston's rice factors was headed for London at the end of the week, and he offered to hand deliver the letters to Father Joshua's office at Dover Castle. In another stroke of luck, the attorney said that he was planning to return to Charleston the following Sunday, and if it worked out for the Scotsman to accompany him on his return trip, it would be no inconvenience. Renty was elated.

Four weeks later, Plowden Weston's Charleston office received its first electronic message transmitted by wire. The telegram stated that Weston's attorney and Angus Burke would arrive the next day. "There's one thing, Renty," Master Weston said. "Have you thought about how your supervisor will feel about living and working on the plantation?"

"Do you mean what will he think about living and working with the People, sir?"

"Yes," Weston replied, surprised at Renty's candor.

"I was the only colored fellow in Dover, sir, and we got along fine. 'Didn't seem to trouble Burke one way or another so long as I did my work. I reckon he'll feel the same about the rest of the People at The Abbey, sir. He's a fine chap."

"Well, then, we'll hope for the best and go from there. You may leave, Renty."

"Thank you, sir."

Burke and the lawyer arrived at the plantation on the same schooner that had brought Renty home earlier. Renty was standing on the landing as the schooner arrived, and when Burke stepped onto the dock, Renty grabbed him in a bear hug. The dock hands were too busy to take note until one of them gasped. Burke looked like a big red monster towering over them, and when they saw him in an embrace with Renty, they thought Renty was being overtaken by a beast. In mass they sprinted down the landing screaming and hollering, thinking the beast was going to eat them next.

Trumpeter Wineglass was also there that day, and although he didn't run after the dock hands, he was surely taken aback. When he got home, Trumpeter told his family that he didn't know that humans came with hair that color.

"I started to run when I first saw him, but then I think, well maybe I don't need to run if Renty says he's alright. And Renty, he ran up to the man and squeezed him so hard that I thought maybe I don't know good character when I see it. There I thought he was a plate-eye or something. After Renty done the 'troductions all round, he and the Scotsman made off for the big house to meet with Master Weston, but before they left, I heard Renty ask the Scotsman if he was carrying a knife. He said he had a *skinny do* in his sock but promised not to use it on nobody. Now, why do you reckon Renty would a' said somethin' like that? I asked the People round me, and everybody say they have no iddy what Renty was talkin' about. T'was a strange thing fo' sure."

Renty and Burke walked toward the big house, and Renty stopped now and then just to take another look at his old friend. "You made you'self scareful to some of the People," Renty said.

"Scareful?"

"You scart 'em lookin' like a bear and all," Renty explained.

"Well, the same God made me as you, so I figured it don't make much difference what we look like," Burke said, thoughtfully. "They'll get used to me soon enough."

"When Master Weston and I was writing your letters, he asked me if you might be the sort o' chap that might not take to livin' with colored people. I tol' him you didn't give me no problem about workin' with me in Dover, so I figured you weren't troubled by it, but the master might be plannin' to ask."

"Hell, Renty. If Master Weston is an Englishman, he was probably wondering if your People would be willing to live with me. Englishmen don't think too highly of Scots, you know. They think we're wild and daft, and they'd be right," he boasted.

"Before we get there, though, I need to know if this Weston fellow kept his word about giving you your freedom. If he reneged, I'm gonna' slit his throat like I wanted to back in Dover."

"Master Weston had the papers all ready for me when I got home," Renty said. "He kept his word; now you keep yours. Don't be threatening him. Jest shake his hand and don't say nothin' lest he asks you something."

"He's a natty dresser?" Burke asked, referring to Master Weston.

"Aye, he is that," Renty replied.

"Then he's an Englishman alright."

"Aye, he's close enough."

"I thought so," Burke said. "I won't insult him, but don't expect me to like the blot, and I ain't gonna call him 'master.' We save that for the King, and unless I'm really turned around, there ain't no king for a thousand miles, which, of course, is just as well because Scotsmen ain't fond of kings, neither. What did your family say when you told them about your freedom?"

"I ain't told them, yet."

"You are bloody kidding me!" Burke huffed.

"No, I'm not," Renty said, thoughtfully. "After I got my papers and all, I jest didn't want to tell 'em. They'd be happy for me, but that wouldn't make no difference in they lives. They have to get up ever-day and work the master's fields whether they want to or not. My life is 'xactly the same as it used to be, so I figured I'd jest keep it to myself for a while."

"Are you ever going to tell them?"

"I'm waiting 'till freedom comes to all the People. It ain't gonna be long; it's in the air."

"Aye, it 'tis. An Irishman on the boat coming over told me that. Ain't no way to live. How can a man call himself a Christian and own slaves? Only the bloody British, that's who."

"Master Weston's a South Carolinian, not a Brit, Burke."

"I know that, but his people were Brits."

"Aye, that they were," Renty said.

Burke's introduction to Plowden Weston was a touch awkward, but it went better than Renty had expected. After the meeting, Renty and Burke went to the carpenter's workshop. Next to it were three new buildings, including two cabins — one for Renty and one for Burke. The other building was a long structure with two doors opening onto a porch. That was the dormitory for the workers they would hire to build St. Mary.

"When you talked about going home to build a chapel, I didn't believe you, Renty," Burke said. "I thought you intended to build one. I just didn't see how you were going to do it all by yourself. Now, I see that you're serious. Do you have the plans we worked on?"

Renty and Burke studied Renty's copy of the architectural drawings on the way to the site where Renty and Master Weston had agreed to put the church.

"Good looking place to put a chapel," Burke said studying the rich sandy soil. "One nice thing you got goin' for you here is the soil. It's flat as a flapjack, and a fellow on the boat said there's no frost line in South Carolina. I thanked him for his thoughts, but I couldn't believe there ain't a frost line here."

"Well, there ain't," Renty said, laughing. "The only kind of frost we ever see here lasts about ten minutes. We build ever-thing on footings, though. Not because of frost, but because of termites. They'll eat your house an' be done with it 'fore you know they're there. We use cypress knees fo' the pilings. Termites got an aversion to cypress."

"Why is that?" Burke asked.

"Cypress juice, I reckon."

"When do we start?"

"When our building supplies get here," Renty replied. "I'm planning to work that furry red arse of yours soon enough. Tonight, my family's throwing you a party like you've never seen. It'll let 'em get to know you. I think some of them still think you're the Devil. Mama's next door neighbor thinks you're a plate-eye."

"I can see 'em thinking I could be the Devil; I am a Scotsman, after all, but I never heard of the plate-eye."

"A plate-eye is the spirit of someone who was murdered, and now they're all cankored up with hate, and they can take on the shape of most anything they want to, like a dog or something. They have big red eyes, and they's mean and vengeful; nobody wants to meet up with a plate-eye. The one good thing is that the plate-eye can't abide foul odors, so the People carry charms filled with gun-powder and sulfur toward the plate-eye offen them."

"I'm not exactly thrilled to spend my afternoon talking to people wearing stink bags because o' me," Burke said. "Tell you one thing, though. I grew up near a bog, and there ain't nothing that smells worse than that. You might say I'm stink proof. Bogs are piles of ancient dung, you know. Ain't nothing worse than that, so we'll see who runs who off today."

Renty hadn't exaggerated about how frightened some of the People were of Burke. When Renty and Burke got to Miss Delilah's house, a bunch o' people from the quarter were standing in clusters out in the lane just a' starring and whispering about Burke. They were kind of quiet with their remarks, though, 'cause they didn't want to take a chance on him hearing their whispers and all. They knew he was the Devil just by looking at him. There were plenty o' pictures of Scratch in the Bible, but he might be on his good behavior 'cause o' Renty. If he showed that black tongue o' his, though, that'd be the time to get to runnin'. Lucifer, he run fast, too, but the People was proud that a black man can outrun anything if he's scart enough. They'd been running from Satan as long as anyone could remember. They know their fastness to be a true thing.

Burke put the surprise on everybody. He talked and played with the babies, and when he laughed, his tongue was pink just everybody else's, and he had Jesus teeth, meaning that they were white and perfect. So, what were the People to do?

They thought about it and decided to give Burke a try, and pretty soon they commence ta' liking him even if he did look like Beelzebub. Burke had a good laugh on him, and when the People didn't under-stand a thing, Renty'd translate and everybody started to laughin' and thinkin' he's an alright person just like the People, only he hatched out the wrong color.

"De Lord don't get ever-thing right all the time," Miss Lillian said. "Looks like he make Burke a right nice person on the inside, an' that's the part that counts."

Once that was all figured out and Burke had Miss Lillian's stamp of approval, he just started bein' one of the People. It didn't happen overnight, of course; some folks were harder to convenience than others, but it was a thing that was done, and after a time, nobody even thought much about Burke being the Devil anymore. They were far more troubled by the fact that Burke wore a skirt with nothing on underneath it.

"Must be why God done give him such a hairy backside," Miss Lillian said during one of her rocking marathons.

The chapel got underway, and the People visited the worksite everyday just to see how things were progressing. The land had already been cleared of rocks and scrub, and they discovered a stash of ballast bricks going back to British times. Renty stacked them up out of the way to use for the front walkway.

"I like the iddy of walking on British bricks," Renty said to Burke.

"'Rather be walking on their carcasses, but bricks'll do fine," Burke said out of the side of his mouth.

The work was coming along on schedule and the eatin' was good 'cause ever woman on the plantation brought a spread by at one time or another. Burke thought a couple o' things smelled kinda funny at first, but after about three-four weeks, he told Renty that the People's food was awful good; fried chicken, sweet potato pie and boiled goobers being his favorites.

"What's a goober?" he asked Renty one day.

"It's a peanut."

"Well, Mr. Information, what's a peanut?"

"It's a nut that grows in the ground. When the tops die back, you pull 'em out of the ground, knock off the dirt off of 'em and boil 'em in salt water. Beer works better, but when we gets beer, we'd hate to waste it on goobers."

"If the nuts are called peanuts, why do the People call them goobers?" Burke asked.

"Cause *goober* is the old word; *goobers* is what they was called in Africa. Like the floodgates out in the rice fields. Ever-place else in the world they're called floodgates, but in Africa the floodgates were made out of tree trunks, so the People call 'em *trunks*. Even white folks call 'em trunks. Don't you have Scottish names for English things?"

"No. We have Gaelic names for English things."

"Gaelic?"

"We speak Gaelic in Scotland."

"I'm confused."

"Well, now you know how I feel."

CHAPTER 11

Rachael and Burke

The Abbey Plantation 1859

"MAMA, IT'S MY TURN to take dinner to the chapel, but Hattie wants to go, too," Rachael whined as she and Mama put the finishing touches into an enormous basket they'd borrowed from one of the neighbors. Rations of flour, sugar, and molasses were running low, being the end of the month and all, so Mama and Miss Lillian had to borrow the extra they needed. But, they could still put on a handsome spread with butter beans from their own yard, slabs of fatback salted away since hog killing time last January, hoe cakes made from flour, salt and water, pickled sweetbreads, and apple pie made from apples grown in the old apple orchard next to the Cuba Garden. Rachael and Hattie together couldn't carry the basket more than ten feet. It was too heavy.

"Stop complaining," Sheila hollered back. "Go get that wheelbarrow from the paint shed. I never seen such babies."

Rachael hadn't met Burke or Renty, yet. She'd been too busy working on an embroidery project at the big house to do any socializing, but that was finally over, and she was looking forward to doing anything other than sewing. It'd been two years since the incident with the Middleton boy, time for Rachael to understand that despite her looks and her insatiable desire to have something exciting happen to her, there was no way in hell it was going to happen as long as she and her family lived in slavery. She could pray for it, she could do Indian dances, she could holler, and she could plead, but it wasn't gonna happen, no matter how much she wanted it. She might as well have prayed for a fancy new pair of red shoes. It just wasn't happening. Exciting things happened to white girls dressed in silk taffeta dresses with ribbons in their glossy hair and slippers on their feet made from fine kid leather, not to colored girls, no matter how pretty they were. Mama and Miss Lillian didn't help any, harping as they did from morning 'till night about marriage.

"You're a marriageable girl, Rachael. You need ta be thinkin' 'bout your future. The boys in the quarter are trippin' over each other tryin' to get your eye, but you neber give them the time of day. Now, why is that about?"

"I don't want a boy, Mama," Rachael would say. "I don't want nobody."

"Well, you can't keep this up forever. You need to think about it real hard, Rachael. Promise you'll think on it."

"I promise, Mama."

The chapel site was about a quarter of a mile from the Wineglass's cabin, downhill, mostly, and there was a worn path leading almost all the way there. Pushing a wheelbarrow wasn't a glamorous job, but it wasn't going to be a difficult one. Rachael was planning to talk Hattie into doing most of the work, anyway. Pushing a wheelbarrow could raise blisters, she'd say, and she had to protect her hands so she could continue to do the delicate embroidery she was so good at. Hattie certainly wouldn't want to upset the mistress, now, would she? When she brought it up with Hattie, though, Hattie told her to put a sock in her pie hole and to leave her alone. Little sisters have a gift for seeing through the bull shit. After a couple of starts and stops when Hattie threatened to run the wheelbarrow off into the pond next to the People's cemetery if Rachael didn't help with the pushing, Rachael and Hattie finally arrived at the building site where a half dozen men were already gathered. One look at Rachael even pushing a wheelbarrow and the work came to an abrupt halt. The men gawked and stared and generally make fools of themselves because she was so pretty and all, but nobody was as smitten as Burke. He could barely move.

"Well, that one's a bobby-dazzler," he whispered to Renty.

"A bobby-dazzler?" Renty asked.

"A pretty girl."

"She did a lot of growing up while I was gone," Renty said, studying Rachael for the first time. "Her papa's Trumpeter Wineglass, a friend of mine."

"Wineglass?"

"It's a long story," Renty said, "but he's a fine fellow, and we've been friends since we were little."

"You're related to everyone on the plantation," Burke said, laughing. "This girl's beautiful; is she old enough for an introduction?"

"She's got to be 'bout seventeen now, maybe older," Renty said. "Old enough. I still think she's too young for you, Burke. She was attacked by a white boy a few years back, made her skittish. Give it some time to get used to you, first."

Burke honored Renty's advice, but it didn't keep him from acting like a giddy kipper every time he saw the girl. She was just so bloody beautiful, but as Burke was making eyes at Rachael, the most surprising thing happened. Rachael started making eyes at Renty. She was horrified by her emboldened behavior. It was too much like the goo-goo eyes she made at the Middleton boy. It made her feel trampy. At the same time, though, it made her feel good. Renty had just turned twenty-six; he was no boy. Was that the difference? Was that why she was attracted to him? She had no idea. His hair was short beneath his wide-brimmed hat, and he was careful with his appearance even when he was swinging a hammer or supervising a gang putting up a ceiling joist. Delilah used to brag that he could work all day without breaking a crease on his work pants. Renty looked smallish next to Burke, but Rachael was certain that he was stronger than he looked, and he had to be smart because he seemed to understand every word that ugly red-furred person uttered.

Burke's skin was white — pinkish-white — and even though he was red-furred and didn't look anything like the Middleton boy, he was always going to be white, so Rachael cut him a wide berth. Renty's voice was pleasing, and his accent was a cross between where he'd grown up and where he'd been. Rachael liked it. Rachael liked everything about Renty. Of course, that didn't separate her from the gaggle of young women who felt the same way. Renty had set out for England as a carpenter, but he'd returned a heartthrob. The first few times Rachael was close enough to study him, she wondered if this was the excitement that she'd been looking for. Maybe she was drawn to Renty because he was a man of the world; he'd been places. Was that it?

Renty was oblivious. He'd never put too much stock in the importance of keeping time with a woman. It wasn't that he didn't find them attractive — a blind man could see how beautiful Rachael was — but Renty was always in a hurry to finish a project or eager to start a new one to spend more than five-seconds thinking about women.

Rachael could change his perspective, though. As Renty got to noticing her, he realized that coming or going, Rachael was, what did Burke call her? A bobby-dazzler? She was dazzling. 'Couldn't argue with that, but it was as clear as day that Burke already had his cap set for her. He was agog every time he saw her, and he was Renty's best friend, so Renty backed away. Burke showed up at work one morning with a black cloud over his head. He was down, and for the first time he was wishing he had a bellyful of single malt.

"What's the matter?" Renty asked, while he and Burke worked together to set up a plumb line.

"The lass I have my eye on told me this morning that she wasn't interested in me. She said to stay away from her, and that if I was ta' come courting, she'd hide under the bed."

"I'm sorry, Burke," Renty said, hoping that his excitement wasn't showing, knowing that it was Rachael Burke was talking about. "Now that they know you ain't a plate-eye, they're lots of women interested in you," Renty pointed out.

"I ain't interested in them, though," Burke said, heavy on the brogue. "I'm only interested in one lass, and she ain't interested in me. I need the company of a woman. It's been a long time. And I don't want one who will hide 'neath the bed when I come calling. I want a lusty young woman with big bobbies and fair pink skin and hair redder than me own."

"Missing home?"

"Aye, that I am. I miss the pubs and rough-housing with my mates. I want to hear the pipes, and play darts and take a good long piss facing Edinburgh Castle. I want to get shit-faced and sleep it off in a whore-house. I want to kiss girls named Molly and Fiona and Annabel. How I'd love to lift my kilt for a fair Annabel. I even miss the harshness of Scottish winters. I thought that Trumpeter's daughter would make me forget my longing, but when she turned me down this morning, she did me a favor. She made me face the truth. I miss home."

"I felt the same way in Dover," Renty said, sympathetically. "I didn't dream of girls named Molly or Fiona, but I missed my family. Are you planning to leave?" Renty asked.

"Hell, no, I'm not leaving 'till this chapel is finished, not a day sooner; I just miss home, that's all."

"Maybe we can find you a woman in Georgetown," Renty said, smiling at having hatched a plan. "There are taverns along Front Street. How do you get along with seamen?"

"Mariners and me get along fine as long as I don't get too gassed," Burke said. "How 'bout we go there tonight?"

"I can't go into a tavern. What are you thinking?" Renty exclaimed. "You're a free man. Nobody at the tavern will give a shit. Most o' them wouldn't be able to read my manumission papers even if they wanted to. I'd just be one more n.... They'd beat the tar outta me just for walkin' in the door."

"Bloody fools," Burke mutters.

"Well, that's the way it is. Freedom doesn't change ever-thing, but you should go. You should go this afternoon."

Burke took Renty's advice and hired one of the laborers at the chapel site to row him to Georgetown after work that day. It was a seven-mile trip to Winyah Bay, and the tide was going out at about six knots that time of day, so they got to the bay in an hour. The trip to Front Street was another hour, but Burke enjoyed every minute of it. A two-hour trip to reach accommodating women with red curls and overhanging balconies was a bargain. Burke fell in love twice in the first tavern and another time in the second. He would have settled for an Irish lass or even a Welch one, but lass Number Three was a red-haired girl born near Bonnyrigg, a small town less than eight miles south of Edinburgh.

"A Scottish lass for a Scottish lad!" Burke bellowed. "God Bless America!"

Burke was gone for three days, and when he did come dragging in the door, he was a married man.

"Me and Mairghread here are husband and wife!" Burke roared after finding his way to the job site. "Gather 'round lads and meet the misses."

Renty was in the rafters of the sanctuary at the time, and it was a good thing he'd tied himself to a crossbeam; otherwise he'd have fallen to the ground for sure.

"Mrs. Burke, good ta' meet you," he said, after unhooking his safety belt and winching himself down to the floor of the chapel.

"You can call me Mairghread," Mrs. Burke said, shyly. "It's Gaelic for Margaret. You can even call me Margaret if you like. Mairghread's a mouthful."

"Mairghread suits you," Renty said, noting how much Mairghread and Burke favored.

Mairghread had the same unruly hair, piercing blue eyes, and skin the color of boiled shrimp. Mairghread was a large woman with rounded parts in all the right places and a sweet smile. She was young, Renty guessed; she was no older than Rachael—maybe even younger.

"Tell me you're surprised," Burke said, planting a playful slap on his bride's rump.

"I'm that, alright," Renty said, still studying the girl.

"I admit it was a bit sudden," Burke said, "but when you find the right girl, you just want to jump on it, so to speak. Do you think his highness will mind?" Burke asked, referring to Master Weston.

"Don't know," Renty replied, honestly. "Nothin' like this has ever happened. The plantation's kind of old fashioned and set in its ways. We need a change around here, though, and you're a sight for sore eyes, Mairghread. Why don't you have Burke take you to your cabin."

"We get our own cabin?" Mairghread said, gleefully.

"Well, it ain't much. We weren't expecting a lady," Renty said. "Give us a little while, though, and we'll find you some food and extra blankets an' a cook pot and such, so's you'll be comfortable. Take the rest of the day off to help Mairghread get squared away, Burke. I'll talk to you after supper."

A Katherine Wheel—a firework that spins like a whirling clock face and shoots off flames and sparks in every direction—might best describe how the news of Burke's marriage flew around the plantation. By the time the story had gotten back to Renty, Mairghread either looked like a fairy princess or a female plate-eye, depending upon who you asked. Some said she was burlier than Burke, which was pretty ridiculous seeing as to how nobody was bigger than Burke, at least not in South Carolina.

Everyone seemed to agree that she was a sweet spirited young girl and a pretty one even though she was oddly colored. Her questionable background troubled some of the old-livers, but the younger ones, especially those who knew Burke, were happy for him. Burke wasn't like most of the white folks the People were familiar with; he was a regular person who never acted like he was better than anyone else. Maybe that went back to his unusual coloring, but the People didn't care as long as he was a good chap to be around, and they were willing to extend the same courtesy to Mairghread.

After Burke and Mairghread moved to the plantation, Renty was happier than he'd ever been because he was free to court Rachael, and it wasn't long before he asked Trumpeter and Sheila for their permission to marry her.

CHAPTER 12

Wedding Bells

The Abbey Plantation 1859

HE FOUND TRUMPETER and his family sitting on the porch. Trumpeter was smoking his pipe, Miss Lillian was in a rockin' frenzy, Lacey and Hattie were in the yard picking bouquets of Lady's Breath, and Sheila was sitting on the steps of the porch shelling peas. Rachael was in the cabin, and she was as nervous as a cat. She was afraid that Renty might back down because he couldn't get his words out, being so quiet and all, but Renty did fine, and when Trumpeter stood up and slapped him on the back, Rachael rushed out. Everybody jumped up and started kissing each other.

Then Burke and Mairghread and Miss Delilah and Renty's brother, Amos, and everybody started coming down the lane, and everybody was rejoicing and talking about happy times. Then they all got ta' talking about the wedding, and everybody asked Renty and Rachael if they were going to wait until the chapel was finished to have the wedding, and they said no. They didn't want to wait that long, and that's when Sheila came up with her plan.

"They can still be married in the chapel," she said. "Who says it has to be finished? God's already living there. If we sweep it up a little bit, who cares if the windows aren't in or the pews aren't ready yet? It's still God's house."

Then Trumpeter asked Renty when he was planning to ask for Master Weston's permission, and Renty said he didn't know.

"Why don't we go right now and get it over with?" Trumpeter asked.

"Thanks for coming with me," Renty said as they neared the big house.

"It ain't nothing." Trumpeter said. "Besides, you're going to be my son-in-law."

They were ushered into Master Weston's study, and Renty had a feeling that Master Weston had already heard the news, 'cause he was so free with his permission. Renty felt better and had just let out a sigh when Master Weston reminded him that even though he was free to come and go as he pleased, Rachael still belonged to the plantation and wasn't permitted to leave it without permission. Renty said he'd already thought about that and that it was a thing that would be done according to the rules. Master Weston said good, and then a young girl came to the door to show Renty and Trumpeter out.

When they were out of ear shot from the big house, Trumpeter turned to Renty and said, "Renty, what did Master Weston mean when he said you were free to come and go?'"

"He was referring to me being a freedman, Trumpeter."

"A freedman?"

"I got freedom the day I come home from England," Renty said. "Master Weston and me, we signed the papers that very day."

"You mean you been free ever since you come home?"

"Uh-huh."

"So, why did you stay on, and why didn't you tell nobody?"

"It wouldn't have changed anything. This is where I want to be, to live on the plantation and to build the chapel. I didn't want anybody else to build it, and what good would it do to tell ever-body about being free when they're still slaves? I couldn't do it. I wanted to wait until freedom comes to ever-body."

"Does Rachael know?"

"No, I ain't told her. I ain't told nobody but you."

"Tell her before the wedding," Trumpeter advised. "Don't have a secret this big going into a marriage. Little secrets, maybe, but not big ones like this."

"Alright, Trumpeter," Renty said. "I'll tell her tonight. Do you think she'll be surprised?"

"I think she'll bust a gut, but in a good way, Renty. Rachael wants to be free as bad as we all do. She'll be happy 'bout it."

Rachael wasn't happy when she heard the news that evening; she was confused, and she asked the very same questions that her papa had asked. Then she asked another one that tore at Renty's heart.

"If you're free, does that mean that I'll be free, too, when we're married?"

"No, Rachael," Renty said, holding back his tears. "Our children will be free, but not you, my dear. Freedom's coming soon for ever-body, though. We just have to wait, and we'll do it together."

Three weeks later on an early spring day that smelled like green grass and daffodils, the plantation bell rang to mark the day of the wedding. Rachael wore a white lace gown made from fabric given to her by Mistress Emily. As a special gift, the seamstresses in the laundry house made a veil out of spare netting and embroidered tiny flowers and vines on it until it looked like something a fairy might have worn. Sheila and Trumpeter wore their Sunday best. Hattie wore her yellow dress, and Rachael had made Miss Lillian a new dress as a surprise.

Rachael was the most beautiful bride anyone had ever seen. The chapel looked beautiful, too, even though everyone had to stand and to sing without the organ, which was still stuck in Charleston. But nobody cared, and that wasn't even the best part.

Rachael wasn't the only bride that day. Although Mairghread and Burke had been legally married back in Georgetown, it had taken place in a bar, and the judge who performed the service had bragged that he hadn't been sober in twenty years.

It just didn't seem right, so when Rachael and Renty heard that Mairghread had always wanted to be married in a proper church, they offered to share their wedding day. Trumpeter was sure right about the People having some happy days. He surely was.

CHAPTER 13

The Little Red Chair

The Abbey Plantation 1859

A FEW WEEKS LATER, Trumpeter was told to deliver a load of lumber to the carpenter shop, and he asked Sheila if Hattie could go with him. Sheila said she could go once she put the children down for their naps, so Trumpeter said he'd pick her up then. Trumpeter had even more status on the plantation now because he had just become Renty Tucker's father-in-law, and he was feeling pretty good about everything, but as they neared the carpenter shop, Trumpeter warned Hattie not to ask about the chapel, or they could be there all day. For a man of few words, Renty sure did like talking about the chapel. "It's gonna be finished by Christmas," Trumpeter said. "You can ask your questions then."

Trumpeter reminded Hattie one last time to shush up about the chapel, and then he pulled his mule in front of a trough filled with fresh rice straw.

"That worthless old mule can smell rice straw a mile away," Trumpeter said with a laugh. "He's a real case, ain't he, Hattie?"

After Trumpeter jumped off the wagon and started unloading the lumber, Renty Tucker stepped out into the sunlight from the workshop.

"Afternoon, Renty. 'Thought I'd bring Hattie along with me today."

Now, Hattie had taken on some extra status, too, being that she was Renty's new sister-in-law. Because of her age, though, Sheila had suggested that they call each other cousins, which suited ever-body just fine.

"Hattie," Renty said, "come inside my workshop. I think I might have something in there you'll take a shine to." After looking over at Papa for approval, Hattie excitedly followed Renty through a cavernous maze of work tables and storage shelves. Dust motes and sawdust swirled around them as they passed, reminding Hattie of a sorcerer's cottage in a fairytale she'd heard. There was less sunlight in the rear of the workshop, and what little there was cast shadows that looked like stick figures prancing about. *Maybe witches lived there,* Hattie mused.

Renty got to the back wall, and then he stopped and turned back toward Hattie.

"Ah, here we are," he said. "What do you think?"

In front of her was a waist-high shelf containing four Windsor-style chairs just her size. Two were green. One had been left in its natural wood tone, and one was painted Chinese red. "I learned to make these chairs a long time ago," Renty said, as Trumpeter joined them. "If you'd like to have one, Hattie, all you have to do is pick it out."

"Oh, the red one! The red one!" Hattie cried.

"The red one it is," Renty said as he removed the chair from the shelf. "I have to tell you a story about this chair, though. This one has a mighty fine story 'tatched to it. I didn't make this one. It come straight from the big house."

"'Old Master Thomas Dunhill died seven or eight years ago," Renty began, "and his daughter, Miss Charlotte, ask me to come to the big house to see about some furniture she needed to get rid of 'cause she was getting the house all spruced up for her brother, George, to be the new master. She showed me the furniture and said that I could have anything I wanted, so I just said I'd take it all. She said that was fine, so I loaded it onto my wagon. This little chair was wrapped up inside a' old wardrobe with angels painted on it. I didn't know it was there for a long time, and by the time I found it, I figured Miss Charlotte hadn't missed it, so I just hung it up in my workshop. Now it's yours. See the letters carved into the seat? They're called initials. I had to think a long time about whose they belonged to. Then I remembered they belonged to Master Theodore, the little boy who died in the ice house. Broke his neck, I think. One of the People had made the chair for the little boy's fifth birthday; that's what my granny said. That was a long, long time ago, though — probably more than fifty years," Renty added, realizing that he may have upset Hattie by telling her the story.

"Look, Papa," Hattie said pointing to the initials.

"If you put your fingers on them, you can feel them," Renty explained.

"The first one is a 'T,' the second one is an 'M,' and the third is a 'D.' It stands for Theodore Madison Dunhill, the little boy in the cemetery."

"Try the chair on for size, Hattie," Trumpeter suggested, changing the subject so's Hattie didn't ask Renty to teach her to read or some other smart aleck thing.

Fearing that the beautiful little chair might break if she sat down too quickly, Hattie settled into it so slowly that Renty and Papa began to laugh. "You ain't gonna break it, Hattie. It's made for sitting," Renty said.

"I've never seen such a beautiful thing. I'll take care of it my whole life," Hattie promised.

"I'm sure you will, Hattie," Renty replied. "I'm sure you will."

Hattie wanted to sit in her chair in the back of the wagon on the way home, but it was too cold, and Papa said the road was too bumpy. "You might just tumble right out, Hattie. You can rock in it all you want to when we gets home. I want you to share it with Lacey. She didn't get no chair."

"Renty said he'd give her one next time, Papa," Hattie said.

"Well, I'm happy about that one," Papa said. "It should cut down on the tears when we get home."

CHAPTER 14

The Tree of Africa

The Abbey Plantation 1859

HATTIE BROUGHT HER CHAIR out into the yard the next morning so she could see the initials in the sunlight. She didn't get much looking done, though, because it was Saturday, and she and Mama had to put in a half day at the nursery. After that, Hattie, Lacey, Mama, and Miss Lillian would spend the rest of the afternoon refreshing the mattresses. They'd miss Rachael's quick stitches. Collecting fresh wadding to re-stuff the mattresses was a pain in the neck. Even Trumpeter was expected to help out, and he hated it.

Practically every evening he'd come through the door and hand Sheila a bunch of pine straw, or Spanish moss, or discarded rags, and then he'd act pissy about it. "Ain't fittin' for a man," was his excuse, but Sheila just let it roll off her back.

"Adding stuffing to a mattress never kilt nobody," she'd say, so Trumpeter would just let it go and ask what was for supper. It'd sure been easier to live in cotton country. Mattress stuffing was hard work because everything had to be boiled in lye water and dried good before going into the mattress. Then the mattress stuffers would sit in a big circle and stuff until their fingers ached. Sheila and Miss Lillian were always grateful that they didn't have to worry about making blankets. Everybody in the quarter slept beneath woolen blankets imported from England. Indigo blue in color, the blankets were distributed every year on a rotating schedule. One year, a new one would be given to each child in a family. The following year the adults in the family would receive a new one. The People always joked about the old days when the indigo that dyed their English-made blankets was probably grown at The Abbey.

Quilts were another matter, and just like the other women in the quarter, Sheila and Miss Lillian spent evening times quilting by the fire. Most of the quilts they made were simple ones made out of scraps saved from worn out work clothes, but sometimes they made special ones decorated with patterns depicting scenes from Africa or the Bible.

"When you get married," Mama used to say, "I'll be giving you a Tree of Africa quilt just like my mama gave me."

Hattie and her sisters descended from one of the most important women to ever live at The Abbey—Aunt Hattie. Aunt Hattie, of course, had already passed away before Hattie Wineglass was old enough to remember her, but she continued to be a legend among the People because of her skills at dyeing—not the mortal kind of dying, but dyeing fabrics. Small and hunchbacked, Aunt Hattie used to disappear into the woods and spend hours collecting ingredients for her dyes. Then she'd return, tie her findings into bunches, and hang them from the ceiling above the fireplace in her cabin. When she was asked to dye something, all she needed to ask was, "What color would you be wanting?"

Aunt Hattie knew that the leaves from the elm, cherry, and red oak trees made red dyes; Spanish moss and onion skins made yellow; walnut shells made brown dye; indigo made blue dye; and grasses made greenish-colored dyes. According to Aunt Hattie, she could make dye out of practically anything.

Her most powerful dye, the one she called rusty nail red, was made by digging a hole in the red clay that was down by the pump house, filling the hole with water, and stirring the water until it worked itself into a soupy red slush. That's all there was to it. Anything thrown into the hole would stay dyed forever; the trick was in knowing how long to leave it there before it started to rot. That's why you needed Aunt Hattie; she had an instinct for such things. Combine Aunt Hattie's glorious colors with cotton batting bartered from cotton plantations in Georgia or the Sea Islands, and your Tree of Africa quilt could be the only one like it in the whole world.

Every family in the quarter had at least one Tree of Africa quilt, and they were precious possessions. Hattie's quilt, which Mama and Miss Lillian had already finished and put away, had a stylized tree in the center with big blue-green leaves. Stick figures representing Hattie's ancestors were depicted in a field of rice to remind Hattie that her ancestors had grown rice for centuries. Hattie's Abbey family, including Mama, Papa, and Miss Lillian, were also on the quilt. The border of the quilt was decorated with stylized heads of golden rice and lilies of the field. Quilt backs were traditionally white, but Hattie's was rusty nail red. Hattie's people were from Guinea and Sierra Leone on Africa's westward coast where the People had been growing rice for hundreds and hundreds of years.

"They was so good at it that slave traders got top dollar for our hides," Miss Lillian told Hattie. "We'd probably be back in Africa if we hadn't been so good at it."

"You mean you and me and our family might be livin' in Africa right this minute?"

"I surely do," Miss Lillian said. "We was only brought here 'cause we could grow rice."

"For true?"

"For true," Miss Lillian said, nodding her head.

"What do you think we'd be doin' right now if we was back in Africa?"

"We'd probably be sittin' in our house just like we are right now. 'Course it wouldn't look like this house—it'd probably be made out of grass and mud bricks and shaped like a circle or somethin', but it'd be our house, not the master's house or nobody else's. An' the rice we grew would be our, too, same as the pigs and cows and guinea hens. They'd be all our."

"It'd be a fine thing, wouldn't it Granny?"

"It surely would."

CHAPTER 15

Christmas in the Quarter

The Abbey Plantation 1860

HARVEST TIME FLEW BY that year, and Christmas time was knocking at the door. The People loved Christmas, but getting ever-thing ready for the Baby Jesus was hard work.

The houses in the quarter had to be white-washed and scrubbed from top to bottom with lye soap and soda ash until they smelled as sweet as clover. Then the decorating commenced. Sheila draped garlands of holly and magnolia above the door and windows and filled her Mason jar vases with bouquets of fragrant Scotch pine. She rousted Hattie and Lacey from their warm beds before dawn and fed them their breakfasts whilst they were getting dressed. Tomorrow was Christmas Day, and there was work to be done. Hattie's cousins were already down at the well preparing to tote water for the families. Then they were going to help Papa and Uncle Ted butcher whatever they'd trapped in the woods the night before.

Hattie's first job of the day was to help Lacey make up the beds and sweep the floor. Snapping beans was next. Mama handed Hattie a large ceramic bowl filled with butter beans and said to get going.

No instructions were necessary for that job — the girls knew they'd be spending the rest of the morning snappin' beans out in the yard. It wasn't a job they wanted to rush, though. A worse job was coming up next. Killing chickens was woman's work, and Hattie and Lacey were the ones expected to do the killing. There were two ways to kill a chicken. One was to break its neck by whirling it around in a circle, but it was a horrible method because the chicken's head would usually come off, and the rest of the chicken would go flying. Another problem with that particular method was that the chicken flopped around on the ground for a long time before it died. If its head was off, all that flopping sprayed chicken blood on everything in sight, including the ones doing the killing. So, the Wineglass girls chose method number two, which was to catch the chickens with a wire hook and to tie the birds upside-down on the fence, so they could cut their heads off without all that flapping. The chicken catching part went well, and tying them to the fence went well, too. The girls were almost home, but when Hattie pulled out the butcher knife, Lacey started bawling.

"I ain't gonna murder a chicken, an' you can't make me," she screamed.

Hattie called her a sissy girl and a few other choice names. Then she pushed Lacey out of the way, beheaded the chicken, and intentionally squirted chicken blood in Lacey's direction. Lacey howled, but Sheila didn't even look up. Lacey was a sissy girl.

Chickens' guts smell to high heaven. There's never been a good smelling chicken, and there never will be. Maybe God intentionally made chickens stink so much so you don't feel bad about killing them. According to Hattie, they should all be rounded up and sent to New York or some other country where it already stinks, and the chickens could run around unnoticed. The decapitated chickens were hung from the fence for an hour or so. Then Sheila blanched them in boiling water for about thirty-seconds. Blanching made it easier to pluck the chickens, and that was considered woman's work too. About fifteen-seconds into the process, Lacey realized that she hated plucking chickens even worse than killing them.

"Mama," she said, "these chickens stink. They're gonna make me keck up my breakfast." That was it.

Sheila was worn out with Lacey's whining, and she had a hot tempter. She was getting mad, so she came off the porch and stood over Lacey looking like a tree.

"You've got five seconds," she said.

"Yes, Mama," Lacey whispered. Mama meant business, so Lacey stuffed her nostrils with cotton batting and kept on plucking. Once the chickens were clean, Mama cut them into recognizable parts and dropped them into a skillet of hot lard.

Papa roasted the turkey, possums, and the ducks on an open fire out in the yard.

CHAPTER 16

Jumpin' de Broom

The Abbey Plantation 1860

HATTIE AND HER FAMILY cooked up their Christmas supper, while Renty and Burke made their way toward St. Mary. They were fixing to install the lockset onto the chapel's front door, and it was the last job. Renty and Burke wanted to put it in together. The lockset was a gift from Mistress Emily, and it had been in her family for more than two hundred years. The size of a thin cigar box, the lockset was brass, and it was richly engraved with cherubs and curlicues. Renty and Burke had barely said a word to each other that morning, not that they were out of sorts with each other; it's just that they'd worked every day for the past year to complete the chapel, and now that it was finished, it left a vacant place in their hearts.

"I feel empty inside," Burke said, breaking the silence.

"Me too," Renty admitted. "I thought I'd be happy about finishing the chapel, and I am. I am, but I wish it could go on, too. I didn't 'spect to feel hollow inside."

"Me neither," Burke said. "We slaved over this chapel—pardon the pun—and here we are standing in its doorway with nothing left to do. I guess now we have to turn it over to some fat parson and walk away. You know, you and me are free to hire ourselves out to build other chapels."

"I thought about that," Renty said, as he studied the lockset. "Tucker and Burke, Chapels, Builders of St. Mary of the Fields, Waccamaw."

"Burke and Tucker, Chapels, it does have a nice ring to it," Burke said, laughing in his unfettered way. "Let's take some time off and think about what we want to do."

"What about Scotland?"

"I think Mairghread and I will stay here for now," Burke replied. "She likes being an American girl and all. Besides, she has a bun in the oven."

"A bun in the oven?"

"A baby, you daft dunderhead."

To no one's surprise, Matilda and Homer Lee announced their plans to marry on Wedding Day, which was the day after Christmas. So, when Renty and Burke put in the last of the six screws in that held the lockset in place, the whole plantation was relieved. They were going to have themselves a wedding in the finished chapel. For as long as anyone could remember, weddings between slaves had always been held on the piazza of the big house, but St. Mary of the Fields changed all of that. Renty and Burke had both said their vows there, of course. But Matilda and Homer Lee would be the first couple to be married in the completed chapel, and the People were certain that from now on their weddings would top anything on the river. Renty and Burke made their final walkthrough of the chapel when they heard the chatter of women.

The invasion was on. Delilah, Hattie, Sheila, Rachael, Mairghread, and a half-dozen other volunteers showed up with brooms and mops, scrub brushes, and mop buckets to prepare the church for the upcoming Christmas service. Sheila had been saving her stash of worn diapers and lemon oil for a special day. And it didn't get more special than this, so she parceled out the diapers and sat the bottle of lemon oil on the communion table so everyone could use it as they needed it. The women got to dusting, sweeping, washing, scrubbing, and polishing every square inch of their magnificent new chapel. Ladders were set up so that Rachael and Hattie could clean the stained-glass windows, but they were told to use a light touch. The windows were fragile and virtually irreplaceable, so Rachael and Hattie slowly climbed to the top of their ladders and cleaned the windows with vinegar and water.

"Go light," Delilah cautioned. "And if yo' get ta' falling, fall this a' way."

The girls got down from their ladders. The diapers were collected. The lemon oil was put away. And it got all quiet-like. "I think we're done cleaned ever-thing there is to clean," Delilah said, breaking the silence. "I'm feeling mighty prideful."

"Me too," said her new daughter-in-law, Rachael. "This is a kind of proudfulness that I never felt before. Like we did somethin' that will last forever. We the People did this."

"And Burke," Mairghread added.

"I'm sorry, Mairghread. I was countin' him as one of the People, and you, too," Rachael said reaching out for Mairghread's hand. "It's just that ever since the Middleton boy, I've been mad. Even when I married Renty, I was still a little bit mad. Mad at God or somebody. I don't even know who I was mad at, but today, I feel joyful just like a new baby being born and bouncing into a world of happiness. I don't know what has gotten into me."

"I know," Hattie said. "I know what it is. It's the light, the light through the stained-glass windows is magic, magic straight from God. It's kind of like God is smiling on us, telling us that He is proud of our good work on the chapel."

When the People arrived the following morning, the chapel nearly took their breaths away. Sunlight streamed through the stained glass, casting fanciful prisms of light everywhere, like fairies let loose from a cage. The windows were called lancet windows because they formed a point at their apex like the point of the lances that the knights in shining armor used to carry into battle. The archways within the chapel mimicked the shape of the windows as did the doors. The oak pews had been custom made in Charleston.

Bunches of magnolia, cedar, and other evergreens were placed at the base of each window and tied to the end of each pew. A large silver cross sat on top of the communion table, and it was engraved with words: *This Do In Remembrance of Me.*

The marble baptismal font came from Mistress Emily's ancestral home in Somerset, England, and it stood near the pulpit.

The Christmas service was the most glorious one ever, everyone agreed afterwards. The hymns soared to the top of the beamed ceilings, and Brother Kirby's words about Jesus and the angels of the Lord praising Glory to God in the Highest, made every person in the church reach for their handkerchiefs. The only thing the People didn't like was that Master Weston and Miss Emily attended the service, and their presence threw everything off. Brother Kirby had to keep his thoughts about freedom to himself, and the choir director felt pressed to turn down the volume of the music to more closely resemble the music that the Westons were used to at All Saints' Church. It was something the People just had to live with.

The Westons didn't know, of course, and nobody was going to tell them—the chapel had been their idea, after all, so the People kept a special pew near the back of the church just in case they decided to stop by. When the Westons weren't there, the women were free to shout "Hallelujah!" or "Amen!" if they wanted to and to wave their kerchiefed hands in the air. But they were also free to jump, or to run up and down the aisles, or to faint dead away if they wanted to. Those displays were too intimate to share with the master looking on even if he did pay for the chapel.

Matilda and Homer Lee's wedding was held the next day, and it was one of those days when the sun was at its most brilliant, the sky was the bluest anyone could remember, and there wasn't a breath of wind. "It sure is a fine day," Homer Lee said to his sister that morning.

"It surely is Homer Lee," she replied.

"Like it say in the Bible, God is in His heaven, and all is good. They's some nasty looking storms looming over Georgetown, though. We best get on wid this wedding before God dumps all that storm on top of us."

As Homer Lee's sister laid out his wedding shirt and pants that she had made for him as a gift, she asked, "Are you happy about Matilda and all? Is she de woman for you?"

"Oh, Matilda's the one, alright," Homer Lee said, giving his sister a kiss on the forehead. "I loves that woman, and she loves me. Today, I feel outta my mind with joy and happiness. Praise Jesus!"

On the other side of the quarter, Matilda was biting her nails. What had she gotten herself into? What was she doing promising a man that she would marry him? Matilda don't need a husband; she needed a tonic to give her the strength to back out of the wedding. Her wedding dress was laying on the bed, spread out like a fairy dress.

Rachael and the other women who worked in the laundry house had stitched every square inch of that dress to make it resemble a dream catcher. Mistress Emily had given Matilda ten yards of silk brocade to make her dress out of, and it ended up being the most beautiful one that could be imagined. Matilda, however, wasn't about to set foot in it. If she did, she'd have to go through with the wedding.

"Matilda, why are you out on the porch in your underwear?" Rachael came out to ask. "You need to get in here and get dressed. We need to get on to the chapel so's you can get married before the storm comes blowin' in, and we get sopped."

"I ain't gettin' married today," Matilda told a stunned Rachael.

"What do you mean you ain't gettin' married today? Who do you think this wedding dress belongs to? It don't have my name on it. It don't say RACHAEL. It says MATILDA on it, and that's you."

"I ain't doin' it."

"You and me have been sewing on this wedding dress for months, and you jest happen to pick this 'xact moment to change your mind?"

"Well, I guess I did," Matilda says, staring at the ground.

"What's the matter, Mattie?" Rachael said, reaching out for her friend.

"I'm scared," Matilda said. "I'm scared of having a husband who tells me what to do and when to do it. I don't need nobody orderin' me around and tellin' me that I'm trash and ain't no better than horse piss."

"Homer Lee compared you to horse piss!"

"No, Homer Lee never said nothing like that. Homer Lee's a good man. He's never said an unkind word to me."

"Then why don't you want to marry him?"

"'Cause men change when they get to be husbands. They get mean."

"No, they don't," Rachael insisted. "My papa never done anything bad to my mama, and Renty loves on me all the time. I'd put the whomp on him if he ever did something mean, but he's sweet to me, Mattie. He loves me. Homer Lee's not gonna change from his ways jest 'cause he's getting married. You just married a mean man the first time. Now you got it right. You've got Homer Lee."

"He is a good man, ain't he?" Matilda asked, feeling shameful for her doubts. "I like spending time with him. I like how strong and proud he is, and he has a good hank o' hair."

"Then what are we waiting for? Let's get you into that fancy dress."

When Matilda and Rachael arrived at the chapel, everyone cheered and told Matilda that they'd never seen a more beautiful bride. Of course, everyone always says that on a woman's wedding day, but the difference that day was that everyone meant it. Matilda's dress was made of two parts: a long full skirt with a slight bustle in the back and a blouse designed to cover the waistband of the skirt but not to limit Matilda's ability to move her arms. The blouse had mutton sleeves and rows of tiny tucks running up the front.

Matilda's veil had started out as a lacy kitchen curtain, but Rachael had cut away some of the lace and turned the veil into something that framed Matilda's face and made her look like an angel. Matilda was also wearing white shoes that she borrowed from one of Homer Lee's sisters and white kid gloves given to her by Mistress Emily.

Everybody was there. There wasn't a soul who either didn't love Homer Lee or wasn't kin to him, and they had grown to really like Matilda, so everyone showed up. Besides, there was free food. Hattie and her family was there, of course. Since the incident with Rachael and the Middleton boy, Matilda had become a member of the Wineglass family. The service started when everyone was accounted for, including the groom, of course, along with his large, boisterous family.

Homer Lee was practically as done up as his bride. He had on white wool pants, a white linen shirt, and a cotton vest that his sisters had made for him as a wedding gift. He had black patent leather shoes on and new white socks. He was wearing his daddy's funeral tie that had black and gray stripes. He couldn't have looked more handsome, and he was enjoying every minute of it.

The chapel was filled with wildflowers that had been added to the evergreens from Christmas Day and two dozen white tapers, yet another gift from the mistress. The chapel smelled like yellow jasmine. When the organ player started up with his rendition of "Here Comes the Bride," Matilda latched onto Homer Lee's arm and gave him her biggest smile ever.

Rachael had been right; Homer Lee was going to stay the man he was, and Matilda wasn't going to spend another day of her life feeling guilty for being happy. At the end of the nave, a white linen sheet had been spread out for the couple to stand on, and a pillow had been placed on the kneeling place. More flowers decorated the communion table. Matilda stopped to do a little curtsey to the Weston's in their private pew near the back of the church and another to Homer Lee's family. Matilda and Homer Lee had come up with the idea to start everything off on the right foot.

Preacher Kirby McLean from McLean Plantation on John's Island married the two. As it turns out, he was on visitation leave to see his Waccamaw family, and he was a fire and brimstone kind of preacher, which the People were particularly fond of, so he was asked to perform the wedding. After freedom, Preacher McLean split his time between publishing a small newspaper in Columbia and being an evangelist. As Preacher Kirby uttered his last prayer, the crowd began to whisper and to shuffle their feet.

"Time to jump de broom!" they shouted. "Time to jump de broom."

Jumping the broom was a symbol of tying the knot, of course, but at The Abbey, it was more of a contest between the bride and groom for control of the marriage.

Women like Matilda were strong women who, in many instances, performed jobs that were just as grueling and dangerous as men's, and they didn't like being told what to do. Jumping the broom served as a tiebreaker. Taking turns, the bride and groom would jump backwards over a broom held approximately twelve-inches above the ground. The bride would go first and then the groom. Whoever jumped the broom without touching it was proclaimed to be the head of the household. If it was a tie, as in Matilda and Homer Lee's case, it was ruled a draw, and the decisions would be made jointly.

The wedding reception was as wonderful as the wedding had been. Master Weston had always put on a lavish reception because he believed that it encouraged the People to pair up and marry. He was a big proponent of marriages between slaves, even though they weren't considered legal in the eyes of South Carolina law. Marriages built families, and families brought stability to the plantation, Weston often said. "That's reason enough to put on the dog." And put on the dog, he did.

Large tables were placed in the yard in front of the big house, and they were laden with freshly butchered beef, hogs, and chickens. There were mounds of sweet potatoes, fresh baked bread, macaroni salad, collards, orange slices, wine, and a wedding cake slathered with white icing and topped with a bride and groom holding hands. It was a wondrous thing.

Master Weston's special gift to the bride and groom was a cabin of their own with a bed, a kitchen table and two chairs, crockery to cook with, a new mattress and fresh blankets, and a large stewpot. The newlyweds were also given a three-day honeymoon away from work. In his speech, Master Weston just happened to mention that any woman on the plantation who had six children or more all alive at one time would be given Saturdays off. Home grown slaves were the best kind.

CHAPTER 17

Freedom's A'Coming

The Abbey Plantation 1861

A COPY OF *THE NORTH STAR* was smuggled into the quarter just as the wedding and the Christmas festivities were settling down. The newspaper was published by a runaway slave named Frederick Douglass, and it was filled with the promises of freedom. The son of a slave woman and a white slave owner, Douglass had a voice that sounded like God's own, and he had but one message—freedom.

Renty was the best reader among the People at The Abbey, but he and Angus were working on their plans to start their own business in Georgetown. Renty's sister could read, but she was on her deathbed, so it was up to Daddy Tom to read the newspaper, and he could only read a little. Late at night he'd sit on the porch of the laundry house and sound out Mr. Douglass's words to a crowd of spellbound listeners. *What had been possible for him to accomplish was possible for others,* he wrote, but he stressed that *as long as people lived in ignorance, they would never command the respect of others.*

The folks in the quarter didn't know much about the politics going on in Washington, but they'd heard of Abe Lincoln and about him being honest and all, and they'd heard about freedom from the lay preachers who'd been preaching about it for months. So, when they heard Douglass's words, they figured that freedom was surely on its way.

"Freedom's a'coming," Titus Small could be heard whispering. "Freedom's a'coming. I feels it a'coming. Hallelujah!"

Trumpeter Wineglass also believed that freedom was on its way but not because Frederick Douglass said so. Trumpeter believed that he and his family would eventually be set free because deep down he'd never really seen himself as a slave even though he'd never known anything other than slavery. He knew the names of his ancestors all the way back to Ghana, and "they weren't no ordinary people, no sir," he used to say. "They was kings and queens. When you got royal blood in your veins, it's something you don't never forget."

Maybe the prideful way Trumpeter felt about himself and his kin was the reason he could never understand how Master Weston—or anyone else for that matter—could own him the same as you would own a horse or a cow. How could anyone own another person, especially one with real live royal blood flowing through his veins? It just wasn't right.

The Best Gift

The Abbey Plantation 1862

HATTIE'S OBSESSION TO LEARN to read grew completely out of control after watching Daddy Tom making Frederick Douglass's teachings come to life just by looking at his words on a piece of old newsprint. If it ever happened for Hattie, though, it would take a miracle, and miracles didn't just happen to little slave girls in the middle of South Carolina. Miss Lillian always said that God worked in mysterious ways, though, and Hattie had no way of knowing that He was already working on it. The miracle got underway when a man named Master Rosa arrived on Waccamaw to take over the job as headmaster at All Saints' Academy, a school for the children of local planters. For twenty dollars per semester, All Saints' Academy offered classes in Greek, Latin, English literature, painting, guitar, and world geography. Even if Papa had been able to scrape together the tuition, Hattie wouldn't have been allowed to go. Hattie couldn't have attended that school or any other school because she was the child of slaves.

"They'll get too uppity." "They'll run away." "They'll turn on their masters." White folks said these things about enslaved people who could read. So, a law was passed saying that if a white person taught a slave to read or write, he or she could be put in jail for up to six months. Hattie felt like her own life was at a standstill, although life around her was spinning like a water spout.

War was on its way; ever-body knew it, and the planters along the Waccamaw nervously began to move their families to safer locations inland. The migration forced Master Rosa's to close the academy. Then he accepted an offer from Master Weston to teach religious instruction to the children in the quarter. Master Rosa and his family were to live in a cottage near the big house that was once lived in by Master Weston's mother. Master Rosa made it clear from the beginning that he opposed the laws forbidding him to teach slave children to read, but jobs were scarce, and he was unwilling to jeopardize his family's future, so he stuck to teaching catechism. As it turned out, that was just part of the miracle because Master Rosa's views on the unfairness of the law had rubbed off on his son, Tooker.

Tooker was sensitive about being skinny. Thirteen-year-olds were like that, but Tooker had another strike against him: he had a lisp. It wasn't the worst lisp anyone had ever heard, but it hung like a sack of rocks around Tooker's neck. Except for Sundays, Tooker wore plaid work shirts—the kind farmers wear—with patched britches and a wide belt with an extra-large buckle. His shirttail was always out, and his boots needed polishing. He was a sight.

The first time Tooker met Hattie was at her favorite fishing hole on the narrow creek on the southern border of The Abbey. He hadn't planned to go fishing that day; he was just exploring his new surroundings and stumbled upon her by accident. The instant she saw him, of course, Hattie knew to immediately pack her things and leave. She had no business talking to a white boy under any circumstances, let alone being alone with one. The Middleton boy had been friendly at first, Rachael warned her during one of their late-night talks. He'd called her a pretty girl, and he'd acted real nice.

"They're all the same," she warned. "They want to stick their thing into you and fill you with jissom taboo, their slimy seed that the Devil spits into their plonker while they sleep."

"I never heard of jissom taboo," Hattie replied, praying that her parents weren't listening to their conversation.

"You mean Miss Lillian never taught you about jissom taboo? I thought the two of you had magical powers, and you knew ever-thing like that."

"Well, she never taught me about jissom taboo, and she never told me what a *plonker* is."

"Jissom taboo is their seed, stupid, and they stick their *plonker* into your lady parts to make babies."

"Their *plonker?*"

"Their winky, you simpleton. That's where mixed babies come from, Hattie. That's why they're treated shameful by the People because they are half white and that makes them evil."

"Surely, they're not all evil, Rachael."

"Yes, they are, Hattie. White boys are the devil's children, and when they die, they go back to their father in hell."

"How do you know all this stuff?"

"After what happened to me with the Middleton boy, the women I work with in the laundry house told me all kinds of things. Ever-day they warned me about white boys, but they didn't need to 'cause I already know they're vile. You ever smell a white boy, Hattie?"

"The only white person I ever smelled up close was the mistress, and she smelled good."

"I'm not talking about white women; I'm talking about white boys. They stink. They smell like back water from the river—worse than chicken guts."

"I never knew that," Hattie said. "Do they outgrow it? Does Master Weston stink like that?"

"I don't know, Hattie, and I don't care. I'm staying away from all of them, and you should, too."

"I don't know any white boys."

"Well, good. Stay away from them, or you'll end up with a white baby in your belly just like I almost did. I want you to stay safe, Hattie."

"I will, Rachael. Thank you for telling me about Jessy taboo."

"Jissom taboo, Hattie. Jissom taboo."

The day that Tooker and Hattie met, Tooker picked up on Hattie's discomfort. She was so jittery he couldn't have missed it. So, he immediately promised to stay on his side of the stream if she wouldn't run away. Hattie apprehensively agreed but only because she was too frightened to run or to even open her mouth.

Tooker did most of the talking. "I grew up on a farm near Croton-on-Hudson, that's in New York," he explained. "The streams there are colder and clearer than they are here. You can see all the way to the bottom, even in the holes where the fish hide out. The streams here are so muddy that you can't see much of anything," he said. "Guess it's hard to catch anything around here, I mean since you can't see 'em and all."

With that, Hattie pulled her stringer out of the water to expose ten half-pound bream. "My Papa and I caught a sturgeon in the river last year, and it weighed a hundred-and-fifty-pounds," she said with a note of pride. "Can't see nothing in the river, either."

"You got me on that one," Tooker said laughing. "My name's Tooker, Tooker Rosa. What's yours?"

"A white boy beat up my sister two summers ago," Hattie blurted out. "He almost kilt her, and I'm not supposed to talk to white boys, ever."

"If that had happened to my sister, I wouldn't want to talk to white boys, either," Tooker said, empathically. "I'll leave. I'm real sorry."

"My name is Hattie, Hattie Wineglass," Hattie said, surprising herself even more than Tooker.

"I thought you didn't want to talk to me?"

"I'll talk to you as long as you stay on the other side of the stream. One step this way, though, and I'm gone."

"That's alright with me," Tooker said thoughtfully. An awkward pause followed, and Tooker finally broke the ice. "Wineglass," he said, struggling with the S on the end. "Where'd you get a name like that?"

"Well, my Papa wanted to have the most impressive-sounding name he could think of, so he decided on Trumpeter Wineglass after the biggest wineglass they make."

"That's as good a reason as any, I 'spect," Tooker said, taking it all in. "I've never seen a trumpeter wineglass, but I have to admit that it does sound impressive. I was named after my mother's family; Tooker was her maiden name. My real first name is Delmar just like my father, and I think they're both pretty awful names."

Tooker's observation made Hattie laugh despite her reservations. "Hattie's not the greatest name in the world, neither," she said. "My sister says it sounds like something you should be wearing on your head."

Tooker and Hattie became friends that day despite Hattie's trepidations, and they continued to meet up at the fishing hole whenever they could. They talked about simple things like fishing and the weather, and Hattie was comfortable talking about such things. One day, however, Tooker was absentmindedly dragging his fishing line in the stream, musing about things that boys think about, when he asked Hattie what she wanted to do when she grew up.

The question took her by surprise, at first, and then it made her mad. "What makes you ask me that?" she hissed. "I ain't your fancy white girl! I'm a slave, Tooker! I'm a slave! I'm nothing but somebody else's property," she said, jumping to her feet to leave.

"Don't go," Tooker pleaded. "Sometimes I forget you're enslaved. We didn't have slaves in New York, Hattie. I just didn't think."

"Well, you shoulda," Hattie said repositioning herself back down on her fishing rock. "You have any iddi what it's like for my papa ta have his own children see him say, 'Yes, sir' and 'No, sir' to some no-account overseer day after day, not to know that my parents worry about something happenin' to Master Weston and a new master takin' over the plantation. A new master could split up my family, Tooker. He could take my sisters an' me an' sell us like we was little pigs. There ain't no future for me 'til the People are free," Hattie screamed. "You know what I want more than anything?" she asked, rhetorically. "I want to learn to read, but I can't 'cause there's a law against it. If your papa was ta teach me, he could go to jail."

"I didn't know," Tooker cried, running toward the woods. Papa'd warned him not to have anything to do with the People. They were unpredictable, and they could be dangerous, he said, but Papa didn't know Hattie. She wanted the same things everybody did.

Hattie stayed clear of the fishing hole until she had a chance to think everything over. She meant every word, but she was sorry she'd taken it out on Tooker like that, so the following week she went back to the fishing hole, and there he was sitting on his side of the stream waiting for her. She was sorry, she said.

"I was wrong, Hattie. I'm the one who's sorry. Friends?"

"Friends."

Then he told Hattie to stay right where she was. "I have to go home for a minute, but I'll be right back. I have a surprise," he said. Hattie waited, and before she knew it, Tooker reappeared with something wrapped in tissue paper held behind his back.

"This is for you, Hattie," Tooker said, placing the gift in her lap. "I think you're gonna really like it."

It was October 16, 1860, an ordinary date to some, but to Hattie, it was the day that the heavens realigned and swallowed her whole. Had she shaken hands with Jesus that day, it wouldn't have been a more monumental day because the tissue-wrapped gift was a worn copy of a small book entitled, *McGuffey's Pictorial Primer.*

"I'll teach you to read it," Tooker said. Right out of the clear blue sky, he had given her what she wanted most in the world. It was a miracle.

"It's against the law." Hattie whispered.

"It is," Tooker said. "Papa told me. It's the Negro Act of 1740, and it was passed after a slave rebellion on John's Island. Papa said the law improved living conditions for slaves, but it also tightened controls on everything, including teaching slaves to read. Papa could be sent to jail, but I figured they wouldn't throw a kid in jail. We should still be careful, though, and I think we need a better meeting place than this fishing hole. What about on the porch of St. Mary or beneath the big chestnut tree near the People's cemetery?"

"I don't care," Hattie cried. "I'd meet you anywhere."

A week later, Hattie could read and spell ax, box, cat, dog, elk, fan, girl, hen, ink, and jug; and within two more weeks, she had mastered the entire primer. They moved on to *McGuffey's Eclectic First Reader.* By early spring, Hattie could read from the Bible and Tooker's science books.

Secrets were impossible to keep on the plantation, so before long, everyone in the quarter knew that Hattie and Tooker were studying together. Rachael refused to speak to Hattie; she was so mad. Miss Lillian didn't have too much to say about it, though. Hattie figured she hadn't made up her mind, yet. Granny was sure to have reservations, seeing as how the Middleton boy treated Rachael, but Miss Lillian's head for knowing told her that white boys weren't all alike any more than colored boys were. That didn't mean she was happy about the arrangement, but at least he was a plain boy, not one of those fancy rice princes who was better than anybody else. The People were worried and purely mystified by Trumpeter and Sheila's reaction to the whole thing.

Trumpeter had wanted to kill the Middleton boy and would have had he gotten the chance, but here Hattie was meeting up with this white boy on the steps of the chapel, and Trumpeter hadn't said a word. It felt dirty to the People, and they didn't like it.

One evening Uncle Titus and some of the other men on the planta-tion warned Hattie's family that if the overseer got wind of what was going on, Hattie could be beaten or even married off. After all, she was going on thirteen. Sheila and Trumpeter stood their ground. They'd prayed about it, Trumpeter said, and they didn't trust no white boy a hundred percent, but they figured it was gonna be Hattie's only chance to learn to read, and they weren't going to take it away from her.

"Ever-day the Lord uses ordinary people to do great things," Trumpeter told them. "After freedom, Hattie can teach other children to read—freedmen's children. You could change lives," he said to Hattie in front of everyone. "You could do that, girl." So, she studied hard.

A month later, on April 19, 1861, Frank Small from Belle Terra Plantation came to The Abbey to visit his brother, Titus, and to tell everyone the latest news. South Carolina troops had fired on Yankee troops stationed at Fort Sumter in the Charleston Harbor five days earlier. The North and the South were at war! Frank had even brought part of the front page of the *Charleston Daily News* with him, which he tentatively handed to Hattie at Trumpeter's coaxing. Axle grease from Frank's pants had soaked into some of it, so she couldn't read it all, but she could read most of it.

April 14, 1861, the efforts on the night of April 10 were truly grand and terrific, the news story began. *When daylight descended upon the harbor, it was clear that the proud Confederate troops had forced Ft. Sumter to surrender, and the radical ideas of Lincolnism had been soundly defeated.*

After Hattie said she couldn't read any more of the story because of the grease, someone in the crowd said, "Does that mean that Mr. Lincoln's already whupped?" Then another asked, "Is the war already over?"

Those were the questions they asked themselves. After they thought on it, though, they agreed that a war that had been building for years surely couldn't have ended in a single battle. "It mustn't be the end of the war," they concluded. "It must be the beginning."

An elderly woman was the next to speak. "For years we've prayed for freedom," she cried. "We've prayed 'till the rooster crowed for the day, and now freedom's on the way. Glory! Glory!"

"It ain't gonna be easy, children," Brother Obadiah warned. "It ain't gonna be easy. Pray hard, children. Pray hard."

The People stayed together throughout that night, praying and worrying. What was war going to bring? What was freedom going to bring? And how long would it take before the People were free? The old folks worried about going hungry; the women worried about their children and their houses; and the young men swore to run away to join up with the Yankees.

Plowden Weston, a dead ringer for Robert E. Lee and the brightest scholar among the princes of rice, according to a Charleston newspaper, *sounded the first alarm warning of an upcoming war.*

In a speech he gave to his fellow planters at a meeting of the Charleston Agricultural Society, Weston bragged about how splendidly they had solved the problem of two different races living side by side. "Now I see a revolution coming, a complete overturning of society driven by those determined to emancipate the slave. If it comes, it will come with the force and havoc of a tornado."

As that horrible day drew nearer, Emily Weston became more frightened by the minute. Riots and rumors of riots were whispered about in church pews and other places away from prying eyes. The Westons were like every other plantation family—deep down they were skittish about their slaves, even those they professed to love, and now they were tittering on the brink of paranoia.

Emily had bitten her nails down to the nubs, and she scarcely let Plowden out of her sight. They both wore side arms—his tucked into his belt and hers beneath her skirts. Loaded shotguns were at the ready in the Weston's study, and they locked their bedroom door at night. Their throats could be slit during their sleep, or a simple poison could be added to a meal, killing them both. Food poisoning it would be called if the conspiracy held, murder if it didn't, but they'd be dead all the same, and the plantation would be thrown into chaos. There'd never been a hint of insurrection at The Abbey, but it was happening on other plantations, especially those near Charleston.

Emily usually managed to keep her composure during the day, but at night, her fears haunted her. Before long, she barricaded herself into her room at night and sat in a chair with a shotgun across her lap. Master Weston tried to comfort her, but after one of her friends was stabbed to death during her sleep, Emily couldn't be consoled, so they gathered up what they could and traveled north to Conwayboro to live in a rented farmhouse called Snowy Hill.

Simple fare by plantation standards, the farmhouse was off the beaten path, too plain perhaps to attract the interest of the Yankees. Emily Weston and her English woman servant set up house at Snowy Hill, but Plowden Weston was determined to join the war despite his wife's protestation. Weston officially joined the Confederate Army as a colonel in November, 1861, but he contributed far more to the Confederacy than his own service. It was customary for wealthy men to bankroll his own military unit. A common number was twenty men, but Weston assembled more than a hundred men for which he supplied the uniforms, weapons, horses, food, wagons, and wages.

The following spring the unit was scheduled to pass near The Abbey, and Emily sent a note inviting her husband's men to an impromptu supper back on the plantation. Colonel Weston was surprised by Emily's willingness to return to the plantation, but she pulled the meal off seam-lessly. Large tables were placed about the yard, and Emily and her staff treated more than a hundred soldiers to a Sunday supper served on the Weston's finest china with silver tableware. Emily closely supervised the food preparation, and guards were posted just in case. "It was good eats, ma'am," one of the men said, tipping his hat to Emily following the meal. "Might fine eats."

Soon after, it was rumored that Plowden Weston's health was in decline. It was gradual at first like it is with most people, but people began to notice, except his wife, who often commented to her friends about how handsome he still looked in his colonel's uniform. His political friends were shaken. His noble face was ashen and his eyes—once so dark—were dull and colorless windows onto his weakened soul. His perfectly tailored uniform hung from his shoulders like a jacket on a scarecrow.

So, they conspired to get him out of the military and into a less taxing civilian job by seeing to it that he was elected Lieutenant Governor, a glamorous-sounding job without any responsibility other than to oversee the legislature, which wasn't in session, of course, because of the war. Master Weston was told to stay home and enjoy his fabled library until his health improved, and then he could join his friends in Columbia at the opening of the next session of the legislature. It was a pipe dream.

No one had any idea if or when the South Carolina legislature would ever convene again, and no one believed that Plowden Weston was ever going to get better. He was going to die; it was only a matter of time. Plowden Weston also knew that his life was about to end, and against Emily's wishes, he made a list of people he wanted to say goodbye to, including a number of his fellow planters on the river and a lifetime of friends from Charleston.

They came as quickly as they could, two here, a half-dozen there. Their numbers were a testament to the character of the man. The South had been crushed, fortunes had been lost, and thousands were dead; and yet, those who could come to say goodbye to Plowden Weston did so. Along with the lofty individuals he wanted to see, Master Weston also wished to say goodbye to Trumpeter Wineglass, Renty Tucker, and Matilda Lee. Trumpeter had saved many crops during his time as trunk minder, and Renty Tucker had worked his own magic at The Abbey, but as the two men were rowed up river to Snow Hill Farm, they were taken aback by how silent Matilda Lee was.

"You alright, Matilda," Trumpeter asked every now and then. Matilda was family or as close as you could get to being family, and Trumpeter was genuinely worried.

"I'm fine," Matilda finally replied. "I just can't for the life of me figure out why Master Weston wants to see me. I just can't figure it."

When the boat landed, the three were taken up to the house where they were met by Joseph, the Weston's butler. Tearstained and gaunt, Joseph immediately ushered the three into the front parlor where Master Weston was lying on a makeshift bed. Behind him stood Miss Emily who looked like a ghost of herself with wide, sad eyes and a far-off look.

"Come in," the master said in a weak voice. "Come in."

Trumpeter and Renty followed Matilda, and when he saw Renty's shoulders shaking, Trumpeter pulled out his own handkerchief. Matilda Lee, however, showed no emotion.

Master Weston spoke to Renty, first, thanking him for having built the Weston's summerhouse and especially for St Mary Chapel. "You created something even beyond my dreams," he said. "I will never be able to thank you, Renty."

Then he looked up at Miss Emily who handed her husband's favorite pocket knife. "This is for you," Master Weston said. "You are a fine man, Renty."

Then Master Weston motioned for Trumpeter and Matilda Lee to approach him together. Looking at Matilda, he said, "I called you here to thank you for helping to straighten out my nephew. The woman looked shell shocked, and Trumpeter let out a gasp. "You didn't know about Matilda, did you, Trumpeter?" Weston asked.

"Know what, sir?"

"That it was Matilda who rescued your daughter."

"No sir, I didn't know 'till just now," Trumpeter said, looking down at Matilda.

"I can't officially thank you for what you did, Matilda, but I can tell you that I respected your bravery. As for you, Trumpeter, you saved The Abbey more than once, and I wanted to thank you. When you get home, I also want you to tell Miss Lillian that I am proud to have known her."

Then Master Weston looked up at his wife to be handed another personal gift, but she had nothing left. So, Master Weston motioned for her to remove the studs and cufflinks from his shirt he was wearing.

"No," Emily whispered.

"I have no use for them now," Master Weston said.

"These are for you," he said, handing the studs to Matilda Lee, "and these are for you, Trumpeter. Now that you are a free man, you will need a good pair of cufflinks. "Wear them well."

Then everyone except a few family members were ushered from the room. Not knowing how to make his exit, Trumpeter made an awkward bow to Master Weston and another to Miss Emily, and then he turned and left the room. Plowden Weston died the following morning. Lt. Governor Weston was forty-four.

As Trumpeter and Renty exited the house, they openly sobbed. They had been enslaved by the Weston family for as long as they could remember, but when it came down to saying goodbye, it tore at their insides. It was a thing that couldn't be explained.

Matilda accompanied the two men back to the plantation, and nothing was said during the journey. When they pulled up at the plantation landing, however, Trumpeter reached for Renty and hugged him. Then they shook hands, and Renty walked away.

To Matilda, Trumpeter said thank you in a voice that was unfamiliar to him. It didn't seem to matter, though. Matilda replied that he was welcome, and then she turned to walk away. "You and Homer Lee join us for supper," Trumpeter called out. "It'll just be us family."

"We will," Matilda said. "We'll see you then."

Renty and Burke had lousy timing starting up a business two weeks before the outbreak of war! They called it their chapel business, but only fools would expect to see orders for chapels roll in at the onset of a civil war. They'd rented a workshop on Scrivener Street in Georgetown, and Burke and Mairghread and their little boy, Joshua Tucker Burke, moved into a small apartment over the shop.

Renty and Rachael, of course, stayed on at The Abbey, but Renty spent most of the week in Georgetown, sleeping in the back of the shop. When Renty heard that the Westons had left the plantation to live inland, he made a move that in days past would have gotten him arrested. He and Rachael moved to Georgetown. He didn't say a word to anyone; they just left. It was a risk. Master Weston could send his overseer or the sheriff or even a military detachment for Rachael, but Renty figured Master Weston just didn't have the stomach for it anymore. What could the disappearance of a nineteen-year-old girl mean when the whole world was at war?

Renty and Burke struggled to keep their new business afloat, and no job was beneath them. They repaired docks and boat landings, built privies, restored fireplaces, replaced window glass, built fences, laid brick walkways, and made wooden headstones, which they sold for a dollar.

Mairghread took in laundry, and Rachael worked as a seamstress. They got by, and neither Renty or Rachael was ever questioned about Rachael's disappearance from the plantation.

CHAPTER 19

Sweet Potatoes

The Abbey Plantation 1862

WAR DIDN'T COME TO THE plantation as quickly as everybody had expected. The People had expected to hear the crack of cannon fire and the whiz of bullets the day after they had heard the news about the war. Some people in the quarter even buried food only to dig it up again weeks later. Once war was officially declared, though, Tooker and his family kept to themselves. He and Hattie caught a glimpse of each other now and then, but they never got to speak again in person.

Tooker, however, did leave letters for Hattie near the chestnut tree, and even though the letters lacked the intimacy the two had shared before the war, the letters made Hattie miss him all the more. Trumpeter said it wasn't proper to be seen with him anymore, anyway.

"He ain't a boy no more, Hattie. He's a young man, a white man old enough to be a soldier, and you ain't a child no more, daughter. You're a marriageable young colored girl."

Trumpeter needn't have worried about Tooker and Hattie ever seeing each other again because as the war continued, Tooker and his family spent most of their time living in a small rented creek house on Pawleys Island, returning to the plantation each Saturday to give the children their weekly catechism classes. Daddy Tom arrived one day with a letter from Tooker, and before he would give it to her, Hattie had to promise to read it aloud to everyone. She would, she said, so Daddy Tom handed it over. It was a patented Tooker letter, filled with astute observations and the unusual events that always seemed to happen to him. This letter was about the day that a Yankee gunboat hove into sight and started shelling off the southern tip of Pawleys Island. "The cannons belched fire from afar," he wrote, "and when the shells landed on the beach, they sent geysers of sand into the air. It resembled a fireworks show," he observed, but when it was over, Tooker surveyed the beach and found a cannonball stuck in the wall of his neighbor's house. Tooker wanted to dig it out of the wall, but his neighbor was afraid it would explode during its removal, taking down half of the house with it.

"No deal," he said. "It's staying where it is."

As a postscript, Tooker noted that it had been two weeks, and the cannonball hasn't moved. Some of the old salts on the island, however, are taking bets about how long it will last before exploding. Two years was the longest bet so far. "A hundred to one odds," Tooker said.

Another story followed, and Hattie thought it was even better than the first one. It was about a blockade runner who either accidentally or intentionally tossed hundreds of yards of silk overboard near Pawleys Island, and it eventually washed ashore, where Tooker gathered it up, washed the salt out of it, and spread it out on the beach to dry. Tooker didn't say what he did with the silk after it dried, but Trumpeter said with the cheapest calico going for ten dollars a yard, Tooker could have driven some hard bargains. As the war continued to drag on, food became scarce even for those who still had money to spend.

When Christmas of 1862 came to The Abbey, Sheila and Miss Lillian and the other women in the quarter were spoilt to having some fancy ingredients for their Christmas tables. But now they were worried about what they were gonna serve up. Molasses was good if you didn't have nothing sweet, but brown sugar, now that was something to shout about. It was Christmas Eve morning, and the women in the quarter were busy bartering for this and trading for that, when they suddenly heard the familiar blast of a boat whistle: ttssssssssssssss!

"Praise the Lord!" they shouted as they spotted Mistress Weston on the plantation landing. Just when they figured she wasn't gonna show up that year because of being scared and all, there she was with crates of holiday ingredients to distribute like always. Only it wasn't like always. The People had expected the usual Christmas stuff: coffee, white flour, white sugar, baking powder, cinnamon, and cloves, but those treasures couldn't be had at any price. Emily Weston couldn't even get them for her own kitchen, and she'd heard that a cup of real coffee sold in the streets of Charleston for five dollars!

There had been a bumper crop of apples at Snowy Hill that year, though, and the Mistress gave out at least one hundred, fifty-pound burlap bags filled with them, along with similar bags containing potatoes, carrots, potatoes, and beets. The Mistress also passed out figs and currants, hoping that they could be stretched far enough to make Christmas pudding for everyone in the quarter.

Hattie read in the Charleston paper that even President Jefferson Davis's wife was suffering hardships. "The Christmas season at the Confederate White House in Richmond, Virginia, was ushered in under the darkest of clouds," the newspaper said quoting Mrs. Davis.

"It says here that there were no currants, raisins, or other ingredients to make mince pie," Hattie read. "They had apples, though, so they used them as substitutes."

"That's just like us," one of her listeners commented.

"Just think! Mistress Davis is making mincemeat pies out o'apples, just like us."

"For Christmas," Mrs. Davis wrote, "President Jefferson Davis received a pair of new leather riding gloves embroidered on the back with his monogram in red and white silk."

Mrs. Davis received cakes of soap made from the grease of boiled ham, a collection of songs bound in wallpaper, and a gold thimble from a young man in England. General Robert E. Lee sent Mrs. Davis a wagonload of sweet potatoes."

CHAPTER 20

Now And Forever, Free

The Abbey Plantation 1865

MOST OF THE NEWS about the war had to do with battles in cities and towns that the People at The Abbey had never heard of—Chancellorsville, Chickamauga, Sharpsburg, Manassas, Vicksburg, and Gettysburg. They were beginning to think that freedom would never reach the plantation. Then on February 14, 1865, almost four years after war had been declared, a Yankee gunboat, accompanied by a large schooner, docked at the plantation landing. The shriek from a steam whistle aboard the gunboat alerted everyone on the plantation to come a'running. They were met by an officer wearing a blue uniform with gold epaulets and dirty white gloves. Standing in the center of the landing, he motioned for the People to cluster around him so they could hear his words. The People nervously obliged, seeing as it was a Yankee doing the talking, but they were curious. So, they came together and held their breaths, and then the words were said. Everyone on the plantation was "now and forever free."

"Did Mr. Lincoln say we was free?" one of the people shouted out.

"Who else do you think did it, you bone-headed n...."

As the People stood transfixed, trying to take in the news, some of the soldiers aboard the ships broke rank and ran ashore yelling and whooping. Then the People got all riled up, and everything got crazy. Some of the Yankees stole chickens from the hen house and ate raw eggs right out of their nests. Others shot every four-footed animal they could find and set fire to everything in sight except the underground corncrib, which the People begged them to spare.

One soldier was so crazed that he ripped the kerchief right off of Miss Lillian's head.

Then the soldiers moved on to the overseer's house where they herded Mr. Turner and his housekeeper into the yard. As the house-keeper pleaded for them to stop, one of the soldiers tore a ring from her finger, while his companions plundered the rest of Mr. Turner's house. Then they ransacked Master Rosa's house and herded the Rosa family into the yard, where Hattie later learned that the soldiers tore at their clothes and jewelry. The big house was next. Even though the Westons had walked away from the plantation a year and a half earlier, most of their belongings were still in the mansion.

Within minutes, the soldiers, now joined by a cheering throng of newly liberated men, women, and children, had tossed dozens of bottles of Master Weston's prized Madeira out of the attic window onto the lawn.

Then they moved onto the china and crystal, the furniture, Old Master Weston's collection of rare books, the Axminster carpets, and Mistress Weston's cherished pianoforte that they dumped over the edge of the piazza just to see it crash to the ground. From there they moved onto bigger things. They ripped out the banisters, the doors and door frames, and smashed the windows. They pulled up the floorboards looking for hidden stores of food or silver and ripped up the portion of the attic where one of the servants had told them the Westons had hidden a cache of smoked hams.

After more than two hours of whooping and hollering, the Yankees finally loaded what they could aboard their ships and sailed off as quickly as they had arrived. What they couldn't take with them, they left in the yard, and the People fought over it like chickens. *After all, Master Weston owes us,* they told themselves. *He owed us for all those years of slavery.*

About ten days after the Yankee's onslaught on The Abbey, Jesse Belflowers, the overseer at The Thicket, a plantation across the river from The Abbey, wrote a letter to The Thicket's owner. A week later the letter was fished out of the river near The Abbey, and Hattie was asked to read it.

The Thicket, March 1, 1865

Mrs. Aston,

Yours letter has been Recd and I am wishing you to Know that it is not safe for you to come here. The People have behaved Verry badly & I do think if you had been on the Plantation that you would have been hurt.

Yesterday, two yankeys come up & tole the People they could distribet the hous which they did, taking out ever-thing & then to the smoke hous and Store Room doing the same as in the hous.

They took the Plough oxen & Kild some of them. The hogs in the Pen is Kild & all the Stock is taken a way. The Pore mules has been Road to death.

The People have Puld down the fenceing, brok down the old Stabel & the Carpenter Shop. They also take all the rice & ever-thing, even dogs, Salt and Cotton.

Several weeks after things finally began to settle down at The Abbey, Sheila told Trumpeter that there was something that she'd been hankering to do. "I want to visit Georgetown. I've never seen a real city before, and I surely would like to see one."

Trumpeter had been to Georgetown enough times to last a lifetime, but Sheila's request had been so forthcoming he figured she had been thinking on it a long time. So, the next morning he loaded the family into a borrowed rowboat and headed south. After crossing Winyah Bay and spotting the outline of the city in the distance, Sheila squealed with joy.

"Oh, my," she exclaimed. "I didn't know it would be so big."

Once they tied up at the landing and stepped out of the boat, however, they almost wished they hadn't come. The landing opened onto Front Street that was dominated by the town hall famous for its tower that was nearly forty-feet-tall. The tower had been built specifically to accommodate a bell that Master Weston had donated to the city the year before the start of the war. The building had once been the pride of the city but not anymore. A target for Union twelve-pound field cannons, the bell now lay in a pile of rubble at the bottom of the tower, and the tower's tin roof looked like a half-opened can of sardines. As for the surrounding buildings, they looked even worse. Even though many of the buildings were still standing, they looked like rows of month-old jack-o'-lanterns littered with debris and scarred with soot.

Shop windows were shattered, fires had been set, and looters had made off with everything they could carry. As the family tentatively walked from Front Street onto Queen Street and then on to Prince, they realized that the same fate had been shared by the city's wealthiest residents.

"Looks like the rich folks done boarded up their houses and got outa town," Trumpeter said. "The poor folks didn't have no place else to go; I expect they lock their doors and hide beneath the covers."

Wherever the rich folks ended up, it was apparent that their attempts to save their homes by boarding them up had been a waste of time. Thieves had not only robbed the homes of their furniture, rugs, pots and pans, draperies, and chandeliers, they had even ripped up the stairs and floorboards.

"Before the war," Trumpeter said, "city folks — even some of the rich ones — kept chickens, ducks, and sometimes even cows in their yards or in small pens behind their houses. When the war got dark, though, it looks like ever-thing that could be ate got ate," he reckoned as he and his family returned to the landing. "Even good folks will steal when it come down to feeding they children."

CHAPTER 21

Hattie, You Can Read,
and You Are Free

The Abbey Plantation 1865

AS FREEDOM SPREAD throughout the Lowcountry, it brought jubilation and chaos all at the same time. On one plantation after another, when the People learned they were free, some of them packed up their things and left the plantation forever. Most of them, like Trumpeter and Sheila, however, had families to feed and had no place else to go, so they stayed. About twenty people left the plantation, including two of Hattie's cousins. One was headed for Texas where he heard the ground was littered with gold and silver nuggets the size of a man's fist. His younger brother was setting out for "Luzanna," where there are so many fish they'd jump into your boat just to get away from each other.

There was crying that day and the next. They'd be back to visit someday ever-body promised, but the ones doing the telling along with the ones doing the listening knew better. Ain't nobody coming home to the plantation. Ain't nobody gonna do that. Hard times got harder. After Master and Mistress Weston had left the plantation for their rented farm, the People refused to work the master's fields, so they were left fallow, and fallow fields meant lean bellies. The corn and rice bins were empty, the smokehouse had been burned to the ground, and the food stuffs the People had buried to help themselves get by when the hard times came had rotted in the ground. The only good news was that some of the pigs and chickens had escaped the Yankees' onslaught, and most of the cows had been grazing in the upper fields the day the Yankees came, so they were safe, but now they needed feeding and guarding around the clock. Bands of hungry former slaves roamed free, hijacking and stealing everything they could get their hands on—everything they could sell or eat. And a fine fat cow would have been right at the top of their list.

So, the People who stayed on the plantation had to work together to stay alive. Freedom surely wasn't free. No one was willing to do the jobs they'd done when they were enslaved, though. They wanted to be their own bosses, so they waited for the Yankees to give them the forty acres and a mule they had been promised. Two months, three months, five months passed, and still they waited.

Finally, Trumpeter, Titus Small, and some of the other men from the plantation went into Georgetown to make their demands. The Yankees told them that since Master Weston had died just as the war was ending and that Miss Weston had returned to England to live with her family, the matter would have to be settled by the courts.

"Go on home boys," the men were told. "You're on your own."

Dejected, they went home in tears. "Before the war, I belonged to Old Master Weston," Trumpeter's uncle said. "The last time I was sold, I sell for $2,300. Now, I ain't worth a plugged nickel."

The fields went unplowed that summer, and it wasn't long before everything was in shorter supply than it had ever been during the war. The old people had been right to worry about the war bringing hunger. Everybody was hungry. Sheila and the other women on the plantation sent their children out into the fields and creek beds to dig up roots and edible grasses, while the men and boys fished the river and seined the saltwater creeks.

Before long, half-starved Confederate soldiers—some in bare feet—also filled the roads, while Union gunships patrolled the Waccamaw River. It was the worst of times; danger was around every corner. The only bright spot was that Hattie received another letter from

Tooker. Covered with handprints, it looked like it had been read and refolded more than once, but Hattie was just glad to have gotten it at all.

September 29, 1865

Dear Hattie,

We have seen better times. After the Yankees came to The Abbey, my family and I started living in Master Weston's creek house. We were glad to have a roof over our heads.

Papa and I took on odd jobs when we could find them, while Mama and children fished and crabbed for our supper. We probably ate better than most.

Three weeks ago, a sheriff knocked on the door waving a document from the probate court in Georgetown, demanding that we vacate the property within forty-eight hours.

Papa tried to stall, but the sheriff said he'd be back the next time with a shotgun. So, we left. We moved into an abandoned house in the Marysville section of Georgetown, just south of Winyah Bay. We are the only white family here, but we have been treated well by our neighbors.

The house is on the marsh, so we can still find food, but Mama is despondent. Papa is such a kind man, and he has an education that anyone would wish for their son, and yet, he has to work as a day laborer. "Being able to teach Latin," he says, "won't put food on the table in times like these."

Things may be looking up for us, though. Mama finally heard from her family in Massachusetts, and they have offered to help us get back to New England. All we have to do is get ourselves to the nearest town where the trains are running again.

I just turned eighteen; can you believe it? I'm a man now, and I'm eager to live on my own and to have a real job and to do what other young men do.

I even thought about joining the army once (I won't tell you which one), but Papa talked me out of it. He didn't have to talk very hard, though; I didn't want to go in the first place.

This war was wrong. I think a hundred years from now, people will look at us and think we were fools to kill each other like we have, but I am happy for you and your family, Hattie. I know how much you waited for this day. I hope you've kept up with your studies. Papa says you were the brightest student he ever saw.

You probably won't be hearing from me again, Hattie. I have no idea where we are going to end up or how we're going to get there, but I can promise you one thing—I will remember you always.

Fondly,
Tooker

Hattie read Tooker's letter aloud to the rest of her family, and then she read it again and again to herself. "I will always remember you, too," she said before placing the letter beneath her mattress. It was during that turbulent time that Trumpeter came up with an idea that would change Hattie's life. "Hattie, I've been thinking, and I decided that this is the perfect time for you to start a school."

"A school!" she exclaimed. "Who can afford to send their children to school, Papa? Besides, a school is a building with desks and a blackboard and books. The only books I have are the ones from Tooker. We don't have any of those things, Papa."

"I know things is hard, Hattie, but they're going to ease up now that the government finally split up the plantation like they promised. And don't forget, you have the two things that matter most. You can read, and you are free. Remember what Mr. Douglass said. 'As long as the People live in ignorance, they won't never have respect.' Ain't nothing more important than that, Hattie. Your students could learn to read sitting on the front porch just as well as they could in a school house," he said. "And they don't have to own their own books. They could share Tooker's books. I know you'd like to have a blackboard, but you can manage just fine without one. As for your pupils practicing their ciphers, they can take a stick and draw 'em in the dirt."

Two weeks later twelve barefoot children and two elderly women found their way onto Hattie's front porch. The women sat in Mama and

Papa's porch chairs while the children had to make do with the porch steps, all except the littlest, a five-year-old girl named Mariah, who got to sit in a small red Windsor-style chair. Hattie became a teacher that day. She was seventeen, had never been more than twelve miles from her home, and was so nervous she could barely put one foot in front of the other; but she had dreams to share and things to do. So, as she stepped out onto that porch on that sticky South Carolina morning. She gave up being Hattie Wineglass to become Miss Hattie, Teacher.

Latta Plantation in Huntersville, NC, closed unexpectedly in 2020. When it reopens in the future, it is rumored to be renamed: Latta Historic Farm or Latta Place.

Photographs by author

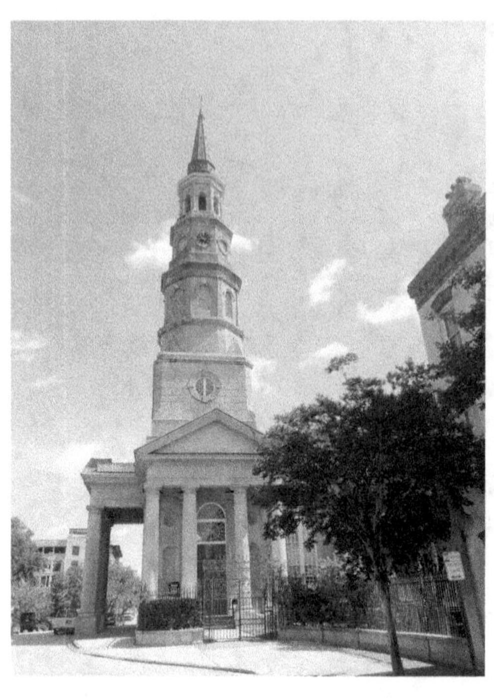

St. Philip's Church, Charleston, SC. Author's photos

One of the original kitchens at Hampton Plantation in McClellanville, SC.

This structure on Arundel Plantation on the Pee Dee River in Georgetown County. It is thought to be a former slave chapel because of its lancet windows and door.

These stained glass windows are in Prince George Winyah Church in Georgetown, but they once adorned the slave chapel at Hagley Plantation. Following the Civil War, they were moved for safekeeping. The slave chapel burned to the ground in 1939. AUTHOR'S PHOTO

The graffiti above is carved into one of the pews at Prince George Church. Its carver was probably a young bored parishioner who was in love with schooners like the one to the left. In their day, schooners were as high-tech as military aircraft.

AUTHOR'S PHOTO

With a seating capacity of 300, the slave chapel on Hagley Plantation was thought to be the largest of its kind in the South. The chapel was destroyed by fire in 1939.

The chapel was built by the plantation's head carpenter, Renty Tucker. I used Renty's true story as inspiration for my story about Rachael Wineglass in this book. After the Civil War ended, Renty became the coroner in Georgetown, SC, and was an important member of the burgeoning freedmen's community.

THE NYPL DIGITAL COLLECTIONS
RLIN/OCLC: NYPGR2105767-B
NYPL CATALOG ID (B-NUMBER): B22096049

This beautiful bride isn't the fictional Matilda, but she could have been. This extraordinary photograph is housed in the New York Public Library.

The Pelican Inn still stands on Pawleys Island. It was originally built to be a summerhouse for the Plowden C.J .Weston family in the 1840s and it is rumored that the Weston's gave it a very peculiar name—Zooland or Zoolander.

The last owner of Hagley Planation before the War Between the States, Weston was rather peculiar himself. Fastidious about his appearance and a dead ringer for the handsome Robert E. Lee, Weston was extremely fond of swimming, but always did it fully clothed. Weston died of tuberculosis in 1865. He was 44.

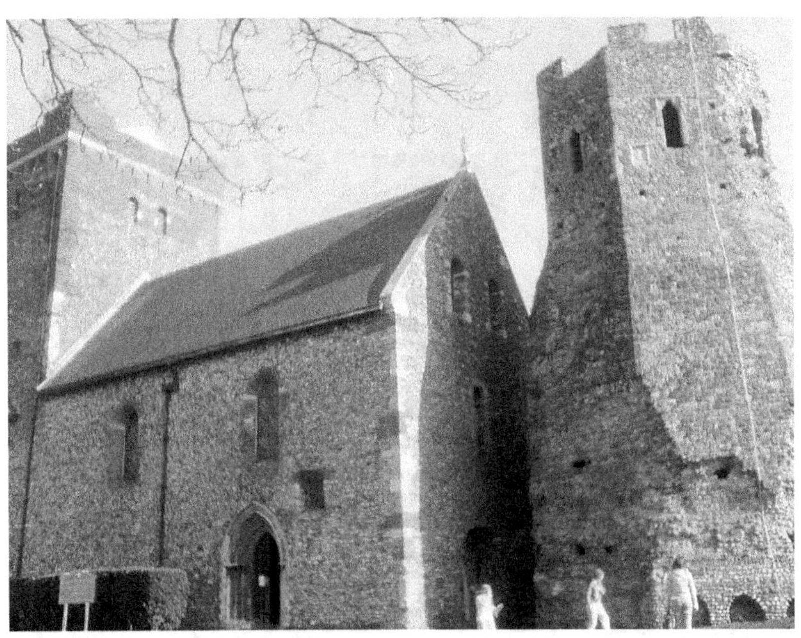

St. Mary Castro, Dover, England

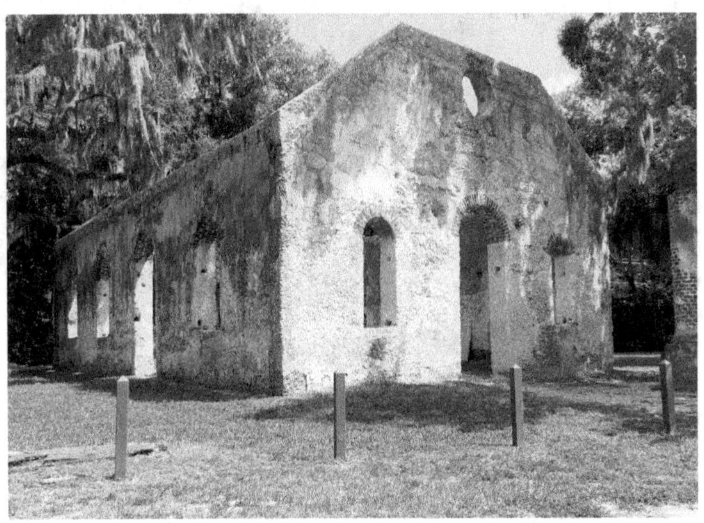

The Chapel of Ease on St. Helena Island. Beaufort, SC 1740

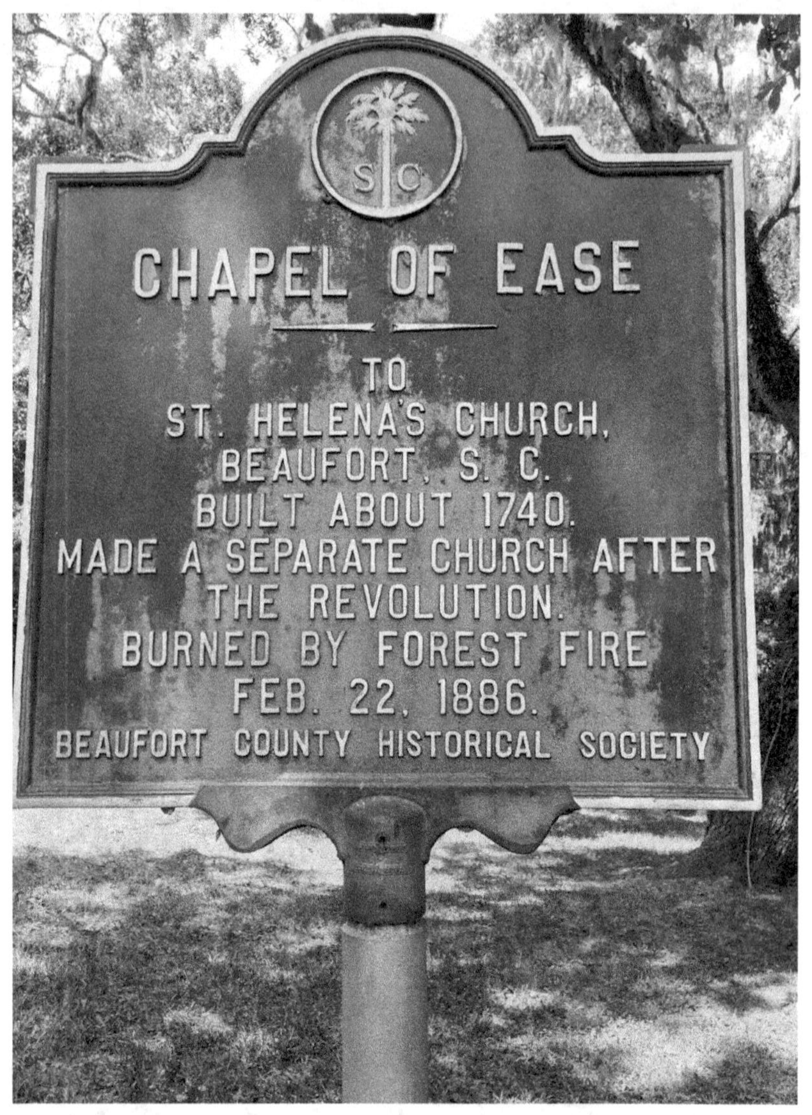

The lane leading to the Chapel of Ease on St. Helena Island.

New Wappataw Presbyterian Church McClellanville, SC

St. James Parish Church on the Santee River near McClellanville, SC

The house on True Blue Plantation that was inspiration for "Donna's Story" in this book. The house, probably built by the Skinner family around 1900, burned to the ground in the 1980s.

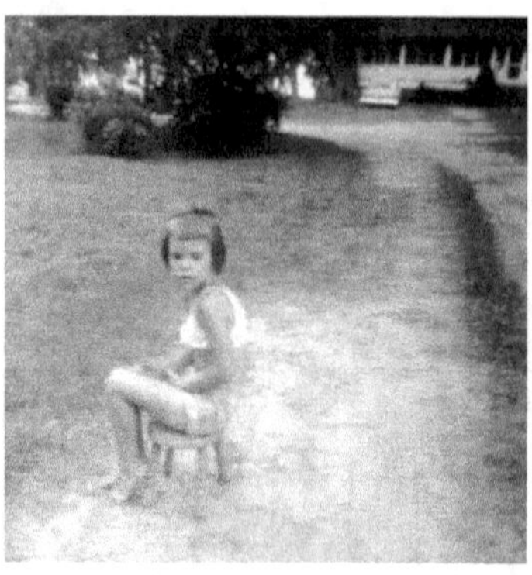

The real Donna Jackson Phillips

The alligator pond

When this photograph was taken in 2004, the church in the background was named All Saints Parish Church. Today, after years of controversy over original ownership of the property and numerous other things, the church's official name is All Saints Episcopal Church Waccamaw. The sanctuary in the background is the church's fourth (1916-17). The original congregation was founded in 1739 and it has always been an integral part of the lives of the Waccamaw River planters and their families.

Since historic churches were unheated, parishioners relied on foot warmers like the one to the right, to warm their feet during services and the long carriage rides home. Hot charcoal or coal nuggets were placed into the thin tin boxes and feet were toasted by placing them on a wooden block built into the top of the foot warmer. This foot warmer was expensive in its day. It is dated: London 1880.

The landing that once served Hagley Plantation is still in use everyday.

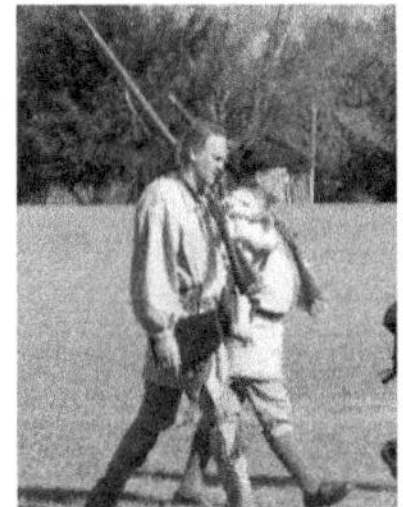

A re-enactment similar to the one Donna and Grandma saw at Boone Hall.

The Champion Oak in the town of Georgetown, is possibly nearing 600 years old, and threatens the historic house adjacent to it.

Plantation findings including 18th century and 19th century English pottery, Native American pottery, arrowheads, a thimble and a marble.

Madelyn Daggett Haskell (1894-1980) was my friend's maternal grandmother. I was going to use her image for the cover of my book, but the gray tones just didn't work. Her sweetness is evident in this photograph, however, and I often thought about her when I was writing about the little girls in my story.

The portrait to the right is a painting of Martha Pawley LaBruce, who was a member of the Pawley family from True Blue Plantation. She died in 1822, and because of her social position would have know the women from all of the powerful planta-tion families along on the Waccamaw River.

Courtesy of Mabel Bradly Garvan Collection, Yale University Art Gallery

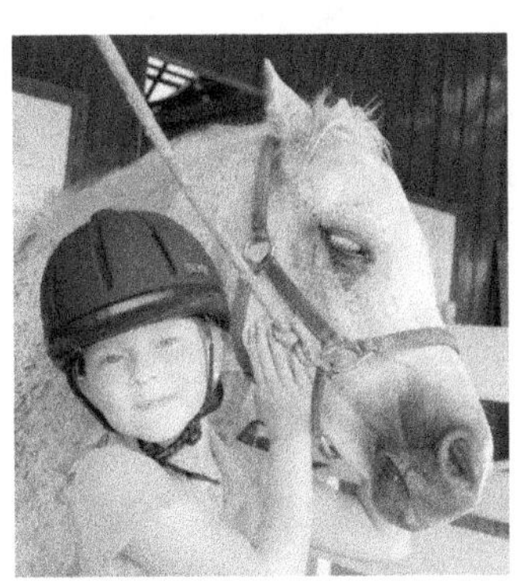

The picture to the left is of my granddaugh-ter, Grayson, when she was eight years old. I was often influenced by her because of her unpredictable silliness and love of horses.

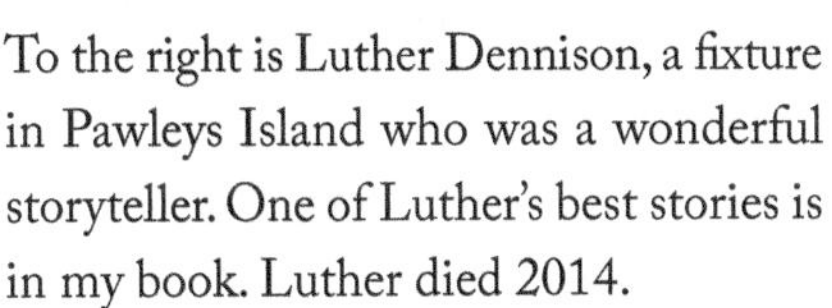

To the right is Luther Dennison, a fixture in Pawleys Island who was a wonderful storyteller. One of Luther's best stories is in my book. Luther died 2014.

MARIAH'S STORY

Julia Named the Baby Mariah

The Abbey Plantation 1860

FIVE YEARS BEFORE FREEDOM came to The Abbey, a baby girl named Mariah was born, and it was the only time Granny Rose ever uttered a curse word. Who could blame her? Mariah fell out into Rose's worn black hands as white as any white child ever born. The secret that Granny Rose's daughter, Julia, had so jealously guarded had finally revealed itself. Granny Rose had known all along that Julia had become pregnant while she was doing some special sewing at Laurel Hill Plantation and that she had been sent home in disgrace.

Julia had refused to tell her mother anything about the man who was responsible for her pregnancy, though, so Granny Rose just naturally assumed that the baby's daddy was a man from the quarter at Laurel Hill. Now, she knew that he wasn't an enslaved man; he was a white man just as Rose's own father had been.

Eighteen years ago, God had asked Rose to raise a high yellow child, and now He was asking her to raise a white one. As she hurriedly put a blue chalk thumb print on the baby's chest before the spirits could get at her, Rose raised her eyes toward the heavens and exclaimed, "Jesus, have mercy on us all!"

Then she gave her new granddaughter a good looking over, wrapped her in a calico quilt, and placed her on the bed next to Julia. Out onto the porch, she collapsed into her rocking chair, flooded by the memories of birthing her own mixed-race child. Even as a teenager there had been something out of the ordinary about Rose; everybody said so. Tall and thin, her slender neck and wide shoulders were punctuated by a gait that reminded the People of the big cats back in Africa. She was a princess, alright, and it wasn't long before she started drawing unsolicited attention from the plantation overseer—an ill-tempered, tobacco-spitting man named Jacob Manning. Manning trapped Rose unaware near one of the boat houses one day and had his way with her. After it was over, Rose fled to the safety of her home and into the arms of her mother.

She was scratched, skinned-up, and bleeding, but what she didn't know was that she was also pregnant. In the fall of 1842, sixteen-year-old Rose gave birth to a daughter who had a mop of light brown hair and pensive green eyes. Rose named the baby Julia for no particular reason, and then she handed her off to the midwife, exhibiting less interest in the baby than she might have shown a newborn puppy. It was a rocky beginning, but within a few days, Rose had fallen in love with her little yellow baby despite her best intentions, and she and Julia settled into the everyday rhythm of living.

Once the novelty of having a mixed-race child in their midst had worn off, the folks in the quarter just stopped noticing, and for the most part, the same could be said for Mariah. Mariah wasn't the least bit aware of her particular predicament until she was going on four or five. Of course, she knew that granny's skin was brown and that hers was white, but she accepted the difference with indifference. It wasn't until she was old enough to occasionally overhear others asking Granny Rose where her white granddaughter had come from that Mariah began to have questions of her own. Julia and Granny Rose answered Mariah's questions as routinely as they did everything else in their lives.

"You're white because that's the way you was born," Granny Rose told her. "You're a part of this family, though, and we love you just the way you are, and that's all you need to know. So, we don't need to be talking about this ever again."

Grubs, Snakes and Wars

The Abbey Plantation 1861-1865

MARIAH WAS BORN ONE YEAR before the start of the Civil War, and although fighting never took place on the plantation, talk about the war was as common as everyday dirt.

When freedom comes began and ended every sentence. The People had big plans. They would buy some land and build themselves fine houses just like the white folks lived in. Their children would go to school, and they wouldn't have to work hard, and they would get rich. Yes, sir! Everything was going to be fine once freedom come.

Mariah was five the day a Yankee gunship tied up at the landing, clanging and banging, and raising hell. A mob of soldiers spilled out of its belly, whooping and hollering all about Mr. Lincoln and 'mancipation.

"'Mancipation? Does that mean freedom?" one of the plantation's dock workers yelled out to the soldiers.

"Of course, it does you stupid n...."

The plantation bell was singing at the top of its lungs, and the People were cheering and hugging each other for the sheer joy of it all. Freedom's come! Freedom's come! Their collective voice turned to a gasp, though, when the soldiers on the boat broke ranks and fell onto everything within their reach. In a systematic sweep of the plantation, they smashed what they couldn't carry off and stole what they could (including Granny Rose's patent leather shoes). Then they dragged their treasures aboard the gunboat and disappeared down the river.

The Abbey was destroyed. A hundred and fifty years gone within an hour's time. The big house, rice barn, mill house, smoke house, and winnow house were burned to the ground. The stables, dairy barn, carriage house, fowl houses, and some of the privies — gone — stomped into the ground along with the master's famed collection of Madeira. The only thing the soldiers didn't destroy was the chapel, but everyone figured that was because they hadn't known it was there.

The Yankees even carried off the pigs and ducks, except for those they shot for sport. They pissed into the wells and set fire to the fields. They sank the flat boats, pulled up fences, and pried up the boards on the boat landing. It's a wonder they didn't rip up the avenue. It was as if the Philistines had swept down upon the People like in the Bible and scorched the earth beneath their feet. The quarter was the only thing still standing, so the People would have roofs over their heads, but there was little else.

Julia and Granny Rose agreed to stay put, but some of the People, mostly the younger men, packed up and left. With the plantation ripped apart, Julia and Granny Rose worried that they might not survive on their own, so they joined forces with an elderly couple named Maum Harriet and Uncle Joe.

It was a brilliant plan. Granny Rose and Maum Harriet would share the household and babysitting duties, and that would free Julia to make the three-mile walk to the saltwater creek beds every day to scavenge for food. Uncle Joe's job was to keep on doing what he always did — bring home fish.

Maum Harriet was a savvy woman; she could put on a spread with little more than the weeds growing in the backyard. She and Uncle Joe lived alone near the far end of the quarter, but to make things easier, they decided to move their things into an abandoned cabin next door to Julia and Granny Rose. To supplement the fish and whatever else

Uncle Joe could trap and bring home, Julia foraged for roots and anything else that would fill up the stew pot. Before freedom, the People were selective about what they ate; after freedom, everything including grubs and snakes were fair game.

A Little Red Chair

The Abbey Plantation 1866

SOMEONE HAD RANSACKED St. Mary. Scratches had been gouged into the pews, and the communion table was busted. Handprints covered the walls, urine was fermenting in the baptismal font, and the brass alter cross was missing. When the People heard the news, they were crushed, but to a one, they were grateful that it hadn't been a thousand times worse. The chapel could have been torched and the precious stained glass destroyed.

An English nephew of Plowden Weston currently owned the plantation, but permanent ownership was up to the courts, and it could take years before a verdict was rendered. So, the nephew managed the plantation through his attorney in Charleston, reluctant to set foot there for fear that someone might take a potshot at him. Protecting the windows at St. Mary, however, was something that had to be done, no matter the cost or the danger. Three days after learning the news, the nephew arrived at the plantation with a crew of construction workers and woodcrafters from Georgetown who had come highly recommended.

When the People learned that the windows were going to be taken down, they were disappointed, but with times being what they were, they understood the necessity of protecting them, at least for the time. They could be stored somewhere safe until things settled down, and then they could be put back where they belonged. That wasn't the plan, though. The part about them being removed was true, but they weren't going into storage. They were going to be relocated to Prince George Parish Church in Georgetown. An Anglican church before the Revolutionary War, the church was an Episcopal church now, and if that didn't stick in everybody's craw, Renty and Burke's construction company was the one hired to do the job. Renty and Burke were just as shocked as the People were when the lawyer representing the estate offered them the job.

"My client is determined to protect the windows at all costs. Did they want the job, or not?"

Of course they wanted it; it paid a hundred dollars, US dollars. Besides, who else could be trusted to remove them? Renty cried when the lawyer walked out of the workshop. "I can't do it," he said.

"Yes, you can," Burke replied, reminding Renty that they were only removing the windows for safekeeping. "We'll replace them with clear glass for now, but someday, we'll put them back where they belong."

"Prince George is one of the wealthiest churches in South Carolina," Renty said. "It's the planters' church. Master Weston went there. Ain't no way the windows will ever leave there. It's as good as done." Renty was right, of course. Ain't no way the windows would ever leave Prince George.

Mariah signed up for Miss Hattie's school the first day, and since she was the youngest, she got to take her lessons in Miss Hattie's little red chair. Mariah had a facility for reading and language, Miss Hattie told Julia. A gift, she called it, so Mariah studied hard. Julia was amazed how easily letters and words came for Mariah.

The rules of grammar made sense to her, unlike her mother, and Mariah spent hours memorizing the rules that dictated the ways that proper sentences were constructed. Over time, *de, dat,* and *dis* was replaced with *the, that,* and *this.* Ain't never also flunked the test, as did *I don't rightly knows,* and *I 'spects.*

As the changes in her speech became apparent, Mariah grew a big red target on her back.

"Hey, Miss High and Mighty, you think you're better than us, don't you?" some of the kids from the quarter jeered. "You got white skin; now you wanna talk like you's white, but you ain't no different from us. You always gonna be a n.... just like us."

When Mariah was twelve, Uncle Joe was fishing his favorite fishing hole off the landing when he suddenly grabbed his chest and collapsed. He died as he was being carried home and was buried the next night in the old slave cemetery. Granny Rose, Julia, and Mariah sat up with Harriet throughout that moonless night, and it was hard to tell who cried the most. It was Mariah's first time losing someone close to her, but it wouldn't be the last. Soon after, she and Julia noticed that Granny Rose's mind was beginning to wander. She was only forty-seven, but she'd been worked hard. Like an old dog, she was too crooked to stand on her own anymore and spent most of her days in her rocking chair staring off into space. A pasty white film covered her pupils, and even though she couldn't see her hand in front of her face, she still had that stare.

Maum Harriet said it was all part of God's plan. Once a body has seen everything they need to see on earth, God gives 'em that stare, so they can see their way into heaven. Soon after Harriet's comments, Granny Rose died in her sleep. Julia and Mariah decorated her grave with her favorite teacup—the one with the pink and purple roses painted on it.

A few months later, Julia decided to marry a man from the quarter named Samuel Weston on account of him asking her every day for the past year, she said. Julia seemed real happy, though, and Samuel (who Mariah called Daddy Sam) couldn't have been nicer to Mariah and Maum Harriet. A year later, Julia gave birth to a son that she insisted upon naming Joseph after Uncle Joe.

"The next one we'll name after you, dear," she told her husband. Little Sam arrived the next year, and the following year saw the arrival of twin daughters, Rose-of-Sharon and Amethyst Pearl.

Soon after the arrival of the twins, Maum Harriet took Julia aside to tell her that she had a fire in her belly that was getting more painful every day. Julia wanted to call the doctor, but Maum Harriet refused.

"I'm dying," she said, "but I'm ready to go. I miss Uncle Joe. I miss the life we had, and I miss his stories. If the Lord says it's my time to go, that's alright with me. Then I can be back with my husband, back with Joe."

Harriet died two months later. After a real good cry, Julia and Mariah put Harriet's body on the kitchen table and scrubbed her clean as they could so'd she look her best when she met Jesus, and then they dressed her in her Sunday dress and sewed her into a sheet.

The next evening they buried Harriet next to Uncle Joe in the People's cemetery and decorated her grave with sea shells and her cherished crystal goblet. When Harriet and Uncle Joe were newlyweds, Joe had bartered a whole day's labor for that goblet, and he had presented it to Harriet with a piece of blue yarn tied around its stem.

"My, it do sparkle, don't it?" Harriet used to say each time she took it down from the shelf above the window. "My, but it do sparkle, so."

CHAPTER 4

My Stage Name is Stella Bright

Pawleys Island, SC 1877

MARIAH WAS SEVENTEEN, and she'd heard through a church lady that there was a white woman spending the summer in a rented cottage on Pawleys Island who was interested in hiring a live-in maid. Since the cabin Mariah shared with her mother, stepfather, and their new family was fairly bursting at the seams, Mariah decided to apply for the job. Mariah talked it over with her mother first, but Mariah was already determined to do it. Fortunately, Julia agreed—at least about going to meet the lady in question.

The following day, Mariah walked the mile and a half to Sister Dennison's house to ask her if the job was still available. Sister Dennison was a cook at the summer house where the woman was staying, and she told Mariah she'd check into it the next day. Sister Dennison's grandson showed up on Mariah's porch the next afternoon to tell Mariah to be at the Old Foster creek house the next morning at ten o'clock sharp to talk with the white lady. Mariah wore her Sunday dress and her best pair of shoes for her long walk to the white lady's house.

When she reached the narrow spit of land that led over to the island, however, she decided to go barefoot the rest of the way so as not to fill her shoes with sand. Everyone knew where the Old Foster house was; it was a fixture in those parts. The two-story house had large piazzas on all four sides with fancy scrollwork painted every color of the rainbow. Once there, Mariah was hesitant to knock on the front door, but it was the only entrance she could find. Front doors were for white people. She finally found the courage, though, and before she knew it, she was standing eye-to-eye with a woman almost as wide as the door.

"Come on in, darlin'," the woman said. "Come on in. I've been eager for you to get here. Now, don't just stand there; take a seat right over there."

Knocking on the front door of a white woman's house was one thing, but being asked to take a seat in her parlor was another, Mariah thought. Mariah was too nervous to argue, though, so she sat as lightly as she could on a small ladies' chair with a fluffy pink seat cushion.

Although Mariah was nervous about looking at the white woman, her curiosity got the better of her, so she took one long look. She'd never seen anyone like that in her life. The woman looked like a pork sausage with a wild cluster of red curls on the top that reminded Mariah of a bird's nest. A pink satin dressing gown barely covering her enormous breasts was wrapped around her like a condom, and she was wearing pink satin slippers. Her eyelashes were long and fluttery, and her eyebrows were arched halfway up onto her forehead. Her face was unnaturally white except for red splotches on each of her cheeks, and she had the reddest set of lips Mariah had ever seen.

The only thing Mariah knew about white women was by studying the ones who visited The Abbey, but they didn't have chalky faces and clumps of red curls where their hair ought to have been. So, Mariah got to wondering if this was how all white women looked away from the plantation or if this pink lady represented an entirely different breed of person.

Bolting for the door was an option that was starting to look pretty good, but Mariah's thoughts were interrupted when she noticed that even though the white woman was so fat that she made a swishy sound when she walked, she was as graceful as a cat.

"Well, now that you've gotten a good look at me," the white lady said, "I've got some questions for you. Oh, but first, I imagine you'd like to know my name—it's Miss Stella, Stella Bright. It's not my real name, of course, but after I left New Orleans to become an actress, I decided I needed a stage name. It's a good one, don't you think? Of course, I was never much of an actress. All I could do was bat my eyes and wiggle my ass, but then I got a late start. Remind me to tell you the story, sometime."

After asking Mariah a few questions about herself and her education, Miss Stella stopped in mid-sentence and blurted out, "Mariah, I just have to know. Are you sure you ain't a white gal?"

Mariah was so taken aback that she just sat there quiet as a statue for a long time. *I've been here five minutes and a crazy white woman just asked me if I'm white, too,* Mariah said to herself. Then she managed to stammer: "No ma'am. My papa was white, and my mama's papa was white. Legally I'm a quadroon."

With that, Miss Stella threw her head back and laughed until she had tears in her eyes. "I should a' known," she said wiping her tears with the sleeve of her dressing gown. "I should a' known because that's what I am. I ain't white either; I'm a quadroon just like you only I've been passing myself off as white for the last twenty years. I swear I can't believe I'm telling you this, but I've kept this a secret for so long. Maybe I'm getting soft in the head," she said, "but I like you, Mariah.

"A long time ago, I had a baby daughter. If she had lived, I'd like to think she might have looked just like you. She's probably the reason I'm telling you all of this. There ain't another reason that comes to mind. Anyway, remember a few minutes ago when I told you I got a late start on being an actress? And then I told you to ask me to tell you the story, sometime?

"Well, you deserve to hear it now," Miss Stella said. "Like I said before, I was raised in New Orleans where there just ain't the stigma about black and white mixing like there is here. Hell, placage made it easy. I'm sure you've never heard of the word, Mariah, but placage was the custom of free women of color—mostly quadroons like me and you—becoming mistresses to wealthy white men.

"I went to my first quadroon ball when I was sixteen, but I didn't get an offer until I was seventeen. That's when I met a man who owned a plantation a few miles from New Orleans. After he made his intentions known and I accepted, he spoke to my mother who acted as my agent. The two of them cut a deal that would allow me to live in high style as his mistress.

"He was free to break our agreement any time he wanted to, but he had to promise to pay five hundred dollars for each child that we might have together. It was a good deal all around," Miss Stella insisted. "We kept that arrangement for seven years until he told me one night that he wanted to move on because he had found someone younger.

"I didn't mind all that much, and since we didn't have any children except for the one we lost, I wasn't even expecting any money, but before I moved out of his house, he gave me two thousand dollars. The day he handed me that money is the day I decided to dye my hair and to start passing for white, and I've been doing it ever since," she said figuring she'd overwhelmed Mariah with her tales. "Now, Mariah, you shouldn't be surprised by all of this. It happens every day. Do you really think I'm the only gal to pass? Well, I'm not, and I'll tell you another thing. I've buried three husbands—all of 'em white and all of 'em rich. Do you think I could have done that if I hadn't been passing?"

"It's illegal to pass," Mariah said in a half-whisper.

"Only if you get caught, and before that happens, you might just manage to have yourself a career and get rich. 'Sure beats being a maid or housekeeper. It's 1877. What other kind of jobs are open to a colored gal? Nothing. You know it, and I know it. So, what are you going to do?" Stella asked.

"What am I going to do about what?" Mariah replied. "Do you mean pretending to be white? Are you telling me that I should start passing myself off as white?" Mariah gasped.

"No, I'm not telling you to do it. I'm suggesting that you think about it," was Stella's reply. "This is the deal, Mariah. I need a maid or companion or whatever you want to call it, and you need a job. In a few weeks, I'm heading out for Charleston where I'm going to spend the season. Come with me. What do you have to lose? You are well-educated, and you sure don't sound like somebody off the plantation. No one will ever know."

"I'd really like to come and work for you," Mariah finally managed to say, "but I don't know about the rest of it. I'll have to think about it."

"Good enough, Mariah. You can do whatever you want to about that, just don't mention our conversation to anyone, alright?" Miss Stella asked. "Now, why don't you pack your things tonight and move in with me tomorrow afternoon sometime, and then we'll play it by ear."

When Mariah got home, her mother was waiting for her at the top of the lane leading to the quarter. "Are you going to work for the white lady?" she asked.

"I'm leaving in the morning," Mariah said apologetically. "I hope you won't miss me too much, but it's time for me to go out on my own. Besides, you can put some of the kids in my bed. It'll be good for all of us, at least I hope so. I just want to know one thing. If I don't like working for the white lady, can I come home again?"

Tears welled in Julia's eyes as she reached out for Mariah and hugged her close. "I'll always want you with me, Mariah. You're my first born, and I'll always want you with me."

Mariah didn't sleep during her last night at home. She listened to the hoot owl that lived in a pine tree near the edge of the cabin. She listened to the crackle of the fire and to the soft little sounds the children made as they slept. She listened to the frogs croaking in the pond and to the splash of the alligator. She wanted to remember even the smallest sound because they were all the sounds of her childhood.

The following morning, Julia fixed Mariah a big breakfast and helped her set out her clothes. Besides her Sunday dress and shoes, there wasn't much to pack: two skirts, two calico blouses, a short work jacket, two camisoles, a white blouse, a pair of work boots, one night gown, a head scarf, and a pair of mended silk stockings. Julia and Mariah folded everything and placed it into a small tapestry satchel that Julia had kept under her bed since before Mariah was born. In addition to her hair brush and a small mirror, Mariah's only other possession was the Tree of Africa quilt, but that was going to stay right where it was until Mariah had children of her own, and that might be a while, yet, Julia said.

Mariah kissed each of the children, waved goodbye to Daddy Sam out in the field, and gave Mama the longest hug ever. Then she whispered, "I love you," and hurriedly set out for the Old Foster creek house.

Her chest felt like an empty place that her heart wanted to be free of, but Mariah kept her eyes on the road, knowing that if she turned around, she'd never leave home again.

CHAPTER 5

Chocolate Spoons and Pickle Forks

Pawleys Island 1877

MARIAH'S BRAIN WORKED on overload during her two-hour walk to the creek house. Some of her thoughts were of home and Mama, but others were about the advice that Miss Stella had given her yesterday. She'd never thought about passing for white, but she had to admit it was tempting. How wonderful it must be to walk down a road or pathway and not have to step away to let the white folks pass or to be called *miss* instead of *gal* or worse.

If she were white, she could eat in a restaurant or clerk in a store or even visit a library. She could stay in a hotel or in a boarding house; she could take piano lessons if she wanted to or even attend a lecture or concert. If she were white, she would be protected from soldiers and ship hands who thought that yellow gals were fair game for their lusty appetites. If she were white, she'd be free to be anything she wanted to be.

Mariah settled into her new life, slowly getting used to the finery that Miss Stella took for granted—rugs on the floors, tablecloths for every day, and the table set with matching dishes. Mariah's room had a small brass bed with a horsehair mattress and a coverlet called a bedspread that had pink roses on it. Instead of newsprint, the walls of the Old Foster house were covered with wallpaper that Miss Stella said had come from China. In the dining room, there were asparagus tongs and pickle forks, chocolate spoons, and ladles just for soup. There were beautiful little bowls designed to hold bars of soap, plates that looked like the inside of an oyster and even cups just for eating boiled eggs out of.

Miss Stella's room reminded Mariah of one she'd read about where Blackbeard once kept a harem girl he had rescued from an Arab sheik. Everything in the room was upholstered in rose-colored satin and gold fringe: the bed and chaise lounge, the drapes, the pillows, and the folding screen where Miss Stella did most of her dressing.

Perfume bottles of every shape and size took up half of Miss Stella's dressing table, while the other half held a dozen or more large jars–the size that horse ointment usually came in—containing Miss Stella's prized cosmetics.

"Now, Mariah, you be extra careful with my cosmetics," Miss Stella said over and over. "They're not ordinary cosmetics; they're theatrical cosmetics, and they came from New York. I'd just look like such a fright without them; I don't know what I'd do."

Three weeks after going to work for Miss Stella and endless days of homesickness, Miss Stella said she'd had her fill of the ocean and told Mariah to start packing for Charleston. Everything except the fancy wallpaper was going, and it was going to be a monumental job. Miss Stella hired local church women to help Mariah get everything ready, but even then, they barely finished before the boat for Charleston arrived.

Once everything was aboard and accounted for, Mariah and Miss Stella had little to do but to talk and to rest up for the unpacking work that was ahead of them. "Well, Mariah, have you been thinking about what we talked about the day of your interview?" Miss Stella asked.

She had, she said, and she knew that if she was going to do it, now was the time. She just didn't want to embarrass her family. "They wouldn't have to know, would they?"

"Well, darlin', I don't know. You see, it was different for me. My mama was already gone by the time I started passing," Miss Stella replied, "but even if she'd been alive, I would have done it anyway. I just had to get out into the world, and that was the only way I could think of to help me survive on my own.

"It's hard enough being a woman, Mariah. Being a colored woman, well, that's pretty much a death sentence if you're trying to make something of yourself. Don't forget, as a yellow gal the best you can hope for is to be someone's maid or someone's wife," she said. "Maybe you'll get lucky, maybe you won't, but you won't know 'till you try."

"Mariah Weston's going to be my new name," Mariah said, trying to avoid the word pass. I'm going to be Miss Mariah Weston of Georgetown County, South Carolina. My stepfather selected that name after freedom came to the plantation, and he's a fine man, so that's the name I'm going to use."

Miss Stella's attorney, Charles Mayeaux, was waiting for them on the wharf in Charleston and escorted the women to their carriage for the short ride to Miss Stella's rented house near the corner of Tradd and Legare Streets. Mayeaux stayed behind to oversee the unloading of Miss Stella's possessions. A courteous man in his early thirties, Charles Mayeaux was an old-line Charlestonian, a blue-blood, alright. His family was one of the founding families of Charleston's influential Huguenot community, and the Mayeaux name was respected throughout the city. Charles Mayeaux had been trained from infancy to wear the mantle of respectability. Bringing shame to the Mayeaux name would be unthinkable.

The house on Tradd Street was a beautiful townhouse filled to the brim with locally made Chippendale-style furnishings. *How will we ever fit all of Miss Stella's things in here?* Mariah wondered as she looked around the main floor of the house. Then she started to laugh. If Miss Stella wanted something, she'd figure out a way to get it. "I don't know how, but she'd do it," Mariah said out loud. Mariah was right. Within a week, Miss Stella and her team of hired furniture movers had rearranged practically every room in the house.

"I told you to stop worrying about finding a place for everything, Mariah," Miss Stella said. "While you're still young, you need to learn what's worth worrying about and what's not. My theory is, if it ain't goin' be seen on a galloping horse, it ain't worth worrying about."

Mariah had never seen a city as large and sophisticated as Charleston, and Miss Stella reminded her a thousand times that she was seeing the city at its worst. Yankee shelling had destroyed entire city blocks, leaving them looking like rock quarries. If she looked closely, though, she could still see the city's overt symbols of wealth: cobblestone streets, spiraling church steeples, glittering street lamps, hotels and businesses, and most of all, of course, mansions that seemed to line every street. Mariah hadn't known there was that much money in the whole world.

CHAPTER 6

I Was Nervous at First

Charleston 1878

A FEW MONTHS AFTER moving to Charleston, Miss Stella sat Mariah down and suggested that it was time for her to venture out. "You need to have some fun," she said. "You need to meet some new people. You can't just stay in the house with me all the time."

"I'm afraid someone will discover that I'm a fake," Mariah explained. "I don't fit in anywhere. The servants I meet at the market are colored, and they won't have anything to do with me, but if I go to a concert or to the library where there are white people, I'm afraid they won't have anything to do with me, either."

She had to take the chance, Miss Stella replied. "You won't know until you try. There's a concert to benefit the Ladies of the Confederacy Benevolent Fund on Friday afternoon, and I want you to go. I'll have Juniper escort you there and return for you around four. I know it won't be easy, but you're bound to meet some young people there. What do you say?"

"That's what I'm most afraid of," Mariah admitted. "What if I do meet some young people--young white people—and they want to talk to me? I don't know how to talk to white people."

"Sure you do," Miss Stella replied. "You just open up your mouth and say something nice. You can do it. And you're forgetting one thing—you are three-quarters white—you are more white, at least on the outside than you are colored.

"I know you were raised to be a colored woman, and I suppose that's what you will always be on the inside, but you can't deny your white heritage, especially when everyone, including me, sees you that way. And you don't just walk up to someone and say, 'Hello, my name is Mariah Weston, and I'm white.' You simply let them assume what they will. I've never told anyone that I'm white in so many words, except for the census man, and he only comes every ten years."

Mariah would take Miss Stella's advice about the concert, but what should she wear? She'd wear one of her new dresses, perhaps—a dusty blue cotton day dress with darker blue stripes running through, and yes, it did bring out her eyes just like the saleslady said it would. Just before it was time to leave for the concert, Miss Stella placed Mariah's new hat squarely on her head, tucked in a few curls, and proclaimed that she looked beautiful.

"Mama wouldn't recognize me," Mariah said, after studying her image in one of Miss Stella's looking glasses. "I don't know if that's a good thing or a bad thing."

"It's a good thing, Cinderella," Miss Stella said, giving Mariah a noisy kiss. Now, get goin'."

Mariah and Juniper, who remained a respectful three feet behind, walked the three blocks to the square where the concert was to take place. There were benches there—thank goodness! At least she wouldn't have to sit on the ground. She selected an empty one and sat on the far end praying that she would have it all to herself throughout the concert. Before long, though, she was joined by a young mother and two small children who reminded Mariah of fat little puppies. Within minutes, they were climbing in and out of Mariah's lap and pulling at the ribbons on her hat.

"Sally! James! You're being rude to the nice lady," their mother scolded.

Mariah assured her that she didn't mind—she had younger brothers and sisters, she said, and before she had time to think about it, she was conversing with the young woman as easily as if she had been talking with one of her childhood friends.

The young woman's husband owned a tavern on Broad Street, and she had grown up in Charleston. When Mariah told her that she was the companion to a former actress, the young woman seemed delighted. "An actress! Oh, Miss Weston, wouldn't you just love to be on stage and have men fall at your feet?"

The two chatted and giggled throughout the concert and promised to look for each other at the next concert. Back at Miss Stella's, Mariah talked about the fun they'd had.

"I was nervous at first, but once we started talking, I stopped worrying about it. She was really nice."

CHAPTER 7

Back Home

The Abbey Plantation 1878

THE WEEK BEFORE CHRISTMAS, Miss Stella asked Mariah what she would like most for Christmas, and without hesitating, Mariah replied, "A trip home."

"I thought you'd say that, so I've already got it planned," Miss Stella said. "You leave next Monday. You're sure you can manage without me?"

"Sure, I can," Miss Stella said. "Besides, you'll miss me so much, you'll want to come back. We couldn't do without you around here, you know. Who'd get me outta bed in the morning, and pay the bills, and go to the market?

"I don't know who taught you so much about buying fish, but I've never known anyone who can buy fish and shrimp as fresh as you can. Hell, you must find 'em when they're still flopping. If I was to go to the fish market by myself, they'd sell me some smelly mud fish, and I wouldn't know the difference."

Mariah was as nervous about going home as she had been the day she left, but when she saw the plantation's landing coming into view and watched the deck hands aboard the ferry preparing to pull alongside, she broke into tears. Daddy Sam was standing on the landing with his youngest son, James.

"Daddy Sam! Daddy Sam!" Mariah cried. "I'm back."

Julia had moved the children out of Mariah's old room so she could have it all to herself just like before, and it was just as Mariah had remembered, only had it always been that small, and had the ceiling always been so low, and had it always been this dark, and had the bed always been so lumpy?

Mariah couldn't wait for Christmas Day to give everyone the gifts she'd brought them, so she started handing them out as soon as she unpacked the cardboard grip she borrowed from Miss Stella "Oh, Mariah," Julia squealed as she saw the bright blue store bought dress that came tumbling out of paper that her gift was wrapped in. "Mariah, it's beautiful. Why, I'll have to wear it to services on Christmas Day!"

Joseph was reticent to open his gift with everyone watching, but he eventually managed to do it. Inside he found a wooden paddle boat with The Spirit of Charleston painted on the wheelhouse.

"Oh, thank you, Mariah," he said, giving his big sister a snuggly hug. "I've been wantin' to have me a paddle wheeler."

For Little James, Mariah had selected a navy-blue corduroy jacket and matching britches. For the babies, she bought pink sweaters and little knit hats with white pom poms on them. To Daddy Sam, she gave a pen knife with a handle carved from the antler of a deer.

After all the excitement of the gifts had settled down, Mariah curled up at her mother's side near the fireplace and slept. It was so good to be home. After supper she helped Julia clear away the table and wash the dishes in the washtub. For the first time, Mariah noticed how many of the dishes were chipped and stained. Had they always been that way? She couldn't remember.

Four days into her stay, Mariah found herself missing Miss Stella and her new life in Charleston. It's not that Mama or their cabin in the quarter had changed, it's just that Mariah had changed and wasn't aware of the change until she went home.

The next day as she watched her things being placed aboard the ship that was headed back to Charleston, Mariah hugged and kissed her family goodbye, but it wasn't as painful as the first time. It made her melancholy, though, but when she saw the spirals of St. Philip's and St. Michael's off in the distance, she knew that Charleston was her home.

Miss Stella's Place

Charleston 1878-1879

LIFE WENT ALONG SMOOTHLY for Miss Stella's makeshift family that now included Mariah, a parlor maid named Pansy, a cook named Beulah Mae Brewer, and her husband, Juniper, who stopped by every day or so to move a piece of furniture or to do a little carpentry work. Once a month, Charles Mayeaux also stopped by, but he was always there to discuss business with Miss Stella, so Mariah had little to do with his visits until the day she was asked to join them in Miss Stella's salon.

"There's something I need to talk to you about," Miss Stella began. "You know all about my acting days, such as they were, and my three husbands, but between husbands number two and number three, I spent some time in Birmingham that I need to tell you about, now.

"After my second husband died, I knew I was too old to pick up my acting career, and I was too young to just sit around, so I decided to buy a business. I ended up buying a brothel in Birmingham, which I renamed Miss Stella's Place. The business was registered as a boarding house; all bawdy houses call themselves boarding houses, you know, but everyone in Birmingham knew what was really going on at Miss Stella's, and we really did it right.

"My girls were beautiful and young and really something to look at. We traded services with town officials for protection from prosecution, and like I said, we did alright. I'd probably still be there today if I hadn't met my third husband. But he didn't like me being in the business, and I was starting to pork up a little, and I didn't like him being around my girls. So, one day I up and sold the place to the sister of the chief of police.

"That husband—who was my last one—died about six months before I rented the creek house on Pawleys Island, and you know the rest," she said, "but you don't know where I'm going with this, do you?

"Well, I've decided to buy another brothel here in Charleston. The best one in Charleston is on King Street between George and Society Streets," she explained. "It's on the second floor above some fancy shops, and it's for sale, or at least it was until this morning. Mr. Mayeaux just stopped by to tell me that he cut a deal with its owner today, and I am the proud new proprietor of Miss Stella's King Street Brothel."

Mariah was dumbstruck. Mariah had always known that there were bawdy houses in Georgetown, but she'd never seen one of those women up close, and now Miss Stella was telling her that she had just bought the biggest whorehouse in Charleston!

"Why are you telling me this?" Mariah finally managed to say.

"Because I want you to come with me, Silly Goose. I want you to come to King Street with me."

"You already have me... well, you know," she managed to say just before blurting out the fact that she was pretending to be white. "And now you want me to become a bawdy!" Mariah shouted.

"I would never allow you to work as a bawdy," Miss Stella said. "I just want you to continue to be, well, to be my daughter; it's just that instead of continuing to live here, we're going to live on King Street. Do you think you can do that?"

"Yes," Mariah replied, almost shouting. "I can do that, but I'm not going to work as a bawdy." That night after Mariah had time to think about the events of the day, doubts began to creep into her head. *I'm in Charleston where I don't belong in the first place; I'm living with a white woman who isn't a white woman, and I'm passing for white, too, and now I'm planning to live in a brothel! Miss Stella is insane. How can I live in a brothel without being seen as a bawdy? The whole thing is ridiculous! I love Miss Stella, but how can I be happy living in a whore house?*

The next morning, Miss Stella talked Mariah into accompanying her to King Street just to take a look at the new property, being careful not to call it a brothel or to use the bawdy word. Mariah agreed—but only to look around. To access the building, they had to enter a small courtyard off of the alleyway at the rear of the property. Once inside the courtyard, they had to climb a long stairway leading to the second-floor entrance. The fat on the inside of Miss Stella's legs made her stockings rub together so furiously as she made her way up the stairs that Mariah half-expected sparks to fly. Nothing of the sort happened, of course, but Mariah was positive that she smelled something burning.

The exterior of the building looked like any of the city's fabled hidden gardens, but once inside, the walls were covered with red silk brocade as were the furnishings. *Now I know where Miss Stella gets her taste in bedroom furniture,* Mariah thought.

Servants' quarters containing a kitchen and three small bedrooms took up about one quarter of the first floor of the brothel. An apartment used by the former owner, Madame Legrand, took up another quarter, and a parlor, complete with a grand piano, occupied the rest of the space.

Upstairs on the third floor were eight bedrooms designated as client entertainment rooms and five smaller rooms that were used by the bawdy women as shared sleeping quarters during the day. The servants' quarters and the five small third-floor bedrooms were almost institutional-looking in their austerity, but the rest of the house, including Miss Stella's new apartment, had fringe and tassels dripped off of every surface. The beds in the client rooms had silk brocade canopies with gold tassels hanging from all four posters. "The color may be a little garish," Miss Stella said to Mariah's utter surprise, "but for now, I think it will do. We can make changes as we go along."

"One of us isn't sure we want to do anything, as yet," Mariah said.

"Well, we'll see," Miss Stella said taking a close look at one of the tassels. "One never knows, does one?" It took three weeks to talk Mariah into moving to King Street, and Miss Stella only managed to do it by playing on her sympathy.

"I need you, Mariah. I can't do this without you." Mariah finally agreed to the move, providing that Miss Stella promised to give her two days off each week, so she could establish a life of sanity away from the red brocade asylum. Miss Stella would have agreed to three to keep Mariah happy but thought better of telling Mariah that she had underplayed her hand. The physical move to King Street took longer than it should have because of all the gawking done by the men Mr. Mayeaux had hired to move Miss Stella's belongings. Once inside the brothel, they couldn't help but stare at the floor-to-ceiling decadence.

"Lord, this red chariot will take your butt straight to hell," Mariah overheard one of the men saying as he deposited a packing box in Miss Stella's apartment.

At full capacity, the house was built to accommodate ten working women, but when Madame Legrand sold the brothel to Miss Stella, only six planned to stay on. That meant that Miss Stella had to hire four additional women, and she had to do it in short order. Miss Stella's grand opening was to be in two weeks, and she didn't want to have to turn away business because she was understaffed.

So, she put that word out on the street but figured the best way to find additional girls for her house was to talk to the six girls who were staying on. Before she interviewed them, however, she called Mariah into her parlor and locked the door behind her.

"Mariah," she said, "now that I'm about to talk to these girls, it's important for you to hold the line, if you know what I mean. We can't have these girls knowing that you and I ain't lily white. Even bawdies have standards, and there ain't gonna be no white girls working for no colored woman. You can bet your behind on that one. So, if you feel a moment of honesty coming on, you've got to promise to keep it to yourself. I love you darlin', but this is business."

CHAPTER 9

This is a Real Nice Place to Live

Charleston, SC 1878-1879

MARIAH WOULD KEEP QUIET, she promised, so Miss Stella called in Josie Russell, who reminded Mariah of a caged chipmunk. Narrow hipped with dark wiry hair and black eyes, Josie darted about the house with the energy of an exposed nerve.

By the time she stepped into Miss Stella's parlor, Josie had already had her third run-in of the morning—this time with a nine-year-old boy that Josie accused of intentionally splashing mud on her dress in the alleyway behind the brothel. Josie's earlier altercation had been with the new downstairs maid. Josie said the maid tried to trip her as she came down the stairs that morning; even earlier, Josie had sworn at the sugarcane vendor for making voodoo eyes at her.

Josie was always at odds with someone, but Madame Legrand had insisted that she was one of her best girls. "Men like spunk in their women," Madame Legrand said. Josie told Miss Stella that she knew half-sisters who worked at a bawdy house in Georgetown and were interested in relocating to Charleston. She'd contact them, she said. Miss Stella slapped her rubbery thighs in delight.

"We've got half our problem solved, Mariah! Let's talk to some of the other girls."

The next two girls, Maud Harris and May Dell, weren't much help, but it was only noon, and they said their brains weren't fully functional until after four or five in the afternoon, so Miss Stella dismissed them. Then she turned to Mariah and said, "If either one of those girls has a brain, you can bet it's the size of a pea."

Even though Mariah had been a snit for two weeks over the prospects of living in a brothel, she couldn't control her laughter on that one. She loved Miss Stella. She'd love her more if she hadn't asked her to live in a brothel, but she couldn't deny that she would love her no matter where they lived. It was at that moment that Mariah decided to exchange her bad mood for a good one and to try to make the best of things. After all, she could be back on the plantation scratching out a living with the rest of her family, but because of Miss Stella, Mariah was well-dressed and well-fed, living in the most beautiful city in the South. She also made enough money to send more than half of her earnings home every month. She could never thank Miss Stella enough for that, not ever.

Massie Gray was the next girl to meet with Miss Stella. Seventeen, Massie had grown up in Anderson County, but her nickname was Georgia Peach. That's because her skin was the palest pink, her hair strawberry blond, and her eyes reminded folks of periwinkles. She was stunning to look at and had an innocence that drew men like flies.

The other women who had worked for Madame Legrand had been involved in the business long enough to seem comfortable with it, but Massie was still a girl. *She's my age,* Mariah thought. *How did she end up being a bawdy at the age of seventeen?* Miss Stella knew Massie's story, but some things you keep to yourself. If Mariah had known Massie back in Akin, she might not have asked herself that question. Massie Gray was one of eleven children born to a Scotch-Irish dirt farmer and his wife.

The youngest of six girls, Massie slept on the floor until one of her older sisters ran away from home and left a vacant spot in the girls' bed. Massie's parents tried to do right by their children, but there were too many mouths to feed to worry about schooling or anything else other than filling empty bellies once a day. Massie was always hungry, but after she turned fifteen, hunger was the least of her worries. One hot, sticky night, Massie met up with two of her older brothers and their friends on her way to the privy. The boys were all liquored up after a night of carousing, and they were looking for trouble. What they found was an angel standing there in the moonlight in her thin cotton nightgown. Massie ran away the next day. She was only fifteen, but she had learned an important life lesson. If she was going to have to spend her life being mistreated by men, she was going to be paid for it.

Massie apologized for not knowing any available bawdies and thanked Miss Stella for keeping her on. "This is a real nice place to live," Massie said as she left the room.

"I really like my room, too. It's real nice."

The oldest of the women was Isadora Barron, who admitted to being twenty-six and was probably closer to thirty. Miss Stella said she was still young enough to take on her share of clients, though, and experienced enough to help Miss Stella manage a house full of women, so she was welcome to stay.

Rosa Laid was a petite young woman with soft brown hair and blue-gray eyes. She had a sugar-sweet accent and a turned-up nose, and she would talk nonstop if you'd let her. She was best friends with Massie, all except sometimes she'd get mad at Massie for being so pretty and all, she said, but that didn't come up too often; besides it wasn't Massie's fault.

So, she tried to just let it roll off her back just like a chicken or a duck; she couldn't remember which. She didn't know any girl interested in making a change, but she'd ask around. A girl from a house down the street and the two half-sisters from Georgetown joined Miss Stella's household just in time for the grand opening.

Free liquor flowed all night, and the maids had to work in tandem to keep fresh sheets on the beds in the clients' rooms. The next morning found the cash register overflowing and the girls too exhausted to come out of their rooms until suppertime.

"Do you think we'll be this busy every night," Mariah asked as she and Miss Stella surveyed the damage from the night before.

"We will if we pay off all the right people," Miss Stella said from years of experience.

"I'm worried about getting along with the girls," Mariah said. "I'm afraid they're going to think I'm some kind of princess."

Miss Stella said she should give the girls more credit. "This is the deal. Even though most of them didn't have much say about how they got here, they kind of view it as a career choice. Just because you don't want to be a bawdy doesn't mean that they are going to hold it against you. The only reason they'd be mean to you is if you are rude to them. So, try it."

Although Mariah refused to show her face during business hours, she was involved in everything that happened behind the scenes, and she soon realized that running a successful brothel was hard work. Mariah did the bookkeeping, and she also ordered the food and flowers, paid the bills, and oversaw the domestic staff. After everything was up and running, Mariah decided to do some exploring on her first day off.

CHAPTER 10

Miss Mariah Weston

Charleston, SC 1879

SHE'D ALWAYS LOVED BOOKS, so she began with the Charleston Public Library, the oldest one in the country. Colored people weren't allowed in the library; there was a sign. Mariah studied the sign before entering the library. She hated pretending to be something she wasn't, but at that moment, she'd lie to her own mother to get through that door.

She had never seen so many books, and that musty smell was intoxicating. History and geography books occupied most of the shelf space, but there were hundreds of other books on everything from botanical drawings to agriculture displayed near the back of the first-floor exhibition area. Mariah wasn't particularly interested in books on agriculture, but her feet were killing her, and there were two large library tables there, so she sat at the empty one nearest the window. Moments later she was joined by a young man, wearing an expensive-looking brown suit, carrying a beaver skin hat and a stack of books too tall for him to see over.

"Sorry," he said to Mariah as he noisily deposited the books on the other end of the table. "They were heavier than I thought." Then he looked over at Mariah and his jaw dropped. He adjusted his collar as if to clear his throat and said, "Please forgive me, miss. I hope I didn't frighten you."

He hadn't frightened her, Mariah assured him, smiling "Why don't you sit down?"

"I will. My name's Wilson Hassell."

"Mariah Weston," Mariah said as coolly as if she had been born with the name.

Wilson Hassell, Mariah was soon to learn, was related to practically everyone on Charleston's social register including a number of Westons, but he said he was sure that if he had ever met Mariah, he would have remembered. After nervously running his fingers through his light brown hair, Wilson asked if Mariah was related to the Washington Westons of Beaufort or to the Paul Westons of Goose Creek.

"Neither one, I'm afraid. My people are from Virginia," she said, deciding at the last minute to say Virginia rather than Georgetown. "My papa planted tobacco, but with the war and all...."

"I know what you mean," Miss Weston. "My family was planters, too, but we lost practically everything during the war, so I'm studying to be a factor. I graduated from college last year, and now I work at the Cotton Exchange. In six months, I'll receive my license as a cotton broker and go into business with two of my older brothers."

Three hours flew by before Mariah realized that it was almost five o'clock. "Oh, Mr. Hassell, it's getting late; I had no idea. I really must be getting home." Getting home! What was she saying? If Mr. Hassell was the gentleman she thought he was, he'd offer to walk her there, and how could she let him know she lives in a brothel!

She had to think fast. "I've got to run," she said jumping to her feet. "I'll be here next Thursday afternoon. Goodbye Mr. Hassell."

Mariah tiptoed through the back door of the brothel headed for her room when she heard the familiar sound of Miss Stella's voice. "Oh, Mariah, darlin', I need to see you for a minute."

Now what? Mariah put on her sweetest smile and tapped on Miss Stella's door. It'd been weeks since they'd made the move to King Street, but entering Miss Stella's apartment with its silks and velvets, tassels and fringe was still jarring.

"Well, Missy, I just wanted to know how your day went," Miss Stella said in her motherly way. "Did you have fun? Did you meet anyone?"

"Sometimes I think you have eyes in the back of your head," Mariah said, maintaining her smile.

"I do have eyes in the back of my head, suga', but I also know that Patsy just saw you running down George Street with your skirts hiked up to your knees."

"I met a young man today, Miss Stella," Mariah admitted. "I met a wonderful young man at the library. His name is Wilson Hassell, and he's studying to be a cotton factor, and he was really, really nice."

"I'm thrilled," Miss Stella said.

"He's white."

"What does that have to do with anything? Excuse me. Do you think he went home to his mother and told her he met a nice white girl today?"

"No. It's just so hard. My people…."

"I know, darlin'," Miss Stella said, wrapping her arms around Mariah. "It'll get easier, I promise."

Mariah continued to meet Mr. Hassell on her days off. They talked about everything and nothing; they giggled and laughed and hid their faces behind books. They were happy, that is until Wilson said he thought it was time for them to meet each other's families.

Mariah must have turned six shades of purple because Wilson jumped to his feet trying to reassure her. "It won't be that bad, Mariah. My mother is so gentle and kind, you'll love her. My father is older than Mother and he's old school, but he has a kind heart even though he may not show it until he gets to know you better."

"What about your family, Mariah? When can I meet them?"

Mariah had been dreading this conversation for so long, and now that it was here, it was worse than she had even imagined. Here was this wonderful young man, and she could never, ever introduce him to either of her families. Mama, this is Mr. Hassell, the young man from Charleston I wrote you about. Mr. Hassell, this is my mother, Julia. Or, Miss Stella, this is Mr. Hassell the young man I've told you so much about. Mr. Hassell, this is my guardian and second mother, Stella Bright.

And while I'm at it, I'll tell you the rest of the story. I was born a slave just like my mother, and the reason I've been so evasive about where I live is because I live in the best bawdy house in Charleston. Mariah suddenly leapt to her feet and fled the library without looking back. Wilson was running after her, pleading for her to stop. She ran south on King Street until she was forced to stop to catch her breath, giving Wilson time to catch up.

"Did I offend you in some way?"

"You didn't do anything wrong. I just have a lot of things to sort out. You've been a perfect gentleman."

"Then let's walk for a while and see if your spirits improve," he said, offering his arm.

They walked south on King Street near the intersection of Beaufain Street and continued past Market Street. From there it was on to Princess and Fulton streets where they stopped every few minutes to peer into shop windows. In the next block was a row of small shops that included two dress shops and a secondhand furniture store, and at the end of the block was a leather goods store that was separated from the other shops by a small alleyway. As Mariah and Wilson made their way down the block, Mariah's black mood began to improve, and she tried to concentrate on the joys of being on the arm of a handsome young man. Then the unthinkable happened.

Just as they walked past the last dress shop, a young colored boy carrying a stack of hat boxes darted out of the alleyway and crashed into Mariah. The hat boxes flew in all directions, and Mariah landed on her backside in the middle of the sidewalk. Her petticoats were above her knees, and her bonnet was in her lap, but Mariah was far more embarrassed than hurt. She grabbed her shoes and with Wilson's help, got back up on her feet. The boy was staring at Mariah with eyes the size of charger plates, but his apology was drowned out by the insults hurled at him by Wilson.

"You idiot," Wilson began. "You stupid idiot; I should beat the hide off you. Now, get out of my sight!" The boy fled, leaving the hat boxes where they lay, and Wilson turned to Mariah. "I'm sorry, Mariah, but you know how worthless blacks are."

You know how worthless blacks are .... *You know how worthless blacks are* .... played over and over in Mariah's head. Then something rushed over her, and she saw red.

"Get away from me, Mr. Hassell," she said through clenched teeth. "Get away from me!" Her anger surprised Mariah as much as it surprised Wilson. She'd never raised her voice to anyone in her entire life, but then, she had never been as repulsed by anyone as she was at that moment by Wilson Hassell.

"Mariah, what happened?" Wilson replied. "Do you need a doctor?"

"No, you bastard!" Mariah said, fighting to regain her composure. "All I want you to do is to get your hands off of me and to walk away. Don't look back, and don't say another word."

"But...." he stammered.

"Go!" Mariah said. "Just go."

Wilson disappeared, and Mariah ran into the alleyway and threw up. Then she wiped her face with the hem of her dress and walked home. She could barely see her eyes were so swollen. She'd lost her bonnet, and the heel was missing from her left shoe. *Just let me get to my room unnoticed. Please, please, please!* she prayed.

But Miss Stella caught her tiptoeing down the hallway and rushed to see what had happened. "Mariah," Miss Stella cried. "What's wrong? Were you attacked? Your hair.... And there's vomit all over the front of your dress! What happened, Mariah? What happened?"

With that Mariah fell into Miss Stella's arms and sobbed. "I can't be like you; I can't pass for white, and I can't pretend it doesn't matter because it does. Wilson asked today to meet my family. I have two families that I love, but I can't introduce him to either one. He would never understand, Miss Stella. Wilson would never understand."

"Maybe it will just take some time, Mariah," Stella said.

"No, he's incapable of it," she added, choosing not to tell Stella the rest of the story.

"Well, it's alright, darlin'; everything will be alright," Stella said in her soothing way. "I see now that the path that was right for me wasn't the right one for you. Forgive me, Mariah. I just wanted the best for you because I love you. Now I see that you will have to find your own way."

As Massie, Rosa, and some of the other girls from upstairs clustered in the hallway nervously speculating about what had happened to Mariah, Stella and Pansy removed Mariah's torn clothing, washed her face, put her into a fresh cotton nightgown, and tucked her into bed like a little child.

Miss Stella shooed Pansy and the girls away and wedged herself into a small bedside chair next to Mariah's bed. She took Mariah's hand and did something she swore she would never do again — she cried for the first time since the day she left New Orleans.

Mariah woke up in the wee hours of the morning to see Stella slumped over in the chair next to her. Stella was snoring softly, and her carrot-colored hair looked like a nest caught in the wind. Her lip rouge was smudged; there were mascara stains down both cheeks, and her eyes were as puffy as Mariah's. Yesterday it had been Stella's turn to take care of Mariah; now it was Mariah's turn. Mariah could hear footsteps and the slamming of an occasional door, so she knew that some of the girls were still entertaining guests. That meant that Juniper and Patsy should still be up, so she grabbed her dressing gown and went to find them.

Back in Mariah's room, she and Juniper freed Stella from her chair, and the two of them rolled Stella onto Mariah's bed. Pansy removed Stella's beloved feather headpiece and shoes and covered Stella with a cotton coverlet.

"I hope Miss Stella's happy 'bout her sleeping arrangements when she wake up," Pansy said. "You know how fussy she is 'bout her beauty sleep."

"She'll be fine," Mariah said, noticing Stella's resemblance to a drawing she had recently seen of a sleeping Buddha. Then she bent down, kissed the forehead, and slipped out of the room.

The following afternoon, Miss Stella and Mariah sat down together on the piazza, overlooking the garden at the back of the house. Mariah was wearing a cotton shift but little else except for a pair of house shoes and cotton stockings rolled down to her knees. Miss Stella was still in the dressing gown she had slept in the night before and was in desperate need of a heavy-duty application of make-up (the theatrical kind of cosmetics from New York, of course). Both of the women were nursing hangovers, even though neither of them had had anything to drink.

"I'm sorry about yesterday," Miss Stella said as she adjusted the cold compress that was covering her burning eyes. "We really had a time of it, didn't we darlin,' but I've always said there's nothing like a good cry."

As the afternoon shadows lengthened, Mariah told Miss Stella the rest of the story. Then she said that she had decided to go back to the plantation, back to The Abbey.

"I won't be there forever," she promised after seeing the hurt look on Miss Stella's face. "I just need to go back where I don't have to pretend to be something that I'm not. I think if I'm there for a while, I can figure out where I should go from here. I don't know what the answers are, but I think that's where I'll find them."

CHAPTER II

A Letter from Bal-t-more

The Abbey Plantation 1879

TWO DAYS LATER, after countless hugs and tearstained kisses from Miss Stella and the girls, except Josie Russell who preferred to watch from a distance, Mariah boarded The Carolina Gal bound for Winyah Bay. From there she took the ferry over to the mainland and a small river boat that took her upriver to The Abbey. Mariah arrived exhausted but happy to be back on the plantation.

She had sent word to her family to expect her, but she wasn't sure if they had received the news until she spotted Daddy Sam and some of the little ones waving to her from the old landing.

Once she and her luggage were safely ashore, Daddy Sam told Mariah that she was in luck. Maum Harriet's old house was empty again because the elderly woman who had been living there had just moved in with her kin seeing as to how she was all stove up with arthritis.

Mariah could live in the cabin as long as she wanted to.

Mariah was delighted at the prospects of having her own place, and she moved her things into the cabin the very next day. Maum Harriet's affliction had drastically limited her housekeeping capabilities.

Everything in the cabin was covered in dust and soot, and the newspapers that Maum Harriet had glued to the walls so long ago were peeling so badly they looked like birch bark.

The cabin was sound, though, Daddy Sam assured her. "The rest will just take a little spit and polish to get it like you want it, Mariah," he said.

It took more than spit and polish, but Mariah didn't complain; she looked forward to scrubbing floors. It was a surefire tonic, and Miss Stella had just given her an absurd amount of money, so she didn't have to worry about figuring out a way to earn a living.

It took several days to get the cabin livable, but it was time well spent. Mariah gradually began to feel like her old self again and welcomed falling into her bed at night too tired to dream.

She had been right about returning to the plantation; this is where she needed to be.

Days turned into weeks, and weeks into months — six months, to be exact — when Mariah heard Joe Tom, the son of one of her neighbors, shouting her name as he sprinted down the lane toward her cabin.

"Miss Mariah! Miss Mariah!" he cried. "Here's a letter for you and the man who give it to me said it is utter important. It come all the way from *Bal-t-more, New York*."

Mariah smiled at Joe Tom's comment about Baltimore, New York, but after thanking him for the letter, she felt as if her feet were nailed to the porch.

She'd never received a letter from anyone other than Miss Stella, let alone one from Baltimore. It must be a mistake. Who would be sending her a letter from Baltimore?

Then she looked at the envelope and it was addressed to:

Miss Mariah Huger, daughter of Julia
The Abbey Plantation Waccamaw
All Saints' Parish, South Carolina

Who was Mariah Huger? Then Julia studied the return address:

Grayson Harris, Esquire
Harris and Comings Law Firm
132 Governor's Street
Baltimore, Maryland

"This letter is from a lawyer. It has to be a mistake," Mariah said as she spotted her mother running up the lane in a cloud of dust.

"Mama!" Mariah cried. "What's the matter?

"Don't run like that, you're going to hurt yourself!"

"I heard about the letter," Julia said as she came to a stop in front of Mariah. "I've got to talk to you before you open it.""Let's sit on the porch then, Mama," Mariah suggested.

"No," Julia said looking back at the crowd gathering in the lane. "We need to go inside." After Mariah closed the door, Julia placed her hands on Mariah's shoulders. Her touch was light and her hands were shaking.

"Mariah," she said, "I don't know anything about your letter, but I do know that it's your name that's on the envelope. Your real name is Mariah Huger; and your real daddy was Brooks Huger—Brooks Dunhill Huger from Baltimore, Mar-land."

"But Mama," Mariah said.

"Who...?"

"Stop, Mariah," Julia said putting her finger to her lips. "Let me tell you everything before I lose my courage. Your papa was twenty-years-old when I met him," Julia began. "It was at Laurel Hill Plantation. Laurel Hill's mistress was Miss Huger, one of Miss Weston's cousins, and she visited The Abbey every now and then.

"One day she asked Miss Weston if she could borrow one of The Abbey's seamstresses to work on her daughter's wedding dress. 'I need someone who's 'specially good at embroidery', she said, so the mistress picked me."

"Mama," Mariah pleaded. "I don't want to hear a story about a wedding dress. I want to hear about my father."

"I'm getting to that part," Julia promised. "I just had to explain why I was at Laurel Hill. Now, don't get to crying again or I'll never be able to tell you.

"So, I'd been there about a week," Julia said picking up on her story. "One morning I rounded off a corner near the upstairs sewing room and slammed straight into your papa. He was the nephew of Master Huger visiting from Mar-land. He was tall with fine hands with light brown hair pulled back from his face, and I'd been staring at him from a distance ever since I got to the plantation.

"I'd never seen a man like that, so when I got the chance to stare at him up close, I just kept on staring. Then I got all scared that he would beat me for running into him, but he was real nice, instead. He apologized for running into me and even helped me off the floor.

"The next day he followed me around, teasin' and tauntin' until I agreed to meet him after supper in the master's tack room. I knew not to go, Mariah. Miss Lillian raised me not to do such things, but I went anyway and that's when we fell in love. I know it sounds impossible that a boy from a powerful family—a white boy—could fall in love with a no-account person like me, but he did.

"He said slavery would end soon, and that I was as good as anybody else, and that someday we could be together out in the open. He was just a boy and I knew better, but I wanted to believe him.

"We were together one day shy of six weeks when we got caught and I was sent back to The Abbey. I was goin' to tell Brooks something real important that day, Mariah, but I didn't get a chance. I didn't get a chance to tell him about you," Julia said falling to her knees.

Mariah knelt beside her mother and wrapped her in her arms. Julia didn't respond, other than to continue to sob, but she didn't need to. Mariah finally knew the truth. After a time Julia regained her composure, at least enough to enable her to get up off the floor, and then she slipped into Maum Harriet's rocking chair next to the hearth.

Taking a seat beside her on the floor, Mariah slowly opened the seal on the back of the envelope.

Dear Miss Huger, the letter began, *My firm represents your late father, Brooks Dunhill Huger in the matter that concerns you.*

"Mariah," Mamma interjected. "Does that mean he's dead?"

"Yes, Mama," Mariah replied looking up at her mother's tearstained face. "It means that he has died."

After a time, Mariah continued on with the letter:

Enclosed you will find a letter from Mr. Huger addressed to you along with a copy of a bank draft drawn in your name which represents your portion of your father's estate. The actual funds are currently held in trust at the Bank of Baltimore. I suggest that you hire counsel in this matter at once.

If I can be of further assistance, do not hesitate to contact me.
Grayson Harris, Esq.

"Mama," Mariah said softly. "I don't understand."

"Read the letter," Julia said firmly. "Read the letter from your papa."

So Mariah placed Mr. Harris's letter in her lap and opened the enclosed letter that was from her father. Before she could read it, however, the copy of the bank draft that Mr. Harris had referred to glided out between the pages of the letter and landed face-up beneath Mama's rocking chair.

Mariah reached down to retrieve it and gasped. "Mama, the bank draft is for $175,000 (today's equivalent of $5.2M). That's more money than God has! That's the most money in the whole world!"

Now it was Julia's turn to do the soothing. "Mariah, we have to read the letter," Julia said. "We'll understand this better after we read the letter."

Dear Mariah,

I have instructed my attorney to send this letter to you following my death. I have been extremely ill these last months and death will offer me relief from my pain, so do not mourn.

When Julia heard Brooks' words, she placed her face in her hands and cried softly, but when Mariah stopped reading the letter, Julia encouraged her to continue.

Every word from Brooks was precious.

I am sorry that I never got to see you, but I want you to know that I have loved you since the day you were born.

I learned about your birth from Vashti, your mother's friend at Laurel Hill. Vashti told me that she received a note from your mother the day after you were born. I think the man who delivered your mother's message was a servant from The Abbey.

"It was Papa Gilmore," Julia said. "I'd almost forgotten. The day after you were born, I asked to see him in private, and I asked him to deliver a small note to Vashti at Laurel Hill.

"In it I told her about your birth and asked if she would get the message to Brooks. I think a part of me believed that he'd come rescue me and take me back to his home in Mar-land. It didn't happen, of course. So, I had to accept things the way they was.

"I didn't even know until now that the note got there because Papa Gilmore and I never talked on it again."

After a moment, Mariah continued with the letter.

I hope your mother is still alive and well. She was extremely circumspect when I first met her—for good reason, of course. We were so young, but I loved her when you were conceived, and a part of me will always love her. How sorry I am that circumstances kept us apart.

I have always regretted that I didn't fight to keep her, but I was young and I did what I was told.

I know you are extremely surprised to be receiving this inheritance, but it is important to me that you have the advantages that were denied your mother.

There are no strings attached to this money. Do whatever you want to with it. All I ask is that you make your mother proud.

Your loving father, Brooks Dunhill Huger

Your loving father... Mariah repeated those words to herself. Then she carefully folded the letter and placed it back into the envelope.

"Mama," she said, "I've dreamed of this so many times. Not about the money, but about having a father who cared about me. He was there all the time and I never knew."

"I know, Mariah," Mama said between her tears. "So many times over the years I almost talked myself into believin' that Brooks never really existed—almost as if I had just dreamed him up.

"Then I'd look at you and see his beautiful face staring back at me and I'd be reminded that he was real. I've been missing him so much over the years... Now I know he missed me, too. Are you alright?" Mama said, reclaiming her role as Mariah's mother.

"I'll be alright," Mama," Mariah replied. "I just have a lot to think about. How about we work on it together?" she said. Then she placed a kiss on her mother's cheek and prepared to walk next door to her own cabin.

As she passed the window, however, she realized that half the population of the quarter was standing in a large semicircle just beyond the edge of the porch. "Mama, look!" Mariah exclaimed. "Everybody's out in the yard. What are we going to do?"

Just then, Daddy Sam stepped into the room casting an enormous shadow on the fireplace wall. He had rushed home so quickly after hearing about Mariah's letter that he still had his hoe in his hand.

He figured it was bad news, so after pausing to prop the hoe against the door frame, he stepped back into the cabin and said in his gentle way: "Everything's gonna be just fine, Mariah. Now, Mama, don't you worry about this."

Then he returned to the porch and addressed the crowd. "Go on home, now," he said. "Ain't nothing going on here to be worried about." The crowd grudgingly dispersed knowing that Daddy Sam wasn't a man to mince words. If he said "ain't nothing going on" he really meant, "ain't nothing going on that's any of your business."

So they left, but they didn't like being turned away. Mariah's letter was the most exciting news to hit The Abbey since 'mancipation; and Lord knows, the People could use some excitement.

Back inside, Daddy Sam took Mama's hand and then he turned toward Mariah. "I don't know what happen here," he said, "but if you want to talk about it, we can do that. If you don't want to talk, we can do that, too."

After receiving an almost undetectable affirming nod from her mother, Mariah sat back down on the floor next to her mother's chair and reread her father's letter in a slow, almost inaudible voice.

Then she folded the letter much as she had after reading it the first time and stared at the floor waiting for Daddy Sam to speak. Mariah half-expected him to curse or to beat his hands against the wall, or to even leave the room after hearing about Mama's love affair, but he did nothing of the kind.

"Mariah," he said, "I'm happy that you had a papa who loved you. A young girl needs that. I'm just sorry that it was so late a' coming. As for you, Julia, sounds like you chose a fine young man to be Mariah's papa. Just don't be forgetting that I love you, too."

"I love you too, Sam," Julia said reaching out for his rough, scarred hand. Mariah felt awkward witnessing such an intimate moment, so she slipped out the door as inconspicuously as she could without saying another word.

Once inside her own cabin, she drew the curtains, curled up on her bed, and cried until she was out of tears. The following day she sat down with Daddy Sam and Mama to talk about what she should do next, and it didn't take long before they agreed that Mariah should return to Charleston, and contact Miss Stella's attorney, Charles Mayeaux.

"I never thought nobody in my family was ever gonna need a lawyer," Daddy Sam said. "I surely do feel gratitude for Miss Stella. I surely do."

CHAPTER 12

One Hundred and Seventy-Five Thousand Dollars

Charleston, SC 1879

MARIAH ARRIVED BACK in Charleston the following week to find Juniper waiting for her on the wharf. "How was your travels, Miss Mariah?" he asked. "We sure did miss you back at Miss Stella's. Seems like you've been gone a year."

After loading Mariah's belongings into the back of the wagon, Juniper helped Mariah climb aboard, and then he joined her, spit a stream of tobacco juice onto the street over his left shoulder and picked up the reins.

"Ol' Nag," he shouted to his mule. "Let's get a' goin'. Let's be a' gettin' home."

How wonderful it was to be back in Charleston. Had it been six months? Mariah thought so. Juniper's rickety wagon came to a stop near the street entrance to Miss Stella's, and Mariah spotted Miss Stella in all her rotund glory waving her arms and shouting "Hallelujah, my baby's home."

She was surrounded by Josie, Maud, Massie and Isadora. Josie, as usual, had a small cigar perched between her lips, and all four of the women were causing a spectacle because of the way the afternoon sun backlit their flimsy dressing gowns, but Mariah was touched to see them there; after all, they hadn't been up very long. It was hours yet, before the evening's guests would arrive.

Mariah jumped down from the wagon without waiting for Juniper to assist her, and Juniper scolded her: "You is gonna break something doing that. Now don't you be getting ol' Juniper in trouble with Missy Stella."

Mariah was too happy to worry about offending Juniper. All she wanted to do was hug Miss Stella. That evening Miss Stella let the brothel run itself as she and Mariah talked over the incredible events that had caused Mariah's sudden return to Charleston.

After reading the letters from the attorney and her father, Mariah looked up at Miss Stella and asked, "What do I do, now?"

"Well, darlin'," she began, "I agree that the first thing to do is to see Mr. Mayeaux. One hundred and seventy-five thousand dollars, that's a piss pot full of money. I bought out Madame Legrand—lock, stock and barrel—for $2800 cash. So, you can only imagine what you could do with $175,000.

"Let's contact Mr. Mayeaux first-thing tomorrow morning," she said, "And in the mean time Mariah, don't mention any of this to anyone. Charleston's famous for its gentility, but it's infamous for its share of scalawags. I love the girls and all, but you can never be sure as to who's gonna walk through my door. Even an honest man could be tempted by $175,000."

The next day, Mariah and Charles Mayeaux had their first of many meetings. It took place in Miss Stella's private parlor and Mariah had insisted that Miss Stella be present. "I'm not going to meet with that man or any other man without you," Mariah told Miss Stella. "So don't try to talk me out of it."

Mr. Mayeaux arrived promptly at one o'clock and was politely ushered into Miss Stella's parlor by Pansy. Mayeaux had no idea why he had been summoned. The message he had received that morning, which had been hand-delivered by Juniper, only stated that it was urgent that he meet with Mariah and Miss Stella as soon as possible.

Spurred on by the unusual nature of the request, Mayeaux had hurriedly rearranged his schedule, and made the short carriage ride to

Miss Stella's. Accustomed to seeing Miss Stella decked out in garish lace-trimmed costumes, Charles Mayeaux was surprised to find her soberly dressed in a simple dark gray day dress.

Miss Weston was similarly dressed in a gray and white striped day dress, although Mayeaux observed that it did little to distract from her youthful beauty.

Once Mr. Mayeaux was seated, Mariah explained that she had just received a letter from an attorney in Baltimore, and that she wanted him to read it, but when those words were out of her mouth, she knew she was simply trying to put off the inevitable. She had to tell him everything.

"That's not exactly true, Mr. Mayeaux, at least it's not the whole truth," she said, squeezing Miss Stella's dimpled hand for support. "There's something else that you need to know before you read the letter.

"To begin with, my real name isn't Mariah Weston; it's Mariah Huger. I was born on a plantation on the Waccamaw River. I wasn't born in the big house, though, I was born in the quarter.

"My mother was a slave, who was conceived during the rape of my grandmother by the plantation overseer. My father was Brooks Dunhill Huger—yes, one of THE Charleston Hugers, Mr. Mayeaux," she said, responding to the look of surprise on Mayeaux's face.

"My father and my grandfather were both white," she said, turning her gaze to the other side of the room, "but my mother was enslaved, which, of course, means that I was born enslaved." Looking back at the attorney, Mariah paused and said, "I wanted you to know the whole story because you may not wish to represent me anymore."

Even though he was stunned by Mariah's disclosure, Charles Mayeaux couldn't help but respect the young woman seated in front of him. In post-war South Carolina, one drop of Negro blood legally constituted nonwhite status. Mariah had shown a great deal of courage by telling him her story.

He'd never had any dealings with members of Charleston's nonwhite society, nor had any of the other partners in his law firm. Taking on a mixed-race client could have enormous ramifications within the legal community and he couldn't help but remind himself that he had already been criticized for managing the affairs of the owner of a brothel.

There was a possibility that this situation could damage his reputation beyond repair and severely hurt his business. The smart move was to turn his back and walk out the door, but Mariah Huger had demonstrated such courage.

Besides, it wouldn't cost anything to hear her out. If she was planning to ask him to represent her in some kind of legal claim against the Hugers, he would flatly refuse. He couldn't be sure what she was up to, so he decided to stay, at least for the moment.

"Continue, Miss Huger," he said after an awkward pause. "I'll help you if I can."

Mariah was so certain that Mr. Mayeaux would remove himself from her case that she stammered a bit before reestablishing her train of thought.

"The specific reason I asked you here," she finally managed to say, "is because a few days ago I learned that I have inherited a great deal of money from my father. I won't trouble you with the details, unless you're sure you wish to stay on."

A great deal of money, now this is getting interesting, Mayeaux said to himself. "Go ahead, Miss Huger, I'm here to help you."

"Then I'll begin by reading the letter from the attorney in Baltimore, unless you'd rather read it, yourself," Mariah said.

"I would rather read it, myself, if you don't mind," Mayeaux said, taking the letter from Mariah's outstretched hand. After reading the letter, Mayeaux told Mariah and Miss Stella that during his career he had had many dealings with Grayson Harris' firm and that it was considered to be one of the finest in Baltimore.

Then he asked to read the letter from Mariah's father. Just as it had with Mariah, the copy of the bank draft that accompanied Brooks Dunhill Huger's letter, spilled out onto the floor when Mr. Mayeaux opened the letter. In the process of retrieving it he saw the amount of the draft.

"Good lord!" he said out of character. "This is an enormous amount of money, Miss Huger. It is far more than I had expected."

Mariah and Miss Stella sat quietly while Mr. Mayeaux read and reread Brooks Huger's letter. Then he folded the letter, handed it back to Mariah, and apologized for the necessity of having to read such a personal letter.

"I'll look into the case for you, Miss Huger," Mayeaux said after some thought. "Whatever I do must be done very quietly, though. It shouldn't be too difficult to check into the inheritance laws both here and in Maryland," he said, "but I have enormous concerns about the law here in South Carolina.

"According to South Carolina law," he explained, "a child born of a white father and a Negro mother may inherit from the father, but only if the father continued to live with the mother after the birth of the child.

"In your situation, of course, that didn't happen. And another factor is that this inheritance isn't coming from your father's will, it is coming directly from him. If this was taking place in South Carolina, we would be in trouble. But since your father lived in Maryland, I think we'll be alright. Besides, Mr. Harris's letter certainly suggests that it is quite legal.

"My main concern is that your father's legal heirs could choose to contest this bequeath—they certainly could here in South Carolina. The issues associated with race can be complicated," he emphasized. "I'll do what I can, but I am unwilling to argue this one out in a South Carolina court.

"You couldn't win, and my standing within the legal community would be destroyed. This is high-risk poker, Miss Huger." He'd get back to her soon, he said. Then he climbed aboard his carriage to make the return trip to his office.

"Whew! I'm glad that's over," Miss Stella said, kicking off her shoes. "I've never sat still that long in my life. The hardest part was having to keep quiet. Did you notice that I never uttered a single word?"

"The hardest part for me was telling Mr. Mayeaux the whole story," Mariah admitted. "I didn't realize until we sat down together that I would need to explain everything before we read the letters. I've never said those things to anyone, let alone to an attorney. I was afraid he'd leave when he learned the truth about me, and I wouldn't have blamed him if he had," she added.

"I think he came close to leaving, but was too much of gentleman to go through with it. I thought he might leave, too," Miss Stella said,

"But he ain't one to turn tail, Mariah. Like you said, he's a gentleman. Besides, he probably figures there's some money in it for him. Money talks, you know."

Mariah and Miss Stella waited six long weeks before Mr. Mayeaux finally sent a messenger to Miss Stella's house requesting a second meeting. "He must have news," Mariah said as she let out her breath and rolled her eyes towards the heavens.

Mr. Mayeaux wasted no time sharing his good news once he was ushered into Miss Stella's parlor. "Mariah, I have just received confirmation that you are indeed the legal heir to the estate left to you by your father, and that his legal heirs have no claim against you. As I said before, it's a good thing that this was issued in Maryland. We would have had problems if it hadn't been."

Mariah grabbed Miss Stella's hand and gasped. "Think what good we can do with this money," she squealed. Then she admitted to the lawyer that she didn't know what to do with the money yet, but she wanted to do something important with it.

"Will you help me?"

"Of course, Miss Huger, but first I want you to know everything I have learned." After shuffling through a large stack of papers, he found the documents he was looking for and handed them to Mariah.

"This will tell you more about your father's life after he returned to his home in Baltimore, but if you like, I can summarize it for you now." Mariah wanted him to continue, so Mr. Mayeaux explained that after returning to Baltimore, Mariah's father finished his formal education at Princeton University and apprenticed with a large law firm in New York City.

"There he met and later married the daughter of one of the city's most influential families. Your father and his wife had three sons. Two live in Philadelphia and the other lives in Sussex, England," Mr. Mayeaux added.

"You were his only daughter, but you weren't mentioned in the will, so my guess is that they don't know anything about you. I'd urge you to keep it that way."

"Of course," Mariah said in a whisper.

CHAPTER 13

A Schoolhouse for Miss Hattie

Charleston, SC 1879

MARIAH AND MR. MAYEAUX met a number of times during the next several weeks. The first thing on their agenda was to arrange to move Mariah's inheritance from her father's bank in Baltimore to a local bank in Charleston.

Once that had happened, Mariah needed to decide what to do with it. She had a short list. She wanted to build her mother and Daddy Sam a place of their own—a farm with a two-story farmhouse that had a wrap-around porch and real glass panes in all the windows.

Mariah's other wish was to build Miss Hattie a schoolhouse complete with desks and blackboards and a school bell that could be heard for miles around.

Even though Miss Hattie had started her school fourteen years earlier, her only classroom was still the front porch of her house. The porch had been expanded a time or two—Daddy Sam had seen to that—but it still wasn't a proper place for learning.

The last time Mariah visited The Abbey, she spent time with Miss Hattie, catching up on all the news. It was about three o'clock in the afternoon, and school was out for the day, so Mariah walked to Miss Hattie's house hoping to see her in her garden.

Mariah knew that she must follow the unwritten rule; Miss Hattie's private time was to be respected. Since the death of her parents some years back, Hattie had lived alone. When she was tending her garden, it was fine to stop and chat; but when she was inside her house, no one was to knock on her door unless it was urgent.

The dilemma for the People was that Hattie was also the local seer (although she refused to call herself such), and her gift of predicting the weather, interpreting dreams and undoing spells, was as important to most the People as her ability to teach their children to read and write.

So it remained a quandary as to when to disturb her, and when to leave things to providence. The last person to disturb Miss Hattie unnecessarily was bitten by a six-foot copperhead on his way home. Of course, no one would come right out and credit Miss Hattie with the unfortunate incident, but it couldn't be disproved, either.

Fortunately for Mariah, Miss Hattie was standing just inside the gate to her house as if she had just been waiting for Mariah to stop by.

"Miss Hattie," Mariah said, waving. "I just wanted to say hello."

"Come on in Mariah," Miss Hattie said cheerfully.

"Come sit on the porch." As Mariah stepped onto the porch and heard the familiar slam of the screen door, she automatically looked to her right, and there it was—the little red chair.

"Oh, Miss Hattie," she said, "I'm so glad to see the little chair. Every time I sat in it, I felt so important. Do you still use it?"

"For special occasions. The child who wins the weekly spelling competition gets to sit in it. You'd be surprised how their test scores improved when I implemented that rule. I should have done it years ago, but it still would have been your chair, Mariah. You were the best student I ever had."

Back in Miss Stella's parlor, Mariah asked what Mr. Mayeaux thought about the possibility of building a schoolhouse.

"Do you think we could build a building that was large enough to have a school on the ground level, and Miss Hattie's living quarters on the second floor? I just thought it would be nice if she only had to walk a few steps to get to her classroom. Do you think it could be done?"

"I'll certainly try."

To Mariah's surprise, buying the land for her two building projects turned out to be more challenging than getting the actual buildings built. Since Miss Hattie, Mama and Daddy Sam had insisted upon remaining at The Abbey, Mr. Mayeaux had to find not one, but two suitable building lots on the grounds of the original plantation.

The lot for the school had to be located within reasonable walking distance for Miss Hattie's students, and the other lot had to be large enough to accommodate a small farm.

God had his stamp on this one. Only months before Mr. Mayeaux's inquiry, a portion of the old plantation had been put up for sale. Mr. Mayeaux was able to buy a two-acre lot for the school, and a thirty-acre parcel for the farm.

The contractor on the farmhouse project started hollering and running through the yard one day. His workers tackled him and tried to hold him down, because they thought he was having a fit.

He was fine, he said, but it was a happy day. He'd found something important. He'd found the stonework of the original plantation house. That proved that the big house had stood on that exact same spot.

Did Miss Weston want the contractor to remove the foundations, or to build on top of them? Build on top of them, Mariah said, and so it was done.

After the house was completed, Mama and Daddy Sam gave a party out on the lawn. Freedom had come to the plantation only fifteen years earlier, and now two of The Abbey's former slaves owned a new house on the very spot that the big house had once stood.

"It seems fittin' somehow, don't it?" Daddy Sam said to Julia.

"Praise Jesus," she replied.

Opening onto King's Highway and less than thirty feet from the original entrance into The Abbey, the schoolhouse was the size of a country church, with whitewashed clapboard siding and lancet windows.

A matching pair of doors dominated the front of the building making it appear especially grand from the road, and the whole thing was topped off with a shiny tin roof and copper-clad downspouts.

A throng of well-wishers including Mariah and her parents, showed up for the dedication. It was springtime, so the women and girls gathered there were all wearing their white First Sunday outfits, including Mariah and Miss Hattie.

Mariah laughed when one of the women exclaimed that it looked like "a swarm of butterflies had done gathered 'round." As for playing the role of benefactor, Mariah dreaded being called upon to give a speech, but Daddy Sam assured her later that she had handled it with the "grace of the Lord, Himself."

CHAPTER 14

Logan Street

Charleston, SC 1880

AFTER RETURNING TO CHARLESTON, Mariah worked on Miss Stella's books. Miss Stella was a woman of many talents, but bookkeeping wasn't one of them. Mariah's bookkeeping was meticulous.

At a glance she could tell Miss Stella exactly how many bed sheets they had on hand, what they paid for food last month and how many customers each of the girls had entertained last year. Under Miss Stella's supervision, nothing added up correctly, and there was hen scratching in the margins.

Mariah also had to get caught up on the latest news. Maud and Rosa had left the brothel together headed for California hoping to find husbands. Josie Russell had taken up with a tavern owner on East Bay Street and Massie had married one of her best customers, a rosy-cheeked butcher. Other girls took their places, of course, but it wasn't the same.

Once Mariah finally had the account books in a semblance of order, she decided that it was time to buy herself a house. It had to be within easy walking distance of the brothel, and in a mix-race neighborhood.

She wasn't going to lie anymore. Better to start out in a mixed-race neighborhood than to be run out of an all-white one.

She expected it would drag on for months, but she found the perfect house in less than a week. The traditional two-story house was on Logan Street in the heart of Charleston's fashionable new mulatto district.

A Charleston single house, the structure was designed so that each room in the house had a wall of windows to take full advantage of the breezes coming in off of the ocean. The result was a long, narrow structure that sat lengthwise on the lot. Entry from the street was through a door at the end of a narrow piazza that ran the length of the house.

The front door to the house was located near the center of the piazza. Pale green clapboard with cream-colored shutters, the house had been advertised in the paper for $1385 and even though Mr. Mayeaux assured Mariah that it was a fair price, Mariah had insisted on negotiating. She ended up buying the house alone with most of its contents for $1215.

Mariah had grown up in a two-room cabin with newspaper on the walls and rough-sawn planks for flooring. There were no screens or panes of glass in the windows, only wooden shutters to trap in the smoke and keep out the cold. At night, alligators helped themselves to the odd chicken or duck roosting beneath the cabin, and the fireplace offered the only source of light.

Now, Mariah found herself living alone in a house with carpets on the floor and a sturdy set of stairs, a second-story sleeping porch, two fireplaces and three brass beds with chintz dust ruffles, but best of all, an indoor toilet and a claw foot bathtub with its own cast iron water pump.

She had to add boiling water from the stove, but it was beyond her dreams.

She cried herself to sleep the first night, not from loneliness, but from guilt. "I don't deserve this," Mariah said to Miss Stella the following afternoon. "I didn't do anything to deserve the money other than to be born."

"Mariah, it doesn't matter how you got the money, it only matters what you do with it from here on out," Miss Stella said.

"I ain't a religious woman. Why, the Lord'll probably have me dragged outta heaven by my hair, but I do know that He does things on His own schedule. You've just got to give it some time.

"And while we're on the subject, I might as well point out to you that you ain't a girl any more. You are twenty-two years old and what you need more than anything is a man. You need to find yourself a husband. And while you're looking, I recommend you stick to good looking ones with big muscles and full heads of hair."

"Miss Stella!" Mariah blushed. "Are you trying to get me married off?"

"No, I'm not," Stella replied. "I'm trying to find you a good-looking man who can teach you wonderful things and make you happy, but I know you. You won't do it without a wedding ring on your finger, so let's go out and find you a husband."

"Miss Stella," I love you, but you make me crazy," Mariah fired back.

"I came here today worried about what to do with my life, and your advice is to jump into bed with the first hairy man I meet." Then she giggled. "I'll think about it, I promise; just promise me that you won't wear red shoes to my wedding."

"I promise," Miss Stella said. "I'll even let you pick them out for me, providing of course, that they have bows on them. You know how much I like bows."

"I know, Miss Stella," Mariah replied. "I know."

I Met a Man

Charleston, SC 1880

A FEW DAYS LATER Miss Stella told Mariah that she had asked around and learned that only a few of the new mixed-race elite attended Charleston's traditional black churches.

Instead, they tended to either be Presbyterians or Episcopalians. So the following Sunday, she talked Mariah into putting on her most conservative dress and walking the eight blocks or so to St. Mark's Protestant Episcopal Church on the corner of Tucker and Warren Streets.

Mariah had never attended any church other than St. Mary back on the plantation, and was one step away from being sick at her stomach at the prospects of showing up at a strange church, especially unescorted, but she kept reminding herself that the only people she knew in the entire city were bawdies, the owner of a brothel, a cook, two parlor maids, Juniper and an aristocratic white lawyer.

If she wanted to make a quiet entrance at St. Mark's it wasn't going to happen with anyone she knew, she had to risk going alone. She slipped into the sanctuary as quietly as possible and took a seat near the back.

Reluctant at first to even raise her eyes above the back of the pew in front of her, Mariah spent the next few minutes making a big fuss out of adjusting her skirt, but she knew she couldn't keep that up forever, so she took a deep breath and tilted her chin upward.

She was almost brought to tears. The interior of the church was nothing short of magnificence. Mariah had seen stained glass windows before; St. Mary had three of them, but they weren't nearly as large or as grand as these.

And the nave, why it must have been three or four times longer than the one at St. Mary. The colors of the walls were similar, though — pale aqua green and white — but St. Mark's also had gilded corbels and niches, and richly carved moldings that traversed the arched ceilings at every imaginable angle.

Mariah was so intent upon studying her surroundings that she didn't notice the commotion going on beside her until she heard a small voice asking, "Is this seat taken?" She looked down to discover a young girl, perhaps seven or eight, smiling back at her from beneath a bonnet wrapped in purple grosgrain ribbon.

"No, it's not taken. You're welcome to sit there," Mariah managed to reply.

"Thank you," the child said. "My name's Grace Cutler and I'm saving the rest of the pew for my family. They sent me ahead to find good seats. Are you waiting for your family?"

"No, I'm all alone, today" Mariah replied. "As a matter of fact, this is my first visit here. The church is beautiful, isn't it."

"Yes, Papa says it's just as pretty as St. Michael's and St. Philip's where the white people go to church," Grace said, repositioning her bonnet and adjusting the petticoats beneath her violet-colored skirt. "By the way, what's your name?"

"Oh, my name is Mariah, Mariah Huger," Mariah replied, taking note of Grace's delicate profile and light skin. Then she looked away. It was all so easy for Miss Stella, but Mariah was uncomfortable with the notion of skin color and race and mulattoes and quadroons... At The Abbey you were either one of the People or you weren't. There were no in-betweens.

Mariah may have grown up with green eyes and white skin, but she never doubted who she was. Now she was being forced to face it head on. Lord, give me strength.

Grace's family arrived in full force—fourteen in all, if Mariah had counted correctly. There appeared to be aunts and uncles, cousins and grandparents all descending on the pew in mass.

"I told you there were a lot of us," Grace leaned over and whispered.

"Which ones are your parents?" Mariah whispered back.

"My mama's dead," Grace replied. "But that's my papa over there with Granny. His name is William, William Cutler."

William looked over to check on Grace and was surprised to see her speaking to a beautiful young woman, who he had never seen before. Mariah could feel his eyes on her, and suddenly she turned her head, zeroed in on William, and stared back at him as bold as you please. It only lasted a moment, but it was long enough.

Mariah would have left at that moment if her legs hadn't turned to rubber, and the service hadn't already begun. So, she sat back in her seat and tried to concentrate on the words of the choir and the unfamiliar, yet comforting customs observed by the congregation.

As the service finally came to a close, Mariah was about to make her exit when Grace grabbed her hand and insisted that she meet her family. "It'll only take a minute, Miss Mariah. You'll like them, I promise."

Mariah was trying to make her excuses when she realized that the man with rippling muscles and a full head of hair was standing right in front of her. She was going to die! But she didn't of course. She rose to her feet and extended her gloved hand as if she had practiced it a thousand times.

"Miss Huger," William said.

"I realize we have just met and it is terribly forward of me to ask, but the family is planning a picnic in the park, and we'd be very pleased to have you join us. It would mean a great deal to Grace and I promise to get you home safely."

Mariah started to say no, not because she didn't want to go, but because it might not look right. After all it was bad enough that she had attended church without an escort, but when she opened her mouth to say no, it came out as a resounding yes.

A smile came over William's face and they were on their way.

The family set up their picnic on the southwest corner of Marion Park, the portion of the park obviously frequented by Charleston's mix-race population.

Not again! Mariah paused to remind herself how much things had changed during her short lifetime, and she whispered a prayer of thanks. She couldn't help laughing when she looked around to see that everyone in William's family was carrying a picnic basket.

She had never seen so much food in her life: ham and biscuits, fried chicken, pork ribs, speckled butter beans, coleslaw, macaroni salad, bread and butter pickles, canned peaches, cherry cobbler, sweet potato pie and three kinds of cake including a lemon pound cake, an angel food cake and cake that Mariah had never seen before called a Lady Baltimore.

Baltimore. It was a sign from God!

Mariah didn't know exactly when it happened, but she fell in love that afternoon.

Maybe it was when William told her about his wife who had died in childbirth, or the way he laughed after dropping coleslaw on his shoe; or it might have been when he allowed Grace to run barefoot despite his mother's insistence that it wasn't proper.

As William walked Mariah home, he told her that he owned a funeral parlor called Cutler Undertakers. Mariah had to admit that she didn't even know what a funeral parlor was, so he explained it all to her.

For many years now, he said, the affluent white population of Charleston had hired professional undertakers to bury their dead, instead of doing it themselves as it had been done in the past.

During the past ten years, the mixed-race population of Charleston began to attain their own level of affluence, and they wanted the same kind of professional service, but the white funeral parlors refused to take them, so William started his own company.

"Now, I own three funeral parlors, "William explained. "I run the largest one and my brothers run the other two."

Mariah had already told William every other detail of her life, but she didn't elaborate on her inheritance, other than to say it had enabled her to buy a house.

She would save that for another day, a day when lightning bolts didn't shoot through her body every time she felt William's gaze and her hands didn't tremble with his slightest touch. Saying goodbye was almost painful, but had to be done because the family was waiting for William back in the park.

"May I see you again, Miss Huger?" William said with his face less than three inches from her ear.

"Yes," Mr. Cutler, "I would love to," Mariah replied as she fumbled for the doorknob to her front door. "But when?"

"Tomorrow," William said as he turned to walk away. "I'll be here at six."

When Mariah was sure that William had had plenty of time to clear the block, she opened the door, raced out into the street and sprinted all the way to the brothel.

"Miss Stella! Miss Stella!" she cried taking the stairs leading up to the brothel two at a time. Miss Stella was inventorying the pantry at the time, but she could hear Mariah's cries as if they had come from the next room.

"Mariah!" she cried. "What's the matter? Are you alright? You like to scared me to death!"

"Oh, Miss Stella," Mariah gasped as she rushed through the door and attempted to catch her breath. "I just had to tell you...."

"Tell me what?" Miss Stella asked as she put her arms around Mariah and led her to a chair in the kitchen.

"I met a man — a big strong man with a full head of hair and he is gorgeous!" Mariah shouted. "I know I said the same thing about Wilson Hassell, but he couldn't compare to Mr. Cutler. His name is William, William Cutler and he's beautiful and wonderful and he's not a boy, he's a man. Can you fall in love with someone the first time you meet him, Miss Stella? Does it make you feel all hot inside like you've swallowed hot coals, except it doesn't burn, it just feels wonderful? Oh, and can it make you feel tingly and sweaty and can it make your ears ring?"

"I don't know about making your ears ring," Miss Stella said as she planted a kiss on Mariah's cheek, "but it can sure warm up your innards. Oh, and I can assure you that you can fall in love the moment you meet someone; I've done it lots of times. So, tell me more about him," Miss Stella said. "Where did you meet him, tell me you met him at a respectable place."

"Of course, I did," Mariah replied. "Where do you think I met him? In the brothel!"

"No, sweetheart, I don't think you met him here. It's just that I want everything to be as perfect as you think it is," Miss Stella said.

"I want him to be perfect."

"Well, he is," Mariah said, "and I met him at St. Mark's; I met him at church. His name is William. Did I tell you that already? Anyway, he has a daughter named Grace, and he's wonderful."

"We've already established that he's wonderful, Mariah, so you don't have to tell me that part anymore, but if he has a daughter, it stands to reason that he could also have a wife. How about it, Mariah, is he married?"

"He was married, but she died two years ago," Mariah replied.

"So, what does he do for a living?" Miss Stella then asked.

"He owns an under-something parlor," Mariah said trying to remember Williams's exact words.

"He does funerals."

"It's undertaker, not under-something, Mariah," Miss Stella interrupted. "Oh, that's where I've heard that name. That's the name of the family that came here as freed-blacks a couple of generations ago. They're from the islands, I think, and they've made a lot of money, here. They're one of the most respected mulatto families in the city, but it doesn't change the fact that he's an undertaker! Couldn't you have picked someone who doesn't make his living touching dead bodies, Mariah!"

"I don't care what he does for a living," Mariah replied. "He's wonderful just the way he is, and he wants to see me again tomorrow. "I don't know where he planning to take me or what he's planning to do, and I don't care.

"I've been thinking about what you said about having to have a wedding ring on my finger, first. I'm not so sure I care about that anymore, either. Yesterday I didn't even know he existed and today I'd die if I thought I'd never see him again. I think maybe I've gone completely mad."

"You've done no such thing," Miss Stella said, patting the back of Mariah's hand. "You're just in love, darlin'. I told you that you needed a man, but I didn't think you'd find one so fast. I have to ask you, though, did you tell him about your family? Does he know about the brothel and did you tell him about the money?"

"Yes and no," Mariah replied. "I told him about Mama and The Abbey, and I kind of told him about you, although I left out the part about the brothel. I mentioned an inheritance, but I didn't tell him the details. I just mentioned that it had enabled me to buy my own house. I figured I'd tell him the rest, later."

"That's probably a good idea," Miss Stella said thoughtfully. "That kind of information could get in the way when you're trying to get to know somebody. It could complicate things, you know. I think you are right to keep the rest of it under wraps for a while—especially the part about me running a brothel. So when do I get to meet him?" Miss Stella said, selecting a jar of bread and butter pickles from the pantry shelves. "Well, on second thought, you might want to keep that under wraps, too. I'm not exactly what one expects in the relative department. I mean, how many girls get to bring their beaus home to a brothel and a redheaded madame with pink bows in her hair and theatrical cosmetics all over her face?"

"I don't know," Mariah said, laughing. "Only the lucky ones, I guess."

Who in the World is Camille?

Charleston 1881

MARIAH AND WILLIAM were married six months after their first meeting in one of the most lavish weddings ever held at St. Mark's. Mariah wore a gown of cream-colored shantung silk with a veil trimmed in lace that touched the floor and was held in place by a circle of orange blossoms.

William wore a cutaway and spats and an English-made top hat. Grace wore a dress of baby blue silk, and in her hair, there was a circle of orange blossoms just like Mariah's.

Although Mariah was concerned about what Miss Stella might wear to the wedding, she refused to see her outfit ahead of time; "I know you'll look beautiful," she said repeatedly, and Mariah was right.

Miss Stella looked like a duchess in a sophisticated silver-blue silk gown adorned with a double strand of smoky-gray pearls. Her make-up was toned down and her hair, which usually resembled a waterspout, was discreetly tucked beneath a matching hat.

Even her shoes were out of character in that they also matched her dress, although she had taken one liberty; she had added bows, small ones, to each.

Mama, Daddy Sam and Mariah's younger siblings also attended the wedding, although it had taken Mariah forever to talk her mother into it. Julia said she wasn't itching to see any city, especially one the size of Charleston, but Daddy Sam and the children were thrilled at the prospects and Mama finally gave in.

They stayed in Mariah's new house (where Mariah and William had agreed to live after the wedding) and Mariah ordered new outfits for each of them. When Juniper drove them to the church, Mariah barely recognized them. In his worsted wool suit and top hat, Daddy Sam looked like a fashion plate and Julia, dressed from head-to-toe in pale pink silk, was glowing like a young girl.

"Oh, Mama," Mariah cried when she saw her mother moments before the ceremony. "You look so beautiful! You even have on powder! How did you know how to do that?"

"Camille did it for me as a surprise," Julia replied with a smile that suggested a conspiracy.

"Camille?" Julia said.

"Who in the world is Camille?" Mariah asked.

"It's Miss Stella," Julia replied. "Stella Bright is just a stage name; her real name is Camille Devereaux. She told us all about herself dur-ing supper last night, and that's when she asked us to call her Camille. I guess you were too busy staring at William to pay attention. She told us everything, Mariah, even the part about Louisiana and the quadruple balls. She said that being as we're family and all, she figured we had a right to know.

"'I'm mighty thankful,' she told me. If she was a real white lady... well, it'd just make things complicated."

The wedding ceremony went off without a hitch, except that every thirty-seconds Miss Stella blew her nose, drowning out the saying of the vows. No one seemed to mind, though, least of all, Mariah. Mrs. Mariah Cutler, that is; and there had never been a happier bride.

CHAPTER 17

Some Fancy Horse Dung

Charleston, SC 1881

MARIAH EMBRACED HER NEW role as wife and mother with the enthusiasm that grass exhibits in springtime, and she was concerned about telling William about the extent of her inheritance.

Perhaps she shouldn't have waited until after the wedding to tell him. What if William blamed her for keeping it a secret? She'd just have to take her chances.

"William," she said over dinner one night. "I have to talk to you about something really important—it's a good something, not a bad one," she added smiling. "Since Grace is spending the night at Nanny's, I thought this would be the perfect time."

"Well, I have no idea what you're planning to tell me, but you sure got my curiosity up, woman," William said, returning her smile. "Why don't you just get on with it?"

"It all has to do with my real father. Remember when I told you that he was the nephew of the owner of the plantation where Mama went to work on that wedding dress?" Mariah began, "Well, I never knew who he was until two years ago while I was visiting Mama back at The

Abbey, and I received a letter from an attorney in Baltimore. The letter was from my father's lawyer notifying me that he had died and that he had left me an inheritance."

"You told me that, the day of the picnic," William reminded her.

"I know, but I didn't tell you the extent of the inheritance."

"Maybe so, but I figured it must have been a lot because it enabled you to buy a house," William replied. "I've never known anyone who inherited enough money to buy a house."

"I could have bought a lot of houses, William. I could have bought the whole block. He left me $175,000. I've spent $5,894.50 of it, but all the rest is in the bank."

William was speechless. "One hundred and seventy-five thousand."

"Yes, one hundred and seventy-five thousand," Mariah replied. "Now you know why I was nervous about telling you. I hope you're not angry at me for waiting until after we were married. I just didn't know when to bring it up."

"I'm not upset with you. I'm just surprised that it is that much money. Who was he?"

"His name was Brooks Dunhill Huger. Yes, he was one of the Hugers," she confirmed.

"Wow!" William exclaimed. "There's probably only one or two families in all of Charleston with that kind of money, anymore."

"That's what Miss Stella said," Mariah replied, "and that's why I've kept it very quiet. Even my attorney warned me that if the wrong people knew, they'd be feeding like mud fish. I feel a responsibility to do something important with the money. Other than buying this house, I also built a schoolhouse for Miss Hattie, my teacher back at The Abbey, and a farm for Mama and Daddy Sam, but that's all, so far. I just don't know what to do with it."

"You keep on surprising me," William said, smiling. "I'll tell you what, let's sit on the money for a while so you can take your time. It's not like we need it; I made more than $5,000 last year. Why according to last year's Post and Courier, I'm an 'up-and-coming member of Charleston's burgeoning mulatto middle-class.' How's that for some fancy horse dung."

CHAPTER 18

What's that Sound, Mommy

Charleston, SC 1883-1886

IT WAS 1883—one of the best years of Mariah's life. She was a twenty-three year-old who loved her new husband and daughter so much it embarrassed her. People were probably laughing at her behind her back, but she didn't care, and just when she thought things couldn't get any better, she learned that she was pregnant, possibly with twins, just like Mama.

William Huger Cutler and Julia Camille Cutler arrived right on time, and after learning that Mariah had named one of the babies after her, Miss Stella proclaimed that they were the most beautiful babies ever born.

The following spring and summer brought temperatures hot enough to melt the pavement. It was the end of the world, some folks thought. In August, alone, there had been eighteen consecutive days when the temperatures exceeded ninety degrees, and the entire city had taken on the dusty veneer of the Wild West.

Charleston's tropical façade was nowhere to be found. Keeping her family comfortable became Mariah's priority. She dressed the children in lose-fitting clothing made of cotton gauze, and she refused to wear a corset or petticoat—even to church. She flung the doors and windows open night and day, and cooked everything on the top of the stove rather than heating up the oven.

On August 27, 1886, Mariah made an exception. It was the twins' first birthday, and she was determined to bake them a birthday cake no matter how much it heated up the house. So at four o'clock in the afternoon, she and Grace made a double batch of lemony-vanilla cake, poured the batter into two large cake pans and carefully slid the pans into the oven.

Seconds later, Grace was fixing to lick the bowl, she and Mariah heard a strange sound. "What was that, Mama?"

"I don't know, sweetheart," Mariah replied, trying to hide her concern. "It was a rumbling noise that sounded like it came from the Ashley River. I don't hear anything now. Do you?"

Just then, the house shuttered slightly, and then it was enveloped in an unworldly yellow fog. "Rotten eggs, Mama! It smells like rotten eggs!" Grace cried.

"I know," Mariah shouted back. "Run through the house and close the windows and doors while I get the twins," Mariah screamed. "Hurry!"

Grace raced through the house as if she had skates on, then she ran back to the kitchen. "What happened?" Grace cried as Mariah reached out to put her arms around her.

"I don't know. Maybe Papa knows. He'll be home soon."

William got home late, but he had news. A casket salesman had told him that the rotten egg smell had come from some unexplained landslides along a three-mile stretch of the Ashley River. Later that evening, he and Mariah joined some of his neighbors in the street in front of the house. The smell had dissipated by then, but everyone was still on edge, including William.

"If it was twenty years ago, I'd think the Yankees were up to no good," said an elderly man from down the block. "You know how them Yankees are."

"I don't know much about Yankees," another neighbor said, "but when I lived in Uruguay, I saw the same thing happen, once. If we were in South America instead of South Carolina, I'd be worried about an earthquake."

CHAPTER 19

Earthquake!

Charleston, SC 1886

THE FOLLOWING TUESDAY, August 31, was stifling, and everyone in the Cutler household was miserable. The twins had whined all day, and Grace, who usually had a sunny disposition, had been a holy terror.

Mariah couldn't wait to get them settled in for the night. William came home later than usual, and found Mariah bathing for the third time of the day. "I'll be ready for bed, soon. How about you?" he said as he peeled his shirt away from his sweaty back.

"I'm ready right now," Mariah said.

"The children are asleep out on the porch and I haven't heard a peep out of them for the last hour. They were so cranky today, I hope they can stay asleep. Why don't you take a quick bath, William, and I'll fix you some dinner."

"It's too hot to eat. I'm just going to try to cool off and go to bed," William replied.

At 9:51 p.m., just as Mariah turned to leave the bathroom, she heard a sound that the newspaper later described as the "bellowing of wild animals, the grinding of immense rocks and the horror of human agony all rolled into one...."

A split second later, the earth beneath the house belched and heaved upward, ripping the rear of the house from its foundation. Then the earth recoiled, and the house fall back onto its foundation, shattering glass, caving in ceilings and causing a back draft of dust and debris that slammed Mariah onto the floor.

"William!" Mariah screamed.

"I'm here," William yelled. "I'm in the doorway to Grace's bedroom. Are you hurt?"

"I don't think so, but the children, William! They're sleeping on the porch!"

Barefoot and dressed only in his suit pants, William crawled close enough to Mariah to reach out to her. "What happened?" Mariah cried after feeling her husband's reassuring arms around her.

"It was an earthquake, Mariah, a really big one, I think, and I'm betting there are going to be aftershocks, lots of them. We have to get the children out of here, now."

Just then, something exploded at the end of hallway, followed by the sounds of boulders crashing to the ground.

"I think the chimney in the kitchen just collapsed," William said above the roar, "but it sounded like it fell away from the house in the opposite direction of the porch." Mariah and William crawled through the darkness towards the sleeping porch, when they suddenly heard Grace's voice.

"Papa! Papa!" she cried. "Where are you?"

"Grace!" William replied. "Oh, thank God you're alive. Are you hurt?"

"I'm not hurt, Papa, but I'm so scared!" she cried. "Where are you?"

"Mama and I are right here. Do you have the twins?"

"Yes, Papa!" Grace screamed. "I found them underneath a mattress and some wooden posts from the porch railing, but I think they're alright. They're just scared." Mariah and William tunneled through the debris that was blocking the door to the porch, and then they saw the children silhouetted against the city's burning skyline.

"Make it go away, Papa!"

"I can't make it go away, Grace; you know that," William said trying to calm his hysterical daughter. "We have to get out of the house, Grace, and we will need your help. Can you do that?"

"Yes, Papa," Grace said trying to be heard above the cries of Camille and William, Jr.

"William, we can't go back downstairs. How are we going to get out?" Mariah whispered.

Just then, William's premonition about aftershocks came true. At 9:59 p.m., just eight minutes after the initial earthquake, a second shockwave slammed into the City of Churches with the same intensity as the first. Mariah and William clung to their children, as the house beneath them started to break apart.

The bookcase in the foyer crashed to the floor, dishes flew out of the kitchen cupboards and in the dining room, the neatly stacked set of china that Miss Stella had given Mariah and William as a wedding gift, fell to the floor like poker chips raked into a hat.

The cantilevered roof above the porch was practically brand new. It had been completely replaced less than five months earlier, and it held fast, but a huge section of the porch railing pirouetted to the ground, taking a portion of the porch's floorboards with it.

"I just thought of something, William," Mariah cried. "The stairs to the porch, if they're still intact, we could use them to get out of the house."

"Of course," William said. "Grace, you take the twins and stay with Mama while I check on the stairs." Grace and Mariah held their breaths as William crept across a field of debris on his way to the stairs. "I'm almost there," William said every few feet. "I'm almost there."

After tripping over an overturned rocking chair and letting go of a few choice words, William was finally close enough to peer over the edge of the porch. The stairs were still there! The banisters were missing, but the stairs were still intact.

Mariah and her family crept down the fragile stairway, and Mariah couldn't help but think about the houses of cards that Miss Stella's girls liked to build together during their spare time. They reached the ground, and rushed out into the street to join neighbors who had already gathered there.

Covered in mortar dust and dressed in tattered night clothes, the frightened group more closely resembled refugees from the spirit world than the well-dressed assemblage they had represented just hours before.

A sense of urgency took hold. The men formed search parties, and a group of the women set up a triage area. Mariah's concerns were for Miss Stella.

"William," she cried. "You have to check on her! She could be hurt!"

William was extremely reluctant to leave, even though he knew how much Mariah loved Miss Stella, but his parents and brothers were also out there, and he was desperate to know that they were safe. So, he prepared to leave, promising to return as quickly as he could.

William's parents shared a house with William's younger brother, his wife and their two small children. Until that night, William could have walked there blindfolded, but the landmarks that were so familiar to him were gone now, and in their places stood nothing but darkness.

Every street looked eerily like the last. People were rushing through the debris screaming for their loved ones, buildings swayed, trees were uprooted and downed telegraph lines were everywhere.

At one intersection, William came across a bloodied flock of hens and the body of a small pig. At another, he heard a dying man confessing his sins to an indifferent group of strangers.

After an hour, William began to panic because he felt no closer to finding his parents' house than he had when he left his own, and then he ran into Willy Petigru who lived two doors down from them.

"Willy!" William shouted.

"Have you seen my parents?"

"They be just fine, William," Willy assured him. "Ain't much of their house left. Ain't much of my house left, but they be fine. I just seen 'em. You take care of yourself, boy."

"Thank you, Willy," William cried as he raced off to find his family.

"Thank you."

Just as Willy had promised, William's family was less than a hundred yards away. When they spotted William, his mother exclaimed, "William! Mariah and the children, are they alive?"

"Yes, Mama," William said, noting how his mother's tears had formed little rivulets in the thick dust that covered her face. "We had a hard time getting out of the house, but we're all safe. Is everyone here alright?" William asked.

"Mama may have broken her ankle," his brother replied, "but except for that, we're all safe — at least for now. I don't know what will happen, though, if we have another quake. Do you think the worst is over, William?"

"No," William admitted candidly. "I think we may be in for several days or weeks of aftershocks, but then, I've never been through an earthquake, I've only read about them. I have to leave. I promised to check on Miss Devereaux," he said avoiding the use of Miss Stella's stage name.

"I'll be back in the morning, I promise. Stay here if you can. I'm afraid if you go somewhere else, we'll have a hard time finding each other again. I love you."

"I'll pray for you, William," Mama said.

"Pray for us all, Mama."

CHAPTER 20

Marie Antoinette

Charleston, SC 1886

THE BROTHEL WAS ABOUT the same distance from his parents' house as his own house was from his parents', but it seemed twice as far that night. Dust choked William's nostrils and burned his lungs, and the cuts and scratches he had sustained along the way were beginning to sting, but Mariah had to know what had happened to Miss Stella, so William pressed on.

King Street wasn't a residential street. It was lined with shops and storefronts, so it was easily recognizable when he finally made his way there. The difficulty was that because of the damage to the storefronts, they all tended to look alike. William thought he was probably just north of the brothel—no more than a block or two, but he wasn't sure.

As it turned out, he was practically standing in front of it. And he needn't have worried about figuring out where he was because when he stopped to acclimate himself, he saw a familiar face walking toward him.

It was Miss Stella. She was wrapped in a pink satin dressing gown; her lip rouge was smeared from ear to ear, and her enormous breasts looked as if they had been put on sideways. One of her prized beauty spots was stuck to her left eyelid, and in her dust-encrusted wig, she looked like a macabre Marie Antoinette. She was a sight for sore eyes, though.

"Mariah and the children, are they safe?" she cried.

"Yes, at least they were when I left them," William said. "I've been gone a long time and I have to get back to them as soon as possible."

"But my girls!" Miss Stella cried pointing to the crumbled remains of the brothel. "I can't leave my girls! Some of 'em are still in the house, William! We've got to get 'em out."

After wading through the debris that led up to the King Street entrance to the brothel, William had little hope for anyone trapped there. Miss Stella's main salon and private apartment were still discernible, but the girls' rooms were completely gone.

"Have you heard any cries from the girls?" William asked as tactfully as he could.

"Not a one, I haven't heard a peep," Miss Stella replied. "I called out to 'em over and over, but they didn't answer me. We've got to look for 'em, William."

"We can't do it tonight," William said firmly. "It's too dark, and it's too dangerous. There will be search parties when it's light, and I promise to come back in the morning, but we can't look tonight, Miss Stella. We have to go home to Mariah and the children."

"Oh, yes, Mariah, Mariah and the children," Miss Stella said more to herself than to William. "We need to go home to Mariah," and so they set out for Logan Street. For the first half hour, Miss Stella was in such a fog, she barely noticed the sights and sounds around her.

As they neared a pharmacy on the corner of Hudson and King Street, a portion of the pharmacy came crashing to the ground throwing dirt and ash all over her. She barely flinched.

William had never seen Miss Stella with her guard down. She suddenly looked shockingly old and vulnerable. The pee and vinegar that had always defined her was gone, at least for the moment. She reminds him of something out of the Wagnerian opera Mariah dragged him to last year. He hoped she doesn't stay that way forever.

Halfway home, another aftershock hit and even more of Charleston fell to its knees. Once the quake had ended, William realized that Miss

Stella had been thrown to the ground about twenty feet away, and that her left leg was trapped beneath a layer of cobblestones.

"Miss Stella!" he cried as he rushed to her. "Miss Stella! Can you tell if you're hurt?"

"I have a pain in my left leg just up from my ankle," she replied, gagging on the choking dust. "The rest of me's skint up, but I don't think anything's seriously hurt."

"Don't move," William commanded. "I'm going to get the debris off your leg, but you're going to have to hold still while I do it."

"Don't talk; just do it," Miss Stella said, demonstrating some of her old spunk.

As William carefully raked away the rubble, he expected to uncover a badly broken leg. Instead, it looked as though the rough edges on some of the cobblestones had punctured Miss Stella's leg rather than breaking it. It was a deep cut, though, at least he thought it was in the semidarkness.

"It's just a cut," he said, noticing that Miss Stella's collection of stomachs kept her from being able to see it. "It's pretty deep, I think, but it's not bleeding bad right now. Do you think you can stand on it?" he asked.

"Damn right, I can," she replied as if she had finally regained her senses. "You've got to get home to your family, William, and I'm not going to slow you down anymore. Let's get going." With that, she pulled herself to her feet with William's help and they were off.

At three a.m.—an hour after the last aftershock, William and Miss Stella finally staggered onto Logan Street.

"Mariah!" William began to call out. "Mariah!"

"We're here, William, we're in front of the Gibbes' house. You found Miss Stella! When the aftershocks came, I was afraid you were both killed. Did you find your parents?"

"Yes, they lost the house just like we did, but when I talked to them earlier tonight everyone was fine except Mama. 'Looks like she may have broken her ankle," William replied, "but I'm more worried about what has happened to them since then. Have you heard anything?"

"No," Mariah replied, "but you know what they always say, no news is good news. We'll check on them when it's light. Oh, Miss Stella!" she cried noticing her bandaged leg for the first time.

"What happened?"

"Oh, we just had a little accident during our evening stroll through the city," Miss Stella said laughing. "Lordy!" she exclaimed after shaking some of the ash from her hair and inspecting her tattered dressing gown.

"What an awful night. I guess by now, everybody in the world knows what I look like with gray hair. I can tell you one thing, though, when I run across some soap and water, they ain't gonna see it again. Did William tell you about my girls?" she said, dropping her voice as well as her bravado. "We couldn't find six of my girls; Mariah. Pansy, Beulah Mae and Juniper got out, though. William promised to go back and look for them in the morning," she added. "I think they're all dead, Mariah. I think God took 'em home."

"We won't know anything more until tomorrow," Mariah said. "Why don't we rest over here with the children until morning comes, then we can decide what to do."

CHAPTER 21

Aftershocks

Charleston, SC 1886

EVERYONE IN THE CITY clamored for official news, and it was anything but forthcoming. For the first two days, the newspapers were unable to publish their papers. It wasn't until the third day that they were back in business.

From their new living quarters in the rear of the funeral parlor, Mariah and her family read the grim news: It was estimated that as many as a hundred people had been killed, although reports were still coming in, the papers said.

The initial earthquake had been followed by eight aftershocks with the eighth being the worst. Estimates on the damage sustained by existing structures in Charleston were in the ninety percent range with the hardest-hit areas located along the Ashley River and in the Lower Peninsula.

Water mains had burst and sinkholes and fissures—some up to thirty-feet wide—had been reported. The quake was felt from Cuba to New York State, and it was said to be the worst earthquake to ever hit the Eastern Seaboard. A hundred miles to the west of Charleston, a four-foot wall of water from a ruptured dam had knocked a train off its tracks, and another was washed away by an eight-foot wave near Horse Creek.

Inside the city limits, tent cities, including one in Washington Square, had been set up to accommodate the city's homeless, and a shantytown had sprung up across the street from the German Lutheran Church.

The Citadel overlooking Marion Square had suffered extreme damage, and citizens were warned not to set up temporary housing there. The front portico at St. Philip's had collapsed. On Meeting Street, the entire façade of the Hibernian Hall was gone, and a huge crack had opened up beneath the second-story windows of the courthouse on Broad Street. White's Granite Works on the corner of Meeting and Market Streets, however, had survived completely unscathed, and yet, the monuments and headstones displayed in its yard had been twisted from their foundations at exactly the same angle.

Private homes had suffered the same fate as most of the city's landmark buildings, and in a few instances, entire families had died without ever leaving their beds.

One of the newspapers made note of a particular building on King Street—398 King Street to be exact—Miss Stella's brothel! The bodies of six young women, some only partially clad, had been recovered from the rubble there. The earthquake had occurred during business hours, but there was no mention of any men's bodies having been recovered. The women were officially listed as boarders, and the news of their deaths, of course, was old news to Miss Stella and the Cutler family.

CHAPTER 22

Something in Common

Charleston, SC 1886

TWO DAYS AFTER THE QUAKE, Miss Stella orchestrated an extraordinarily touching funeral for her girls in a small black church near Goose Creek. "I don't reckon they'll mind too much being buried around black folks," Miss Stella reasoned. "At least they have each other."

In the same newspaper that sensationalized the story of Miss Stella's brothel, there was also a small story entitled *Little Lost Children.* Less than four inches in length, the story described how three starving Negro waifs had been discovered foraging for food near the crumbled remain of the Charleston Police Station. What is to become of the city's starving children? the story asked. What is to become of the city's Negro orphans? *Starving orphans....*

"William!" she exclaimed. "I know what to do with the money," she said with tears welling in her eyes. "After all the months, now I know! We'll start an orphanage, and we need to do it today. I don't mean here at the funeral parlor, of course, but someplace where children can be safe. There's got to be something we can either buy or rent. Oh, and food, we'll need food and blankets and cots and...."

William found a two-story piano store on Elliott Street that had sustained only minor damage from the earthquake, and by offering triple wages, he hired a work crew to do the necessary repairs.

The paint had barely dried when Juniper and Ol' Mule pulled up with a wagon loaded to the gills with blankets, nappies, canned food, cots, pots and pans, a bright blue kitchen table, seven chairs, and a small cast-iron stove.

"Miss Stella," how did you find all of those things?" Mariah exclaimed. "I thought there wasn't a blanket left in the whole city!"

"Well, darlin', some things you're just better off not knowing, and this is one of 'em. Let's just say they were generously donated by some of my more publicity-shy clients."

While William had been shopping for real estate and Miss Stella had been extorting booty, Mariah collected needy children from the city's predominantly black churches.

Within three days, she had gathered a ragtag group of thirteen between the ages of three and twelve. Six were known to have been orphans before the earthquakes and had been living on the streets; two were orphaned during the quakes; two, including the three-year-old, had recently been abandoned on the steps of Zion Presbyterian, and the status of the rest was unknown.

That night, Mariah looked at herself in the mirror and groaned. Her eyes were bloodshot and her feet were killing her. "I don't think I've ever been this tired in my entire life," Mariah admitted to William after getting the last of children settled into their new home. "I just thought I was tired when I used to complain about chasing the twins around all day."

"I'm exhausted, too," he replied. "I hate to be indelicate, Mariah, but I have a crew of gravediggers who are working around the clock, and we still have bodies waiting to be buried. There's not a coffin or a flower of any size, shape, or color to be had at any price in this city. Every day I have grieving families begging for our services. I can't turn them away."

"I'm sorry, William. I've been so centered on my own needs that I've been oblivious to yours. Forgive me?"

"You're forgiven."

"It's just that I'm so frightened," Mariah said. "I'm proud of getting these children off the streets, and yet I don't know what to do next. Maybe this was a bad idea—a crazy idea. I can't even remember the children's names."

"You're just tired, Mariah; you won't think it's a crazy idea in the morning. But you can't do this alone, even with Miss Stella's help. So, tomorrow we're going to hire Juniper and Beulah Mae to work at the orphanage full-time, and then we're going to run an ad in the local papers for a live-in nurse and a full time teacher."

The ad read, "HELP WANTED: Live-in nurse and full-time teacher needed. Inquire at the Orphanage for Colored Children on Elliott Street."

Mariah received ten applications in the first two days. Jobs for women were few and far apart with the earthquake, but construction workers and gravediggers (who were all men, of course) were making triple wages.

Mariah found a nurse right away. She was a large Mother Goose-type woman with arms the size of swan wings that wrapped around a child at the slightest provocation. Her name was Prudence, and she needed a place to stay because her family's house was in the bottom of the Ashley River. "It was hard times for her family", she said. "The worst hard times ever."

She had ten-year's experience working for a colored doctor in Goose Creek, but because of the earthquake and all, he decided to retire. Prudence tried to get on at the local hospital, but it didn't accept colored nurses or colored patients. "People don't want to be around colored people when they're sick," she was told, as if that was the most understandable thing in the world. Mariah said it was a bunch of horse piss and hired her on the spot, informing her that the children were to call her Miss Prudence. Prudence said that would be real nice.

The first teacher Mariah interviewed was a twenty-two-year-old white woman who must have assumed that Mariah was also white because she admitted during her interview that she didn't think colored children were capable of learning very much, but since she needed the job, she was willing to give it a try. She was so desperate for work, she said, that she would even consider living in the orphanage, at least for a while, but she insisted on having her meals served separately and being able to lock her door at night. Miss Stella had walked in on the last half of the interview, and she got so mad that her ears were practically smoking.

"Get out," she said to the girl. "Get out a' here, and don't you ever come back." The frightened girl bolted from her chair, and ran from the room shrieking.

"I'm sorry, Mariah, I shouldn't have horned in on your business," Miss Stella said, "but people like that just tick me off. Oh, by the way, do you think you could learn to call me Miss Camille? Now that I've decided to leave the brothel business and go into the orphanage business, I thought I might need a new image. What do you think?"

"You don't need to change your name. I like you just the way you are," Mariah said, laughing.

"I appreciate that, darlin', but I don't have the greatest reputation in this town, you know. I just figured I needed a makeover, although I draw the line at giving up my theatrical cosmetics. Even so, I thought a name change might be in order."

"Well, this is the way I see it," Mariah said. "William's family has been wonderful to us, and so have the people at St. Mark's. I'm sure that there will be some raised eyebrows now and then, and a few people in this town may not have anything to do with us, but for the most part, I'm hoping we'll be judged by our good works and not for our pasts."

"You don't have a past, Mariah," Miss Stella replied as she turned to leave the room.

"I love you, Miss Stella," Mariah said, mockingly.

"I love you too, puddin'."

Three days later, Mariah's second applicant for the teaching job showed up on her doorstep. A fresh-faced girl with dark brown skin and a bright yellow dress, the young woman walked up to Mariah, extended her hand, and said that she hoped the job was still available.

"Yes, yes, it is," Mariah replied impressed with the poise of the young woman. "Do you have any teaching experience?"

"I've never taught on my own," the girl said, "but I've been an assistant teacher for the past two years. I have a letter here that will tell you all about it," she added, handing the letter to Mariah. The letter was addressed to Mariah. How could that be? And the handwriting looked very familiar.

Dear Mariah, it began.

I read about your new school in the Charleston newspaper and wanted to introduce you to my newest protégé. She has been my assistant for the past two years and she has the makings of a fine teacher. I think you two will get along very well. Oh, and by the way, you both have something in common — a little red chair.

The letter was signed: *Miss Hattie.*

Donna's Story

Rita Hayworth

The Abbey Plantation 1957

DONNA AND MAMA LIVED in a small rented house next door to Angelo's Barber Shop on Main Street in Marion, South Carolina. Donna was eleven and, if pressed, would have described herself as a lump with corkscrew hair the color of acorn squash.

Mama's hair was auburn, and it was wavy, and she looked like Rita Hayworth — everyone said so. Daddy was on the road most of the time selling everything from whisky to tractor parts, so it was mostly just Mama and Donna, but Donna could remember each time Daddy had come to visit. He'd bring her presents, and she'd pretend that this time he was home to stay, but just when she and Mama got used to putting three plates on the supper table, he'd up and leave again, and Donna would find Mama sobbing on the sofa.

"Don't cry, Mama. He'll come back. He always does." Donna was just a little kid, though, and she didn't understand the hold that the road had on a traveling man. The last time Daddy waved good-bye, he didn't come back. It wasn't long before Donna couldn't remember him anymore, except that he always smelled like Burma Shave.

Mama worked at the lunch counter at Walgreens Drug Store and sometimes waitressed the graveyard shift at Trucker's World. One night she left her shift at the truck stop and started walking home when she was hit by a car and died before they could get her to the hospital. Mama was twenty-six. In her pocketbook, they found two sticks of a fruit gum, a tube of red lipstick, and a coin purse containing $12.37.

After Mama's funeral and her ascent into heaven, Donna went to live with Grandma and Granddaddy Jim on the grounds of a rundown rice plantation named The Abbey, where Granddaddy Jim worked as its caretaker. "Why did Mama have to die?" Donna asked as she and her grandmother unpacked Donna's meager belongings and positioned them around her new room. "And don't tell me that God needed her in heaven like Mrs. Chills said after the funeral because He didn't need her as bad as I did."

"I know, dear," Grandma wearily replied. "I don't know why she died. I just don't know." Then Grandma took a seat on the edge of the rump-sprung mattress and motioned for Donna to join her. "Your Mama was my youngest child," Grandma said, reaching for Donna's hand. "She was sweet and loving, but she didn't know much about human nature. She was only fifteen when the war started, and she met your papa. She was so young, she didn't even finish school, but she wouldn't listen to me or anyone else. So, she married her young soldier, and before long, she had you.

"After the war, jobs were scarce — especially here in South Carolina — and at first your papa did the best he could to make a living for you and your mama. After a while, though, I think he just lost his way. As for your mama, I don't know why she died. She'd made some bad choices, of course, but she was working hard to turn her life around, and she would have made it if it hadn't been for the accident. The one thing you always need to remember is that she loved you more than anything."

CHAPTER 2

Rode Hard and Put Away Wet

Charleston, SC 1957

QUEEN ELIZABETH I ONCE SAID that though she had the body of a woman, she had the heart and stomach of a king. Donna always thought that statement equally applied to Grandma. Grandma had grown up on a hardscrabble cotton farm near Hartsville, South Carolina. The oldest of seven children and one of three girls, Grandma didn't have much time to devote to being a girl. Most of her childhood was spent with a hoe in her hands, coaxing cotton to grow in overused, worn-out soil. By the time she was twenty-five, Grandma had been widowed twice with four children and another one on the way. She was rode hard and put away wet, is what she used to say.

After her children were out on their own, Grandma met Granddaddy Jim at a dance at The Hot Spot, a juke joint across the road from the cotton gin in Dillon. Knox Culpeper and his band, the Culpeper Five, had just fired up their rendition of the "Tennessee Waltz," when Granddaddy Jim spotted Grandma, extended a calloused hand, and asked her to dance.

"I'd love to," Grandma replied. She was wearing a blue cotton dress, mended stockings, and the only pair of shoes she owned, but Grandma rose from her chair like a queen, and that's the moment that Granddaddy Jim said he fell in love. Their life together hadn't been an easy one. Money was always scarce, and they had to work hard just to put food on the table, but in their quiet way, they never stopped loving each other.

Without having to ask, Donna understood that Granddaddy Jim always saw Grandma as that young woman in a blue cotton dress, and despite Granddaddy Jim's gruff exterior, he continued to be Grandma's handsome, sun-baked stranger. Grandma never seemed to mind being poor, but she'd throw a fit when someone questioned her bloodlines.

"Just because kittens are born in an oven doesn't make 'em biscuits," she always said, and the same went for Southerners. "Being a southerner was more about genealogy than it was about geography, and children like Donna were born knowing the difference."

CHAPTER 3

Grandaddy Jim

The Abbey Plantation 1958

AS CARETAKER, GRANDDADDY JIM couldn't predict when his job might turn into a twenty-four-hour-a-day job, so he and Grandma lived on the plantation in an old farmhouse. The plantation was a mystery to Donna when she came to live at The Abbey, and she didn't like it all that much at first because she missed Mama so much.

Grandma was fascinated with every inch of the plantation, and she could tell you something about every rock or blade of grass on the property. Nobody could tell a story better than Grandma, and before Donna knew it, she was drawn into the middle of them. Grandma could tell a story about anything, but some of her best were about the old farmhouse they lived in.

Most people'd just seen an old rundown farmhouse with a tin roof and a screen door that went *creeeeek!* every time it was closed, but Grandma saw the bones of The Abbey's fabled big house. You see, she knew there were massive foundations and footings beneath the farmhouse—way too big to support the farmhouse. They were mansion foundations, she'd say. "They were built back in colonial times. Then they built a mansion right on top of them, and they did it without trucks or earthmoving equipment or electricity and lumber yards. "What they could buy—bricks, window glass, doors, slate, and fancy mantles for the fireplaces—came up river from Charleston; everything else came from the plantation. They milled their own lumber, made shingles from cedar trees they found along the marsh, and even made their own tabby," she said.

"Do you have any idea how hard it is to make good tabby?"

Now, Donna wasn't sure if Grandma was actually expecting a response or not. Sometimes, when she was on a roll with her storytelling, Grandma wanted to do all the talking, herself.

So, Donna just kept her mouth shut. Then she got to thinking and realized this whole story was going over her head because she had no idea what tabby was, so she sheepishly asked, "Does it have anything to do with cats, Grandma?"

"No, it has nothing to do with cats," Grandma replied, letting out a dramatic sigh. "Tabby is homemade concrete made out of oyster shells, sand, and water, and if you make it right, it will last forever. You have to know what you're doing, though. You take a pile of oyster shells and burn them over an extremely hot fire for eight or nine hours—maybe more—until the shells disintegrate into lime. Then you soak the salt out of the lime and mix the lime with water and sand and ground oyster shells used as an aggregate. You know how you can see seashells embedded in the foundation of our house, well they're part of the original tabby, and it's more than two hundreds old."

"Holy Cow!" Donna exclaimed.

It didn't take long before Donna thought that The Abbey was about the neatest place there was. She would have been the first to admit that her perspective on things was limited, though. She'd only been out of South Carolina once, and all she knew of the rest of the world was what she'd seen on *Howdy Doody* and *American Bandstand,* and she could only get a picture by keeping her hand on the tinfoil that Granddaddy Jim kept wrapped around the rabbit ears.

She'd never liked the house, though. Why was it so plain inside? And who in the world would build a two-story house without putting stairs to the second floor? The only way to get there was to climb a ladder that was nailed to the outside of the house and then to crawl through a window. Once there, you could see that the entire space had beautiful heart-of-pine floors; but there was nothing else there, not even walls. Grandma said it was spooky.

Grandma and Granddaddy Jim's house was built on top of the foundations of the plantation's original big house, so it was laid out just like the big house with four large rooms: two on one side of a center hallway and two on the other.

The big house also had a full second story and a large attic. Grandma said that during plantation times, The Abbey's attic held one of the largest collections of Madera for miles around. It was a real showpiece, she said of The Abbey's mansion, but most of the work on the plantation happened in the smaller buildings, not the least of which was the dependency kitchen, which was a separate building from the big house.

"The smoke, soot, heat, and chaos generated by a plantation kitchen wasn't something you wanted to show off for your guests," Grandma said, while listing some of the reasons for separating the kitchen from the big house. "The main reason, however, was fire. You couldn't call the fire department, you know, and once a fire got going good, it had to burn itself out. Fire was the thing they feared the most."

"Same as us, huh, Grandma?" Donna said.

"Yeah, same as us."

There wasn't much left of the dozens of small buildings that were part of The Abbey. There were the foundations to five slave houses plus one intact chimney. There were some other chimneys, the remains of a tool shed, and a fowl house, a roofless dove cote, and a small smoke house that was in surprisingly good shape. Grandma's farmhouse had been updated somewhere along the way, she said, including the addition of an indoor kitchen, two bathrooms, and a lean-to that ended up being Donna's bedroom. Daddy Jim said the original farmhouse had been built to last, but the additions looked more like they'd had been put up with bubble gum.

The house had white clapboard siding and black shutters. It had four fireplaces and the pilings it rested on were tall enough for Donna to walk beneath the entire house without bumping her head.

One of the pilings had a carving:

Samuel + Julia

1880

Grandma said she didn't know who painted the interior of the house the last time, but he must have found the paint on the clearance rack. Everything including the walls, the woodwork, the kitchen cabinets, and the ceilings was painted one color — hospital green. The house had ten-foot ceilings, and the windows went all the way down to the floor, and they worked just like doors.

The house wasn't much to look at by the time Grandma and Granddaddy Jim moved there, but Grandma said it'd been a beautiful house in its day. She ran Donna and Granddaddy Jim ragged, though, complaining about the furniture — Fanny Farmer furniture, she called it, from a 1920s Sears and Roebuck catalog.

Pepper Sauce and Grape Soda

Charleston, SC 1958

GRANDDADDY JIM DIDN'T HAVE the constitution for traveling. 'Said he was too busy taking care of The Abbey. Grandma managed to talk him into it now and then, but it was hardly worth the effort. If they planned to travel any farther than Charleston, he'd insist on leaving by four in the morning, like the time they drove to Virginia to visit Aunt Myrtie (Grandma's first cousin once-removed on her mama's side). It was pitch black when Granddaddy Jim started rousting everyone out of bed by threatening to play the bugle he'd brought back from the war—the Big One: WWII.

"Jim Jordan, if you play that bugle one more time, I'm going to chunk that thing in the river," Grandma bellowed. "If you could play something on it, it'd be different."

"I just lost my lip, but I can still play one note, and that's enough to wake the dead. So, get out of bed, woman."

Donna dressed while Grandma fixed a breakfast of biscuits, sausage, and grits. Then they shoveled it down like hoe hands. Donna cleared the breakfast dishes and packed the picnic basket with things from the icebox that Grandma had put there the night before. Without even looking, she knew exactly what was going to be there: hard boiled eggs, sweet pickles, quarts of sweet tea, bologna and cheese sandwiches, meatloaf sandwiches, leftover pound cake, and oatmeal cookies, her favorite. Oh, and, grape soda—six whole bottles all for her. Donna packed the food on top of the red and white tablecloth and a plastic tub that held Grandma's mismatched picnic silverware, baby food jars containing salt and pepper, Granddaddy Jim's church key, and a bottle of pepper sauce. But when Grandma reappeared, she took everything out of the basket and repacked the whole thing. Donna wanted to complain, but she didn't because she was afraid Grandma might cut back on the grape sodas. Grandma was just throwing in some extra napkins when Granddaddy Jim started honking the horn.

"It's gonna be light soon, and we need to hit the road," he hollered.

So, Grandma brought out the picnic basket and put it in the back of the truck along with the valises, Grandma's train case, and two care packages for the relatives that included canned peaches; canned tomatoes; canned string beans; pear jelly; strawberry jam; apricot and watermelon preserves; and four loaves of fruit cake.

Then Granddaddy Jim fired up the Old '41 and proclaimed, "We're gonna keep rolling until we need gas, so if you girls need to watty-potty, now's the time."

Donna had to sit in the middle, of course. There was no heat, no radio, no air condition, no nothing to do except sit there and pray that they ran short on gasoline before she was forced to pee her pants. Donna didn't take it personally, though. She understood that Granddaddy Jim simply wasn't one to waste time. Time was money—he'd learned that as a kid. You waste a day, and you might not eat at the end of it.

Granddaddy Jim must have had a hundred care-taking jobs. Now and then, he'd even have to work on Sundays. Sometimes, he'd let Donna go but only if she promised not to get in his way. It didn't take long before she'd learned more than she wanted to know about repairing fences, painting boat docks, rebuilding gates, dredging drainage ditches, and chopping weeds! At certain times of the year, one of Granddaddy Jim's most important jobs was control burning. A controlled burn consisted of setting the underbrush within a forest on fire without igniting the mature trees in the process.

"Tedious work," Granddaddy Jim called it, and it didn't take a genius to spot a good burn. If you did it right, the underbrush would lay in ashes, and the trunks of the mature trees would be scorched and sooty, but according to Granddaddy Jim, "A whole lot healthier than they were before."

Grandaddy Jim hated thunderstorms. Lightning made him nervous because of fire and all, but hurricanes were the worst. Another important job was keeping an eye out for hunters sneaking onto the plantation to poach deer. Even when Granddaddy Jim was sound asleep and snoring to beat the band, he'd pop up like a cork the instant anyone took one step on the plantation. Grandma said it was a gift.

A Comet in the Kitchen

The Abbey Plantation 1958

LIVING WITH GRANDMA and Granddaddy Jim was hard at first. Donna had never been around people who worked from daylight 'till dawn and still had jobs to spare. One thing she learned for sure was that wishing on stars and moaning over something you can't have was wasted time, time better spent preparing to go after things that are within your reach and enjoying the things you already have.

Grandma liked to say she'd been happy and poor everyday of her life. The plantation was like a cranky old man who enjoyed surprising folks now and then. His dirtiest trick was lightning. Of course, they were used to lightning at The Abbey. The house was built on a bluff overlooking the river and was the biggest target for miles.

"That was just about the stupidest thing I've ever seen," Grandma used to say. "For the life of me, I don't know why they did that."

Even so, they had always been able to see the storm clouds coming, that is until one evening when Granddaddy Jim was smoking his pipe in the living room, and Grandma and Donna were sitting on the porch watching the sun setting across the river. There wasn't a cloud in the sky or a breath of wind, and Grandma had just commented on what a beautiful evening it had turned out to be; that's when it happened.

Overhead they heard something that sounded like a giant bed sheet being ripped in two, and a half-second later, a ball of fire slammed into one wall of the kitchen and exited the other. In the blink of an eye, it had bored a hole completely through two walls of the oven, blown a chunk out of the kitchen sink, and knocked Granddaddy Jim right off his chair, singeing his pants in the process.

"Grandma!" Donna screamed. "Was it a comet? I think it was a comet."

"It wasn't a comet, Donna," Granddaddy Jim said, making sure his pants weren't on fire. "It was lightning, a direct hit. We should be dead." Just as he said that, the rain came, and they caught a good one. The next day it looked like someone had poured gallons of water on Grandma's fresh-scrubbed linoleum floor.

A month or so later, Donna was riding her bike on the road near the back of the house when she heard a huge explosion — not another comet! And then the ground shook like a bomb had gone off, and it was followed by a giant splashing sound. Donna thought sure the Russians had landed at The Abbey and were on their way to rip out everyone's fingernails. She high-tailed it for home.

"Grandma!" Donna screamed as she raced through the kitchen door. "What happened?"

"Oh, it's nothing to worry about," she said in her no-nonsense way. "Granddaddy Jim just dynamited the pond; that's all."

"He did what?" Donna asked.

"He dynamited the pond. He said he was going to get back at the alligators for eating his chickens. I told him it would be a whole lot easier to just move the chicken house away from the edge of the pond," she said. "But you know how Granddaddy Jim is. He likes doing things his own way."

When Donna ran back outside, she sprinted toward the pond, but as she neared, she stopped dead in her tracks. Chicken feathers and dead alligators littered the ground. Most of the alligators were baby alligators, the kind you could buy at the pet store for ninety-nine cents, and there were dozens of them, but Donna knew right away that the blast had also killed a couple of five and six footers because she could see them floating on their backsides in the middle of the pond.

Granddaddy Jim said he was sure they were the ones that had helped themselves to his chickens, but after supper, he admitted that he was wrong to have dynamited the pond.

"My intentions were good," he said. "I was trying to protect my chickens, but I need to think of a better way."

CHAPTER 6

Green Goopy Stuff

The Abbey Plantation 1958

THE SUMMER BEFORE Donna came to live at The Abbey, Granddaddy Jim discovered a small cemetery about three-hundred-yards east of the house. *Well, what 'a we got here,* he asked himself, as he stumbled upon the edge of the cemetery. He wasn't expecting to find a cemetery; he was looking for a pump house. For a moment, he thought he'd found it. 'Turned out, though, what he thought was part of the pump house was a rusted roll of chicken wire. Then the underbrush thinned out, and he saw a crypt stone that read, *Sacred to the memory of Anne Elizabeth Haddrell.*

There were more graves and a raised vault and a broken headstone that read, *Thomas...something.* Granddaddy Jim hauled off the old fence and built a new picket fence around what he estimated to be the cemetery's perimeter and painted the fence green with leftover paint he found in the chicken house. He didn't like going there, though. It felt like someone had just been there.

One day Grandma told Donna that she was going to introduce her to a very important person. "Her name is Anne Elizabeth Haddrell. Clean up that mess you made on the porch, and we'll go."

Donna had no idea who Anne Elizabeth Haddrell was, but she figured it wouldn't hurt; besides, she didn't have any say over it anyway. She stuffed her drawings under her bed and set out down the lane with Grandma.

The pathway was narrow and overgrown, but it still looked like it had once led to something important. The path made a sharp right turn about a hundred yards from the house. Then it meandered over a small rise, made a slight turn past a magnolia tree, and there it was—a cemetery.

"Anne Elizabeth lives in a cemetery?" Donna asked.

"Well, in a way she does," Grandma replied. "Miss Anne has been living here for more than a hundred and twenty-five years. That's her grave marker. See? It says that she died in 1824."

Anne's gravestone wasn't the kind that pointed up towards the sky. It was one big slab of marble that sat parallel to the ground and covered her entire body. Grandma called it a crypt stone. Piles of crumbling red bricks held the crypt stone about a foot above the ground. Just to the left of Miss Anne's grave was a large broken headstone, and just beyond that was another headstone encased in vines and covered with slimy green mold.

"It looks pretty awful, Grandma," Donna said.

"That may be, but it's a miracle that the cemetery has survived at all. I'm pretty sure it stopped being used as a burying ground during the early years of the War Between the States, which began in the spring of 1861; so, no one's been here since then to keep it clean."

"How do you think that headstone next to Miss Anne's grave got broken?" Donna asked.

"Could have been during a hurricane. Maybe a tree fell on it, or it could have been damaged during the earthquake in 1886. Who knows?"

Four huge oak trees that were at least a hundred years old had sprung up in the middle of the cemetery, and their roots were so long that they threatened everything there, except for the area around Miss Anne's grave, which was still smooth as a baby's butt.

Grandma hadn't noticed that there were two smaller headstones just to the right of Miss Anne's grave until Donna discovered them that day. The first one was only three feet from Anne's grave, but the base of a large tree had grown around about half of the headstone, and it was pretty much hidden from view. When Donna spotted it and realized what it was, she hollered to Grandma who was just on the other side of the fence.

"Grandma! Grandma! Here's another grave. A little one that's all caught up in the trunk of this tree. Oh, wait," she cried. "There's another one, and they have engraving on them—initials, I think, but I can't read them because there covered in green goopy stuff."

"Let's go," Donna said as Grandma climbed through the underbrush to join her.

"What do you mean, go? We just got here."

"This place smells like a septic tank," Donna replied, holding her nose.

"Oh, don't be such a baby. Let's see if we can figure out how to read the inscriptions. We're gonna need some cleaning supplies, a toothbrush, a bucket of water, and a little dab of bleach from the house."

"Let me guess who's going to go get it," Donna said. "Me, right?"

"Right, you are, my dear," Grandma said. "Now, get cracking. Oh, and why don't you bring back some sweet tea? I'm parched."

CHAPTER 7

Miss Anne and Her Babies

The Abbey Plantation 1958

DONNA RETURNED TO THE cemetery with a bucket of bleach water and a Mason jar filled with sweet tea, and Grandma was able to scrub enough of the moss off the headstones to make out the initials. The first read, TMD; the second read, MMD.

"Grandma!" Donna cried out. "I know who they are!"

"So, do I," Grandma replied. "They're Miss Anne's babies."

The top half of Miss Anne's crypt stone read

SACRED

To the Memory
of
Anne Elisabeth Haddrell Dunhill
Wife of Thomas Dunhill
Daughter of John and Elisabeth Hebert Haddrell, who was born in Stono
January 7, 1782, And departed this life, July 24, 1823
This amiable Lady, remarked her early

Piety, exemplary fulfilled the duties of
Wife, Mother and Mistress
She lived beloved and died regretted

The second half of her epitaph, however, was even more poignant.

Mary Margaret Dunhill. born October 21, 1808, died October 26, 1813
Ann Haddrell Dunhill, born January 12, 1812, died September 6, 1814
Elisabeth Anne Dunhill, born January 1, 1817, died September 11, 1820
Theodore Madison Dunhill, born March 26, 1814, died September 14, 1820

Donna was crushed that the headstones had belonged to such young children. It didn't trouble her so much to think about someone as old as Miss Anne dying—after all, she was forty. She was practically ancient, but the children, that wasn't as easy. Picking up on Donna's discomfort, Grandma changed the subject by pointing to another grave on the other side of Miss Anne's grave.

"Who's buried there?" Grandma asked.

"I don't know," Donna replied. "It's covered with so many vines, I can't read the inscription."

"Then we'll remove the vines. Geez," Grandma sighed, and once they did, they learned that the grave belonged to Dr. James Richards Dunhilll. Once a few more vines were out of the way, they learned that Dr. Dunhill had died in 1855 at the age of thirty-one years, eleven months, and twenty-one days.

"He didn't get much doctoring done, did he Grandma?" Donna asked as she pried the last vine from the foot of the vault.

"He sure didn't. See the last three lines of the inscription? It says, *Dr. Dunhill became an occupant of a silent tomb after battling a mysterious illness. He leaves behind a wife and two noble boys.*

"It sounds like he might have died of something pretty sudden." Grandma and Donna later learned that Dr. Dunhill was another one of Miss Anne's sons, and they were glad that he had outlived her.

"Parents aren't supposed to outlive their children," Grandma said from experience.

Granddaddy Jim didn't like the cemetery, but Grandma and Donna loved it. Sometimes Grandma went there after working in her garden. Donna often rode her bike there, and sometimes they walked there together. Grandma was fixing Granddaddy Jim's favorite dinner of butter beans and rice one morning when she announced that she and Donna were going to form a Dunhill Family Cemetery Committee of two.

"We're going to figure out if there are any other people buried in the cemetery," she said, "and then we're going to clean it up."

The next afternoon, they set out for All Saints' Church to look through the parish registers. They knew the Haddrell's had been members of the church for many generations. One of Thomas Dunhill's ancestors had even donated the land for the church, but they didn't expect to get as lucky as they did. Within ten minutes, they found the names of nineteen additional people who had been buried in The Abbey graveyard. The first burial had taken place in 1711; the last had taken place in 1849 (that, of course, was Dr. Dunhill). Notations made in pencil in the margins of the register stated that the list included four generations of masters and their wives, two spinsters, two veterans of the Revolutionary War (one American and one English), an English woman, four young children, and a stillborn infant.

CHAPTER 8

Grave Robbers

The Abbey Plantation 1958

AFTER GRANDMA AND DONNA finished their research at the church, Grandma said it was time to go high-tech. So, she rushed into the kitchen and returned with a trowel, a pair of scissors, and a paper sack filled with cake flour. While she tucked everything into the pockets of her apron, she told Donna to grab a pencil, a pad of paper, and the string jar (a mayonnaise jar she kept her string in) and to meet her out on the porch.

"We're heading out for the cemetery," Grandma announced. "Let's get a move on." On the way, Grandma stopped to cut a small branch from a tree—about as big around as a cigar and stripped off the leaves as they walked. Donna had no idea what Grandma was fixing to do with it, but she kept her mouth shut because she knew that Grandma would have to tell her once they got to the cemetery because she was the only other member of her committee.

Once inside the cemetery's gate, they said hello to Miss Anne just as they always did, and then Grandma walked over to the fence post that was closest to the lane leading up to the house. Then she started counting the pickets leading away from it. When she got to the fifth picket, she told Donna to pull the end of the string out of the string jar and to tie a loop around the bottom of the picket. And then she told Donna to run the string from that picket to the fifth picket on the side of the fence that was directly across the cemetery. When that was done, Donna was supposed to count five pickets from there and do it all over again. *Grandma's making a grid out of string to help us map out the cemetery,* Donna suddenly realized. *She's a genius*—her own grandmother!

After they had the strings lined up in one direction, they strung up another set using the pickets on the two sides of the fence that were perpendicular to the first. Only two or three inches off the ground, the strings were easy to see and easy to step over if you were careful. Once they had the grid up, Grandma took the stick she had prepared earlier and started piercing the ground along the string lines. The ground was surprisingly soft, and she had only made a few holes when she hit something solid.

Was it a tree root or—was it a grave? After a few more *thunks,* she got down on her knees and dug into the soil with her trowel. That's when she and Donna discovered that the soil beneath the surface of the cemetery was like compost, so it tore away in chunks the size of dinner plates. Four dinner plates later, Grandma uncovered something made of unpolished marble. On closer inspection, it was the corner of a box, and it had a smooth, beveled edge. It took a moment, but Donna suddenly knew what they had uncovered. *It was the lid to a vault! They'd dug up a body! They were grave robbers!* Poking around in a cemetery was suddenly very uncool. Donna's hands got sweaty, and she started imagining all kinds of creepy things. A beast!

The kind in the movies that bites the girl in half while she's scream-ing her head off was going to come boiling up out of that vault any second. She was sure of it. She could practically smell its putrid flesh! Grandma caught her in mid-flight with one leg over the fence and the other one halfway off the ground—nabbed inches away from safety!

"Young lady! Where do you think you're going?" Grandma asked in her sternest voice.

"I don't like this place, anymore," Donna replied. "I'm afraid of these people; there are dead people everywhere. Why do we have to do this?"

"Because it's the right thing to do and because we're the only ones to do it. How are you ever going to become a respected historian if you're afraid to learn? Miss Anne is no stranger to you; you know all about her. You even know the names of her children that she buried here. During her lifetime, Miss Anne was mistress of this great plantation, and I imagine that everyone up and down the river knew her and respected her. Now they're all gone," Grandma pointed out. "There's no one left to even remember her name. If we don't do it, it will be as if she never lived at all. So, I've decided that she and the rest of her family should become honorary members of our family—yours and mine. That way they won't be forgotten. If we have to poke holes in the ground or even dig up a headstone or two, they won't mind. They would want to be remembered just as much as we would. We only have another hour before we have to head back to the house and start supper. Do you want to stay or not?"

Donna stayed, of course, and after a while, she realized Grandma was right—*damn it, she was always right.* Miss Anne and the other people buried there had been there a long, long time, and it would be positively sinful to allow their graves to simply disappear. Pretty soon she even got into the swing of things and helped Grandma do the poking. And as it turned out, it was fun—kind of like hunting for buried treasure with a magic wand. After a while, they could even identify what they were hitting just by the sound it made. A tree root, for example, made a dull thud, but a vault made a hollow sound. They soon discovered that the vaults had matching lids, which were also made of marble. The lids, however, weren't hinged or cemented to the vault; their weight was enough to keep them in place. Every time Grandma and Donna heard that hollow sound, Grandma would mark the spot with flour from the sack in her apron. Pretty soon, they had five vaults clearly outlined and then ten—ten new members of the family.

"I sure am having fun," Grandma said, feeling around in her pocket for more flour. "How about you?"

"Yeah, I'm having fun, too."

CHAPTER 9

The People's Cemetery

The Abbey Plantation 1958-59

ON THE WAY BACK to the house, Donna started thinking about the enslaved people who had lived at The Abbey. There would have been hundreds of them living on the plantation over the years. After all, she and Grandma knew that the plantation dated back to the early 1700s because they'd seen a copy of The Abbey's original land grant that was dated 1711. Even if the plantation wasn't up and running for several years after that, slaves must have been living on the plantation by the 1720s—more than two hundred and thirty years ago. So, when they died, where were they buried? You'd need a big cemetery, a really big one.

"Grandma," she said after chucking a pebble into Granddaddy Jim's alligator pond. "Where were the enslaved people buried? The ones who lived on the plantation. Where were they buried?"

"You mean you haven't seen the People's cemetery, yet?" Grandma asked surprised.

"They had their own cemetery?"

"Yes! There's one just upriver from the house, just beyond the path that leads to Grandaddy Jim's new pump house. It doesn't look like much, though. It's an overgrown mess, but it's got a fence around it, so it's easy enough to find. Are you sure Granddaddy Jim never showed you that cemetery?"

"I'm positive."

"Well, he's not fond of cemeteries, say's they give him the creeps, so that's probably why. He did put the fence around it, though."

"Can we go there?" Donna pleaded.

"I've got to fix supper tonight, but we can go tomorrow if you want to. Remind me in the morning," Grandma said.

"What are we having for supper?"

"My two favorite vegetables—snap beans and macaroni and cheese."

"Macaroni and cheese isn't a vegetable, Grandma."

"In South Carolina it is."

"What about in other places?"

"We don't care what they call it in New York or any place else for that matter," she replied. "We only care about what it's called here, and here it's a vegetable."

During supper, Grandma and Granddaddy Jim told Donna about the slave cemetery. It might not have seemed like the ideal dinner conversation to some, but Donna clung to every word.

"When Grandma and I moved here five years ago, the slave cemetery was so hidden beneath brush and undergrowth, I didn't even know it was there," Granddaddy said. "I don't remember how I found it; maybe one of my workers mentioned it. I can't remember, but when I did know that it was there, I felt kind of bad, so I put an old scrap fence around it."

During the first two years on the plantation, Granddaddy Jim said he didn't have his lumber company up and running yet, so times were especially lean. To make some extra money, Grandma joined a group of church ladies who hired themselves out to clean houses. One of the women, a lady named Mrs. Greene, descended from enslaved people from over in Plantersville. She knew a thing or two about slave cemeteries, only she called them graveyards. Mrs. Greene figured out real soon that Grandma was the only one in the group who never tired of her stories, so in between house cleanings, she'd save up stuff to tell her. Grandma said she didn't know what she was going to do with all that knowledge, but now she did. She was going to tell Donna everything she could remember, and it was plenty. As she and Donna made their way toward the People's cemetery the following afternoon, Grandma started in on Mrs. Greene's stories.

"If the enslaved people back in plantation times were given the opportunity to select a location for their own cemetery, they were always quick to select a plot near water," she explained. "The People had an altogether different view of death and the after world," Grandma said. "They believed that once a person died, his or her soul had to pass through a water world to get to Heaven. Being close to water sort of speeded up the process. The water world was so important that people left things on the grave to help the soul of the departed get to the water, especially if the cemetery wasn't close to water."

"Is the cemetery here at The Abbey close to water?" Donna asked.

"It is. It butts up against a tidal pond on the other side," Grandma said.

"What kind of things did people leave at a grave?" Donna asked.

"Things that would hold water mostly, vessels, they called them. Shells were the most common thing to leave on a grave. Sometimes, they would be placed facing up, and other times they would be placed upside down and broken. Mrs. Greene said she didn't know what the difference was, but a shell is a shell, so it didn't really matter. Another thing is that the People had a different way of laying out their cemeteries. You know how the Dunhill family cemetery is laid out on a grid with everybody facing the East? Well, the People's cemeteries couldn't be more different. The People buried their dead every which way, and when they dug a grave, if they accidentally dug into an older one, that was perfectly okay. Mrs. Greene said that they tended to see the cemetery and the whole act of dying more like a family thing or community thing. They wanted to be together in life and in death. I think it's really nice."

"Me too," Donna said.

"It makes the cemeteries look like they are unkept, though, when really, they're left that way on purpose. Mrs. Greene said that's why some people go back into these old cemeteries and clean them up, thinking they are doing a good thing. It's a noble idea, but if you really want to respect an old slave cemetery, you leave it alone."

When they got to Grandaddy Jim's snow fence, Grandma said she'd just remembered some of the most interesting things she learned about the People's graveyard. She'd forgotten to tell Donna about the things that are left behind to honor the dead.

"When the People buried their dead, their family honored them by decorating their grave with something that they loved in life or something that they touched right before passing."

"What sort of things, Grandma?"

"Tea cups, hand mirrors, hair brushes, teapots, eye glasses, shaving mugs.... It could be most anything, but sometimes people were even more creative. Mrs. Greene told me that here at The Abbey graveyard, there's a grave with a large pipe sticking out of the ground that the family used to talk to the person in the grave with. She said that at the cemetery on the old Friendfield Plantation, there's a grave with a steering wheel from a 1930 Cadillac."

"Why, Grandma?"

"Because the man who died used to work as a chauffeur."

"What's that?"

"A man who drives rich people around in fancy cars," Grandma replied. "We're sure to see some whiskey bottles, too, but they're not trash. It means that someone came here and had a drink with the dead person."

"How could they do that?" Donna asked, incredulously.

"They would pour two glasses of whiskey, and then they'd drink one and pour the other one onto the grave. So, when you see a whiskey bottle or any other kind of bottle, leave it right where you found it. Promise me that you won't touch anything. Another thing I want you to know before we go there is that there are people who still bury their dead in these old cemeteries."

"You mean we could see some new graves?"

"We could. It's still the People's cemetery, you know. So, be respectful and watch for snakes. I'm sure there are some here."

"Snakes are everywhere," Donna said.

Donna and Grandma had a difficult time deciding where to climb over the fence. There wasn't a gate; Granddaddy had told them that. But there were some low places, and he suggested climbing the fence there. Finally, they found a spot, but it was still tall enough that Donna snagged her panties on a rough-sawn picket and had to stand there with her leg hiked up while Grandma untangled her.

Once inside the fence, moving about was pretty easy, although they intentionally walked slowly and stomped their feet to warn the snakes to clear out. Even so, Donna said that Tarzan could have gotten lost in the gnarled vines and pricker bushes that grew there. Maybe that was why they didn't see as many graves as Donna had expected.

"The People couldn't buy marble or stone headstones; they had to do with what they had," Grandma explained. "Mrs. Greene said that most of the graves were marked with wooden headstones, but over time, they rotted away and disappeared."

Three of the graves that Donna and Grandma found that day had headstones made out of concrete, but they'd been there a long time. They were getting pretty hard to read, though, other than a date here or a letter or two there. Grandma did spot the grave with the pipe sticking out of it, though, and they happened onto a dozen or more whiskey bottles, a couple of beer bottles, a teapot, a soup ladle, shaving mugs, tea cups, a platter used as a headstone, a rice spoon, and a water pitcher with a rose painted on it.

CHAPTER 10

One Man's Trash

The Abbey Plantation 1958-59

"PEOPLE LIVING IN plantation times weren't very tidy when it came to getting rid of their trash. They didn't have garbage men or trash cans or anything of the like," Grandma said. "They just dug pits in the yard, filled them with trash, and covered them over when they were full. Even then, they weren't very neat about it. From what I've read, they seemed to have had a casual attitude toward trash," Grandma said. "They were more likely to just throw things out in the yard or beneath their houses than they were to put it in the pit. The planters did it, overseers did it, and the People did it. They threw everything out there — everything from chicken bones to broken dishes."

Donna soon learned that you couldn't dig a hole big enough to plant a seed without uncovering something. Practically every time Granddaddy Jim worked in one of the gardens near the house, he'd uncover pieces of old pottery or china. Sometimes, even the chickens would scratch them up. It made sense that soup tureens, cups and saucers, tumblers, platters, mugs, and jugs were occasionally dropped; forks were bent; ladles were separated from their handles; tea kettles sprung leaks; and the pieces and parts found their way into the trash heap. Along with the pottery shards, Donna found clay pipes, buttons made out of mother-of-pearl, English half pennies with King George's portrait on them, a child's tea cup, enough marbles to fill a Mason jar, a rice hook, a butcher knife with a bone handle, and dozens of handmade nails, hinges, doorknobs, and escutcheon plates. She also found enough arrowheads to fill up Grandma's spare button box, the hand grips from an old pistol, and half a dozen musket balls.

CHAPTER 11

Jenny Lou Watson

The Abbey Plantation 1959

LIKE MOST KIDS, DONNA had a love-hate relationship with school. She loved books and reading, and she was a world-class speller, but she hated having to go to school because she didn't like the kids, or to be more precise, she was pretty sure they didn't like her. When Donna was alone, her imagination allowed her to be anything she wanted to be. She could be charming and witty and breathtakingly beautiful. She could glide across a gilded ballroom and make every man in the room fall passionately in love with her with one bat of her long, luxurious lashes.

"Why, if it isn't James Ravenel," she'd gush. "Of course, I'll save you a dance, you scoundrel you," she'd promise with a wave of her fan, and then she'd blow a smoldering kiss to the dashing Reginald Rutledge Huger, fresh from a tiger hunt with the maharaja of Jaipur.

At school, though, she was just a little fat girl with red corkscrew hair. The person she envied the most was Jenny Lou Watson. Jenny Lou was so pretty that when she walked down the halls at school, the traffic parted for her just like the waters did for Moses. Jenny Lou had masses of blond hair, perfect teeth, a Lana Turner nose, and a solid gold charm bracelet. The teachers loved her, the boys thought she was God's gift, and every girl in the whole school wanted to be just like her, including Donna. Jenny Lou was on the student council, she was a cheerleader, a class favorite, and she played the harp. The harp! She was smart, and she was perfect.

Donna figured she was just as smart as Jenny Lou but about as far away from perfect as you could get. Jenny Lou had never spoken to Donna or even looked in her direction. *Why should she?* Donna asked herself. *I just wish she'd say hello to me one time. She wouldn't have to mean it or anything. I just want to know what it'd feel like.*

CHAPTER 12

A Worm on a Hook

The Abbey Plantation 1959

THE DAY AFTER HER thirteenth birthday, Donna and Grandma ran into none other than Jenny Lou and her mother at the meat counter at Marlow's Store. Surrounded by rump roasts, baloney with the skin on, and hams hanging from the ceiling, Jenny Lou twinkled like neon. She was wearing pink pedal pushers and a pink halter top; and although Donna couldn't actually see it, she positively knew that Jenny Lou was wearing a pink bra, too. Her hair was in a ponytail, which swished when she walked in her little pink flats, and her mother was perfect, too.

When Grandma started walking toward them, Donna wanted to die. As they approached the counter, Jenny Lou and her mother never looked at Grandma and Donna or even acknowledged their presence. The perfect pair just stood there bantering back and forth in their perfect ice-tinkling-in-the-crystal-glass Delta Gamma voices. Donna had every right to hate them for treating them like that, but she didn't. She just felt like she and Grandma were two shabby shadows not worthy of a second look.

That was the lowest point in Donna's entire childhood next to the day Mama died, but things have a way of turning around when you least expect, and four hours and twelve minutes later, that's exactly what happened.

That's when Grandma called her out on the porch to read something to her from the front page of the *Georgetown Gazette*. The notice she read announced a statewide contest for young writers. Sponsored by the South Carolina Historical Society, the contest challenged students between the ages of twelve and eighteen to write local histories of their hometowns or neighborhoods. The first-place winner was to receive a $1,000 college scholarship and have his or her manuscript published into a real live book! Entries were due September 1. It took Grandma two days to talk Donna into entering the contest.

"You can write about The Abbey, and that's the best story there is."

CHAPTER 13

Cat Head Biscuits

The Abbey Plantation 1959

DONNA JUMP-STARTED HER PROJECT by crawling beneath her bed to retrieve her collection of spiral notebooks, diaries, and writing tablets filled with research notes. One of them even had some of Grandma's best recipes, including her world-famous biscuit recipe that Donna thought she'd add to her manuscript just to impress the judges. The size of a proper biscuit was a big deal to Grandma. She always said that people from New York traveled to South Carolina, expecting to see biscuits that were two to three inches tall, but that was because they wouldn't know the real thing if they tripped over it.

"Real buttermilk biscuits are not to be judged by their height," she said. "They are to be judged by their circumference."

Grandma was an expert on making biscuits. She made them with red eye gravy practically every day of her life. That was because in addition to being The Abbey's caretaker, Granddaddy Jim also owned a small logging business. Many men had worked for him over the years, including some broken-down, calloused, drifter-types, like Dudley Olinbush. All true Southerners, of course, know a thing or two about biscuits, but

Grandma said she'd never forget the first time she served biscuits and red eye gravy to Dudley.

Supper for the men was served out in the yard on a long table that Granddaddy Jim had made from scrap lumber. The men sat on a collection of old kitchen chairs, nail kegs, wooden crates, and a two-seater made from the guts to a 1930s wicker porch swing. Grandma was serving biscuits to some of the other men when Dudley exclaimed, "Good Gawd, Miss Katie! Them's cat head biscuits!"

"What the devil are you talking about, Dudley?" Grandma asked, turning toward him. "You liked to croaked me yelling like that."

"I'm sorry, Miss Katie," Dudley replied. "It's jest that I ain't seen biscuits like this since I was a kid. Them's as big as cats' heads."

After she copied the recipe onto some notebook paper, Donna drew a cat's head next to it and decided it looked so good that she'd include a couple more recipes.

Deciding which ones to use was the hard part, but she finally came up with two recipes for rutabaga pie. Why two? Because one tasted just like pumpkin pie, and the other one was like a chicken pot pie with rutabagas, potatoes, hamburger meat, onion, celery, and store-bought steak sauce. Donna and Granddaddy Jim loved the chicken pot pie version, but Grandma didn't make it very much unless company was coming because it had a particular sauce in it, and the sauce was expensive. After reading the label and learning that the sauce had been created by a chef for one of the kings of England, Grandma said it was no wonder that it was way out of her price range—a whopping sixty-nine cents a bottle.

CHAPTER 14

Little Bo Peep

Boone Plantation 1959

IF DONNA WAS GOING to write a prize-winning story about life on a plantation, she'd need to know a lot more about slave quarters than she did. Since there weren't any slave cabins left at The Abbey, Donna asked Grandma if they could visit the slave street at Boone Hall Plantation, just north of Charleston.

Although it was more than an hour's drive from The Abbey, it didn't take much to talk Grandma into it because she loved to meander through the plantation's elaborate English-style gardens. Donna liked the gardens well enough, but she was far more interested in poking around inside the plantation's original barns, workshops, and slave cabins. To get the most out of their trip, Donna and Grandma decided to take a free guided tour of the plantation. Their docent was Alberta Mae Davenport, a molasses-laced, aging belle that Grandma said was the spittn' image of Aunt Pittypat in *Gone With the Wind*. A hoop the size of a bathtub held up Alberta Mae's enormous skirts, but she had the hoop thing down pat. It was a thing of beauty.

After negotiating the porch steps as graceful as you please, Alberta Mae curtsied to her little group of visitors and introduced herself. Then she batted her eyes behind a lacy silk fan and announced with a great fanfare that Boone Hall's famous half-mile avenue of oaks had been featured in the movie version of *Gone With the Wind,* as the avenue leading to Ashley Wilke's stately mansion, Twelve Oaks.

After allowing a reasonable amount of time for that bit of history to settle in, Alberta Mae went on to explain that Boone Hall was built in 1743 and that it had stayed in the Boone family for more than one hundred years. The plantation's survival, she emphasized, hinged on the fact that when the cotton market crashed during the War Between the States, Boone Hall fell back on its second industry, manufacturing bricks and roof tiles.

"I wish The Abbey had done that," Grandma whispered. With a wave of her gloved hand, Alberta Mae also pointed out that some of the finest mansions and civic buildings in Charleston were made out of bricks and tiles made at Boone Hall. Since planters along the Waccamaw River built most of those mansions, Grandma said it made sense that some of the planters also used bricks from Boone Hall to build their plantations. Boone Hall brick wasn't used to build The Abbey, though. The Abbey Plantation was too old. According to Alberta Mae, Boone Hall's slave street was one of the few still standing. Made of brick with roofs of overlapping clay tiles, the cabins lined the creek side of the avenue of oaks just as they did in plantation times.

"These cabins were occupied by—shall we say—the upper-level house servants," Alberta Mae noted with a dramatic point of the finger. "The field workers lived in smaller cabins elsewhere on the plantation. Well, that is the end of our tour today," she added, "but we certainly want to invite y'all to stay for the battle—it's very exciting, and it's free to everyone."

"A battle?" Donna said. "What battle?"

"The Battle of Secessionville," Grandma replied. "Didn't you see the sign? We can stay for a while if you want to, but if we do, we'll need a front row seat. Go back to the truck and get the quilt behind the seat. Then go over there and stake out a claim."

Donna found a good spot next to a woman and her two children. As it turned out, the woman was the wife of one of the reenactors, and she was dressed for the part. Her long, shiny blond hair was neatly tucked into a black hairnet and her green and white silk dress looked just like the one Scarlet wore to the barbecue at Twelve Oaks, except it didn't show off her bosoms like Scarlet's dress did. The woman's daughter, Melanie, was seven. She had long blond hair just like her mother's, but Melanie's hair was in pigtails tied at the ends with big blue bows. On her head, she wore a straw bonnet that matched her dress, which was periwinkle blue with little white flowers on it.

Donna thought she looked just like Little Bo Peep and found herself wishing that she had a costume just like that even though she knew that it was one of those things, kind of like red patent-leather shoes. You know you don't need them; you just want them.

CHAPTER 15

The Red Chair

Mt. Pleasant, SC 1959

AFTER SPENDING THE MORNING watching the reenactment, Donna and Grandma decided to stop at the Sudsy Dawg in Mt. Pleasant before heading back to Pawleys Island. While they were there, they spotted a small junk store.

"Let's go see what they've got," Grandma said, savoring her last bite of hot dog. "I could sure use some more plastic containers."

The parking lot in front of the store was so full of furniture and rusted-out farm implements that Grandma ripped her stockings on a bed spring hiding behind a sixteen-gallon galvanized feed tub before she could even get to the door. Once inside, however, she and Donna were faced with a different challenge. It was so dark they could barely see their hands in front of their faces.

"I can't see squat," Grandma said. "How 'bout you?"

"I can't see anything either," Donna replied. "I don't think this is even a store. It's a warehouse or something, and I don't like it. Let's go."

"Oh, you're such a weenie," Grandma said. "I'm not going anywhere until I've had a chance to look around."

Standing side-by-side, allowing their eyes to acclimate to the dim lighting, they heard a howl—the kind a cat makes when he gets too close to the rocking chair—followed by a booming baritone voice resonating from the back of the store.

"Ya'll come right on in and make yo'selves to home," the voice said.

Donna quickly gave Grandma one of those let's-get-out-of-here looks, but Grandma ignored her and took off in her search for plastic ware. Donna followed suit, keeping a watchful eye out for the person who belonged to the voice in the back room.

"Grandma," Donna whispered, "I don't like this place. I'm afraid there are rats in here and that there's a man in the back room torturing cats. I want to go home."

"Donna," Grandma whispered back. "Nobody's torturing cats, and there aren't any rats, here. Why do you think they have cats? Now help me look for one of those fancy cake plates with the see-through covers and the yellow plastic handles. I've been wanting one of those for years."

Just then, Paycheck Quartermain, the owner of the booming voice appeared, and he seemed so glad to see them that Donna figured he hadn't had a customer in months.

"Howdy do, ladies," he said, making a slight adjustment to the waistband on his coveralls. "What can I help y'all with?"

"I'm interested in buying one of those fancy cake plates with the see-through covers and the yellow plastic handles," Grandma replied as if everyone in the world shared her enthusiasm for plastic kitchen accessories.

Paycheck didn't flinch; he acted as if he was asked that question a hundred times a day. "I think I've got two of 'em," he said. "I'm just not certain where they are. Give me a minute. I think they might be back there with the fishing tackle and the Majolica oyster plates, but I'm not sure."

Donna was just about to ask Grandma what in the world a Majolica oyster plate was when something caught her eye just to the left of a stuffed fox squirrel mounted to a tree stump. It was a chair, a child's chair with turned spindles and a gracefully curved back that also formed the arms of the chair. It looked as though it had sat outside for years, but after knocking some of the dust off, she could tell that a long time ago it had been painted red, a funny kind of red like you might find on a

Chinese lantern. In the meantime, Grandma had joined the search for the treasured cake plates at the back of the store, so Donna decided to take a closer look at the chair. After blowing off another layer of dust, she turned the chair upside down where she discovered even more evidence of red paint. And then she righted it again, and that's when she spotted something even more intriguing—the initials TMD. TMD—the same initials she saw every day on a small footstone in the Dunhill Family cemetery at The Abbey.

"Grandma!" she shouted. "Grandma, come see what I found."

"I'll be there in a minute," Grandma replied. "Mr. Quartermain just found the handle to one of the cake plates, so the rest of it should be here someplace."

"Grandma," Donna cried. "I found something really important."

"I'll be there in a minute," was Grandma's only reply. So, Donna waited. Finally, Grandma and Paycheck returned from the bowels of the store, wearing triumphant smiles, each carrying a plastic cake plate with a see-through cover and a yellow plastic handle. Ecstatic over her finds, Grandma had forgotten all about Donna's excited claims, but Donna was about to explode from excitement and practically attacked her as she and Paycheck approached the front of the store.

"Come see! Come see!" Donna insisted. "Come see what I found."

So, Grandma deposited her own treasures on the check-out counter and followed Donna to a spot along the left side of the store just beneath the stuffed head of an elk half the size of Kansas. But when she saw that Donna was pointing to a chair, she lost her sense of humor. "You brought me back here to see a chair?" she asked.

"This isn't just a chair, Grandma," Donna squealed. "I think this is a very important chair. I think this chair came from The Abbey."

"What's The Abbey?" Paycheck asked, interjecting himself into the conversation.

"It's a plantation in Pawleys Island," Donna said, exasperated.

"Y'all own a plantation?" Paycheck asked with eyes the size of half dollars.

"No, we don't own the plantation," Grandma replied. "We're the caretakers; we just live there."

"Well, I was going to say, it's not every day that you meet a plantation owner," Paycheck said. "Come to think if it, I never have. So, what's with the chair?"

"I think it belonged to a little boy who is buried in the cemetery at The Abbey," Donna replied. "See the initials," she said pointing to the inscription. "They're TMD, just like on the foot stone in the cemetery. They're the initials of Miss Anne's son—Theodore Madison Dunhill. I just know it."

"You have no way of knowing who owned that chair, and besides, it would have to be really old if it had belonged to that little boy," Grandma said. "I think he died in 1815."

"No, Grandma; he died September 14, 1820, and I know this is his chair," Donna replied.

Hearing the resolve in her granddaughter's voice, Grandma turned to Paycheck and asked if he knew anything about the history of the chair.

"Well," he said, "I got this off an ol' boy from Charleston a year ago, maybe more, but I don't know where he found it. All I can tell y'all is that it's called a Windsor chair, and it's old. If you study it up close, you can tell it ain't been near a furniture factory. It was made by hand."

"What do you want for it?" Grandma asked.

"Well, seeing as to how y'all perked up my day by stopping by, I'll make you a package deal—four and a quarter for everything."

"Three and half and you've got yourself a sale," Grandma replied.

"Make it an even four and it's a done deal," Paycheck countered, and the bargain was struck.

As Paycheck helped load the chair into the back of Granddaddy Jim's truck for the trip back home, Grandma was about to point out that they would never be able to prove for sure that the chair actually came from the plantation no matter how much they wanted to believe it had when in the sunlight, she saw something carved on the underneath side of the chair.

"Wait a minute, Mr. Quartermain," she said. "Don't load the chair just yet. I think I saw something."

Paycheck responded by positioning the chair so that the three of them could clearly see the name Hattie Wineglass and the date—1855—on the underneath side of the chair.

"Hattie Wineglass!" Grandma exclaimed. "Miss Hattie used to have the school for colored children on River Road. Everyone in town knew Miss Hattie. She lived on the second floor of her school and taught every day until the day she died. She was born enslaved at The Abbey, and I remember when she died because I went to the funeral. It was back in the early 1940s, and there must have been a thousand people there. The governor and his wife came all the way from Columbia. Now that I think about it, there was another really important person there that day. The newspaper said she was a mulatto lady. Her name started with an *M*, I think. Anyway, she had grown up at The Abbey where she had been one of Miss Hattie's students. The lady had donated the money to build Miss Hattie's schoolhouse, and then she went on to found an orphanage and school for the colored children of Charleston. I didn't get to meet her or anything, but I got to see her during Miss Hattie's funeral. She was sitting right next to the governor. I think you're right about the chair belonging to Miss Anne's little boy," she said smiling.

"Oh, Grandma!" Donna cried. "I just knew it! Oh, thank you, Mr. Quartermain! Thank you so much!"

"You're welcome, child," Paycheck said, flashing a toothy smile. "I reckon it was just sitting here waiting for you to take it back home. Now, y'all get on your way, but promise to visit me the next time you're in the neighborhood. And take good care of that chair," he said slamming the tailgate.

"I promise I will, Mr. Quartermain," Donna said. "I promise."

CHAPTER 16

Tooker and Hattie

Charleston, SC 1959

AFTER THEIR TRIP TO Boone Hall, Donna and Grandma decided that it was time to head out for the courthouse to mimeograph wills, deeds, death records, and other court documents that Donna needed to write her story. And even though they found some important records, they were desperate to figure out exactly what happened to The Abbey's big house and barns and other outbuildings. What they needed was an eyewitness. Then they found something that made both of them shout and holler for joy. Just by chance, they ran across a folder in the research room of the library that contained a half-dozen crumbling letters written to Hattie Wineglass by someone named Tooker Rosa.

"Yippee," Grandma exclaimed. "I don't have the slightest idea who Tooker Rosa was, but if he knew Miss Hattie well enough to write to her, maybe we can figure out who he was."

A few hours later, they did just that. They learned that Tooker was the son of a man hired to teach catechism to the enslaved children at The Abbey. Master Rosa and his family—including his son, Tooker—actually lived at The Abbey during the War Between the States. They had an eyewitness to the most historic day in The Abbey's two hundred and twenty-five-year-old history. According to a note attached to the file, the last letter in the series was missing, but the other five were still there. In the first one, Tooker told Hattie that although he had enjoyed his summer at the creek house on Pawleys Island, he missed spending time with her, and if the war didn't come too close to the plantation, he would see her in the fall. Then he bragged about rescuing bolts of silk that had washed ashore near the creek house and told her how scared everyone was the day the island was attacked by a Yankee gunship. In his subsequent letters, Tooker recalled the disheartening news of distant battles and about his mother having to resort to making coffee out of boiled weeds and substituting the ashes from corn cobs for baking soda. He asked Hattie about the health of her grandmother, Miss Lillian, and then he sadly announced that his cousin from Richmond had been killed at the Battle of Shiloh.

Then Tooker described his last day at The Abbey, February 14, 1865.

I don't know if you saw me on the boat landing the day the Yankees came, but I was there. I looked for you, but I didn't see you or any of your family.

Did you see any of the things that happened that day or were you sent into the woods to hide with the other children? Papa made Mama and my younger brothers and sisters to stay in the house, but he allowed me to accompany him to the landing. He told me that if we treated the soldiers with respect, they would respect us in return. Of course, that didn't happen.

When they came ashore, they were so riled up they ate raw eggs right out of the hen house and slapped each other on the back as they took turns shooting the sows in the pig pen. They tore at the skirts of some of the women and set the dairy barn on fire. While a handful of the soldiers set fire to the storehouse and the mill, a second group of men poured hundreds of pounds of rice onto the ground and ripped out every fence post in sight.

Then they drove Mama and my brothers and sisters out of our house and threw everything we owned out into the yard. Mama was pleading with them to leave, but they knocked her to the ground, and one of them wrenched her wedding ring off her finger. Then they set fire to our house with torches soaked in pitch, and then they moved on to the Big House where most of the People were already gathered. About a minute later, I saw a group of men heaving together to push Miss Weston's piano over the edge of the piazza. When it crashed into the yard, a crowd of soldiers roared with laughter, and then wine bottles started flying out of the windows in the attic, and everything just started happening at once.

Dishes and furniture were tossed into great piles in the yards and clothing and bed linens, the likes of which you've never seen, spilled out onto the yard from overturned trunks and linen presses. There was smoke everywhere and people screaming at each other and babies crying and guns going off all over the place.

And then some of the People just started falling on the stuff in the yard, ripping and tearing at it like dogs fighting over raw meat. Some of them ran from the house carrying banisters and chairs and books, while Old Zeus and his sons carried off Master Weston's globe.

Even with all the yelling and screaming going on, we weren't afraid of the People so much. We were afraid of the soldiers. And we were about as scared as you could get, so while all of this was going on, Papa motioned for us to gather round and told us that we were going to have to make a run for it.

"Run for the carriage house," he shouted, "and don't stop for anyone or anything."

He didn't have to tell us twice. We were so scared we took off like jack rabbits — even Mama. When we got there, we harnessed Master Weston's bays to one of his carriages, and Papa and I piled everyone in. Then he told me to peek out of the carriage house to see if our way was clear, and then I jumped aboard, and we took off. As we rushed down the avenue for the last time, we looked back at the plantation, and that's when we saw the flames.

I'll never forget our escape back to the island. It was less than three miles to the creek house, but it took us the rest of the day to get there. The road was a quagmire, and we were never out of the sight of dead things, and the stench was almost unbearable. There were dead horses all along the way, and once we even saw a man's arm sticking out of a shallow grave. What is to happen to us, Hattie?

The letter was signed: *I pray that you and your family are safe. Your faithful friend, Tooker*

CHAPTER 17

Now I Ain't Worth a Plugged Nickel

The Abbey Plantation 1960

THE WAR OFFICIALLY ENDED two months later, but by then, the fields were overgrown, the barns and outbuildings had been burned to the ground, and most important, the river had destroyed the irreplaceable dikes.

"There wasn't enough money in the world to rebuild what had been lost," Grandma said. "The Abbey was one of the most valuable plantations on the river, and now it was gone." Then she said the Yankees eventually took over the plantation, split it up into forty-acre plots, and parceled it out to former slaves. Some people along the river stuck it out for a few more years, including one of the last planters, Elizabeth Allston Pringle. Mrs. Pringle's father was the last governor of South Carolina before the War Between the States, and her family was one of the wealthiest in the state. And yet, toward the end, Mrs. Pringle was so desperate that she once borrowed sixty dollars from one of her family's former slaves. She planted her last crop in 1906."

"It is a thing of the past now," Mrs. Pringle wrote. "The banks are gone, the trunks have been washed away, and there is no money to replace them."

No one could have anticipated a second Yankee invasion, but in the early 1900s, that's exactly what happened. Rich Yankees started buying up the old plantations for ten-cents on the dollar to use as fishing and hunting preserves. South Carolinians found the second invasion more humiliating than the first.

"In one way, though, it turned out to be a blessing," Grandma said, "because it saved The Abbey and the other old rice plantations from having houses or steel mills or power plants built on them during those years."

Donna figured it was a classic case of God working in mysterious ways.

CHAPTER 18

Struttin' Her Stuff

The Abbey Plantation 1960

THE DEADLINE FOR TURNING in her manuscript was September 1, but Donna was so afraid of making a fool out of herself, she kept revising her story. She worked on it on the porch, in her room, and even in the bathroom. Her favorite place, though, was the kitchen table, and that's where she and Granddaddy Jim came to loggerheads. After telling her for the tenth time to get her papers off the table, he accidentally knocked a stack of them all over the kitchen floor. That was it. Granddaddy Jim was pissed and threatened to pull the plug on the whole project. Well, that was just fine with Donna, and she came bouncing into the kitchen thinking that her book-writing nightmare was behind her. Hallelujah!

There was one little problem, though. She'd forgotten about Grandma. "If you think you're getting out of this one, you're dead wrong," Grandma said under her breath. "You're gonna finish that manuscript if it kills us both."

She was showing her teeth. She meant it. She gave Donna two days to finish her paper, and then she drove Donna to Charleston to submit it in person. The volunteers at the Historical Society were unexpectedly helpful, but instead of being one of those really great moments in Donna's life, it turned out to be a perfectly rotten one. While she and Grandma were waiting for the woman at the desk to accept the manuscript, Donna spotted a big pile of other manuscripts on a table behind her desk, and they were beautiful. It was clear that each of them had been typewritten, and most of them were in fancy folders. Donna's manuscript was written in longhand, and it was held together with an ugly red rubber band. A chunk of her heart fell off and died.

School started two days later for which Donna was eternally grateful because she didn't have time to dwell on the contest. Instead, she had to get all of her school supplies together, and Grandma performed the annual task of figuring out what to do with Donna's HAIR! One thing they hadn't anticipated, however, was that all of Donna's school clothes were way too big and way too short.

During the summer, Donna had managed to thin down and grow four-inches all at the same time! She didn't even know a person could do that, but she was sure liking it. Of course, she couldn't take credit for getting taller, but she must have thinned down because she had been too busy to eat all summer. There was a God after all.

Her rangy new body didn't make her like school any better, but she had to admit that she didn't hate it as much as she used to. Her heart still went SPRONG, though, when she saw Jenny Lou Watson. The first day of school, for example, Donna wore a green and white flowered dress with a big white line around the bottom of the skirt where it had been let out.

Jenny Lou wore a lemon-yellow sleeveless blouse with a matching straight skirt and white flats. Donna realized that day, however, that looking perfect probably had its drawbacks. It required a lot of time to look like that, so much so that Jenny Lou Watson hadn't signed up for the writing contest.

Of course, Donna didn't know that was the reason Miss Perfect hadn't signed up, but she was relieved about it just the same. September dragged on and so did October. It seemed as though November was never going to come, and then, of course, it did. The winner of the contest was to be notified by mail, and the letter was to be sent out on November first. November second lumbered by, and so did November third. By then Donna had learned that four other students from her school, alone, had entered the contest, which meant that hundreds, maybe thousands of manuscripts must have been submitted statewide. She also learned that she was one of the youngest entrants. *Well, that was just great!*

Then at 1:23 p.m. on Friday, November fourth, Donna was called to the principal's office. By the time she got there, her ears were making clanging sounds, and she was on the verge of tears. Someone had died, or she had committed an unpardonable sin. Either way, she figured she was in big trouble. When she got there, though, the principal, his secretary, Grandma, Granddaddy Jim, and her fifth-grade teacher were standing there with grins on their faces like they'd been stealing watermelons.

"The letter," Grandma said in her church lady voice. "The letter came.... You won first place, Donna. You won the contest!"

Donna didn't remember much after that. She vaguely recalled Grandma handing her the letter and her teacher kissing her cheek. There'd been some backslapping, she was sure of that, and handshaking, although she couldn't swear to it. She didn't even remember being driven home from school.

An assembly was held the following day to officially announce what had already spread all over town. Donna walked in to take her seat on stage, and everyone cheered.

For the first time in her life, Donna Margaret Jackson, a former little fat girl, was the center of attention. She suddenly had a bad case of the tingles, and her lips were acting crazy, like they didn't know whether to form a smile or to prepare themselves for a good hard cry.

Could fame affect your bladder?

Someone from the Historical Society was there and so was a photographer from the *Georgetown Times*, and after a few minutes, Donna got to thinking it couldn't get any better, when all of a sudden, it did.

After declaring how proud he was to have such a splendid award earned by one his finest students, Principal Sullivan went on to explain that

Donna had won the award not only because she had written a compelling story but because she had done a first-rate job of researching it. Then he asked another of his most accomplished students to introduce Donna, and none other than Jenny Lou Watson rose from her seat, headed toward the lectern. Donna got so lightheaded, she also tipped over her chair.

"I'm just so honored to be here today to introduce y'all to one of my very dearest friends," Miss Perfect gushed. "What can you say about Donna Jackson? Well, I guess you can say she's just about perfect. That's it; she's a perfect little ol' thing. So, without further ado, here she is — my friend Donna Jackson."

Donna stood, staring at the lectern, which looked like it was at the end of a tunnel. She was going to have to get there one way or another, so she took a step to test the waters. She smiled. She had it in the bag. She was heading herself on over to the lectern — the center of the universe at that moment — and she felt like struttin' her stuff and singing out loud. Little Miss Butterfly had never even looked her in the eye, and now they were dearest friends. *Well, kiss my ass!*

After school, Grandma and Donna drove to one of their favorite spots near the boat landing at Sandy Island where they sat for a long time just soaking up the sounds of the river and the wind moving through the saw grass. Donna broke the silence by asking Grandma if she thought that Mama knew about the contest.

"Oh, of course she does," Grandma replied.

"Grandma Liddy said that once a person makes it into Heaven, God spares 'em the bad news back on earth, but He makes sure they know all the good news."

"I figure your Mama knew you won the contest even before you did. By now, she's bragged about you all over heaven."

"Do you think they have lipstick in heaven?"

"Lipstick?"

"I was just thinking about Mama and couldn't imagine her without it."

"Well, I can't imagine her without it, either. I'm sure she's got hundreds of lipsticks."

Grandma turned away, and Donna dried her eyes with the hem of her dress.

"You know who else is proud of you?" Grandma asked, breaking the silence. The women you wrote about: Miss Anne, Charlotte Dunhill, Hattie Wineglass, Miss Cornelia, and all those other women whose names we'll never know," Grandma said. "They're proud of you, too. Oh, and when you were naming the women of The Abbey, you forgot one — the newest one — Donna Margaret Jackson."

"Oh, Grandma…." Donna whispered. "Thank you…."

For the next few minutes, the two sat transfixed, unwilling to break the spell that had fallen over them, wanting only to feel its spell. Then a truck horn sounded in the distance, and they were jolted back to the present.

"I do have one question for you," Grandma said as she shoved the Old '41 into low gear and approached the turn into the entrance to The Abbey. "What are you planning to write about for next year's competition?"

"What!" Donna exclaimed. "I just won this year's competition, and now you're planning next year's."

"Well, yeah," Grandma replied. "If you want to get a jump on the competition, you can't put it off. And don't tell me they won't let you, 'cause I asked."

"But I don't want to work on another manuscript."

"Of course you do," Grandma replied.

"I do?" Donna asked.

"Of course," Grandma said, stopping to wave to Granddaddy Jim who was repairing a fence near the old ram's run.

"Okay," Donna said, after a long pause.

"Good," Grandma replied. "We'll start tomorrow."

About the Author

 **NANCY ROGERS'** passion for history is the result of having spent many years living on the remains of an eighteenth-century rice plantation in Pawleys Island, South Carolina. She is a former biographer of the South Carolina Hall of Fame and is a former docent at Historic Columbia, in Columbia, South Carolina and Latta House, in Charlotte, North Carolina.

Nancy's freelance work has appeared in numerous magazines and newspapers, including *The New York Times*. *The Women of Abbey Plantation* is a sequel to Nancy's first novel, *Sarah's Secret,* a story inspired by a real-life plantation mistress who died in 1723.

Nancy currently lives in Charlotte, where she takes part in various civic projects, gives historic lectures, and occasionally gives cemetery tours specializing in iconography. For more information about Nancy and/or her novels, go to www.nancyrogers.novels.net.

9 781958 032114